THE
NEW ROGER CARAS
TREASURY OF GREAT
CAT
STORIES

g^b

GALAHAD BOOKS
NEW YORK

For text credits, see Acknowledgments on pages vii–ix.

First Galahad Books edition published in 2000.

Galahad Books
A division of BBS Publishing Corporation
386 Park Avenue South
New York, NY 10016

Galahad Books is a registered trademark of
BBS Publishing Corporation.

Library of Congress Control Number: 00–132385

ISBN: 1-57866-098-X

Printed in the United States of America.

CONTENTS

Contents

CONTENTS

Contents

ACKNOWLEDGMENTS

ACKNOWLEDGMENTS

"Noble Warrior" by Andre Norton. Copyright © 1989 by Andre Norton. Reprinted by permission of the author.

"Oscar, The Socialite Cat" by James Herriot. Copyright © 1994 by James Herriot. From *James Herriot's Cat Stories,* by James Herriot. Reprinted by permission of the agent for the author's estate, Harold Ober Associates, Inc., and St. Martin's Press, Inc.

"Phut Phat Concentrates" by Lilian Jackson Braun. Copyright © 1963, renewed 1988 by Lilian Jackson Braun. Reprinted by permission of The Berkley Publishing Group. All rights reserved.

"Schrödinger's Cat" by Ursula K. Le Guin. Copyright © 1974 by Ursula K. Le Guin. First published in *Universe 5.* Reprinted by permission of the author and the author's agent, Virginia Kidd, Virginia Kidd Agency, Ltd.

"Skitty" by Mercedes Lackey. Copyright © 1989 by Mercedes Lackey. Reprinted by permission of the author.

"The Start of the End of It All" by Carol Emshwiller. Copyright © 1991 by Carol Emshwiller. Reprinted by permission of the author and Mercury House, San Francisco, CA.

"Teddy's Tale" by Roger A. Caras. Copyright © 1994 by Roger Caras. Reprinted by permission of the author.

"Touching Is Good for Living Creatures" by Merrill Joan Gerber. Copyright © 1981 by Merrill Joan Gerber. Reprinted by permission of the author.

"The White Cat" by Joyce Carol Oates. Copyright © 1994 by Ontario Review, Inc. Reprinted by permission of the author.

INTRODUCTION

Mankind didn't so much domesticate the cat as we invited the incredible wild creature from the Nile Basin to insinuate itself into *our* lives while making room for it in *our* consciousness. From the very beginning, somewhat over four thousand years ago, the cat has been up front, in our space, in our hearts, beguiling, bewitching, entertaining and mystifying. And it did all of this without revealing any of the secrets about its own feelings. And it is certain the cat does have secrets. Everything about it makes that fact obvious. The mysteries in the original cat's piercing look is still locked away there, defying us to penetrate them and sort them out.

Try as we might, we have never really understood the cat in all of its shapes and moods. We have, at times, worshipped the cat (as Basht or Bastet in Egypt, celebrated in amazing, erotic festivals on barges on the Nile); put people to death for injuring cats; and, a short time later in our history, we actually tortured cats. Today, now that we have achieved our present high cultural status and consider ourselves enormously sophisticated and civilized, we kill cats by the millions because we can't house the kittens that are born each year, ignoring the fact that they are easily preventable. Cats are still purring—we don't know why—and we are still barbaric—and I don't think we understand why!

In short, we are confounded by cats and a great many of us haven't a clue as to how to act in their presence. One thing we have done, though: we have written about them very well indeed.

The cat tracks through our history have created a bewildering trail of ambivalence, guilt, shame, pride and confusion. I don't think that we have ever known how we should feel about cats. Perhaps that is because cats are so enigmatic and we are never quite sure how they feel about us. The trail of bewilderment has spawned a class of literature that reflects this jumble of emotions, for although much of it is very good indeed as literature, it constitutes a perfect muddle as far as our conscience and our bioethic goes. The literature of the cat is really as much a reflection of our own feelings as it is a picture of direct feline matters.

Ambivalence over our domestic animals is not exclusive to the cat. We have worshipped both the cow and the bull, the horse and the ram, yet we have also treated them appallingly. We grow fairly ecstatic over dogs yet force them to endure terrible cruelties. Yet, somehow, our bifurcated relationship with the cat has exceeded all of that. It is to be found in the way people have written about the cat. Part of it could be because of the unique position cats hold on the roster of the domesticated ones. No other major domestication has produced an adored/despised animal of so little economic significance as the cat. It is true that kittens can be sold for hard currency, that cat food is big business, and that people spend a lot of money on catnip–stuffed toys and kitty litter, but compare that with the cow—hides, meat, milk, butter, cheese, glue, bone meal and scores of other products. Compare the dollar value of the cats of the world with the worth of hogs or of the four billion goats now owned by man. Think, then, of wool, lamb and mutton. What is the worth of the camel? Dogs lead the blind, detect bombs, drugs and guns and make the management of livestock possible. What of the draft and farm power of the horse down through history? No one ever went to war on the back of a cat nor did they explore continents that way. What we have then is a heralded domestication that is just about one hundred percent luxury. Perhaps that embarrasses us—or at least adds to the confusion.

So we have a luxury that kills not only our mice but our song birds, a wonderfully soft and amazingly beautiful creature that looks at us like a walking, purring enigma and defies us to strip away and reveal its charade. We know it has been a goddess, we know we have often acted abominably toward it and invited our dogs to tear it apart, we know that as a species we don't know how to act, how to behave in the company of the cat. We don't even know what good manners are, much less ethical behavior. And so we make our way through the literature of the cat to see what we can find out about the history and the magic of that glorious creature—and whatever we can discover about ourselves.

There is joy in the words and ideas that have been organized and compiled by the gentle people among us who have adored the cat. (We note but are not sure we understand why Alexander the Great, Napoleon the Possessed and Hitler the Hideous variously feared and despised cats. Perhaps people who seek to conquer the world hate cats because they have already done it.) Herein we may take joy, reflect, mentally stroke the cat and seek ourselves. It is a delightful, fulfilling collection of wonder and wisdom and represents some of the best cat writing and reporting ever done. We are enlarged by being its witnesses.

Roger A. Caras
Thistle Hill Farm

Cleveland Amory

A CAT FOR ALL SEASONS

It has long been a theory of mine—and I am known, if I do say so, for my long theories—that authors, generally speaking, are rotten letter writers. There are good reasons for this. The good letter writer is writing privately, thinking of one person and writing intimately to that person. The author, on the other hand, who is not particularly accustomed to writing privately but rather to writing publicly, is not thinking of any one particular person except perhaps—and sometimes all too often—himself or herself.

And, speaking of that him and her, it is another theory of mine that women, generally speaking, are better letter writers than men. There is a wide variety of good reasons for this, but the one which I believe has most merit is that women are superior in one-on-onemanship, if they will kindly forgive the male intrusion in that last word.

If authors are not that terrific at letter writing, however, they do appreciate good letter writing when they receive it. Indeed, one of the greatest pleasures authors have is reading letters addressed to them about what they write. I am no exception, and since my most recent books have concerned, among other things, my cat Polar Bear, I am particularly pleased about the number of people who write to me wanting to know more about him. Once in a while of course I wish that at least a few of these writers would also want to know more about me but, as I have often said, you can't have everything—particularly nowadays. You would think, though, that a reasonable number of people would take the time to figure out who did all the behind-the-scenes work, all of the dirty work in the trenches if you will, which made Polar Bear possible. But no, they don't. It's the star they want, and never mind the man without whom Polar Bear would never have been heard of, let alone been a star.

I was not the least jealous of Polar Bear, mind you, but I do want you to know that if the situation were reversed and more people wanted to know about me than about him he would not for a moment have been as philosophical about it as I was. As a matter of fact, I can see him now going right into one of his snits—and I tell you when it came to being jealous Polar Bear could go into the snottiest little snit you ever saw. Kindly remember that jealousy has often been described as "The Green-Eyed Monster," and after you've done that just stop and ask yourself what color eyes do you think Polar Bear had?

There is, though, one question an extraordinary number of these letter writers asked which I found irritating for an entirely different reason from the ones who ignored me, and that was, very simply, the question they asked as to whether or not Polar Bear was still alive. I found these letters particularly annoying when he was still alive, and they are of course much more difficult to answer now. After all, I don't go around asking whether or not someone I know whom I also know that they know is dead yet. Just the same, that is the way "still alive" always sounded to me. In fact, still alive still sounds to me a dead ringer for dead yet.

Letter writers who were, to my mind, more considerate of my feelings were inclined to ask simply how old Polar Bear was. I liked that better, but I do believe that at a certain age, whether it is about cats or people, the question of how old one is has a certain annoyance to it. You do not meet someone you have not seen for some time and suddenly ask how old he or she is. It implies that they are not as young as they were. My answer to that is, who is?

The best answer to this question was given many years ago by a famous friend of mine—and also Polar Bear's—the late Cary Grant. Faced with a wire from a researcher from *Time* magazine which asked, "HOW OLD CARY GRANT?" Cary himself politely wired back. "OLD CARY GRANT, FINE," he said. "HOW YOU?"

In any case, to answer my letter writers, I always made clear, at least until now, when he is gone, that Polar Bear was indeed alive and well. I rescued him, as I made very clear in *The Cat Who Came for Christmas,* on Christmas Eve, 1978, which made him in 1992, fourteen years older than he was when I rescued him.

There remains, of course, the sticky question as to how old he was in 1992. He was at least fourteen years more than when I rescued him, but how much more? In other words, how old was he when I rescued him? Remember, he was a stray, and strays do not come with birth certificates. Susan Thompson, his veterinarian, believes he could have been any age between one and three, but she is the first to admit that veterinarians have a very difficult time estimating cats' ages exactly. Horses, yes, apparently by their teeth, but cats no. Cats have very odd teeth anyway.

Marian Probst, my longtime assistant, believes Polar Bear was less than one, but I don't want you to go to the bank on Marian's opinion about his age, either. For example, Marian is always adding a year to my age for no reason at all, although I've told her a hundred times that because I was born in 1917 and it is now 1992 that does not make me seventy-five, it makes me seventy-four. After all I was *born* in 1917—I wasn't *one* in 1917—I was *zero* in 1917, and I wasn't anywhere near one until 1918. But it is no use talking figures with Marian—you might as well talk the economy.

Anyway, going along with Susan's doubt and ignoring Marian's mathematics, it is quite possible to assume that Polar Bear, who could well have been zero in 1978 was, let us say, zero until 1979. By the same figuring, I was sixty-one in 1979—in the prime of life, if I do say so. Today I am a little past my prime, perhaps, but not much, mind you, just on the rim of my prime. On the other hand, in 1992, Polar Bear was, as I say, at least fourteen. Now, I realize that when it comes to comparing cats' ages to people's ages an extraordinary number of people still believe that old wives' nonsense that seven years of your life is like one year of your cat's life. By that standard Polar Bear was, by a person's age, ninety-eight. How many people do you know who, at ninety-eight, are still alive? I know there are some, but I am asking how many.

And besides this I have literally hundreds of letters from people whose cats are in their twenties, and an extraordinary number whose cats are over twenty-five. That would make them, for a person, 175. The next time you see a person who is 175 please let me know, and while you're at it you might as well also tell him or her that, despite what Marian says, he or she is only 174.

I am, of course, not the only person who has called attention to the fallacy of that 7-to-1 cat-versus-person theory. Not long ago a veterinarian in the Gaines Research Center came up with a new chart—one which I have already published in a previous book but which I am now publishing again, for the benefit of those of you, and there are so many nowadays, who have poor memories. In any case, here it is:

Cat's Age	Person's Age
6 months	10 years
8 months	13 years
12 months	15 years
2 years	24 years
4 years	32 years
6 years	40 years
8 years	48 years
10 years	56 years
12 years	64 years

14 years	72 years
16 years	80 years
18 years	88 years
20 years	96 years
21 years	100 years

To my way of thinking this is certainly a lot closer to the mark than that old 7-to-1 theory, and it is rather remarkable how Gaines refuted that 7-to-1 by having the person go three years while the cat was going only from six months to eight months, and yet having the person at the advanced age of ninety-six go just four years to one hundred while the cat went only one year, from twenty to twenty-one. In any case, Gaines was not by any means alone in changing the 7-to-1 formula. In a British cat book, for example, I found the statement that some experts believe once a cat is nearing "feline old age" you should "multiply its years by 10 to get a true comparison with a person's age." And a British-born veterinarian now living in this country, Ian Dunbar, came up with a shorter revision:

Cat's Age	Person's Age
1 year	3 years
7 years	21 years
14 years	45 years
21 years	70 years
28 years	95 years
31 years	103 years

Shortly after the publication of his findings, Dr. Dunbar was challenged by Washington writer Ed Kane, who took him to task in three specific areas—of his cats' one to humans' three, of his cats' seven to humans' twenty-one, and of his cats' fourteen to humans' forty-five. Mr. Kane also recommended a study of cat-versus-human age by Dr. Tom Reichenbach. This, I learned, first appeared in *Feline Practice,* a veterinary journal, and in it Dr. Reichenbach went so far as to use a computer to compare the ages of some 480 cats and the data obtained from census records on human ages. He also completed a graph which demonstrated the comparison of one- to seventeen-year-old cats with zero- to ninety-year-old humans. You may be sure I was very happy to see that zero recognized. In any case Dr. Reichenbach came up with these findings:

Cat's Age	Person's Age
1 year	17 years
2 years	28 years
3 years	31 years
4 years	41 years
5 years	45 years
6 years	45 years
7 years	51 years
8 years	58 years
9 years	61 years
10 years	61 years
11 years	66 years
12 years	66 years
13 years	71 years
14 years	76 years
15 years	81 years
16 years	81 years
17 years	89 years

I found some of these figures fascinating. For example, in the year when the cat went from five to six, the person stayed at forty-five, and in the year when the cat went from nine to ten, the person stayed at sixty-one. And still again, when the cat went from eleven to twelve, the person stayed at sixty-one. And still again, when the cat went from eleven to twelve, the person stayed at sixty-six. Finally, when the cat went from fifteen to sixteen, the person stayed at eighty-one. It was especially good to know that when Polar Bear was going from five to six and nine to ten and eleven to twelve, I was staying absolutely still. Who says everybody has to keep growing older? You don't, if you put your mind to it.

* * *

One thing was certain. If Polar Bear at fourteen was like me at seventy-four—I know the damned graph said seventy-six, but it could well have been a mistake—we were in a sense roughly the same age. At least we were both by no means old, but in the full bloom of what I would call our maturity. At the same time I realized I would now have to watch out for him more carefully. In just one more year, at fifteen, he would be like me in my eighties. Fifteen might not seem too bad for him to think about, but certainly the eighties were something I did not want to dwell on. What I did want to do was go back to some of the letters I had received from people who had cats over thirty. Dr. Dunbar had given a cat's age at thirty-one as a person's age at one hundred three. I was not really looking forward to being one hundred three, but from where I was sitting it was certainly a lot more appealing than Reichenbach's having Polar Bear being fourteen and me being just four years away from those damned eighties.

No matter. Whatever the age relationship between us, and whether or not I was in the prime, or on the rim, of my maturity, it was time for me to realize that, whatever I was, Polar Bear was no spring chicken. And so, whether he liked it or not, I had better get on with an entirely new health and fitness program for him. The first thing I did was to read everything I could get my hands on pertaining to older cats. One of the first was a book by Harry Miller entitled *The Common Sense Book of Kitten and Cat Care.* "Cats generally begin to show their age," he wrote, "at about 8 years." Frankly, that made me pretty mad. Polar Bear had not done anything of the sort at age eight and in fact at fourteen he still had not. But Mr. Miller went on:

> The elderly cat does not jump and run in play as he used to do. He is no longer capable of sustained exertion, and he may even tire after moderate exercise. He'll want to sleep more, and may be short-tempered about things he once put up with.

Again, that was not Polar Bear. He jumped and ran and played just the way he always did. He certainly did not tire after moderate exercise. It is true he wanted to sleep more, but I have never known him when he did not want to sleep more. Finally, as far as being short-tempered about things he once put up with, he never did put up with things he once put up with, for the simple reason that he never put up with them in the first place.

Frankly that opinion came too close to home for comfort. Finally, there was perhaps the most extraordinary opinion from my old friend Dr. Dunbar. He wrote in *Cat Fancy* magazine about a California cat named "Mother Cat" who, he said, had two hundred kittens and nonetheless lived to be thirty-one. She also, he maintained, liked both other cats and people, but she liked people more and more as she grew older. I could certainly understand that. At least I am sure by that time she liked people better than male cats. Dr. Dunbar, however, proceeded:

> As with Mother Cat, some cats like people more and more as they grow older. Other cats like people less and less, becoming increasingly intolerant of being disturbed and handled, especially by children and strangers.

Since Polar Bear was intolerant of children and strangers by the time I first saw him, he was, by fourteen, totally so. Nonetheless, Dr. Dunbar then went on with a suggestion about how to handle older cats when it came to what he called "even routine visits to the veterinarian."

> Do not wait for your middle-aged cat to become old and grouchy. Do something about it now. Prevention is the name of the game.

Dr. Dunbar was not kidding—and a game was indeed what he had in mind, as we shall see in a moment. First, though, he begins with how to prepare your cat for the experience:

> To prepare the cat to enjoy veterinary examinations, begin by introducing your cat to visitors. A simple and ultimately enjoyable exercise is to invite people over to the house to hand-feed the cat its dinner. Refusal to take food from a stranger is a sign that the cat is stressed. Your job is to remove this stress before your

cat's next routine veterinary examination. Do not rush, however; let the cat do things in its own good time. Forget the cat's dinner for today, and have the stranger try again tomorrow. Remember, it is quite normal for wild *Felidae* to go several days with no food at all. With patience and perseverance, any cat will come around eventually.

With all due respect to Dr. Dunbar, I could visualize all too clearly what would happen if I were to try the very idea of giving Polar Bear his dinner by hands-on feeding from strangers. Even if they were relatively familiar strangers, I assure you, they very soon would have a lot more to worry about than whether or not wild *Felidae* had or had not eaten for days—such as, for example, whether or not they still had the use of their own extremities to eat with.

But Dr. Dunbar apparently had not had that much experience with cats who felt as strongly about strangers as Polar Bear. Because, after the hands-on feeding, he proceeded right on to his promised games:

> When the cat enjoys the company of strangers, it is party time— time to play Pass the Cat. One visitor picks up the cat, offers a treat, performs a cursory examination, offers a second treat, and then passes the cat to the next person. This game puts the cat in good stead for a visit to the veterinary clinic, especially if one or two visitors dress up as ersatz veterinarians—wearing white coats or surgery greens and sporting an antiseptic after-shave.

This one was, frankly, too much for me even to attempt to visualize. I just knew that when stranger A passed Polar Bear to stranger B, let alone on to strangers C, D, and E, that would be it because the stranger never lived who could handle a passed Polar Bear, game or no game.

As for the game preparing Polar Bear for meeting a white- or green-coated "ersatz veterinarian" sporting "an antiseptic after-shave" I think one visit from Polar Bear would, at the very least, persuade a stranger to part company with the white or green coat and the antiseptic after-shave as rapidly as possible. And my advice to said stranger would be, after carefully shutting the door behind him before the advance of Polar Bear, to enter, again as rapidly as possible, some other ersatz field of endeavor.

I do not wish to give the impression that Polar Bear was, in his latter years, more difficult than he was when he was younger. Actually, that would not be fair—in many ways he was less difficult. When, for example, two strangers came to my apartment, he would often not bother to move from the chair in which he was sleeping. When he was younger, one stranger was his limit. Two, and in a flash he was off under the bed or under the sofa, and woe betide the stranger who tried to "Here Kitty Kitty" him from under there. Polar Bear was better when he was older, I believe, partly because it was more trouble for him to move. But equally partly I believe it was because as he grew older he grew more philosophical.

In 1991 *Cat Fancy* magazine did a survey of older cats—approximately one-third of whom were from ages ten to twelve, another third from thirteen to fifteen, and still another third from sixteen to nineteen. An extraordinary number of even the oldest of these cats were still lively and, just as I found with Polar Bear, at least a little friendlier with strangers. I liked best the comment of Andrea Dorn of Nevada, Ohio: "I'm not sure whether my cat's personality has changed or not," Andrea said. "I'll think she has become friendlier, but then she'll meet a new person and make a bad impression, and I realize that she and I just get along better. She hasn't really changed; I've just become more like her."

The more I thought about that story the more I thought that through the years Polar Bear and I had gotten more and more like each other. But I do think I should say that, while I had made a real effort to emulate his good qualities and not his bad ones, I do not feel he made the same effort in that department toward me. All too often I found him not emulating my good qualities, but emulating my very worst qualities. For example, I found him growing increasingly short of patience. I know patience is not my long suit, but I saw no reason for him to emulate that minor fault of mine when he could have much more profitably been working on one of my many major virtues, such as my unfailing courtesy to my inferiors. Which, if I do say so, keeps me very busy indeed.

But no matter. The point is that, generally speaking, we got along famously and, as I have said, knowing Polar Bear was, as the age comparisons showed, aging far more rapidly than I was, I made allowances for his character failings just the way I kept a careful check on his health and fitness. I had particular trouble with his eating. After years when he was younger of trying to keep him from getting too fat, now when he was older I was suddenly faced with the problem of him getting too thin. In the early days he was fussy about food, all right, but only fussy when I tried to put him on a diet. In later days, however, he was just fussy, period. It made no difference what I put down. He would sniff it and look at me, and all but say "You don't expect me to eat this, do you?" So, naturally, I would try something else. I usually had the same response again, and indeed it often took a third choice for him to get interested. Too often his average meal took on the appearance of a smorgasbord.

I was relieved to learn it was not at all unusual for older cats to eat less and to lose weight. But it worried me, and I fussed and fussed over it. I called his vet, Susan Thompson, on the slightest provocation, and when I claimed, as I usually did, that he was too sick to travel to the vet's, she graciously made a house call. She kept reassuring me that he was doing fine, but she also told me the fact was sooner or later I should know he would get sick.

I hated her telling me that. I hated it when Polar Bear was sick when he was younger, but when he was older, and he was in the twilight of his years, I did not think I could stand it. Just the same, I knew it was inevitable, and I tried to be a good soldier and brace myself for it. I also did my best to do everything I could for him.

And then like a bolt out of the blue came the shock—the very last thing I would expect. Polar Bear did not get sick—*I* got sick.

It was really incredible. Me, in the prime or on the rim, as I said, of my maturity, being the one to succumb, while Polar Bear, despite being the one far more precarious on the cat-age versus human-age scale and the one of the two of us who, by any odds, should have politely led the way toward any infirmity, was fine and dandy. Honestly, it was so unbelievable I could hardly make any sense out of it, let alone start to live with it.

As I have tried to make clear from the first book about Polar Bear, he and I were from the beginning two very different individuals when we were sick. When I was sick I wanted attention. I wanted it now, and I wanted it around the clock. Besides this, I wished everyone within earshot of my moans and groans, of which I have a wide variety, to know that I am not only at Death's door but also that I have the very worst case of whatever it is I think I have that has ever been visited on any man, woman, child or beast since the world began.

I stated clearly that if, for example, I had a slight cold and the cold had taken a turn for the worse, I wished people to gather around my bedside in respectful silence. For those with poor hearing, I wished them to gather especially close, and for those with poor memories I wished them to bring pad and pencil so that of course they could take down and transmit to posterity, hoarsely and with extreme difficulty, my last words. In much the same manner I visualized my loved ones gathering around after I had gone to my Final Reward to hear my Last Will and Testament. In this I fully intended to give them further instruction, since they no longer had the benefit of my counsel, on how they were to conduct themselves.

All this, mind you, for a cold. But now I had something far more severe—a combination of an ulcer, a distorted aneurism, and what my doctor, Anthony Grieco, described, after a look at my X-rays, as a "curmudgeonly esophagus." I know I have often been described as a curmudgeon, but to hear one's esophagus described in this way—and by one's own doctor—was a bit unsettling. Furthermore, since I was struck with all these troubles at once, I did not even have the time or opportunity to settle down into my usual hypochondriacal ways heretofore described. Instead I was just another patient—and one who, unhappily, as I believe I have already mentioned, was born without any patience.

The most curious thing of all is what happened to my relationship with Polar Bear. Instead of my looking after him, he was now looking after me. No longer was he the rescuee, as had happened in the beginning when I had found him that snowy Christmas Eve, when I found him outside the garage, now he was the rescuer. It really was a total turnaround from what had been our relationship since that first day.

Of course, he was not the only one looking after me. And Polar Bear was never good at being one of a group doing something together as a team. He was either the captain, or he would not play. In this case, if he could not be chief cook and bottle washer, he wanted to be chief of everything else. During the daytime he would sit at the far corner of the bed nearest the door and monitor all comings and goings with the authority of Horatius at the Bridge. During the nighttime he would hunker down between my arm and chest, making sure the covers allowed him to keep at least one beady eye ready for examining any nocturnal visitor.

If the person entering was Marian, my daughter, a friend, or even a long-standing enemy whom I had returned to grace, Polar Bear would of course motion them through, acting for all the world like a traffic patrolman. On the other hand, if the person were a stranger, out would come not only the paw to stop traffic, but the rest of Polar Bear, too. He did not actually attack people, but he certainly gave every indication of not being above such measures if required.

Watching him, I could not help thinking of a story I had read of another protective cat. The cat's name was Inkee, and he was owned by a woman named Debra Lewis of Detroit. One day, Mrs. Lewis remembered, she and her husband were playing on the floor. Inkee was in another room. Suddenly Mrs. Lewis yelled, "Ouch!" Immediately Inkee arrived on the double. His actions were, she reported, in order, first to sit on Mrs. Lewis' chest as if to say "Are you all right?" second, when Mrs. Lewis assured him she was, to kiss her on the nose; third, to go over to her husband and bite him; and fourth and finally, to run out of the room.

I sincerely believe that, faced with similar circumstances and substituting Mrs. Lewis for myself, Polar Bear would have done all of the above. I am particularly sure he would have done so in the case of the most difficult person with whom he had to cope during my illness—the trained nurse. Polar Bear did not like nurses, trained or not, and nurses did not like Polar Bear. For one thing he is not fond of people in white—on the theory, I believe, that their people-caring is just a front and that, underneath, they are probably veterinarians preparing at any time for a surreptitious assault with a needle.

13

There was another reason that Polar Bear did not like this particular nurse, and that was that he did not like her voice. Whether it was what she said with that voice or whether it was the way she said it—her maddening use of the plural, the endless "How are we?" addressed, of course, to just me—I do not know. But it was certainly one of the reasons he did not like her. There was, finally, a third reason he could not stand the nurse, and that was that I did not like her either, and he was smart enough to know that, and also to know that the reason I did not like her was primarily that she did not like him.

Fortunately this round robin did not last long. Her stay, however, brief as it was, had a bearing on Polar Bear's crowning achievement as watch-and-guard cat. This was the day, or rather the night, he spent with me in the hospital. I shall not tell you which hospital it was. Actually, I was in two of them—in Texas, where the attack first came on, and also in New York. But to spare the attendants of both of them—none of whom, I wish to point out, I actually physically abused—I shall not mention the hospitals' names.

There was a reason Polar Bear was at the hospital. Marian, who could not visit me that day, had a friend bring Polar Bear down in his carrier to see me. The friend was supposed to return before visiting hours were over and take Polar Bear back, but unfortunately an emergency came up and she could not make it. Since that particular day and night the other bed in the two-bed room was unoccupied, I decided that if Polar Bear spent the night he would at least not be bothering anybody else. I even took the precaution of spreading some newspaper in the bathroom for a serviceable litterbox.

If I had asked Marian to leave Polar Bear with me for the night, I very much doubt she would have done so. Marian plays strictly by the book—not, I am sorry to say, always by one of my books—and when it comes to rules and regulations I am firmly convinced that she, not Robert, wrote those rules of order. All in all, I was fortunate that night to have the friend bring Polar Bear and then not be able to return, although I must admit that when it happened I immediately began practicing my favorite winning argument in any situation—that "they" said it would be all right. Those "theys" may have been entirely fictitious, but I promise you they have covered a multitude of sins in my life, and in this case they came through with flying colors.

I did, however, have a serious talk with Polar Bear. I told him that during the night an almost steady stream of people would be passing through our room because that is the way hospitals work—they were sort of like railroad stations. Furthermore, I warned him, most of the people who would be passing in or through the room would be dressed in white, but he would not in any circumstance regard them as veterinarians. Indeed, I told him, he was not to regard them at all because I wished him, from the moment he heard footsteps approaching outside the door, to get under the covers and stay there without leaving in view even so much as one of his beady eyes.

I could tell by his tone of listening—and do not fool yourself, Polar Bear did indeed have a tone of listening—that he did not go along with my idea about this. Clearly, he wanted to know that if this was how it was going to be in the hospital, how in the world could I expect him to do his job of protecting me?

There are all kinds of protection, I told him sternly, just the way there are those who also serve who only stand and wait. They also protect, I added to make it absolutely clear, who only lie and wait. But lie and wait, I added firmly, was just what I expected him to do.

I next told him our first trouble would be the arrival of my supper. The minute I said "supper," Polar Bear could not see what trouble that could possibly be. I explained that it would be trouble because it would probably be brought by a man or a woman in white, and before he started to jump out of bed and up on the tray it would be nice if he at least waited until the man or woman had put the tray down.

I was of course being sarcastic. I didn't want under any condition for him to appear until the man or woman in white had left not only the tray, but also the room.

Polar Bear had the clearest way of asking, "And where, may I ask, do I come in?" The way he did it was by coming as close as a cat can to a cocked eyebrow. I told him he came in because the minute the man or woman went, then and only then could he come out and share my supper. And amazingly enough, it all happened exactly as we discussed it. The minute I heard the wheels of the meal cart outside the door I swooped Polar Bear under the covers and the man came in, put down the tray, and left, all so quickly that Polar Bear did not have time to do anything about it. Once we were alone, however, out he came, and dove for the supper tray. And so, between us, as we so often did at home, we shared and shared alike, his idea of sharing and sharing alike being that he ate both his share and my share of what he liked and left me to have both my share and his share of what he did not like.

When we were through I again placed him under the covers until the man had come in and removed the tray. Afterwards, I warned Polar Bear that we were far from out of the woods yet. Still to come, I told him, were at least three more visits. I also told him that, from then on, one or the other of us should stay awake and that we should schedule watches the way they do on shipboard. Since by this time Polar Bear was already yawning his head off—which was a tendency he often had when I was starting on something important—I decided to teach him a lesson and told him I would take the first shift from ten to twelve, and he could then take what I explained to him was the beginning of the graveyard shift, from twelve to two, and then again I would take over from two to four. There were only two troubles with this beautifully thought-out plan of mine. For one thing, we did not have an alarm clock, and for another we did not know exactly what our battle plan would be when the one who was on watch called the other to action. Actually, Polar Bear was terrific at waking me when he wanted something, but I had no idea how good he would be at waking me when he did not want something or wanted something to stop.

Anyway, we were in the middle of all these plans when suddenly I heard footsteps and the door opened and we had our first visitor. She turned on the light, moved swiftly to my bed, and put down a tray with some water and a pill in a cup. "It's our medication," she said. So far she had not even looked at me or the bed and I was sure she had not seen Polar Bear. But now she was turning and would see Polar Bear. Polar Bear, however, was nowhere to be seen. He was back under the covers. What he had done of course was to see the pill—and all I can say is that if I have ever seen a cat show the white feather I saw it then. I knew perfectly well how Polar Bear felt about pills, but this was too much. When it was all over and he came out, I had to explain to him what showing a white feather meant. I told him that it was plain and simple cowardice. He wanted to know where it came from, and I told him never mind where it came from, he would not remember it anyway. Actually, I learned it came from the belief that a gamecock with a white feather in his tail would not be a good fighter, and I did not see any reason for bringing up such a sordid subject as cockfighting.

I really gave him a very good speech, but the last part of it fell upon deaf ears. He had fallen asleep again. This of course I could not permit. It was now his watch, and people who went to sleep on their watch were often shot. Also I told him I particularly did not want him to go to sleep again before the sleeping pill nurse came—because sleeping pill nurses get very angry when patients go to sleep on them before they have had a chance to give them their pills. I informed Polar Bear sternly I simply would not answer for the consequences if the sleeping pill nurse saw him under such circumstances—it would be bad enough if she saw him under normal circumstances.

Once more I dozed off, and once more it seemed only a short time before the door opened and this time the lights came flooding on as well as the cheerful question, "How are we tonight?" All I could do was reply wanly that I was as well as could be expected. Once more there was, of course, no Polar Bear in evidence. He was under the covers again, sleeping on picket duty—really he was impossible—particularly since we were this time faced with the temperature-and-pulse nurse. First she put the thermometer in my mouth and then reached for my wrist. This was a mistake. Polar Bear almost invariably took exception to strangers attempting intimacies with me. Out came, all too visibly, one of his arms with its paw headed ominously for the nurse's hand. I had a brief thought that what we would now have would be a three-person arm wrestle, but unfortunately the situation was far worse than I thought. The nurse could not fail to see Polar Bear's arm appear from under the covers, but that was not the main trouble. The main trouble was that she did not think the arm belonged to a cat. What she thought it belonged to was far worse—she thought it belonged to a snake. In any case she shrieked her displeasure, jumped up and made a mess of everything, including the thermometer in my mouth.

At this juncture I could hear steps coming down the hall—probably, I thought, the nurse's guard. Immediately I took the thermometer out of my mouth and reached under the covers where, good as gold, Polar Bear still was. I pulled him out and held him up, in all his glory, for the nurse to see. See, I said, no snake, no snake at all, just a dear little cat.

By this time she did not know what to think, but it was Polar Bear who saved the day. He did not hiss at her or do anything threatening, but instead gave a definite purr and then one of his perfected silent AEIOU's. It won her over in an instant—in fact, before her nurses' guard appeared, she had actually helped me to get Polar Bear back under the covers. By the time they marched in I was having both my temperature and pulse taken as if nothing had happened.

Our third visitor was the sleeping pill nurse, and from the beginning we were off to a bad start. Despite what I had explicitly told Polar Bear not to do, he was sound asleep and so—ashamed as I am to record the fact—was I. When this truly ghastly woman banged open the door, turned on the top light, and uttered her war cry, "And how are we tonight?" it was all too much. I wanted to say, "We *were* fine," when, without so much as a by-your-leave, out came Polar Bear. Actually, he felt he had his leave—he thought she was the same nurse as the one before.

She was not, of course. I will say this, though, for the sleeping pill monster—she held her ground. But I knew she would not, like the other nurse, let it go. This was strictly a law-and-order nurse. I had to think of something and I tried once again. "They said it was all right" but to say it fell on deaf ears is an understatement. "And who may I ask *us*," she said, looking of course at just me, "is *they?*" The doctor, I said lamely. With that she moved to the chart at the foot of the bed. Oh, not that doctor, I said arrogantly, the head doctor. "Well," she said ominously, "we"—and for the first time not looking only at me—"will see." And with that she started to march out the door.

I tried to continue with the last argument about my "they" but it was no use. She was in such a state of high dudgeon that she had not even remembered to leave me my sleeping pill. And on top of her departure, out came Polar Bear who—I am not making this up—actually put on, for my benefit, if not for hers, a masterful imitation of a cat's idea of a human's high dudgeon.

In any case, it was masterly enough so she did nothing about him, and I never did know whether she tried to do something about him. All I know is that we had one more interruption, which came the next morning. It was the nurse who came to take blood. I was virtually sure Polar Bear would not stand still—or rather lie still—for this, and he did not. But in more than one way it was my fault. For some reason nurses always go for my left arm when they go for blood, and invariably in that left arm they cannot seem to find a good vein to work with. In vain I presented the other arm and begged my visitor to try it but, nurses being nurses, it was no use. After three tries, however, I had had enough. I pulled my left arm away and demanded she try the right one. She refused. We had come to a Mexican standoff—or at least we had one until out from under the covers came my champion. Out he came in full battle stance and, giving the nurse first the hiss and then a growl, he did his masterpiece—he held up a warning paw. It was his right paw, too.

Immediately the nurse knew she was outgunned. Without a word she moved around to the other side of the bed, took my right arm, and took the blood. And even more remarkable, before she left she at least tried a pat in Polar Bear's direction. "I have a cat, too," she said. "I won't say a word."

Later that morning when the men in white came to get us—and some women in white, too—Polar Bear and I went, as the saying goes, quietly.

Ernest Hemingway

CAT IN THE RAIN

There were only two Americans stopping at the hotel. They did not know any of the people they passed on the stairs on their way to and from their room. Their room was on the second floor facing the sea. It also faced the public garden and the war monument. There were big palms and green benches in the public garden. In the good weather there was always an artist with his easel. Artists liked the way the palms grew and the bright colors of the hotels facing the gardens and the sea. Italians came from a long way off to look up at the war monument. It was made of bronze and glistened in the rain. It was raining. The rain dripped from the palm trees. Water stood in pools on the gravel paths. The sea broke in a long line in the rain and slipped back down the beach to come up and break again in a long line in the rain. The motor cars were gone from the square by the war monument. Across the square in the doorway of the café a waiter stood looking out at the empty square.

The American wife stood at the window looking out. Outside right under their window a cat was crouched under one of the dripping green tables. The cat was trying to make herself so compact that she would not be dripped on.

"I'm going down and get that kitty," the American wife said.

"I'll do it," her husband offered from the bed.

"No, I'll get it. The poor kitty out trying to keep dry under a table."

The husband went on reading, lying propped up with the two pillows at the foot of the bed.

"Don't get wet," he said.

The wife went downstairs and the hotel owner stood up and bowed to her as she passed the office. His desk was at the far end of the office. He was an old man and very tall.

"*Il piove*," the wife said. She liked the hotel-keeper.

"*Sì, sì, Signora, brutto tempo.* It's very bad weather."

He stood behind his desk in the far end of the dim room. The wife liked him. She liked the deadly serious way he received any complaints. She liked his dignity. She liked the way he wanted to serve her. She liked the way he felt about being a hotel-keeper. She liked his old, heavy face and big hands.

Liking him she opened the door and looked out. It was raining harder. A man in a rubber cape was crossing the empty square to the café. The cat would be around to the right. Perhaps she could go along under the eaves. As she stood in the doorway an umbrella opened behind her. It was the maid who looked after their room.

"You must not get wet," she smiled, speaking Italian. Of course, the hotel-keeper had sent her.

With the maid holding the umbrella over her, she walked along the gravel path until she was under their window. The table was there, washed bright green in the rain, but the cat was gone. She was suddenly disappointed. The maid looked up at her.

"Ha perduto qualche cosa, Signora?"

"There was a cat," said the American girl.

"A cat?"

"Sì, il gatto."

"A cat?" the maid laughed. "A cat in the rain?"

"Yes," she said, "under the table." Then, "Oh, I wanted it so much. I wanted a kitty."

When she talked English the maid's face tightened.

"Come, Signora," she said. "We must get back inside. You will be wet."

"I suppose so," said the American girl.

They went back along the gravel path and passed in the door. The maid stayed outside to close the umbrella. As the American girl passed the office, the padrone bowed from his desk. Something felt very small and tight inside the girl. The padrone made her feel very small and at the same time really important. She had a momentary feeling of being of supreme importance. She went on up the stairs. She opened the door of the room. George was on the bed, reading.

"Did you get the cat?" he asked, putting the book down.

"It was gone."

"Wonder where it went to," he said, resting his eyes from reading.

She sat down on the bed.

"I wanted it so much," she said. "I don't know why I wanted it so much. I wanted that poor kitty. It isn't any fun to be a poor kitty out in the rain."

George was reading again.

She went over and sat in front of the mirror of the dressing table looking at herself with the hand glass. She studied her profile, first one side and then the other. Then she studied the back of her head and her neck.

"Don't you think it would be a good idea if I let my hair grow out?" she asked, looking at her profile again.

George looked up and saw the back of her neck, clipped close like a boy's.

"I like it the way it is."

"I get so tired of it," she said. "I get so tired of looking like a boy."

George shifted his position in the bed. He hadn't looked away from her since she started to speak.

"You look pretty darn nice," he said.

She laid the mirror down on the dresser and went over to the window and looked out. It was getting dark.

"I want to pull my hair back tight and smooth and make a big knot at the back that I can feel," she said. "I want to have a kitty to sit on my lap and purr when I stroke her."

"Yeah?" George said from the bed.

"And I want to eat at a table with my own silver and I want candles. And I want it to be spring and I want to brush my hair out in front of a mirror and I want a kitty and I want some new clothes."

"Oh, shut up and get something to read," George said. He was reading again.

His wife was looking out of the window. It was quite dark now and still raining in the palm trees.

"Anyway, I want a cat," she said, "I want a cat. I want a cat now. If I can't have long hair or any fun, I can have a cat."

George was not listening. He was reading his book. His wife looked out of the window where the light had come on in the square.

Someone knocked at the door.

"*Avanti,*" George said. He looked up from his book.

In the doorway stood the maid. She held a big tortoise-shell cat pressed tight against her and swung down against her body.

"Excuse me," she said, "the padrone asked me to bring this for the Signora."

Ruth Rendell

LONG LIVE THE QUEEN

It was over in an instant. A flash of orange out of the green hedge, a streak across the road, a thud. The impact was felt as a surprisingly heavy jarring. There was no cry. Anna had braked, but too late and the car had been going fast. She pulled in to the side of the road, got out, walked back.

An effort was needed before she could look. The cat had been flung against the grass verge which separated road from narrow walkway. It was dead. She knew before she knelt down and felt its side that it was dead. A little blood came from its mouth. Its eyes were already glazing. It had been a fine cat of the kind called marmalade because the color is two-tone, the stripes like dark slices of peel among the clear orange. Paws, chest, and part of its face were white, the eyes gooseberry green.

It was an unfamiliar road, one she had only taken to avoid roadworks on the bridge. Anna thought, I was going too fast. There is no speed limit here but it's a country road with cottages and I shouldn't have been going so fast. The poor cat. Now she must go and admit what she had done, confront an angry or distressed owner, an owner who presumably lived in the house behind that hedge.

She opened the gate and went up the path. It was a cottage, but not a pretty one: of red brick with a low slate roof, bay windows downstairs with a green front door between them. In each bay window sat a cat, one black, one orange and white like the cat which had run in front of her car. They stared at her, unblinking, inscrutable, as if they did not see her, as if she was not there. She could still see the black one when she was at the front door. When she put her finger to the bell and rang it, the cat did not move, nor even blink its eyes.

No one came to the door. She rang the bell again. It occurred to her that the owner might be in the back garden and she walked round the side of the house. It wasn't really a garden but a wilderness of long grass and tall weeds and wild trees. There was no one. She looked through a window into a kitchen where a tortoiseshell cat sat on top of the fridge in the sphinx position and on the floor, on a strip of matting, a brown tabby rolled sensuously, its striped paws stroking the air.

There were no cats outside as far as she could see, not living ones at least. In the left-hand corner, past a kind of lean-to coalshed and a clump of bushes, three small wooden crosses were just visible among the long grass. Anna had no doubt they were cat graves.

She looked in her bag and, finding a hairdresser's appointment card, wrote on the blank back of it her name, her parents' address and their phone number, and added, *Your cat ran out in front of my car. I'm sorry, I'm sure death was instantaneous.* Back at the front door, the black cat and the orange-and-white cat still staring out, she put the card through the letter box.

It was then that she looked in the window where the black cat was sitting. Inside was a small overfurnished living room which looked as if it smelt. Two cats lay on the hearthrug, two more were curled up together in an armchair. At either end of the mantelpiece sat a china cat, white and red with gilt whiskers. Anna thought there ought to have been another one between them, in the center of the shelf, because this was the only clear space in the room, every other corner and surface being crowded with objects, many of which had some association with the feline: cat ashtrays, cat vases, photographs of cats in silver frames, postcards of cats, mugs with cat faces on them, and ceramic, brass, silver, and glass kittens. Above the fireplace was a portrait of a marmalade-and-white cat done in oils and on the wall to the left hung a cat calendar.

Anna had an uneasy feeling that the cat in the portrait was the one that lay dead in the road. At any rate, it was very like. She could not leave the dead cat where it was. In the boot of her car were two plastic carrier bags, some sheets of newspaper, and a blanket she sometimes used for padding things she didn't want to strike against each other while she was driving. As wrapping for the cat's body, the plastic bags would look callous, the newspapers worse. She would sacrifice the blanket. It was a clean dark-blue blanket, single size, quite decent and decorous.

The cat's body wrapped in this blanket, she carried it up the path. The black cat had moved from the left-hand bay and had taken up a similar position in one of the upstairs windows. Anna took another look into the living room. A second examination of the portrait confirmed her guess that its subject was the one she was carrying. She backed away. The black cat stared down at her, turned its head, and yawned hugely. Of course it did not know she carried one of its companions, dead and now cold, wrapped in an old car blanket, having met a violent death. She had an uncomfortable feeling, a ridiculous feeling, that it would have behaved in precisely the same way if it had known.

She laid the cat's body on the roof of the coalshed. As she came back round the house, she saw a woman in the garden next door. This was a neat and tidy garden with flowers and a lawn. The woman was in her fifties, white-haired, slim, wearing a twin set.

"One of the cats ran out in front of my car," Anna said. "I'm afraid it's dead."

"Oh, dear."

"I've put the—body, the body on the coalshed. Do you know when they'll be back?"

"It's just her," the woman said. "It's just her on her own."

"Oh, well. I've written a note for her. With my name and address."

The woman was giving her an odd look. "You're very honest. Most would have just driven on. You don't have to report running over a cat, you know. It's not the same as a dog."

"I couldn't have just gone on."

"If I were you, I'd tear that note up. You can leave it to me, I'll tell her I saw you."

"I've already put it through the door," said Anna.

She said goodbye to the woman and got back into her car. She was on her way to her parents' house, where she would be staying for the next two weeks. Anna had a flat on the other side of the town, but she had promised to look after her parents' house while they were away on holiday, and—it now seemed a curious irony—her parents' cat.

If her journey had gone according to plan, if she had not been delayed for half an hour by the accident and the cat's death, she would have been in time to see her mother and father before they left for the airport. But when she got there, they had gone. On the hall table was a note for her in her mother's hand to say that they had had to leave, the cat had been fed, and there was a cold roast chicken in the fridge for Anna's supper. The cat would probably like some, too, to comfort it for missing them.

Anna did not think her mother's cat, a huge fluffy creature of a ghostly whitish-grey tabbyness named Griselda, was capable of missing anyone. She couldn't believe it had affections. It seemed to her without personality or charm, to lack endearing ways. To her knowledge, it had never uttered beyond giving an occasional thin squeak that signified hunger. It had never been known to rub its body against human legs, or even against the legs of the furniture. Anna knew that it was absurd to call an animal selfish—an animal naturally put its survival first, self-preservation being its prime instinct—yet she thought of Griselda as deeply, intensely, callously selfish. When it was not eating, it slept, and it slept in those most comfortable places where the people that owned it would have liked to sit but from which they could not bring themselves to dislodge it. At night it lay on their bed and, if they moved, dug its long sharp claws through the bedclothes into their legs.

Anna's mother didn't like hearing Griselda referred to as "it." She corrected Anna and stroked Griselda's head. Griselda, who purred a lot when recently fed and ensconced among cushions, always stopped purring at the touch of a human hand. This would have amused Anna if she had not seen that her mother seemed hurt by it, withdrew her hand and gave an unhappy little laugh.

When she had unpacked the case she brought with her, had prepared and eaten her meal and given Griselda a chicken leg, she began to wonder if the owner of the cat she had run over would phone. The owner might feel, as people bereaved in great or small ways sometimes did feel, that nothing could bring back the dead. Discussion was useless, and so, certainly, was recrimination. It had not in fact been her fault. She had been driving fast, but not *illegally* fast, and even if she had been driving at thirty miles an hour she doubted if she could have avoided the cat which streaked so swiftly out of the hedge.

It would be better to stop thinking about it. A night's sleep, a day at work, and the memory of it would recede. She had done all she could. She was very glad she had not just driven on as the next-door neighbor had seemed to advocate. It had been some consolation to know that the woman had many cats, not just the one, so that perhaps losing one would be less of a blow.

When she had washed the dishes and phoned her friend Kate, wondered if Richard, the man who had taken her out three times and to whom she had given this number, would phone and had decided he would not, she sat down beside Griselda—not *with* Griselda but on the same sofa as she was on—and watched television. It got to ten and she thought it unlikely the cat woman—she had begun thinking of her as that—would phone now.

There was a phone extension in her parents' room but not in the spare room where she would be sleeping. It was nearly eleven-thirty and she was getting into bed when the phone rang. The chance of its being

Richard, who was capable of phoning late, especially if he thought she was alone, made her go into her parents' bedroom and answer it.

A voice that sounded strange, thin, and cracked said what sounded like "Maria Yackle."

"Yes?" Anna said.

"This is Maria Yackle. It was my cat that you killed."

Anna swallowed. "Yes. I'm glad you found my note. I'm very sorry, I'm very sorry. It was an accident. The cat ran out in front of my car."

"You were going too fast."

It was a blunt statement, harshly made. Anna could not refute it. She said, "I'm very sorry about your cat."

"They don't go out much, they're happier indoors. It was a chance in a million. I should like to see you. I think you should make amends. It wouldn't be right for you just to get away with it."

Anna was very taken aback. Up till then the woman's remarks had seemed reasonable. She didn't know what to say.

"I think you should compensate me, don't you? I loved her, I love all my cats. I expect you thought that because I had so many cats it wouldn't hurt me so much to lose one."

That was so near what Anna had thought that she felt a kind of shock, as if this Maria Yackle or whatever she was called had read her mind. "I've told you I'm sorry. I am sorry, I was very upset, I *hated* it happening. I don't know what more I can say."

"We must meet."

"What would be the use of that?" Anna knew she sounded rude, but she was shaken by the woman's tone, her blunt, direct sentences.

There was a break in the voice, something very like a sob. "It would be of use to me."

The phone went down. Anna could hardly believe it. She had heard it go down but still she said several times over, "Hallo? Hallo?" and "Are you still there?"

She went downstairs and found the telephone directory for the area and looked up Yackle. It wasn't there. She sat down and worked her way through all the Ys. There weren't many pages of Ys, apart from Youngs, but there was no one with a name beginning with Y at that address on the rustic road among the cottages.

She couldn't get to sleep. She expected the phone to ring again, Maria Yackle to ring back. After a while, she put the bedlamp on and lay there in the light. It must have been three, and still she had not slept, when Griselda came in, got on the bed, and stretched her length along Anna's legs. She put out the light, deciding not to answer the phone if it did ring, to relax, forget the run-over cat, concentrate on nice things. As she turned face-downward and stretched her body straight, she felt Griselda's claws prickle her calves. As she shrank away from contact, curled up her legs, and left Griselda a good half of the bed, a thick rough purring began.

The first thing she thought of when she woke up was how upset that poor cat woman had been. She expected her to phone back at breakfast time but nothing happened. Anna fed Griselda, left her to her house, her cat flap, her garden and wider territory, and drove to work. Richard phoned as soon as she got in. Could they meet the following evening? She agreed, obscurely wishing he had said that night, suggesting that evening herself only to be told he had to work late, had a dinner with a client.

She had been home for ten minutes when a car drew up outside. It was an old car, at least ten years old, and not only dented and scratched but with some of the worst scars painted or sprayed over in a different shade of red. Anna, who saw it arrive from a front window, watched the woman get out of it and approach the house. She was old, or at least elderly—is elderly older than old or old older than elderly?—but dressed like a teenager. Anna got a closer look at her clothes, her hair, and her face when she opened the front door.

It was a wrinkled face, the color and texture of a chicken's wattles. Small blue eyes were buried somewhere in the strawberry redness. The bright white hair next to it was as much of a contrast as snow against scarlet cloth. She wore tight jeans with socks pulled up over the bottoms of them, dirty white trainers, and a big loose sweatshirt with a cat's face on it, a painted smiling bewhiskered mask, orange and white and green-eyed.

Anna had read somewhere the comment made by a young girl on an older woman's boast that she could wear a miniskirt because she had good legs: "It's not your legs, it's your face." She thought of this as she looked at Maria Yackle, but that was the last time for a long while she thought of anything like that.

"I've come early because we shall have a lot to talk about," Maria Yackle said and walked in. She did this in such a way as to compel Anna to open the door farther and stand aside.

"This is *your* house?"

She might have meant because Anna was so young or perhaps there was some more offensive reason for asking.

"My parents'. I'm just staying here."

"Is it this room?" She was already on the threshold of Anna's mother's living room.

Anna nodded. She had been taken aback but only for a moment. It was best to get this over. But she did not care to be dictated to. "You could have let me know. I might not have been here."

There was no reply because Maria Yackle had seen Griselda.

The cat had been sitting on the back of a wing chair between the wings, an apparently uncomfortable place though a favorite, but at sight of the newcomer had stretched, got down, and was walking toward her. Maria Yackle put out her hand. It was a horrible hand, large and red with ropelike blue veins standing out above the bones, the palm calloused, the nails black and broken and the sides of the forefinger and thumb ingrained with brownish dirt. Griselda approached and put her smoky whitish muzzle and pink nose into this hand.

"I shouldn't," Anna said rather sharply, for Maria Yackle was bending over to pick the cat up. "She isn't very nice. She doesn't like people."

"She'll like me."

And the amazing thing was that Griselda did. Maria Yackle sat down and Griselda sat on her lap. Griselda the unfriendly, the cold-hearted, the cat who purred when alone and who ceased to purr when touched, the ice-eyed, the standoffish walker-by-herself, settled down on this unknown, untried lap, having first climbed up Maria Yackle's chest and onto her shoulders and rubbed her ears and plump furry cheeks against the sweatshirt with the painted cat face.

"You seem surprised."

Anna said, "You could say that."

"There's no mystery. The explanation's simple." It was a shrill, harsh voice, cracked by the onset of old age, articulate, the usage grammatical but the accent raw cockney. "You and your mum and dad, too, no doubt, you all think you smell very nice and pretty. You have your bath every morning with bath essence and scented soap. You put talcum powder on and spray stuff in your armpits, you rub cream on your bodies and squirt on perfume. Maybe you've washed your hair, too, with shampoo and conditioner and—what-do-they-call-it?—mousse. You clean your teeth and wash your mouth, put a drop more perfume behind your ears, paint your faces—well, I daresay your dad doesn't paint his face, but he shaves, doesn't he? More mousse and then aftershave.

"You put on your clothes. All of them clean, spotless. They've either just come back from the dry-cleaners or else out of the washing machine with biological soap and spring-fresh fabric softener. Oh, I know, I may not do it myself but I see it on the TV.

"It all smells very fine to you, but it doesn't to her. Oh, no. To her it's just chemicals, like gas might be to you or paraffin. A nasty strong chemical smell that puts her right off and makes her shrink up in her furry skin. What's her name?"

This question was uttered on a sharp bark. "Griselda," said Anna, and "How did you know it's a she?"

"Face," said Maria Yackle. "Look—see her little nose. See her smiley mouth and her little nose and her fat cheeks? Tomcats got a big nose, got a long muzzle. Never mind if he's been neutered, still got a big nose."

"What did you come here to say to me?" said Anna.

Griselda had curled up on the cat woman's lap, burying her head, slightly upward turned, in the crease between stomach and thigh. "I don't go in for all that stuff, you see." The big red hand stroked Griselda's head, the stripy bit between her ears. "Cat likes the smell of me because I haven't got my clothes in soapy water every day. I have a bath once a

32

week, always have and always shall, and I don't waste my money on odorizers and deodorizers. I wash my hands when I get up in the morning and that's enough for me."

At the mention of the weekly bath, Anna had reacted instinctively and edged her chair a little farther away. Maria Yackle saw, Anna was sure she saw, but her response to this recoil was to begin on what she had in fact come about: her compensation.

"The cat you killed, she was five years old and the queen of the cats, her name was Melusina. I always have a queen. The one before was Juliana and she lived to be twelve. I wept, I mourned her, but life has to go on. 'The queen is dead,' I said, 'long live the queen!' I never promote one, I always get a new kitten. Some cats are queens, you see, and some are not. Melusina was eight weeks old when I got her from the Animal Rescue people, and I gave them a donation of twenty pounds. The vet charged me twenty-seven pounds fifty for her injections—all my cats are immunized against feline enteritis and leptospirosis—so that makes forty-seven pounds fifty. And she had her booster at age two, which was another twenty-seven fifty. I can show you the receipted bills, I always keep everything, and that makes seventy-five pounds. Then there was my petrol getting her to the vet—we'll say a straight five pounds, though it was more—and then we come to the crunch, her food. She was a good little trencherwoman."

Anna would have been inclined to laugh at this ridiculous word, but she saw to her horror that the tears were running down Maria Yackle's cheeks. They were running unchecked out of her eyes, over the rough red wrinkled skin, and one dripped unheeded onto Griselda's silvery fur.

"Take no notice. I do cry whenever I have to talk about her. I loved that cat. She was the queen of the cats. She had her own place, her throne—she used to sit in the middle of the mantelpiece with her two china ladies-in-waiting on each side of her. You'll see one day, when you come to my house.

"But we were talking about her food. She ate a large can a day—it was too much, more than she should have had, but she loved her food, she was a good little eater. Well, cat food's gone up over the years, of course, what hasn't, and I'm paying fifty pee a can now, but I reckon it'd be fair to average it out at forty pee. She was eight weeks old when I got her, so we can't say five times three hundred and sixty-five. We'll say five times three fifty-five and that's doing you a favor. I've already worked it out at home, I'm not that much of a wizard at mental arithmetic. Five three-hundred and fifty-fives are one thousand, seven hundred and seventy-five, which multiplied by forty makes seventy-one thousand pee or seven hundred and ten pounds. Add to that the seventy-five plus the vet's bill of fourteen pounds when she had a tapeworm and we get a final figure of seven hundred and ninety-nine pounds."

Anna stared at her. "You're asking me to give you nearly eight hundred pounds?"

"That's right. Of course, we'll write it down and do it properly."

"Because your cat ran under the wheels of my car?"

"You murdered her," said Maria Yackle.

"That's absurd. Of course I didn't murder her." On shaky ground, she said, "You can't murder an animal."

"You did. You said you were going too fast."

Had she? She had been, but had she said so?

Maria Yackle got up, still holding Griselda, cuddling Griselda, who nestled purring in her arms. Anna watched with distaste. You thought of cats as fastidious creatures but they were not. Only something insensitive and undiscerning would put its face against that face, nuzzle those rough grimy hands. The black fingernails brought to mind a phrase, now unpleasantly appropriate, that her grandmother had used to children with dirty hands: in mourning for the cat.

"I don't expect you to give me a check now. Is that what you thought I meant? I don't suppose you have that amount in your current account. I'll come back tomorrow or the next day."

"I'm not going to give you eight hundred pounds," said Anna.

She might as well not have spoken.

"I won't come back tomorrow, I'll come back on Wednesday." Griselda was tenderly placed on the seat of an armchair. The tears had dried on Maria Yackle's face, leaving salt trails. She took herself out into the hall and to the front door. "You'll have thought about it by then. Anyway, I hope you'll come to the funeral. I hope there won't be any hard feelings."

That was when Anna decided Maria Yackle was mad. In one way, this was disquieting—in another, a comfort. It meant she wasn't serious about the compensation, the seven hundred and ninety-nine pounds. Sane people don't invite you to their cat's funeral. Mad people do not sue you for compensation.

"No, I shouldn't think she'd do that," said Richard when they were having dinner together. He wasn't a lawyer but had studied law. "You didn't admit you were exceeding the speed limit, did you?"

"I don't remember."

"At any rate, you didn't admit it in front of witnesses. You say she didn't threaten you?"

"Oh, no. She wasn't unpleasant. She cried, poor thing."

"Well, let's forget her, shall we, and have a nice time?"

Although no note awaited her on the doorstep, no letter came, and there were no phone calls, Anna knew the cat woman would come back on the following evening. Richard had advised her to go to the police if any threats were made. There would be no need to tell them she had been driving very fast. Anna thought the whole idea of going to the police bizarre. She rang up her friend Kate and told her all about it and Kate agreed that telling the police would be going too far.

The battered red car arrived at seven. Maria Yackle was dressed as she had been for her previous visit, but, because it was rather cold, wore a jacket made of synthetic fur as well. From its harsh, too-shiny texture there was no doubt it was synthetic, but from a distance it looked like a black cat's pelt.

She had brought an album of photographs of her cats for Anna to see. Anna looked through it—what else could she do? Some were recognizably of those she had seen through the windows. Those that were not, she supposed might be of animals now at rest under the wooden crosses in

Maria Yackle's back garden. While she was looking at the pictures, Griselda came in and jumped onto the cat woman's lap.

"They're very nice, very interesting," Anna said. "I can see you're devoted to your cats."

"They're my life."

A little humoring might be in order. "When is the funeral to be?"

"I thought on Friday. Two o'clock on Friday. My sister will be there with her two. Cats don't usually take to car travel, that's why I don't often take any of mine with me, and shutting them up in cages goes against the grain—but my sister's two Burmese love the car, they'll go and sit in the car when it's parked. My friend from the Animal Rescue will come if she can get away and I've asked our vet, but I don't hold out much hope there. He has his goat clinic on Fridays. I hope you'll come along."

"I'm afraid I'll be at work."

"It's no flowers by request. Donations to the Cats' Protection League instead. Any sum, no matter how small, gratefully received. Which brings me to money. You've got a check for me."

"No, I haven't, Mrs. Yackle."

"Miss. And it's Yakob. J-A-K-O-B. You've got a check for me for seven hundred and ninety-nine pounds."

"I'm not giving you any money, Miss Jakob. I'm very, very sorry about your cat, about Melusina, I know how fond you were of her, but giving you compensation is out of the question. I'm sorry."

The tears had come once more into Maria Jakob's eyes, had spilled over. Her face contorted with misery. It was the mention of the wretched thing's name, Anna thought. That was the trigger that started the weeping. A tear splashed onto one of the coarse red hands. Griselda opened her eyes and licked up the tear.

Maria Jakob pushed her other hand across her eyes. She blinked. "We'll have to think of something else then," she said.

"I beg your pardon?" Anna wondered if she had really heard. Things couldn't be solved so simply.

"We shall have to think of something else. A way for you to make up to me for murder."

"Look, I will give a donation to the Cats' Protection League. I'm quite prepared to give them—say, twenty pounds." Richard would be furious, but perhaps she wouldn't tell Richard. "I'll give it to you, shall I, and then you can pass it on to them?"

"I certainly hope you will. Especially if you can't come to the funeral."

That was the end of it, then. Anna felt a great sense of relief. It was only now that it was over that she realized quite how it had got to her. It had actually kept her from sleeping properly. She phoned Kate and told her about the funeral and the goat clinic, and Kate laughed and said Poor old thing. Anna slept so well that night that she didn't notice the arrival of Griselda who, when she woke, was asleep on the pillow next to her face but out of touching distance.

Richard phoned and she told him about it, omitting the part about her offer of a donation. He told her that being firm, sticking to one's guns in situations of this kind, always paid off. In the evening, she wrote a check for twenty pounds but, instead of the Cats' Protection League, made it out to Maria Jakob. If the cat woman quietly held onto it, no harm would be done. Anna went down the road to post her letter, for she had written a letter to accompany the check, in which she reiterated her sorrow about the death of the cat and added that if there was anything she could do Miss Jakob had only to let her know. Richard would have been furious.

Unlike the Jakob cats, Griselda spent a good deal of time out of doors. She was often out all evening and did not reappear until the small hours, so that it was not until the next day, not until the next evening, that Anna began to be alarmed at her absence. As far as she knew, Griselda had never been away so long before. For herself, she was unconcerned—she had never liked the cat, did not particularly like any cats, and found this one obnoxiously self-centered and cold. It was for her mother, who unaccountably loved the creature, that she was worried. She walked up and down the street calling Griselda, though the cat had never been known to come when it was called.

It did not come now. Anna walked up and down the next street, calling, and around the block and farther afield. She half expected to find Griselda's body, guessing that it might have met the same fate as Melusina. Hadn't she read somewhere that nearly forty thousand cats are killed on British roads annually?

On Saturday morning, she wrote one of those melancholy lost-cat notices and attached it to a lamp standard, wishing she had a photograph. But her mother had taken no photographs of Griselda.

Richard took her to a friend's party and afterward, when they were driving home, he said, "You know what's happened, don't you? It's been killed by that old mad woman. An eye for an eye, a cat for a cat."

"Oh, no, she wouldn't do that. She loves cats."

"Murderers love people. They just don't love the people they murder."

"I'm sure you're wrong," said Anna, but she remembered how Maria Jakob had said that if the money was not forthcoming, she must think of something else—a way to make up to her for Melusina's death. And she had not meant a donation to the Cats' Protection League.

"What shall I do?"

"I don't see that you can do anything. It's most unlikely you could prove it, she'll have seen to that. You can look at it this way—she's had her pound of flesh."

"Fifteen pounds of flesh," said Anna. Griselda had been a large, heavy cat.

"Okay, fifteen pounds. She's had that, she's had her revenge. It hasn't actually caused you any grief—you'll just have to make up some story for your mother."

Anna's mother was upset, but nowhere near as upset as Maria Jakob had been over the death of Melusina. To avoid too much fuss, Anna had gone further than she intended, told her mother that she had seen Griselda's corpse and talked to the offending motorist, who had been very distressed.

A month or so later, Anna's mother got a kitten, a grey tabby tomkitten, who was very affectionate from the start, sat on her lap, purred loudly when stroked, and snuggled up in her arms, though Anna was sure her mother had not stopped having baths or using perfume. So much for the Jakob theories.

Nearly a year had gone by before she again drove down the road where Maria Jakob's house was. She had not intended to go that way. Directions had been given her to a smallholding where they sold early strawberries on a roadside stall but she must have missed her way, taken a wrong turning, and come out here.

If Maria Jakob's car had been parked in the front, she would not have stopped. There was no garage for it to be in and it was not outside, therefore the cat woman must be out. Anna thought of the funeral she had not been to—she had often thought about it, the strange people and strange cats who had attended it.

In each of the bay windows sat a cat, a tortoiseshell and a brown tabby. The black cat was eyeing her from upstairs. Anna didn't go to the front door but round the back. There, among the long grass, as she had expected, were four graves instead of three, four wooden crosses, and on the fourth was printed in black gloss paint: MELUSINA, THE QUEEN OF THE CATS, MURDERED IN HER SIXTH YEAR. RIP.

That "murdered" did not please Anna. It brought back all the resentment at the unjust accusations of eleven months before. She felt much older, she felt wiser. One thing was certain, ethics or no ethics, if she ever ran over a cat again she'd drive on—the last thing she'd do was go and confess.

She came round to the side of the house and looked in at the bay window. If the tortoiseshell had still been on the windowsill, she probably would not have looked in, but the tortoiseshell had removed itself to the hearthrug.

A white cat and the marmalade-and-white lay curled up side by side in an armchair. The portrait of Melusina hung above the fireplace and this year's cat calendar was up on the left-hand wall. Light gleamed on the china cats' gilt whiskers—and between them, in the empty space that was no longer vacant, sat Griselda.

Griselda was sitting in the queen's place in the middle of the mantelpiece. She sat in the sphinx position with her eyes closed. Anna tapped on the glass and Griselda opened her eyes, stared with cold indifference, and closed them again.

The queen is dead, long live the queen!

Fritz Leiber

THE CAT HOTEL

From the cool patch of floor by the kitchen door Gummitch, an orange cat of endless curiosity and great patience, watched the younger and slenderer gray cat Psycho stand motionless over their water dish, peering down at her reflection. The day was hot, but she did not drink.

Although they were not related, Gummitch felt a big-brotherly concern for Psycho. He wondered if she were studying the mirror world or even considering oversetting the dish to create a water-sculpture as he'd done on occasion.

Or if something sinister were at work.

Kitty-Come-Here, their featherbrained mistress, known to humans as Helen Hunter, stopped in the dining room doorway, a small slender woman in a thin flowered dress carrying a furled green parasol and a small white handbag.

"I've called a taxi, Gummitch," she informed him, "to take me to the Concordia Convalescent Hospital to make polite inquiry of my beloved widowed mother-in-law as to how her broken hip is mending, and sweet worried noises. Though truly it is the great Harry Hunter's place to do that." She sniffed. "Don't you think, Gummitch, his business trips have come most conveniently since the catastrophe? I leave you in charge of the house. Please don't go out and pick a fight with the Mad Eunuch, it's much too sultry. Ah, there's the buzzer. Psycho, if you can stop admiring yourself for a moment and listen to me, be a good kitling and do everything that Gummitch tells you to, bar bedroom stuff. Now goodbye, chaps."

Gummitch himself rather wished that Old Horsemeat were here, not to pay dutiful filial visits, but to consult with about Psycho. Except that of late his strange parent-god had been imbibing rather too freely of the second of the two wondrous and terrible evil-tasting human beverages—not mind-quickening coffee, which had the power almost (but not quite, alas) to gift brutes with human speech, but insidious sometimes-burning alcohol, the mocker and jester—and as a result was not to be trusted as much as formerly.

Kitty-Come-Here, the ginger cat had to admit, was showing flashes of unaccustomed thoughtfulness and reliability—though not many or very bright, he hastened to add. Still and all, beneath her solemn kitteny playfulness, there did seem to be something new, serious and mysteriously sad, growing by fits and starts under the bobbed black hair of the little lady who had come to Old Horsemeat (to use his words) from over the Shortwaved Ocean, in contradistinctions to the Pacific.

The cat heard the front door close.

Somewhat later, at Concordia, Helen Hunter backed smiling and cooing out of Mrs. Hobart Hunter's single dim ground-floor room rather more hurriedly than she'd planned so as not, at all costs, to hear the deep sob she suddenly *knew* was going to burst convulsively from behind the bravely composed face and tightly pressed, serenely smiling lips of the cologne-scented old lady supine in the narrow high bed. For if she did hear it, she'd have to go back and do all her clucking, Harry-excusing work over again, and she as suddenly knew she simply couldn't *bear* that. Panic touched her, and in its unreasoning grip she backed rather faster and farther than she'd intended—all the way into the equally dim double room across the hall.

Gaining some control of herself, she turned around rapidly, surveyed the three beds and three old women crowding the room, and was momentarily shocked moveless and speechless, the contrast with what she had been visiting was so positively scaly.

Her mother-in-law had been tucked in neatly (of course she had a broken hip), while these creatures sprawled all which ways in their nightgowns (after all, it *was* warm) on top of their covers and pillows with all sorts of resultant untidy, immodest, even obscene disclosures.

In the single room there were a few neatly arranged objects on the bedside table and nothing whatever on the top sheet save Mrs. Hobart Hunter's pale flaccid arms extended decorously down her sides. Here all three beds and tabletops were littered with a jumble of soiled crumpled tissues, hair-holding combs and brushes, candy boxes, lunch remnants, paper cups, photographs, books, papers, and magazines, mostly astrology.

Harry's mother had been recently washed and neatly groomed, smelled of cologne.

These women had elf-locked or straggly flying hair, what there was of it, smeared lipstick, were smudged with dirt, looked greasy. They had a variety of odors about them. Really, they stank.

The first old woman had scrawny legs, a chunky pot-bellied body, and a little screwed-up face with squinting eyes and a button nose that would have looked scowly-angry except her small mouth was smiling.

The second old woman was fat like a little bumpy mountain with immense hips, droopy jowls, and large peering pop-eyes.

The third old woman was skinny as death itself, had a blotched pallor all over, a curving beak of a nose, and no chin to speak of. An empty brass cage hung beside her bed.

Helen took in all this in three rapid snapshots, as it were. A couple more seconds and she might have recovered her poise, but just then the first old woman asked with a chuckle, "Lose your way, dearie?"

"Something frighten you, chickie?" the third old woman chimed like a cracked bell.

"Well, you certainly aren't my niece Andrea," the second old woman observed in a voice like suet.

"No, I don't believe I am," Helen started to say inanely and broke off midway, flustered.

"My, what a lovely green parasol," the third old woman continued.

"And what lovely bobbed hair. You do look cool," the first old woman added enviously.

"You look nice enough to eat," the second old lady concluded in her flannel tones.

"Oh, do please excuse me," Helen began and then turned and ran out before she garbled anything more or yielded to the impulse to respond to the last remark with "Is *that* what made you so fat, you dirty old cannibal?"

In her hurry she turned the wrong way in the hall, and rather than repass Mrs. Hobart Hunter's door and risk hearing snuffles, she left the Concordia by the way of the door to the concrete-surfaced "patio" surrounded on three sides by a tall hedge, which was simply the backyard of the one-story convalescent hospital and figured as an airing spot for the mostly elderly patients.

It was empty now, save for a few white tables and chairs in need of a paint job, and very hot. Helen unfurled her parasol and departed by the one exit available if you didn't want to go back through the Concordia, a two-foot gap in the back hedge—she had to tip her parasol to get through.

She emerged in an untidy, unpaved alley with garbage cans. From the newspapers scattered around them the words "Korea," "239 Communists," "McCarthy," and "Rosenbergs" leaped up, reminding her of how Harry had said to Gummitch, "We live in a witch-hunt age, you hear me, cat? They got the diplomats and movie actors. They'll be after writers next, writers and cats. Remember how the Inquisition got after you along with the witches? Maybe the FBI will come for you and me at the same time."

Across the alley was another tall hedge with a matching gap in it, through which she could see a wedge of very green lawn that looked much more attractive than the littered sandy alley, so she pressed on through, tipping her parasol again and noting that the way underfoot was somewhat worn, as if these back exits were in regular use.

The gap was in a back corner of the property she entered. Straight ahead of her, the intensely green lawn stretched to the next street and was so thick and springy underfoot she was reminded of her native England.

There emerged into view a neat two-story wooden Victorian house whose gleaming white paint put the Concordia to shame. By its back door there was parked a shining white motor scooter with a white box fixed behind its sheepskin saddle. A narrow walk of pale gravel led from it close around the house to the next street.

Just next to Helen at the back of the property was a large area enclosed by a neat mesh-wire fence several feet higher than the hedge. Inside it were more lawn, three graceful low trees, some tidy bushes, two flower beds, and a low summer house (it looked) white as the main building with a white scrollwork sign over its open door that read, in much-serifed black letters, "Wicks Cat Hotel."

As she strolled wonderingly forward around the enclosure, Helen congratulated herself that her green parasol and flowered dress suited her very well to this handsome environment. Thank goodness, she told herself, she'd washed her hair and taken a shower just before coming out.

Coming around in front of the enclosure, where there was a latched door in the mesh, she surveyed it more closely, at once spotting a tranquil Himalayan on a tiny platform in one of the low trees and two strolling lilac-point Siamese slender as fashion models. The longer she looked, the more cats she saw ensconced in the bushes, sniffing the flowers, and wandering in and out of the little building, all of them elegant and well behaved, a few rather plain tabbies among the aristocracy, which included a blue Persian, a crinkly coated dark silver Rex, and a Havana brown who positively flamed. She said aloud softly, "Oh, Gummitch, if you could see this. A positive cat heaven!"

"Some persons do voice that reaction. But who is Gummitch, pray?"

Helen turned to face a trim woman her own age, two inches taller, fully as slender, but a degree sturdier than herself. A straw blonde, she wore her hair cropped and white slacks and Nehru jacket at once medical, military, and chic. Her right eye was deep blue, the other brown.

"He's my cat," Helen said eagerly, and when the other did not at once respond volunteered, "I'm Helen Hunter."

"Wendy Wicks," the other responded, extending her hand. "I'm the proprietor. Do I rightly discern in your speech a British accent with the lilt of Wales?"

Nodding, Helen countered, "And I a Scots?"

"Truly enough, though I come from the Lakes. Which makes us fellow countrymen," the other said approvingly, adding an extra squeeze to their handshake. "Would you care to look inside?" She unlatched the mesh door. Helen furled her parasol.

The guests of the Wicks Hotel took no notice of them. Inside the low white building the two women stood comfortably enough, though Helen noted Harry would have had to stoop here. It was all one room lined with about sixty comfortably large cages in three tiers, each with its rug, water and food dish, and cat-box. The floor was occupied only by some hassocks, a climbing frame, and an imposing gray Tudor castle of stout cardboard with numerous cat-size windows and doors.

Helen echoed herself with, "A cat paradise!"

Wendy ended her little talk with, "Some of our guests are quite long-term, while their mistresses go to New York or London for the plays, or on extended ocean cruises," and gave Helen a hotel card on which her first name was spelled "Wendele," had the initials "D.V.M" behind, and there was the subscript "hospital facilities available."

Wendy said, "The next time you're out of town, Gummitch might enjoy our hospitality. That is, unless he's an unneutered male."

"He is," Helen informed her. "My husband, Harry, has very fixed ideas upon that point—"

"I know," the other interposed with a touch of venom, "men are apt to entertain such barbarous notions."

"—and so do I, I was going to say," Helen concluded bravely.

Wendy caught her hand and squeezed it, saying with a disarming smile, "There are, of course, my dear, good arguments, aside from patristic ones, to be made for that position. Even the Amazons had to make compromises. Why, I've taken toms myself in the hospital. Come, let me show you that."

Helen followed her out of the hotel and its grounds up to the back door of the Victorian house. As they passed the motor scooter Wendy touched it, saying, "Our ambulance," then, as she opened the white door beyond, "The Wicks Cat Hospital! No other species accepted!"

Inside was a spotless veterinary examination—and, Helen supposed, emergency room—everything cat-sized and -adapted. Suspended on brass wires from points along the skull, spine, and tail was the complete skeleton of a cat, which struck her as rather grisly. A large 1953 calendar on the wall featured phases of the moon.

Wendy said, "Wait a minute and I'll show you our isolation ward for infectious cases. I'll call you," and she pushed through one of the two inner doors.

Helen peeked after her in time to see her draw a black curtain in front of three cages like those in the hotel, then drew back a little guiltily.

"Come in," Wendy called and when Helen had complied pointed out three glass-fronted large white boxes against the wall opposite the three curtained cages.

"Our isolation cubicles," she explained. "They have their own ventilation system."

Two of the boxes were empty. The other held a young seal-point Siamese, who peered out at them bright-eyed enough.

"I detected a mild respiratory infection in this one of our guests," Wendy explained, "and am treating it with antibiotics. She'll probably return to the hotel tomorrow." The phone in the examination room rang. "Excuse me," she said.

Alone, after a few seconds Helen yielded to curiosity. She crossed the room and started to lift a corner of the black curtain.

"Mrs. Hunter!" the other called from the doorway, "do you realize that cats are subject to certain diseases in which their eyes become temporarily hypersensitive to light? You might have permanently injured one of our patients."

"I'm sorry, I didn't know," Helen said, backing off.

"I think you had best leave," the other went on in a gruff doctor voice, and as she escorted a flurried Helen through the other inside door of the examination room through a long old-fashioned parlor with a large fireplace, continued formidably, "In the past, Mrs. Hunter, persons have gained entry to these premises under false pretences with the intention of kidnapping valuable cats to hold for ransom and for even worse purposes!" Her mismatched eyes flashed coldly.

"You surely don't think that I—" Helen began, more apologetic than indignant.

"No, I suppose not, I guess," Wendy replied with sudden and surprising return to her earlier amiability, "but after all, Helen, I have showed you everything here, and I'm sure that we both have other things to do." She led Helen into a front hall with a wide staircase leading to the second story. Then, as she let her out the front door, where a brass plate read "Wicks Cat Hospital," she gave Helen's hand a final squeeze and said with a smile, "Come back for another visit, dear, anytime you wish. Only remember that I'm another lone Britisher in an alien land and a profession dominated by arrogant males, so I have become overly sensitive and suspicious."

Hastening home by bus, Helen's feelings were mixed. She still felt drawn to Wendy. Such a strong, handsome, competent girl with a really beautiful face if you made allowance (if that were needed) for slightly overlarge upper center incisors and rather long large ears, though growing close to the skull, and of course the intriguing blue-brown eye pair. Why, it was years and years since she'd noticed so much about a person she'd met only once. Am I becoming infatuated? she asked herself with a silent giggle.

But then, on the other hand, the veterinary's sudden exaggerated hostility and the rather shivery details of the cat skeleton and black curtain. What had been behind that, anyway? The light-sensitive story was surely a blind because the light in the "isolation ward" had been on when the doctor'd first gone in and drawn the curtain.

And yet at the same time the whole place had reminded her so much and so nostalgically of England—the lawn, the house and cat motel, the woman herself—half-awakening deep-buried memories of all sorts, some of them, Helen felt sure, very strange.

When she left the bus, the day, though more sultry than ever, had darkened, and when she stuck her key in her own front door, she heard a low rumble of thunder.

Gummitch was waiting inside, uttering a "Mrrp-Mrrp!" in which there was more alarm and indignation than greeting. He ran halfway up the stairs and then paused to look back over his shoulder. Heart sinking, Helen followed him to the upstairs bathroom, where Psycho lay curled motionless in the pale green washbowl as though it was a cat sarcophagus. The young cat seemed only half-conscious; her eyes were filmed, her short gray fur was rough, her nose hot.

Helen carried her downstairs to the phone and dialed the number on the card given her by Wendy, who answered on the third ring, listened to Helen's rapid description, and said only, "Don't do anything. I'll be there."

Waiting would have been easier for Helen if she'd been told to do something. She opened the front door to the gathering dark and low growling thunder. She asked, "Whatever happened, Gummitch? Did Psycho go out and eat something?" But the orangy cat answered only, "Mrrp-Mrrp!" Finally she called a taxi.

As if that had been the proper charm to hurry events, there was a purring "put-put" from down the street. Going to the door with Gummitch close beside her, she saw that the approaching storm had banished twilight and brought on instant night, into which the pale shape of the hospital scooter and rider came like the ghost of a modern centaur. It nosed into the driveway, then rode diagonally across the lawn to park at the foot of the front steps.

Wendy was now wearing additionally a white cap with rather long visor, and she stripped off white gauntlets as she came up the steps, carefully took Psycho into her arms, and briefly examined her.

"She's very sick and must be taken to the hospital at once and given treatment," she pronounced. "I'll have a full report for you tomorrow morning. Don't worry too much: she's a young cat and I believe we've caught it in time. Her chances of complete recovery are very good." All this while carrying Psycho down the steps, gently laying her in the box behind the saddle, which opened at a touch, and getting astride the vehicle, having thrust her gauntlets in the top of her slacks.

"Good-bye, chaps," she called as she drove off carefully at an even pace.

It all happened so fast that Helen, who'd hurried down the steps with Gummitch after her, couldn't think what to call back. But now as they both watched the white scooter disappear down the dark street, she said, "Oh, Gummitch, what have we done to Psycho?"

"Warra warra," the cat replied, concerned and somewhat angry. He hadn't liked the cat doctor's looks, and he also believed that his own close presence was in any case something essential to Psycho's safety and recovery.

Thunder rumbled, closer now.

A taxicab drew up. Its driver got out and, seeing Helen, opened the rear door and came a few steps up the walk.

She arrived at a quick decision, called to him, "I'll just get my bag and wrap; be with you in a second," and ran up the steps into the house, thinking Gummitch had run back ahead of her; cars often had that effect on him.

But the cat had other ideas. He'd circled off sideways into the darkness, made a craftily wide circle through some bushes, and sneaked into the cab when the driver wasn't looking.

Inside he did not spring on the seat, but instead crouched in the dark far corner of the floor. He did not intend the investigations he had in mind to be thwarted. And indeed when Kitty-Come-Here got in, she was so busy giving the driver instructions as to where the Wicks Cat Hospital was, and so agitated generally, that she actually didn't notice him. She slung her light coat on the seat beside her, and it trailed over, further concealing him.

Gummitch congratulated himself on his sagacity. What doesn't move in the shadows, isn't seen. Old Horsemeat had more than once recited to him Eliot's poem about McCavity, the mystery cat modeled on

Professor Moriarty, and if there were a Moriarty, there had to be a cat Sherlock Holmes, didn't there?

When the cab drew up at the newly repainted old white house with the brass plate beside the door and Kitty-Come-Here got out, saying to the driver, "Please wait for me," Gummitch slid out right behind her and immediately ducked under the vehicle, preparatory to beginning another of his wide circles. Geometric evasiveness, that's one more of my methods, he told himself.

Helen mounted to the open porch and pushed the buzzer, and when it wasn't answered quickly, plied the brass knocker, too. But when the door was finally opened, it was by an unsmiling and doctor-faced Wendy, who did not move aside to let her in.

"It's past visiting hours," she said coldly. "Really, Helen, I know you're concerned about your cat, but you mustn't become hysterical. You can't see Psycho now in any case; she's in isolation."

"But you didn't even tell me what's wrong with her," Helen protested.

"Very well. Your cat is suffering from epidemic feline enteritis, the most widespread and dangerous cat plague of them all, one for which early immunization is a necessary precaution observed by all half-way informed owners. But you never had shots for her, did you? No, I thought not. Perhaps your husband doesn't believe in that, either."

Gummitch watched the two from the next to the top step of the stairs to the porch, only his narrowed eyes showing over. When the cat doctor was in the midst of her condescending and reproachful lecture, he flowed up onto the porch and along it to the second window from the door, which was open wide at the bottom, and softly looped through, hugging the wall and sill, into the dim large room beyond.

Outside, the cat doctor continued, "What treatment is she getting? I injected serum and water in proper quantity, gave by mouth a chemical agent I've had good results with, and disposed her comfortably in an isolation cubicle, where she is getting *rest,* which is something even veterinary doctors require and get on rare occasions, and you no doubt could do with yourself. Please do not call before 9 A.M. tomorrow. Good night, dear Helen." And she closed the door.

After a moment of staring at it with both fists clenched, Helen returned to her cab, disconsolate and fuming delicately. The driver asked her, "Excuse me, lady, but did you have a cat with you in there when we came over?"

"Certainly not!" she replied impatiently. "Why do you ask?"

"I don't know," the driver responded warily. "I just thought. . . ." His voice trailed off.

I shouldn't have been so short with him, she told herself. Natural of him to suppose that when you go to a cat hospital you take a cat. Probably thought I had it wrapped in my coat or something.

Nevertheless, the matter worried her a little. Now she wouldn't feel easy until she'd seen Gummitch. But when she did, at least she could speak out her mind to him, relieve her injured feelings a little. Oh, that wicked (but so dashing) doctor woman!

In the Wicks Cat Hospital living room, Gummitch had immediately found a good hiding place under an easy chair against a wall, from which he could survey the whole room, study the black carpet with its curious designs in white lines, and wait until things settled down before beginning his detective work—see which way the cat doctor was going to jump, you might put it.

After shutting the door on Helen, she came rapidly through the living room (Gummitch saw only her trousered legs footed with white oxfords) and went through the swinging door at its back end. Outside, thunder crackled. The storm was definitely getting nearer.

After enough time for Gummitch to go into a half-doze, the cat doctor returned, setting the swinging door wide open, he was happy to see, though he could have managed it himself, he was confident, as well as many knobs and some latches.

She moved more thoughtfully this time, going to one of the bookcases and selecting a volume to take with her, before exiting to the front hall, leaving dimmed lights behind her everywhere. He heard her going upstairs.

Helen was in a quandary. She'd paid off the taxi driver, tipping him generously to make up for her shortness with him, but when she'd gone into the house there'd been no Gummitch to greet her and hear what she thought of the doctor woman. He might have gone out through the cat door, of course, on some business of his own, but wouldn't he have waited to ask her about Psycho? Had the taxi driver really seen a cat? Despite Wendy's warning she dialed again the number on the card, but this time got only an answering service which could just take messages to give the doctor when and if she called in. Outside, thunder boomed. Helen didn't like being all alone in the house.

Back in the living room of the cat hospital, the cat-detective still bided his time under the easy chair. After another period of waiting, during which there were faint footsteps overhead that finally ceased—the cat doctor's and someone else's, still lighter but thumpy ones—Gummitch ventured out and unhurriedly made his way toward the back of the room, frequently pausing to sniff. Outside, the crackling came more often, and suddenly he heard the patter, then the pelting of swift-breaking rain, and from the window behind him felt a breath of chilly storm-breeze.

The white-line pattern on the black carpet was a curious one of triangles and triskelions and swastikas, and just in front of the cold, empty but practical fireplace and with one of its five points aimed straight at it, a huge empty star. There welled up in his mind a murky racial memory of an even wider hearth with a huge fire blazing in it and naked women standing before it in a pentacle and rubbing into each other's bodies an ointment that had a not altogether unpleasing acrid odor.

Gummitch glided into the examination room, saw the hanging cat skeleton, hissed under his breath, then sprang to the table before it, and gave it an experimental pat. The little bones rattled softly and the skull swung a bit, as if to see who its disturber was.

He next entered the isolation ward, the door of which was also set open. Perhaps because of the soft purr of their ventilation system, his gaze fixed at once on the three glass-fronted isolation cubicles, and he leaped lightly to the shelf in front of them.

In the cubicle Psycho lay on her side with eyes closed and ears drooped. He couldn't repress a mew of excitement, then, with his muzzle pressed against the glass, mewed softly twice more and rapped the pane lightly with a paw. She did not stir.

53

The young Siamese in the next cubicle was making motions at him, but Gummitch ignored her, continuing to study Psycho. He could discern her gray chest rise and fall a little, regularly, while her fur looked a little brighter than it had in the pale green washbowl, he thought—or hoped.

He reminded himself then that he was a detective in enemy territory and couldn't afford to give way for long to dumb dutifulness. With an effort he tore his gaze away from Psycho's window, turned to survey the rest of the isolation ward, and saw for the first time the three now uncurtained wire cages against the opposite wall.

The fur on his back rose and his tail thickened.

In the first cage was a little old dog with squinched-up face and beady eyes that glared at him continuously, a black Pekinese.

In the second cage was an animal of the same shape as the little green frogs he'd seen hopping around in the spring. Only this one was bigger and fatter, with warts. And it didn't hop, but just crouched slumpingly and fixed upon him its large cold, cold eyes. It was the same color as the dog.

On a low perch in the third cage was a rather large bird which Gummitch knew to be a parrot because the Mad Eunuch's owner kept a bright green one with a big yellow beak. But this one was mangy and ancient-looking and malevolent-eyed, while its wickedly curving beak pointed straight at him. Both its beak and its ragged feather coat were inky black.

The little dog coughed hackingly, and thunder crashed outside as if the heavens were riven, while the great glare of lightning that simultaneously shone through the open doorway called Gummitch's attention to a fourth ebon beast just now hopped there and regarding him with an intelligence that seemed greater and more evil than that of the others.

It was an animal that Gummitch had never seen before, but thought because of its overlarge front top teeth must be related to squirrels, one of whom had terrified him in kittenhood when they'd first seen each other close from opposite sides of a window. And it had long, tall ears. Gummitch could only imagine it to be a deformed giant tailless squirrel, the product of mad science or vile sorcery.

Now it turned and, as lightning flared again and thunder crashed, hopped—to report, Gummitch was suddenly sure, to the cat doctor. The fearless cat-detective reached an instant decision and leaped down and raced after. The monstrous beast crossed the living room in four long hops, but Gummitch could readily match that speed, he found. In the front hall at the foot of the stairs, the beast turned at bay, making mewling sounds. Gummitch advanced on it stiff-legged and back arched, involuntarily letting out a loud and most undetectivelike caterwaul.

Then he saw beyond it the cat doctor coming down the stairs. She was stark naked, bore in her hand a long yellowish knife with red hilt, and glared at him, the lips of her small mouth parted in a snarl that revealed her large front teeth.

He retreated to the living room. She came after, her knife advanced before her, followed by the black hopping giant squirrel-monster. Gummitch cast one longing look at the open window, but then remembered his responsibilities. To the accompaniment of the storm's hammer blows and flashes, he raced twice around the room to baffle them, then darted through the examination room back into the isolation ward. They came after him relentlessly. From atop Psycho's cubicle he caterwauled defiance. They came up to it.

But then the storm's final and climatic thunder-crash and dazzling lightning-flare revealed to all three of them a new figure framed in the doorway, a rather small person wearing a dripping yellow oilskin and a deep-brimmed sou'wester.

It was Kitty-Come-Here, and she cried out, "Gummitch! I knew I'd find you here!"

Gummitch's fur relaxed a little. Wendy shoved the knife under some papers on the table beside her. The black squirrel-monster mewled innocently.

Kitty-Come-Here eyed the three of them in turn, taking her time about it, and then her gaze went on to the three occupants of the wire cages. At last she cried out comprehendingly, "Wendy, you are a *witch*. And that black rabbit there is your familiar. And although you claim this is a hospital for cats only, you've been treating or boarding the *familiars* of those three dreadful old women (all witches, of course; you probably have a whole coven!) in the Concordia in the room opposite my mother-in-law's. The resemblances are all unmistakable and prove my case. And when there's no outsider to see, you go around naked—"sky-clad" is your witch expression for that, isn't it? And you were chasing Gummitch and trying to do something to him, weren't you?"

Wendy reached a lab smock from a hook on the wall and shouldered into it leisurely. "Why, I never heard a more ridiculous set of ideas in my whole life," she said guilelessly. "It's true I sometimes bend the hospital's only-one-species rule a little, and it wouldn't do to advertise that to the mistresses of our guests. And I have a pet hare; drop a curtsy, dear Bunnykins! Cats are wonderful, but one needs a break from them when one sees them all the time. And I do occasionally doctor or board pets of patients in the Concordia, both apt to be elderly for obvious reasons. Any psychologist will tell you, dear Helen, that people, especially elderly ones, grow to resemble their pets, or else select them with that point unconsciously in mind. I habitually sleep raw, and tonight when Bunnykins and I discovered loose in the hospital what we took to be a stray tom bent on rapine (how could I know he was your Gummitch, dear?), we were seeking to eject him, that is all. There, does that answer your questions?"

"I don't think so," Helen said stoutly. "Why are all these animals *black,* I want to know? And what were you hiding when I came in?"

"I have a deep professional interest in melanism," Wendy told her. "And by the by, how *did* you get in?"

"When no one answered the door, I climbed through the open window, and now I'm glad I did! You still haven't told me—"

A joyous meow! from Gummitch interrupted this interchange. He was looking in Psycho's window. The young grey cat lifted her head a little and opened her eyes, which were no longer filmed with sickness, but bright with cat intelligence. She was smiling at Gummitch and them all. Though obviously still very weak and quite haggard-looking, she was clearly on the road to recovery.

This most happy occurrence rather put an end to serious accusations of witchcraft and other ill-feeling, and when Wendy insisted on serving them tea in a pot with an English Union Jack on it, with milk to go with it and seedcake, and with a saucer of milk for Gummitch, peace was fully sealed. Gummitch drank a third of his milk to please Kitty-Come-Here, though keeping a most wary eye on the cat doctor and Bunnykins, who appeared to resent that name, the cat judged, though continuing to act the innocent fool.

Afterward, going home by taxi, Helen told Gummitch, "I still think she may be a witch, you know, but a rather nice one, just being kind to some dirty old sister witches—ugh, old as *Macbeth!*—and their sick animals. And she did have to admit you were most well-behaved, Gummitch, for a tom. I think that's a lot, coming from her. And you *did* uncover the whole thing, whatever it was, you know, you clever, sneaky cat. You broke through her British reticence, all right. She'd have played snob-doctor all night, otherwise. And did you notice, Gummitch, she had the slimmest and most stalwart body and the darlingest little breasts, almost as small as mine. I'm sure we're leaving Psycho in very good hands. But how should we tell Old Horsemeat about all this, Gummitch, when he comes back from his business revels? Not everything, I think, though of course he'd love it all for one of his stories."

Gummitch decided she was still pretty featherbrained.

Amy Hempel

NASHVILLE GONE TO ASHES

After the dog's cremation, I lie in my husband's bed and watch the Academy Awards for animals. That is not the name of the show, but they give prizes to animals for Outstanding Performance in a movie, on television, or in a commercial. Last year the Schlitz Malt Liquor bull won. The time before that, it was Fred the Cockatoo. Fred won for draining a tinky bottle of "liquor" and then reeling and falling over drunk. It is the best thing on television is what my husband Flea said.

With Flea gone, I watch out of habit.

On top of the warm set is big white Chuck, catching a portion of his four million winks. His tail hangs down and bisects the screen. On top of the dresser, and next to the phone, is the miniature pine crate that holds Nashville's gritty ashes.

Neil the Lion cops the year's top honors. The host says Neil is on location in Africa, but accepting for Neil is his grandson Winston. A woman approaches the stage with a ten-week cub in her arms, and the audience all goes *Awwww*. The home audience, too, I bet. After the cub, they bring the winners on stage together. I figure they must have been sedated—because none of them are biting each other.

I have my own to tend to. Chuck needs tomato juice for his urological problem. Boris and Kirby need brewer's yeast for their nits. Also, I left the vacuum out and the mynah bird is shrieking. Birds think a vacuum-cleaner hose is a snake.

Flea sold his practice after the stroke, so these are the only ones I look after now. These are the ones that always shared the house.

My husband, by the way, was F. Lee Forest, D.V.M.

The hospital is right next door to the house.

It was my side that originally bought him the practice. I bought it for him with the applesauce money. My father made an applesauce fortune because *his* way did not use lye to take off the skins. Enough of it was left to me that I had the things I wanted. I bought Flea the practice because I could.

Will Rogers called vets the noblest of doctors because their patients can't tell them what's wrong. The doctor has to reach, and he reaches with his heart.

I think it was that love that I loved. That kind of involvement was reassuring; I felt it would extend to me, as well. That it did not or that it did, but only as much and no more, was confusing at first. I thought, My love is so good, why isn't it calling the same thing back?

Things might have collapsed right there. But the furious care he gave the animals gave me hope and kept me waiting.

I did not take naturally to my husband's work. For instance, I am allergic to cats. For the past twenty years, I have had to receive immunotherapy. These are not pills; they are injections.

Until I was seventeen, I thought a ham was an animal. But I was not above testing a stool sample next door.

I go to the mynah first and put the vacuum cleaner away. This bird, when it isn't shrieking, says only one thing. Flea taught it what to say. He put a sign on its cage that reads *Tell me I'm stupid.* So you say to the bird, "Okay, you're stupid," and the bird says, real sarcastic, "I can talk—can *you fly?*"

Flea could have opened in Vegas with that. But there is no cozying up to a bird.

It will be the first to go, the mynah. The second if you count Nashville.

I promised Flea I would take care of them, and I am. I screened the new owners myself.

Nashville was his favorite. She was a grizzle-colored saluki with lightly feathered legs and Nile-green eyes. You know those skinny dogs on Egyptian pots? Those are salukis, and people worshiped them back then.

Flea acted like he did, too.

He fed that dog dates.

I used to watch her carefully spit out the pit before eating the next one. She sat like a sphinx while he reached inside her mouth to massage her licorice gums. She let him nick tartar from her teeth with his nail.

This is the last time I will have to explain that name. The pick of the litter was named Memphis. They are supposed to have Egyptian names. Flea misunderstood and named his Nashville. A woman back East owns Boston.

At the end of every summer, Flea took Nashville to the Central Valley. They hunted some of the rabbits out of the vineyards. It's called coursing when you use a sight hound. With her keen vision, Nashville would spot a rabbit and point it for Flea to come after. One time she sighted straight up at the sky—and he said he followed her gaze to a plane crossing the sun.

Sometimes I went along, and one time we let Boris hunt, too.

Boris is a Russian wolfhound. He is the size of a float in the Rose Bowl Parade.

He's a real teenager of a dog—if Boris didn't have whiskers, he'd have pimples. He goes through two nylabones a week, and once he ate a box of nails.

That's right, a box.

The day we loosed Boris on the rabbits he had drunk a cup of coffee. Flea let him have it, with half-and-half, because caffeine improves a dog's trailing. But Boris was so excited, he didn't distinguish his prey from anyone else. He even charged *me*—him, a whole hundred pounds of wolfhound, cranked up on Maxwell House. A sight like that will put a hem in your dress. Now I confine his hunting to the park, let him chase park squab and bald-tailed squirrel.

The first thing F. Lee said after his stroke, and it was three weeks after, was "hanky panky." I believe these words were intended for Boris. Yet Boris was the one who pushed the wheelchair for him. On a flat pave of sidewalk, he took a running start. When he jumped, his front paws pushed at the back of the chair, rolling Flea yards ahead with surprising grace.

I asked how he'd trained Boris to do that, and Flea's answer was, "I didn't."

I could love a dog like that, if he hadn't loved him first.

Here's a trick I found for how to finally get some sleep. I sleep in my husband's bed. That way the empty bed I look at is my own.

Cold nights I pull his socks on over my hands. I read in his bed. People still write from when Flea had the column. He did a pet Q and A for the newspaper. The new doctor sends along letters for my amusement. Here's one I liked—a man thinks his cat is homosexual.

The letter begins, "My cat Frank (not his real name) . . ."

In addition to Flea's socks, I also wear his watch.

A lot of us wear our late-husband's watch.

It's the way we tell each other.

61

At bedtime, I think how Nashville slept with Flea. She must have felt to him like a sack of antlers. I read about a marriage breaking up because the man let his Afghan sleep in the marriage bed.

I had my own bed. I slept in it alone, except for those times when we needed—not sex—but sex was how we got there.

In the mornings, I am not alone. With Nashville gone, Chuck comes around.

Chuck is a white-haired, blue-eyed cat, one of the few that aren't deaf—not that he comes when he hears you call. His fur is thick as a beaver's; it will hold the tracing of your finger.

Chuck, behaving, is the Nashville of cats. But the most fun he knows is pulling every tissue from a pop-up box of Kleenex. When he gets too rowdy, I slow him down with a comb. Flea showed me how. Scratching the teeth of a comb will make a cat yawn. Then you have him where you want him—any cat, however cool.

Animals are pure, Flea used to say. There is nothing deceptive about them. I would argue: think about cats. They stumble and fall, then quickly begin to wash—I *meant* to do that. Pretense is deception, and cats pretend: Who me? They move in next door where the food is better and meet you in the street and don't know your name, or *their* name.

But in the morning Chuck purrs against my throat, and it feels like prayer.

In the morning is when I pray.

The mailman changed his mind about the bird, and when Mrs. Kaiser came for Kirby and Chuck, I could not find either one. I had packed their supplies in a bag by the door—Chuck's tomato juice and catnip mouse, Kirby's milk of magnesia tablets to clean her teeth.

You would expect this from Chuck. But Kirby is responsible. She's been around the longest, a delicate smallish golden retriever trained by professionals for television work. She was going to get a series, but she didn't grow to size. Still, she can do a number of useless tricks. The one that wowed them in the waiting room next door was Flea putting Kirby under arrest.

"Kirby," he'd say, "I'm afraid you are under arrest." And the dog would back up flush to the wall. "I am going to have to frisk you, Kirb," and she'd slap her paws against the wall, standing still while Flea patted her sides.

Mrs. Kaiser came to visit after her own dog died.

When Kirby laid a paw in her lap, Mrs. Kaiser burst into tears.

I thought, God love a dog that hustles.

It is really just that Kirby is head-shy and offers a paw instead of her head to pat. But Mrs. Kaiser remembered the gesture. She agreed to take Chuck, too, when I said he needed a childless home. He gets jealous of kids and has asthma attacks. Myself, I was thinking, with Chuck gone I could have poinsettias and mistletoe in the house at Christmas.

When they weren't out back, I told Mrs. Kaiser I would bring them myself as soon as they showed. She was standing in the front hall talking to Boris. Rather, she was talking *for* Boris.

" 'Oh,' he says, he says, 'what a nice bone,' he says, he says, 'can *I* have a nice bone?' "

Boris walked away and collapsed on a braided rug.

" 'Boy,' he says, he says, 'boy, am I bushed.' "

Mrs. Kaiser has worn her husband's watch for years.

When she was good and gone, the animals wandered in. Chuck carried a half-eaten chipmunk in his mouth. He dropped it on the kitchen floor, a reminder of the cruelty of a world that lives by food.

After F. Lee's death, someone asked me how I was. I said that I finally had enough hangers in the closet. I don't think that that is what I meant to say. Or maybe it is.

Nashville *died* of *her* broken heart. She refused her food and simply called it quits.

An infection set in.

At the end, I myself injected the sodium pentobarbital.

I felt upstaged by the dog, will you just listen to me!

But the fact is, I think all of us were loved just the same. The love Flea gave to me was the same love he gave them. He did not say to the dogs, I will love you if you keep off the rug. He would love them no matter what they did.

It's what I got, too.

I wanted conditions.

God, how's that for an admission!

My husband said an animal can't disappoint you. I argued this, too. I said, Of course it can. What about the dog who goes on the rug? How does it feel when your efforts to alter behavior come to nothing?

I *know* how it feels.

I would like to think bigger thoughts. But it looks like I don't have a memory of our life that does not include one of the animals.

Kirby still carries in his paper Sunday mornings.

She used to watch while Flea did the crossword puzzle. He pretended to consult her: "I can see why you'd say *dog,* but don't you see—*cat* fits just as well?"

Boris and Kirby still scrap over his slippers. But as Flea used to say, the trouble seldom exceeds their lifespan.

Here we all still are. Boris, Kirby, Chuck—Nashville gone to ashes. Before going to bed I tell the mynah bird she may not be dumb but she's stupid.

Flowers were delivered on our anniversary. The card said the roses were sent by F. Lee. When I called the florist, he said Flea had "love insurance." It's a service they provide for people who forget. You tell the florist the date, and automatically he sends flowers.

Getting the flowers that way had me spooked. I thought I would walk it off, the long way, into town.

Before I left the house, I gave Laxatone to Chuck. With the weather warming up, he needs to get the jump on furballs. Then I set his bowl of Kibbles in a shallow dish of water. I added to the water a spoonful of liquid dish soap. Chuck eats throughout the day; the soapy moat keeps bugs off his plate.

On the walk into town I snapped back into myself.

Two things happened that I give the credit to.

The first thing was the beggar. He squatted on the walk with a dog at his side. He had with him an aged sleeping collie with granular runny eyes. Under its nose was a red plastic dish with a sign that said *Food for dog—donation please.*

The dog was as quiet as any Flea had healed and then rocked in his arms while the anesthesia wore off.

Blocks later, I bought a pound of ground beef.

I nearly ran the distance back.

The two were still there, and a couple of quarters were in the dish. I felt pretty good about handing over the food. I felt good until I turned around and saw the man who was watching me. He leaned against the grate of a closed shoe-repair with an empty tin cup at his feet. He had seen. And I was giving *him—nothing.*

How far do you take a thing like this? I think you take it all the way to heart. We give what we can—that's as far as the heart can go.

This was the first thing that turned me back around to home. The second was just plain rain.

Ursula K. Le Guin

SCHRÖDINGER'S CAT

As things appear to be coming to some sort of climax, I have withdrawn to this place. It is cooler here, and nothing moves fast.

On the way here I met a married couple who were coming apart. She had pretty well gone to pieces, but he seemed, at first glance, quite hearty. While he was telling me that he had no hormones of any kind, she pulled herself together and, by supporting her head in the crook of her right knee and hopping on the toes of the right foot, approached us shouting, "Well what's *wrong* with a person trying to express themselves?" The left leg, the arms, and the trunk, which had remained lying in the heap, twitched and jerked in sympathy. "Great legs," the husband pointed out, looking at the slim ankle. "My wife has great legs."

A cat has arrived, interrupting my narrative. It is a striped yellow tom with white chest and paws. He has long whiskers and yellow eyes. I never noticed before that cats had whiskers above their eyes; is that normal? There is no way to tell. As he has gone to sleep on my knee, I shall proceed.

Where?

Nowhere, evidently. Yet the impulse to narrate remains. Many things are not worth doing, but almost anything is worth telling. In any case, I have a severe congenital case of *Ethica laboris puritanica,* or Adam's Disease. It is incurable except by total decapitation. I even like to dream when asleep, and to try and recall my dreams: it assures me that I haven't wasted seven or eight hours just lying there. Now here I am, lying, here. Hard at it.

Well, the couple I was telling you about finally broke up. The pieces of him trotted around bouncing and cheeping, like little chicks, but she was finally reduced to nothing but a mass of nerves: rather like fine chicken wire, in fact, but hopelessly tangled.

So I came on, placing one foot carefully in front of the other, and grieving. This grief is with me still. I fear it is part of me, like foot or loin or eye, or may even be myself: for I seem to have no other self, nothing further, nothing that lies outside the borders of grief.

Yet I don't know what I grieve for: my wife? my husband? my children, or myself? I can't remember. Most dreams are forgotten, try as one will to remember. Yet later music strikes the note, and the harmonic rings along the mandolin strings of the mind, and we find tears in our eyes. Some note keeps playing that makes me want to cry; but what for? I am not certain.

The yellow cat, who may have belonged to the couple that broke up, is dreaming. His paws twitch now and then, and once he makes a small, suppressed remark with his mouth shut. I wonder what a cat dreams of, and to whom he was speaking just then. Cats seldom waste words. They are quiet beasts. They keep their counsel, they reflect. They reflect all day, and at night their eyes reflect. Overbred Siamese cats may be as noisy as little dogs, and then people say, "They're talking," but the noise is farther from speech than is the deep silence of the hound or the tabby. All this cat can say is meow, but maybe in his silences he will suggest to me what it is that I have lost, what I am grieving for. I have a feeling that he knows. That's why he came here. Cats look out for Number One.

It was getting awfully hot. I mean, you could touch less and less. The stove burners, for instance. Now I know that stove burners always used to get hot; that was their final cause, they existed in order to get hot. But they began to get hot without having been turned on. Electric units or gas rings, there they'd be when you came into the kitchen for breakfast, all four of them glaring away, the air above them shaking like clear jelly with the heat waves. It did no good to turn them off, because they weren't on in the first place. Besides, the knobs and dials were also hot, uncomfortable to the touch.

Some people tried hard to cool them off. The favorite technique was to turn them on. It worked sometimes, but you could not count on it. Others investigated the phenomenon, tried to get at the root of it, the cause. They were probably the most frightened ones, but man is most human at his most frightened. In the face of the hot stove burners they acted with exemplary coolness. They studied, they observed. They were like the fellow in Michelangelo's *Last Judgment,* who has clapped his hands over his face in horror as the devils drag him down to Hell—but only over one eye. The other eye is busy looking. It's all he can do, but he does it. He observes. Indeed, one wonders if Hell would exist, if he did not look at it. However, neither he, nor the people I am talking about, had enough time left to do much about it. And then finally of course there were the people who did not try to do or think anything about it at all.

When the water came out of the cold-water taps hot one morning, however, even people who had blamed it all on the Democrats began to feel a more profound unease. Before long, forks and pencils and wrenches were too hot to handle without gloves; and cars were really terrible. It was like opening the door of an oven going full blast, to open the door of your car. And by then, other people almost scorched your fingers off. A kiss was like a branding iron. Your child's hair flowed along your hand like fire.

Here, as I said, it is cooler; and, as a matter of fact, this animal is cool. A real cool cat. No wonder it's pleasant to pet his fur. Also he moves slowly, at least for the most part, which is all the slowness one can reasonably expect of a cat. He hasn't that frenetic quality most creatures acquired—all they did was ZAP and gone. They lacked presence. I suppose birds always tended to be that way, but even the hummingbird used to halt for a second in the very center of his metabolic frenzy, and hang, still as a hub, present, above the fuchsias—then gone again, but you knew something was there besides the blurring brightness. But it got so that even robins and pigeons, the heavy impudent birds, were a blur; and as for swallows, they cracked the sound barrier. You knew of swallows only by the small, curved sonic booms that looped about the eaves of old houses in the evening.

Worms shot like subway trains through the dirt of gardens, among the writhing roots of roses.

You could scarcely lay a hand on children, by then: too fast to catch, too hot to hold. They grew up before your eyes.

But then, maybe that's always been true.

I was interrupted by the cat, who woke and said meow once, then jumped down from my lap and leaned against my legs diligently. This is a cat who knows how to get fed. He also knows how to jump. There was a lazy fluidity to his leap, as if gravity affected him less than it does other creatures. As a matter of fact there were some localised cases, just before I left, of the failure of gravity; but this quality in the cat's leap was something quite else. I am not yet in such a state of confusion that I can be alarmed by grace. Indeed, I found it reassuring. While I was opening a can of sardines, a person arrived.

Hearing the knock, I thought it might be the mailman. I miss mail very much, so I hurried to the door and said, "Is it the mail?"

A voice replied, "Yah!" I opened the door. He came in, almost pushing me aside in his haste. He dumped down an enormous knapsack he had been carrying, straightened up, massaged his shoulders, and said, "Wow!"

"How did you get here?"

69

He stared at me and repeated, "How?"

At this my thoughts concerning human and animal speech recurred to me, and I decided that this was probably not a man, but a small dog. (Large dogs seldom go yah, wow, how, unless it is appropriate to do so.) "Come on, fella," I coaxed him. "Come, come on, that's a boy, good doggie!" I opened a can of pork and beans for him at once, for he looked half starved. He ate voraciously, gulping and lapping. When it was gone he said "Wow!" several times. I was just about to scratch him behind the ears when he stiffened, his hackles bristling, and growled deep in his throat. He had noticed the cat.

The cat had noticed him some time before, without interest, and was now sitting on a copy of *The Well-Tempered Clavier* washing sardine oil off its whiskers.

"Wow!" the dog, whom I had thought of calling Rover, barked. "Wow! Do you know what that is? *That's Schrödinger's cat!*"

"No it's not, not any more; it's my cat," I said, unreasonably offended.

"Oh, well, Schrödinger's dead, of course, but it's his cat. I've seen hundreds of pictures of it. Erwin Schrödinger, the great physicist, you know. Oh, wow! To think of finding it here!"

The cat looked coldly at him for a moment, and began to wash its left shoulder with negligent energy. An almost religious expression had come into Rover's face. "It was meant," he said in a low, impressive tone. "Yah. It was *meant*. It can't be a mere coincidence. It's too improbable. Me, with the box; you, with the cat; to meet—here—now." He looked up at me, his eyes shining with happy fervor. "Isn't it wonderful?" he said. "I'll get the box set up right away." And he started to tear open his huge knapsack.

While the cat washed its front paws, Rover unpacked. While the cat washed its tail and belly, regions hard to reach gracefully, Rover put together what he had unpacked, a complex task. When he and the cat finished their operations simultaneously and looked at me, I was impressed. They had come out even, to the very second. Indeed it seemed that something more than chance was involved. I hoped it was not myself.

70

"What's that?" I asked, pointing to a protuberance on the outside of the box. I did not ask what the box was as it was quite clearly a box.

"The gun," Rover said with excited pride.

"The gun?"

"To shoot the cat."

"To shoot the cat?"

"Or to *not shoot* the cat. Depending on the photon."

"The photon?"

"Yah! It's Schrödinger's great Gedankenexperiment. You see, there's a little emitter here. At Zero Time, five seconds after the lid of the box is closed, it will emit one photon. The photon will strike a half-silvered mirror. The quantum mechanical probability of the photon passing through the mirror is exactly one half, isn't it? So! If the photon passes through, the trigger will be activated and the gun will fire. If the photon is deflected, the trigger will not be activated and the gun will not fire. Now, you put the cat in. The cat is in the box. You close the lid. You go away! You stay away! What happens?" Rover's eyes were bright.

"The cat gets hungry?"

"The cat gets shot—or not shot," he said, seizing my arm, though not, fortunately, in his teeth. "But the gun is silent, perfectly silent. The box is soundproof. There is no way to know whether or not the cat has been shot, until you lift the lid of the box. There is *no* way! Do you see how central this is to the whole of quantum theory? Before Zero Time the whole system, on the quantum level or on our level, is nice and simple. But after Zero Time the whole system can be represented only by a linear combination of two waves. We cannot predict the behavior of the photon, and thus, once it has behaved, we cannot predict the state of the system it has determined. We cannot predict it! God plays dice with the world! So it is beautifully demonstrated that if you desire certainty, any certainty, you must create it yourself!"

"How?"

"By lifting the lid of the box, of course," Rover said, looking at me with sudden disappointment, perhaps a touch of suspicion, like a Baptist who finds he has been talking church matters not to another Baptist as he thought, but a Methodist, or even, God forbid, an Episcopalian. "To find out whether the cat is dead or not."

"Do you mean," I said carefully, "that until you lift the lid of the box, the cat has neither been shot nor not been shot?"

"Yah!" Rover said, radiant with relief, welcoming me back to the fold. "Or maybe, you know, both."

"But why does opening the box and looking reduce the system back to one probability, either live cat or dead cat? Why don't we get included in the system when we lift the lid of the box?"

There was a pause. "How?" Rover barked, distrustfully.

"Well, we would involve ourselves in the system, you see, the super-position of two waves. There's no reason why it should only exist *inside* an open box, is there? So when we came to look, there we would be, you and I, both looking at a live cat, and both looking at a dead cat. You see?"

A dark cloud lowered on Rover's eyes and brow. He barked twice in a subdued, harsh voice, and walked away. With his back turned to me he said in a firm, sad tone, "You must not complicate the issue. It is complicated enough."

"Are you sure?"

He nodded. Turning, he spoke pleadingly. "Listen. It's all we have—the box. Truly it is. The box. And the cat. And they're here. The box, the cat, at last. Put the cat in the box. Will you? Will you let me put the cat in the box?"

"No," I said, shocked.

"Please. Please. Just for a minute. Just for half a minute! Please let me put the cat in the box!"

"Why?"

"I can't stand this terrible uncertainty," he said, and burst into tears.

I stood some while indecisive. Though I felt sorry for the poor son of a bitch, I was about to tell him, gently, No; when a curious thing happened. The cat walked over to the box, sniffed around it, lifted his tail and sprayed a corner to mark his territory, and then lightly, with that marvellous fluid ease, leapt into it. His yellow tail just flicked the edge of the lid as he jumped, and it closed, falling into place with a soft, decisive click.

"The cat is in the box," I said.

"The cat is in the box," Rover repeated in a whisper, falling to his knees. "Oh, wow. Oh, wow. Oh, wow."

There was silence then: deep silence. We both gazed, I afoot, Rover kneeling, at the box. No sound. Nothing happened. Nothing would happen. Nothing would ever happen, until we lifted the lid of the box.

"Like Pandora," I said in a weak whisper. I could not quite recall Pandora's legend. She had let all the plagues and evils out of the box, of course, but there had been something else, too. After all the devils were let loose, something quite different, quite unexpected, had been left. What had it been? Hope? A dead cat? I could not remember.

Impatience welled up in me. I turned on Rover, glaring. He returned the look with expressive brown eyes. You can't tell me dogs haven't got souls.

"Just exactly what are you trying to prove?" I demanded.

"That the cat will be dead, or not dead," he murmured submissively. "Certainty. All I want is certainty. To know for *sure* that God *does* play dice with the world."

I looked at him for a while with fascinated incredulity. "Whether he does, or doesn't," I said, "do you think he's going to leave you a note about it in the box?" I went to the box, and with a rather dramatic gesture, flung the lid back. Rover staggered up from his knees, gasping, to look. The cat was, of course, not there.

Rover neither barked, nor fainted, nor cursed, nor wept. He really took it very well.

"Where is the cat?" he asked at last.

"Where is the box?"

"Here."

"Where's here?"

"Here is now."

"We used to think so," I said, "but really we should use larger boxes."

He gazed about him in mute bewilderment, and did not flinch even when the roof of the house was lifted off just like the lid of a box, letting in the unconscionable, inordinate light of the stars. He had just time to breathe, "Oh, wow!"

I have identified the note that keeps sounding. I checked it on the mandolin before the glue melted. It is the note A, the one that drove the composer Schumann mad. It is a beautiful, clear tone, much clearer now that the stars are visible. I shall miss the cat. I wonder if he found what it was we lost?

Cornelia Nixon

AFFECTION

As a baby, my father claimed, I was a cat. I don't know what hard evidence he had, but at one time I played along with him to the extent that, when introduced to strangers, I fell on all fours (I'm not proud of this) and said meow. Later I acquired every known cat toy: stuffed cats, china cats, cat books and posters, a cat pin, cat erasers, a cat lunchbox and toothbrush, a blue felt circle skirt with appliquéd cats, and sheets with kittens printed out of all spatial sense. I also lobbied without cease for an actual cat, wearing my mother down until she suddenly agreed, apparently out of mere exhaustion, the year my third older brother joined the others in their loud and hungry teens.

Seymour spent his kittenhood in my room. My brothers were forbidden to approach my door, and I tried to stand guard around the clock, until my parents made clear that I would still have to go to school. When the bell rang in the afternoon, I was on my bike before most kids cleared their seats, racing home in panic, trying to beat my brothers. Soaked and panting, I didn't slow down until I made it to my door. But then I stopped, opened it a quarter inch at a time, in case he was behind it.

Sometimes he was hard to find in that wilderness of false cats. He'd be caught halfway up a curtain, big-eyed, mewing for help, or curled in a perfect circle on the bed, surrounded by the rubble of his day, torn magazines and lamps overturned on their shades. Impossibly small and light, at first he was no more than the idea of a cat, a loud purr in electrified fur, a dandelion with claws. Ten times a night I'd wake up afraid of crushing him, feel for him on the bed, and he'd start to purr. Once after dinner he was gone. I panicked, accused my brothers, forced a search of their rooms. Hours later, exhausted from weeping, I opened my bottom drawer and found him curled peacefully on a sweater.

When my brothers were not at home, I introduced him to the backyard. Staggering across the lawn, he recoiled at grass blades, arched his back and hissed, or charged suddenly at nothing, scaring himself. For a long time he was relieved to go back to my room, purred loudly when he found the soft warm bed.

Then one day I saw him leap to the top of my bookshelf from a standing start. When he jumped off the bed, you could hear the thud from anywhere in the house. He sat for hours on the windowsill, lashing his tail as he stared outside, or into the closet with his ears perked, listening for mice. He was a big gray cat with a white belly and paws, like a fish designed to blend both with the dark water, seen from above, and light sky, seen from below. The two-tone scheme extended to his nose tip and paw pads, which were half-black, half-pink. In his green eyes the black could be round and shiny as an eightball, tight as a stitch, or like a watermelon seed. When I opened the door of my room, he loped across the floor, making a break for the outside.

"Yaaaaaaaaaa," my brother Charlie said, eyes crossed, tongue flapping while he jerked his body like Frankenstein, the first time he met

Seymour on the lawn. Dropping to a crouch, Seymour eyed him, and fled sideways, out of the yard.

"What's a cat's favorite drink?" my father said and took the library card out of my book. Removing the pencil stub from behind his ear, he started doodling on it.

I didn't bother to answer. I was only out there on the deck, sitting in smoke and fumes from the barbecue, because inside Hank was torturing his saxophone, and a cat's favorite drink was a very old joke. If I gave the obligatory response (mice tea) there would be no stopping him. What do cats put in their lemonade? he'd want to know. What's their favorite dessert, their favorite weather, their favorite exercise? Where do they take their children on Saturday afternoons?

Solemnly he slid the card back into the pocket at the back of my book. Paying no attention, I secretly worked it out of the pocket to where I could see it. Drawn on the card was a ladybug meeting a Sugar Smack. They were the same shape, ovals, with spots. The ladybug had legs, the Sugar Smack didn't, but the resemblance was close enough. The ladybug gazed at the Sugar Smack, and a heart rose from it. The caption read "Love Stinks."

"So," my father said. "How's your cat?"

"Fine." As far as I knew, that was the case: he stopped by every day to eat, usually in the early morning before the boys were up. He no longer came home at night, and I had no idea where he was spending his time, but he seemed fine.

A boy yelled in the backyard, and David's hightops squeaked across the kitchen floor.

"You weenie!" he yelled, banged open the sliding screen and pounded down the steps to the yard.

"David!" my mother yelled from inside.

David dashed up the steps, giggling, ran into the kitchen, slammed the glass door, and locked it behind him. Charlie ran up panting, put his hands on either side of the door, and lifted it off its runner. He propped it against the wall and plunged inside.

77

Sounds of shouting, feet pounding the stairs. "Did not," we heard, and "Don't you ever." Doors slammed upstairs.

"I thought I saw him the other day," my father said, starting a doodle on a paper napkin. "Across the street. At the new people's house." He paused thoughtfully. "I could be wrong, but it looked as if he was pawing their front door."

"Oh, sure," I said. By no outward sign did I reveal that I had been shot through the chest with a hot dart. "He gets around. Cats have resources, you know—they're not like dogs. They make their own friends. It's an honor when they come around."

He raised his eyebrows without looking up from his drawing. "An honor. Yes, that's certainly true."

Inside, voices started again, my mother's and Charlie's. The front door banged open, and Charlie ran by in the driveway above us, headed for the garage. My mother was close behind him, his motorcycle helmet dangling by its strap from one hand, her arm straight down at her side. He pushed his motor scooter up the driveway to the street. She followed with quick graceful steps, shoulders back, head up, like a diver approaching the end of the board. He reached the sidewalk, paused to throw one leg over the bike. She swung the helmet over her head, straight-armed, slammed it into the concrete. It bounced with a sharp crack.

"That's what's going to happen to you, young man!" she said.

Charlie buzzed away without looking back. My mother walked quickly back to the house, head up, shoulders back. The helmet rolled over twice and stopped, teetering in the driveway. My father stood up and followed her inside.

The new people's house was just across the street, but it was hard to see from where I was. Like most of Berkeley, our street was on a steep hill. We lived on the downhill side, hanging out into air, and the top of our house was only about as high as the sidewalk on the other side. To see anything I had to cross the street, climb up into their yard.

Their red convertible was in the driveway, and most of the windows in the house were open, with curtains blowing out. I didn't have a plan. With anyone else I could have gone over to play with the kids, but the new people didn't have any, not even a dog or a cat. I considered them the most uninteresting family I had ever seen.

At the top of their driveway was a gate, but when I got to it I heard voices in back. Veering away, I crossed the front yard, searching the shrubbery as if for a lost ball. On the other side of the house was a new redwood fence, still smooth and faintly red, not gray and prickling with splinters like ours. Standing on a large ornamental rock, I could see over the top.

The last people that lived here had kids, and in those days the backyard was a dead lawn/dog bathroom, equipped with hula hoops, polo sticks and mole mounds, a tetherball pole in a bare circle. Now suddenly it looked like a picture in a magazine: a new deck, a tall hedge, massed flowers in orderly bloom.

The hedge blocked my view of the lawn, but through it I thought I saw a flash of gray and white. My heart started to pound. I hauled myself to the top of the fence, trying to see better, then dropped to the ground on the other side. I didn't care—let them catch me. I had to find out.

One corner of the deck met the house not far from where I landed. Maybe I could make it, maybe not. The deck was only about four feet off the ground, with azalea bushes planted around the edge. Getting through the azaleas without rustling would be tricky, and when I got there, I tried not to touch them at all.

The people were on the other side of the deck, talking and laughing loudly, and they didn't seem to notice me. Underneath, there was a hint of musty cat box, but the old dead grass was still in place, so I didn't have to crawl in the dirt. From there, I could see the whole yard.

It was Seymour, all right. Across the soft new lawn, in the shade of the hedge, he lay on his side like a lion, looking up, exposing his white underchin and belly fur. His head tracked a bug, he snapped at it, missed. Lowering his chin, he surveyed the yard.

I lifted my head above the azaleas, and he gave me a long intense look. Blinking, he turned away, licked his shoulder with sudden energy.

"So there we were, still in the cab, for God's sake—" a man's voice said, up on the deck. A woman gave a high quick laugh, and another man said "Oliver" in a warning tone.

I could see slices of them through the slats—it was the new people and another man. The new people were both tall and blond, the woman in a white sundress and the man in seersucker pants. The other man, the one named Oliver, was dark and had on white trousers. Through the slats, they all moved in flickers, like an old movie, up there in the yellow light.

"No, you have to believe me, I swear it," the man named Oliver said, and the new people laughed uneasily.

"If it's anything like the last one—" the man who lived there said.

"No, no, it isn't, believe me. So there we were, we'd hardly said eleven words to each other, and there we were—" He went on to describe several forms of torture I'd heard about on the playground, emphasizing how much the woman in the taxi wanted him to do those things to her. The new people's laughter got higher and thinner, with gaspy pauses, until his voice ran down. Nobody said anything for about a minute.

"Oh, kiss and tell, Oliver," the woman said.

Both men laughed quickly, as if surprised. She stood up, walked across the deck and down the steps to the lawn.

My heart was thudding so hard I could see it in my eyes as I shrank down behind the azaleas. Chin pressed to the dirt, I watched her cross the grass. Her dress was printed with red roses, her blond hair in a ponytail down her bare back.

I couldn't see her face, but I knew she was pretty, because I'd seen her once close up. I was passing their house on the sidewalk when she came running down the driveway, chasing the blond man, who was trying to get away from her, striding toward the red convertible, parked at the curb. She was inches behind him, half-laughing the way you do when you're playing a joke on someone, or chasing them and about to make the tackle. She had on jeans, a man's shirt, and loafers, hair pinned to the back of her head, while the man was wearing a suit and tie.

"Just tell me who she is," the woman said. "Just tell me how you met her!"

"No," the man said, opening the door of the convertible.

"Just tell me how you met her! Is she one of your patients? No, you have to—"

The man shrugged her off, closed the door, but she reached in and grabbed the shoulder of his jacket.

"Just tell me how you met her!" She was yelling but still keeping her voice down, quieter than it would have been, and half-laughing.

The man started to drive, the woman running along beside him, still gripping his jacket. As they passed me, he looked right at me and blushed. I was surprised to see that close up his face wasn't handsome at all, almost ugly as he grimaced at me. He drove off, breaking her hold on his jacket. She turned quickly, without glancing at me, and went into the house. I hadn't seen them again until now.

Seymour came out from under the hedge as she approached it and gave a pitiful meow, opening his pink mouth wide as a baby bird's. She stopped to pet his head, and he flopped onto his side, offering her the soft white fur of his belly. She stroked from his throat all down his underside, and he stretched his front legs forward and his back legs back, arching his neck. The tip of his tail started curling and uncurling. In a minute he would take hold of her wrist with his claws and teeth, play-biting, getting harder if she didn't stop.

When he grabbed for her, she laughed and scooped him up. She held him just right, his back supported on her arm, as she walked over to a bench under a low tree. She sat down, stroking his whole body, and he sprawled across her lap, kneading her with his paws. Taking a bit of dress between his teeth, he closed his eyes and kneaded her intently, a spot of cat drool spreading on her dress.

"Look at that, Oliver," the man who lived there said. "Isn't that an inspiring sight? Woman and child—it doesn't get better than that. You're looking at the goddamn inspiration of all great art. Don't you think it's an inspiring sight?"

"Woman and child," Oliver said, and ice clicked against glass.

I expected to be caught every second, but they walked right over me to dinner without seeming to notice. The next afternoon, no cars were in their drive, and I went over again, to see if he was still there. Nobody asked where I was going. These days, my mother said "What!" if I went near her, and once I saw her sitting with her elbows on the kitchen table and her hands over her eyes. She considered "Playing" enough of an answer for where I'd been.

Seymour was there, all right, making free with the house and grounds. I stayed back near the fence, where he wouldn't have to notice me, and he didn't seem to mind. He dozed on the deck, rolled in the flower beds, strolled along the top of the high fence. From an oak tree he leapt to an open window on the second floor. With one quick ripple of his back, he slipped under the sash, calling out a meow. After a while he came out, sat on the sill in the sunshine, and licked his paws. Jumping to the tree, he shinnied headfirst down the trunk. Pausing at the bottom, he blinked, stalked toward the hedge.

Hunched in the shadow, he waited, looking up. The hedge was in bloom, studded with red flowers, and a hummingbird hovered along it, sticking its needle-nose in every one. Flat along the ground, he crept up fast and launched himself into the air, all twenty claws aimed for the bird. The hummer darted just out of reach, chittering angrily, while he crashed down through the hedge, holding his position as if frozen, claws clutching air, and landed in a heap. Standing up, he shook himself and stalked away, thrusting his shoulders forward like a panther.

A car door slammed in the driveway. Seymour crouched under the hedge, and I made it under the deck one heartbeat before she came through the gate with bags of groceries.

Walking back and forth to the car, she paid no attention to Seymour. The third time she passed him with her arms full, he charged out, grabbed her calf with his paws, eyes black and round as if he had scared himself. She laughed, and he darted back under the hedge, drawing himself up fearfully. But when she went by again, out he charged, gave her a two-pawed bat and dashed back in. She crouched down, tried to tickle his chest.

"Am I dead yet?" she said. "Did you get me yet?"

He pulled back, staring at her hand as if she had a knife in it. Suddenly he pounced, grabbed her wrist, pawed her hand with his back feet, and leapt back under the hedge. He pounced, pawed, retreated, pounced, until she got tired of him.

* * *

She didn't let on that she saw me that day, but I was sure somehow she knew. When I saw her in the street, I rode away furiously on my bike, or went wild and yelled something stupid at the nearest kid. Even so, I couldn't stop. Whenever she drove away, I had to sneak up, climb the fence, snoop around their yard, whether he was there or not. If I tried to do something else, I had eyes in the back of my head, pointed at their house, until I forgot everything and raced toward it.

One evening, late that summer, I was near the front door when someone rang the bell. I opened it, not thinking much about it. My heart nearly stopped. It was the woman, and she had Seymour in her arms.

Someone grabbed my shoulders from behind. "Don't you ever open the door at night," my mother said and yanked me back into the hall.

I sat on the bottom stair, where I could watch through the banister. From the living room came boys' voices yelling, "Come on! Come on!" and a distant crowd roar.

"I'm sorry to bother you," the woman said hurriedly, adding her name and where she lived. She was dressed up, in high heels and a linen suit, her hair in a French roll.

"Yes, and you have our Seymour." My mother did not say her own name in return, and she reached for him, pulled him away from the woman before she started to hand him over. The woman looked startled and put her arms out, one second after it was no longer necessary to do so.

"Someone told us he might be your cat," she said in a flat, even voice, as if she were reading it. "And we were wondering—he seems to have some sort of abscess, on his paw—"

I stood up, tried to see around my mother's arm. She took hold of one paw, and he tensed, flipped over, climbed her shoulder. Behind us, my father came up to watch.

"The left rear," the woman said quietly. "We didn't like to take him to the vet without—"

"Thank you very much," my mother said and turned away. She started to close the door.

My father caught it over her head, and she ducked under his arm, carried Seymour to the kitchen. My father stepped into the doorway. He was so tall he had to stoop slightly to get under the frame. "So. Let's see. What shall we call it? Catnapping?"

The woman looked up at him and blushed. "We didn't exactly—I'm sorry, but you see, we didn't think he had a home." She examined my father. "He seemed to be throwing himself on our mercy."

"We thought someone must be keeping him in."

She gasped slightly. "You make it sound like we use little chains and handcuffs. It isn't exactly like that—he begs to come in. We've tried ignoring him, but he wakes us up at night, and he won't take no for an answer. Once he pawed our door for an hour and a half." She held up her hands, palms out, and paddled the air, as if begging to come into our house. "We thought he was hurting his paws."

My father took a step out onto the stoop, lowering his voice. "Alienation of affection, then. You've heard of that? You can sue the corespondent for it, in a divorce."

The woman smiled slightly, looking up at him. "Without of course being at fault oneself."

My father stepped all the way out, pulled the door closed behind him.

"Jesus, don't they know how to get rid of a cat?" Charlie said, laughing, in the kitchen. "There's nothing to it. You just go *yaaaaaaaaaaa.*"

In a flurry of white paws, Seymour shot around the corner. Casting me a black-eyed look, he put his nose to the bottom corner of the front door, batting with a soft paw.

"In a minute," I whispered, picking him up. "You can go back out in a minute. If you go right now they'll catch you, because they're both still out there."

I carried him up the stairs, and he watched nervously over my shoulder. At the window on the landing I showed him: my father and the woman were standing on the sidewalk in the fading light, blocking escape by the front door.

* * *

84

"Cat patrol," my father said a couple of weeks later, throwing down his napkin after dinner. "I'll just go get him, so Jane can have him for a while before she goes to bed."

I followed him out into the hall. "That's all right, Dad. Don't worry about it."

Seymour had been jailed in my room the whole time he was on antibiotics, on orders from the vet. He spent it sitting on the window sill, lashing his tail, or meowing at the door to get out.

"It's okay. I'll see him in the morning, when he comes over for breakfast."

"He's your cat."

"I know. But don't worry about it."

He put his hand on the door knob. "You stay here. I'll be right back."

An hour later he brought Seymour up to my room and shut him in. Heading straight for the closet, he sat in the dark, wide-awake, eyes reflecting light when I opened the door to see how he was. I waited until the house settled down for the night, then let him out by the front door.

Soon we had the routine down: carried back after dinner, he went to sleep on my bed, until some dark and silent hour. Sleep was something he understood, and he woke me up as gently as it can be done: nose close to my face, he purred, or gave a soft chirp. Together we padded down the stairs in the dark, his fur brushing my leg under the gown. I only had to open the door a few inches, and in the fainter dark outside I watched him snake around it. Trotting away up the walk, his ears were alert, fur fluffed with excitement.

"But he comes back every night," the woman said, laughing on our front stoop with my father. It was the first rain of the year, and he and I were out there watching it when she drove up. She waved to him as she got out and called something I couldn't hear, then came across the street, smiling in a tan raincoat. Her hair was getting wet, and my father told her to come up under the eaves.

She smoothed her wet hair back out of her face. "He comes in the window about three o'clock in the morning and jumps on the bed, cheerful as can be. So glad to see us, and would we mind getting up and fixing him a snack? If we close the window, he sits in the tree and yowls, about five feet from our ears. That's a sound that could go through concrete. Cat from Mars, Sam calls him."

My father turned elaborately to look at me, but I was backing through the doorway, into the hall, out of reach.

Down in the darkroom my mother called his name. Soon she came up the stairs, two at a time. Headed for the study, she noticed the open front door and stood still, watching.

"Maybe if he had a way to get back in here at night," the woman said. "Maybe he comes here first, and can't—"

"A cat door," my father said. "We thought of that. But—the raccoons. Have you got raccoons? We've got raccoons, and skunks, and once in a while even—"

My mother stepped out the door. "You have to go get Hank this minute." She took hold of his arm, tried to pull him into the house.

"Okay," my father said, and she let go, stepped inside.

"But if he tried to come in here at night, and he doesn't have a way—" the woman said.

My mother stepped out, took hold of him again. "Right now. You can do this later." She was much smaller than my father but pulling so hard he had to step inside. She closed the door behind him.

"Jesus, Ella," he said.

She yanked his raincoat out of the closet and shoved it at him. "You said you were going twenty minutes ago! What does it take!"

From the window on the landing I watched the woman cross the street, flipping her collar up. When she reached their driveway, Seymour dashed out from under a bush and loped ahead of her with long easy strides. He got to their front door first.

My father ran across the street, holding his rain coat. He caught her arm just before she opened her door. Seymour pressed up against it, arching his wet back, meowing at them until they went inside.

My father didn't say anything to me, but he stopped going over after dinner to bring him back. It wasn't long after that before Seymour stopped coming over for breakfast. I was the only one who noticed at first, and I had time to figure out what had happened before anyone else.

Across the street, the woman's car was gone, and the windows in the house stayed closed for days. The man drove up at night in the red convertible and away again in the morning, always alone. After he left, I'd walk right up their driveway, open the gate and sit on the deck. Along the hedge, hummingbirds sipped the lowest flowers undisturbed.

Once I went over after a hard rain. Fat white clouds were sailing away, over the hill, leaving the sky empty and blue. Steam rose from their deck, shining in the sun. I lay down on the boards and rested my nose in a crack. The wood was warm and smelled of sweet spice, with gusts of cat box underneath. I thought about Seymour as a kitten, how he slept on my chest and mewed, heartbroken, if I put him down. Later he was so tender with my sleep.

Maybe I should have known. One summer morning as I walked by, pretending not to stare at the new people's house, I noticed something on their front stoop. Their curtains were still closed, and I went up quickly to see what it was.

Side by side on the doormat lay two dead mice. They were perfectly lined up, with each other and the door, stiff tails pointing the same direction. One's head was thrown back in agony, exposing a triangle of tiny teeth. The other lay on its side, glassy black eye open, paws curled. Both gray coats were matted with cat spit, but they were almost un-marked, a tiny drop of clotted blood on one, and nothing eaten.

Gardeners policed the new people's yard, packed redwood chips around authorized plants and left no leafy corners along the fence. The lower slopes of our yard, on the other hand, were a tangle of blackberry vines, nasturtiums and bindweed, home to salamanders, mice, and even snakes. After catching the first mouse, he must have carried it in his mouth while he climbed the steps to our deck, passed our kitchen door, climbed our driveway, passed our front door, crossed the street, climbed their steep yard, and placed it carefully on their doorstep. Then he had to go back down and do it all again.

I imagined Seymour on a beach. The woman held him on her lap, both of them in sunglasses. A cool drink was on the table and a bowl of cat food underneath. By now she must know what kind he liked: land animals were only worth a sniff, the dried stuff not even that. Most fish he would eat, though for some kinds he stayed on his feet, drawn up away from the bowl. Only for tuna would he sit all the way down.

Maybe there would be fishing boats pulled up to that beach. Maybe Seymour would meet them, leap aboard, rub the fishermen's legs. Maybe the boats caught tuna. Maybe Seymour stowed away on a tuna boat, lived with the fishermen, left that woman on the beach.

One night my father did not come home for dinner. My mother didn't say anything about it, and she didn't yell at Charlie or say much of anything else. She waited for dinner until we were all half-starved, but none of us talked about it. We just lay around the living room, playing games and pretending to read, and even the boys were quiet. It got to be seven, seven-thirty, quarter to eight.

"Come to the table," my mother said.

"Aw, let's wait for Dad," Charlie said, but she was spooning food onto plates.

She left his place set, pans covered on the stove, and sat in the kitchen, writing Christmas cards, near the wall phone. It rang twice, both for Charlie. It was almost ten before she remembered to send me to bed.

The house was dark and still, and I must have been asleep a long time, when I suddenly woke up. I always slept with my door closed, but now it was open. A soft heavy object hit the floor. The door closed silently, the latch clicked and footsteps went down the stairs.

In the faint light from the window, I saw a shape like a shepherd's crook go by the bottom of my bed. A moment later it came back, twitching slightly. I thought I heard purring. Suddenly the bed compressed, and heavy soft feet stepped on my shins. Even in the dark I could see his white mask. He was purring louder than I'd ever heard, and kneading the bed at every step, claws catching in the comforter.

"No," I said. "You don't live here anymore."

The purr was deafening when he reached my face. He brought his nose close, touched my forehead, gave me one quick lick, as if to see who I was by taste.

"Forget it, Seymour. You made your choice."

Circling around by my chest, he kneaded the covers just right. He curled down against my side but kept his head up, ears pointed toward the door. Purring thrummed through the bed.

"Okay, look. It's late. But only for tonight. No promises. Understood?"

He didn't turn down that diesel purr one bit.

Charlotte Macleod

A LONG TIME SITTING

She had been sitting there a very long time. She had no notion of how long, it didn't matter. Nothing mattered. Nothing had mattered for many years. There seemed to be no life left in her, she sat quite immobile in her rush-seated chair, the folds of her long black gown lying just as they had fallen when she'd last sat down, her eyes fixed on the one red coal that still glowed in the fireplace. Only her mind still worked, carrying her to far-off worlds.

Lost in her thought, she did not hear the taxi drive up the overgrown lane or the key turn in the lock that had not been turned all the while she had been sitting. Yet she was not surprised when the door was pushed open and a woman came into the kitchen, a pale, thin woman who smiled and spoke.

"Oh! How do you do? I didn't expect—that is, Mr. Mowl at the real estate office seemed to think—but what a nice surprise to find you here. Are you Mrs. Hittle?"

Was she? She supposed she must have been, once. For a long time she'd been invisible, apparently that was no longer so. Mowl must have told this woman that the owner of the cottage was dead, perhaps he was right. She moved not a muscle, spoke not a word, the woman seemed not at all disconcerted. She was young, she looked oddly dressed, but perhaps fashions had changed. She was putting a bagful of groceries and another filled with cleaning supplies on the bare wooden table, going back outside to bring in two large blue suitcases. Then she was planning to stay.

The old woman was not surprised to have acquired a tenant, nothing surprised her, but she did feel a small, long-forgotten sense of obligation to her house. The front bedroom must be cleaned, a bed made ready with lavender-scented sheets, a bright patchwork quilt, plump down-filled pillows. It was a tight squeeze, but she managed. The young woman called down, "Mrs. Hittle, it's beautiful!"

Feeling some slight nudge of satisfaction, the old woman willed the groceries into the pantry and the cleaning stuff into the broom closet, wafted a yellow tablecloth over the dingy table top, and directed the kettle to fill the teapot. What next? Food, that was it, there should be something to go with the tea. Scones were all she could think of, a plate of warm scones. It was not until she heard the young woman coming downstairs that she remembered the raisins, she tucked the last one in without a moment to spare and set the fire to dancing.

"How dear of you to make the tea. And fresh scones, too! You really mustn't spoil me like this, Mrs. Hittle, I'd expected to fend for myself. I'm Jenny Wrenne, in case Mr. Mowl didn't tell you. I'm an artist. Sort of one anyway, I paint little vignettes for greeting cards. It doesn't pay much, but it's fun."

While she was chatting, Jenny Wrenne had been fetching the cups, pouring the tea, carrying a cupful and a scone on a little plate over to the old woman before she fixed her own, bringing her chair over by the fire.

Not too close, she wasn't pushy like the animal who was shoving his way in through the leather-hinged cat hole.

"What a gorgeous cat!"

Beauty was clearly in the eye of the beholder. Asphodemus, for that was his name, although nobody but he and the old woman knew it, was overlarge and bony of frame, gangly in the legs, frayed about the ears, lumpy in the tail, ragged and unkempt of pelt. Perhaps Jenny Wrenne's artist's eye was able to penetrate through the disreputable outer integument to the noble heart within, or maybe she was just sick and tired of painting cute kitties with bows around their necks. Anyway, she and Asphodemus took to each other right away although there could be no doubt in the cat's agile mind as to where his true allegiance lay. He rubbed against Jenny's legs, permitted her to serve him a saucer of milk and a corner of buttered scone with the raisins considerately picked out (Jenny ate them herself), then went to curl up in the old woman's lap.

The tea that the new tenant had poured for her silent hostess sat untouched until Jenny went back upstairs to get her painting materials, then Asphodemus made quick work of it and went back to sleep. Jenny would have liked to sketch Mrs. Hittle but didn't think she should go ahead without asking permission; it seemed too early in their acquaintance for that. She did move Asphodemus in her mind's eye to the hearth rug and paint a charming idealization of him with the firelight bringing out red gold glints in his ruddy coat, his ears nicely evened off around the edges, and an expression of content on his face.

The cat would look ever so distinguished, if not precisely handsome, if he'd wash more often and take better care of his whiskers, Jenny thought. As though he had read her mind, Asphodemus woke up and began to tidy himself. Despite his contortions, the old woman did not stir, but sat as she had been, gazing straight into the dancing flames. How long had it been since her fire had last burned clear?

She began willing away the cobwebs that had gathered inside the fireplace, and along the ceiling beams, running her mind like a vacuum cleaner into all the corners where dust had collected. She had been a good housekeeper back then; no dried bats or fillets of fenny snakes cluttering up her kitchen, she had been above such petty chicaneries. Not that she had been a good woman. She had been a particularly wicked woman and a first-class sorceress, until she had committed the arrogant folly of laying an extra-powerful curse without first erecting herself a safety net of protective charms. The curse had backfired, locking her here in limbo bereft of speech, of movement, of all physical functions, with no living soul except Asphodemus to look after her. He was an old cat now, each of his nine lives had been a long one but the last of them was by now nearly spent. She would, and this surprised her, miss him when he crossed over.

Was it possible that she retained some tiny grain of human feeling despite the backfired curse? Was the mild pleasure she'd been getting from utilizing what little power she still possessed to sweep away the cobwebs and conjure up a clean bed for an unexpected guest based on something other than the retained vanity of a once houseproud woman? This was something new to think about, she had not thought about anything new for a great span of time. She willed the woodbox full and sent another log to the fire. Intent on getting Asphodemus's whiskers just right, Jenny Wrenne didn't notice.

The afternoon was wearing on, Jenny began wondering about lamps and candles. There was no electricity in the cottage, Mr. Mowl had told her that much anyway. No telephone either, and no running water. But that pump in the sink must work because Mrs. Hittle's kettle had been full. Mr. Mowl had cautioned Jenny to boil the water before she drank, the house had not been occupied for a long time and he could not guarantee the well.

The taxi driver had laughed when she'd told him she was going to live in the old Hittle house, he wouldn't tell her why. Perhaps he'd known, as Mr. Mowl seemed not to, that the owner was still in residence and that, despite its lack of modern amenities, the house was beautifully kept and very comfortable. Jenny felt rather embarrassed about all those cleaning supplies Mr. Mowl had seemed to think she would need, she hoped they had not offended her landlady. Maybe that was why Mrs. Hittle still wasn't speaking to her.

No, Jenny could feel no atmosphere of disapproval, and she was good at atmospheres. More likely, Mrs. Hittle had suffered a stroke that left her bereft of speech and perhaps awkward in her movements. That would explain why she preferred not to leave her chair in her new tenant's presence. She must manage well enough when she was alone, to have prepared that lovely tea so quickly.

Well, Jenny could talk enough for two, she'd just as soon be doing the chores herself but she wasn't about to quarrel if Mrs. Hittle chose to run the house her own way. She was in no position to quarrel, she'd come here for the sole reason that she couldn't find another place cheaper to rent. Her greeting card designs were nothing special, even so she couldn't turn them out fast enough to earn more money than would barely keep her head above water. Mr. Mowl had been almost contemptuous when she'd told him how little she could afford, he hadn't troubled himself even to show her where the cottage stood.

Perhaps that was just as well. If he'd seen how nice the place was inside, he'd surely have asked a higher rent. It was too late now, she'd signed the lease and paid her deposit, he couldn't back out if he wanted to. Jenny added one last triumphant whisker to the cat's noble face. There, her sketch was done. She did feel a trifle odd about not having tied a red bow around the cat's neck as greeting card convention required, but her artistic soul had rebelled against it. He was not the type for ribbons and frills.

This painting had turned out to be quite different from Jenny's usual style, it was the best thing she'd done in ages, maybe her best ever. She would, she decided, try a whole series of paintings with so splendid a model. But not tonight, it was getting dark, time to clear away her paints and think about supper. She'd planned to have sardines on toast as a special treat for her first night in her new lodging. It would be only decent to share with Mrs. Hittle and the cat, but would one small canful stretch to feed three? Jenny was an optimist and besides, they'd had that lovely tea not so long ago. Too bad the scones were all gone, but she'd brought a loaf of bread.

Making toast over an open fire sounded romantic. However, it might be safer to try the black iron stove where the kettle was singing again, though she hadn't been aware of its gentle purr before now. Nor had she noticed the funny little hatlike contraption that could only be an old-fashioned tin toaster. The cat probably wouldn't care for toast, he could have the sardine oil instead, it would be good for his coat.

The toaster worked well enough. Jenny laid browned slices on two flowered china plates she'd found in the cupboard and arranged an even third of the sardines for each of them, adding a garnish of lettuce and tomato from her grocery bag to provide extra vitamins and make the servings appear less meager. She set what remained in the can down on the hearth for the cat to eat, and carried a filled plate, a cup of tea, a fork and a napkin to Mrs. Hittle, all prettily set out on a tray with more flowers painted on it. This house was full of charming surprises, why had she been led to suppose it was little more than a shack?

The old woman was making no sign that she knew the food was there, but that was all right, Jenny was getting used to Mrs. Hittle's odd ways. She went back to the table and sat down to her supper with an appetite too hearty for the small amount of food before her. At least she'd thought it was; somehow these sardines turned out to be more filling than sardines usually were. She ate them slowly, in tiny bites, thinking how much better they tasted than all the other sardines she'd ever eaten. Perhaps it was the stove-browned toast that made the difference.

The tomato and lettuce seemed almost too much of a good thing, by the time she'd finished the last bite she felt altogether replete and ready to fall asleep. She rinsed her plate and cup under the pump, which worked beautifully, refilled the kettle, set it back on the stove, and excused herself to her landlady and cat. Mrs. Hittle wouldn't mind the new tenant's going, she still hadn't touched her supper, it would be only courteous of Jenny to let her eat in peace.

While Jenny was struggling into the lavender-smelling bed and pulling the bright patchwork quilt up around her ears, Asphodemus was finishing Mrs. Hittle's sardines, toast and all. He didn't even much mind having to eat the lettuce and tomato, meals had been few and far between here over the years. The old woman had been too far off in that other place to give more than an occasional thought to feeding her familiar, he'd had to catch most of his breakfasts and suppers before he could eat them. He was sick and tired of spitting out fur and feathers, not to mention bones and beaks. A cat his age was used to a little pampering and some variety in his diet, though Asphodemus did hope this new member of the household would lay off the tomato next time it was her turn to cook.

Come morning, Jenny woke to the smell of coffee brewing and bacon frying. Mrs. Hittle and her pet must already have breakfasted, an empty plate and cup were draining on the sinkboard and the cat was looking smug. Jenny's plateful of fried eggs, bacon, hashed brown potatoes, and two perfectly browned pieces of toast was keeping warm on the back of the stove. She ate every bite and was glad to get it, when it was all gone she went over and kissed Mrs. Hittle on the cheek. Then she got out her paints and sketching pad, coaxed the big cat outdoors, and spent a happy day on a perfectly splendid painting of him sitting on the doorstep like a king on a throne.

And so it went, Mrs. Hittle never moving, never speaking, but always having Jenny's breakfast warming on the stove no matter what time she got up, Jenny and the cat going off to some picturesque spot where he could pose and she could paint. If it rained, they stayed indoors and found some equally beguiling spot, often one that Mrs. Hittle had arranged for them only moments before they got there, though of course Jenny didn't know that. The cat could not have been a more obliging model, the artist's brush had never before been plied so deftly or so productively.

Somehow the housework got done while Jenny was painting, somehow the limited supply of groceries she'd brought with her had not yet run out. Mrs. Hittle must have both a root cellar and a preserve closet somewhere, though Jenny had not yet seen either. Potatoes, carrots, green stuff, jars of fruit, pickles, even jams and honey would be lying on the table when Jenny and the cat got back from their day's work. Jenny would contribute whatever she could and prepare a meal, always different, always good. The cat's fur was beginning to shine, his gaunt frame to fill out, he was washing regularly and thoroughly now, he was even beginning to purr a little now and then, when he happened to think of it.

As the days passed, Jenny's paintings accumulated, each of them better than the one before. Counting them up, she was astonished to find that she had almost two weeks' worth. How could the time have gone by so fast? She must quit having such a good time and become more businesslike. Much as she loved gloating over her finished works, she could not afford to keep them here, they must be mailed off to the greeting card company before another month's rent came due and she found herself with no money to pay.

It was only a two-mile walk to the village, the taxi driver had told her so. She could ask him to bring her back if she felt too tired to carry the groceries she must buy, she must not continue to batten on Mrs. Hittle's bounty as she'd been doing. Jenny explained all this to Mrs. Hittle and the cat, made up her stack of sketches into a neat package for mailing, and set off down the road. Mrs. Hittle felt a distinct twinge of disappointment when the door closed behind Jenny. Why should this be so? Now she had yet another new thing to think about.

Mrs. Hittle was not the only one to be given food for thought that day. A jowly man with a rather mean-looking mouth was just leaving the post office with his mail when a smiling young woman carrying a large brown envelope said to him, "Why, hello, Mr. Mowl."

At first he didn't recognize her, she looked about ten years younger and a good deal rosier than the pale, thin woman who'd shown up in his real estate office a couple of weeks ago, looking for a cheap place to live. He'd rented her the old Hittle place, sight unseen, there was no other way it would ever get rented. In fact, however, Mr. Mowl had done pretty well out of the old Hittle place over the years, always insisting on a six-month lease, always collecting a deposit in advance, almost invariably having the would-be tenants storming into his office the next morning claiming the place was unlivable and demanding their money back; always letting them know, gently but firmly, that they couldn't have it. This young woman had actually spoken pleasantly to him, what could have gone wrong?

Mowl put out a cautious feeler. "Things going along all right out there, Miz Wrenne?"

"Oh yes, everything's wonderful!" Too late Jenny realized she'd sounded far too enthusiastic, she tried to back off. "That is, it's adequate for my purposes. I'm outside sketching most of the time. Of course without electricity or running water . . ." she couldn't think of anything really negative to say about the Hittle house, she was simply no good at lying.

"Awful nuisance having nothing to cook on but an open fire, though, isn't it? And sitting in the dark by yourself every night must get kind of lonesome."

Then Mr. Mowl hadn't the faintest idea what the house was like, or that Mrs. Hittle was still living there! How could he be taking on tenants and issuing leases without knowing where to send the owner her share of money from the rents? Maybe he thought his client was still in the hospital on account of her stroke. Should Jenny explain that she'd come back? No! It was his to find out, not hers to tell. She was quite put out with Mr. Mowl.

"Oh, I manage well enough," she said shortly. "I'm a working woman, you know, I must get this package in the mail to my publishers. So nice to see you, Mr. Mowl."

It hadn't been nice at all, but polite lies didn't count. Jenny mailed her sketches and went on to the market. As people always do, she bought more than she had intended and was standing on the sidewalk, debating whether she could afford to take the taxi now that she'd overspent her budget buying little dainties to tempt Mrs. Hittle, and how she'd get her purchases home if she didn't get a ride, when who should drive by but Mr. Mowl.

"Hop in, Miz Wrenne, I'll run you back."

Burdened as she was, Jenny still didn't want to accept. "Oh no, I mustn't put you to the trouble."

"No trouble at all. I've got business out your way."

He was out of the car, snatching away her bundles before she could resist. She'd just have to tell him to let her off at the roadside because the lane wasn't drivable, Jenny decided. Actually the lane wasn't too bad, though not very good, but the car was new and elegant, surely he wouldn't want it all scratched up. Anyway, a lift was a lift and she really could not have afforded the taxi. She got in and spent the short ride trying to evade Mr. Mowl's searching questions, which seemed to add up to why she wasn't furious with him for sticking her out at the old Hittle place.

She thought of a few things she'd have liked to ask him in return, but knew better than to start a conversation she might not be able to control.

She might have known she couldn't control Mr. Mowl either. Despite her protests, he swung into the lane and drove right up to the house. Jenny herself had been doing a little weeding and pruning, little could she reck that Mrs. Hittle had beguiled the morning tidying up the house itself: causing shingles to be replaced, straightening the roof line where the ridgepole had sagged, rehanging shutters that had dangled by one hinge or fallen off entirely, even giving them a fresh lick of green paint. Jenny herself didn't notice particularly as this was how her mind's eye had envisioned the cottage all the time, but Mowl almost threw a conniption.

"What the Sam Hill's been going on here?"

"I don't know what you mean, Mr. Mowl," said Jenny with a new dignity that she'd learned from Asphodemus. "May I have my bundles please?"

"B-buh—phm'f—ar—num. I'll carry them in for you."

"No, please don't. Mrs. Hittle may be sleeping, I don't want her disturbed."

"Mrs. Hittle?" Mowl gave Jenny a very odd look. Then he bulldozed his way past her, caught one horrified glimpse of the silent old woman sitting in front of the fireplace, dropped the bags of groceries on the floor, and fled. As Jenny went to pick up the scattered foodstuffs, she was relieved to hear him driving away, a good deal faster than he ought to be driving on that narrow, rutted lane. She hoped he'd stay away.

But he didn't. Mowl's cupidity was great enough to overcome his cowardice. Once back in his own house he sacrificed a couple of perfectly good silver spoons and melted them down to make silver bullets, he told himself that he could always reclaim the bullets afterward and try his hand at turning them back into spoons. He loaded an old horse pistol of his great-grandfather's, it was high time he got some use out of the weapon, and drove back up the lane the following night under cover of darkness.

That young woman who called herself Wrenne, she had to be a witch, or a wizard in disguise he told himself. She, or he, or maybe it must surely be in league with the powers of darkness. How else could she have brought back that evil hag from wherever the old besom had been for the past hundred years or so?

Mowl could remember his own grandparents talking about the old woman in hushed voices. He'd been startled to learn that his great-grandfather had died in some strange and horrible way on account of a woman named Hittle, a woman dressed all in black from head to toe, who'd sat in front of her fireplace still as a statue and worked her devilish spells.

After the earlier Mr. Mowl's terrible death, a few bold souls had gone to Mrs. Hittle's house. Too awed to wreak the vengeance they'd had in mind, they'd found her sitting there in her old rush-seated chair, silent, unmoving. They'd watched her in relays night and day for a whole week long, she'd never batted an eyelid. On the seventh day Mrs. Hittle had gradually faded away and never been seen since. But there was always a coldness in front of the fireplace, no matter how high the fire was built up. And every time anybody tried to move that old rush-seated chair out of the way, it would scoot right back to the spot where she'd been sitting.

That stubborn chair was the main thing that had always so far put tenants off staying, that and the feeling that somebody was in the house, not doing anything, just being there. Nobody wanted an invisible presence butting in on their privacy, Mr. Mowl could hardly blame them for that. What he planned to do with those silver bullets was no more than any decent, respectable resident with a sense of civic responsibility ought to be proud and honored to do for the good of the community.

Fixed up the way it was now, that cottage could be bringing in a pretty penny in local real estate tax dollars, not to mention a hefty commission for a smart real estate agent. Mowl would have to fiddle the paperwork, that would be no great problem except for the lease he'd got Miz Wrenne to sign. Well, that was just too bad for Miz Wrenne, there was a sinkhole down back over the hill plenty big enough to hold both the young witch and the old one. Who'd ever know? He tossed off a heartening jolt of whiskey to prove he wasn't a bit scared and set off on his civic betterment project.

The moon had been shining brightly when he'd left the village. Now a cloud must have come over it or something, it was pitch black out here on the back road. He'd have missed his turnoff if it hadn't been for a damn great big tomcat's green eyes catching his headlights as he rounded a curve. Mowl had always hated cats, he swerved deliberately to run this critter over, missed it, but found himself just where he wanted to be, heading straight for the old Hittle place.

Fortune favored the brave, or the slightly drunk. Grasping his horse pistol, making sure his powder was dry, Mowl left the car and advanced on the cottage. Something scooted ahead of him and seemed to pass right through the closed door. He almost dropped the gun, then emitted a sigh of relief. Only that cussed cat going in through its cat hole. Might have known a witch could keep a cat around. Well, she wouldn't have it much longer, he'd see to that. The door wasn't locked. That figured, the old key was iron. Witches wouldn't touch iron. He turned the knob and strode inside.

Yes, there she sat, stiff as a waxwork, just the way he'd seen her the day before, only now the cat was up on her lap. Great big orange thing with eyes like a panther's, he'd teach it to glare at him like that. Mr. Mowl raised his pistol.

Consarned trigger was stuck, it wouldn't budge. Mowl worked at the gun frantically, in a panic now, all his cowardice to the fore. "Damn you, fire!" he roared.

His shout woke Jenny, she leaped out of bed and flew down the stairs in her nightgown and bare feet, spied the frenzied man waving the pistol and the spitting cat standing up on Mrs. Hittle's lap, back arched, eyes flashing green fire. She rushed to shield them with her own body.

"No! Don't hurt them!"

Then everything happened at once. Asphodemus sprang clear over Jenny's head, straight at Mr. Mowl. The gun went off, the first silver bullet passed straight through the cat and struck Jenny in the shoulder. Stunned by the impact, she dropped to the floor beside the murdered cat. Mowl reloaded, cocked the pistol again, sent his second bullet into Mrs. Hittle's back, turned and fled the house. Still too stunned to move, Jenny heard his car start and go pell mell down the lane. He would crash. He did. The car exploded, the blast brought Jenny to her feet. Her first coherent thought was for the old woman.

"Mrs. Hittle! Mrs. Hittle! Oh, please speak. Are you badly hurt?"

"Yes, my dear." The voice was gentle, almost musical. "Be happy for me, I am released. I'll be going now, you stay here. Asphodemus will take care of you, as he did of me."

"Asphodemus? The cat? But—but he's dead. Mr. Mowl shot him. And I never even knew his name!"

"It's all right, Jenny. Everything will work out. I promise." Rising with no sign of stiffness from the chair she had so long occupied, Mrs. Hittle put her hand for a moment on the wound in Jenny's shoulder. At once the bleeding stopped, the bullet hole healed, the bloodstains faded from Jenny's nightgown, and a small tear in the cloth was invisibly mended. Mrs. Hittle then stooped over the body of her late familiar, and whispered something Jenny couldn't hear. He vanished, Jenny could not repress a sniffle.

"I hate to see him go. I—I loved him so."

"Don't worry, Jenny, Asphodemus will be back. You may kiss me goodbye if you want to."

Perhaps it was the kiss that broke the spell. Mrs. Hittle was gone, Asphodemus was gone, Jenny was alone. Strangely, she didn't mind. She knew there was no sense in her going to see what had happened to Mr. Mowl, whatever it was, he'd asked for it. But now whom would she pay her rent to?

Time enough to think of that later. She went back to bed and slept soundly, waking up an hour later than usual because there was nobody left to fix her breakfast. She made toast and a pot of coffee, she was sitting at the table drinking her second cup when a man came to the door, a youngish man with hair the color of burnished brass with coppery highlights and a beard to match. It was a beautiful beard, short and silky, that matched his hair and all but covered his face. His eyes were a magical clear green. He was carrying a kitten, a tiny orange tiger, adorable as all kittens were but somehow not the type to have a ribbon around its neck.

"Good morning," said the man. "Is this your kitten? And are you Miss Hittle?"

"No, I'm only a tenant. My name is Jenny Wrenne. Mrs. Hittle has—passed away."

"Then there are no Hittles left around here at all?"

The taxi driver had told Jenny there weren't. "None," she said. "She was the last."

"But this is the old Hittle house?"

"Oh, yes."

"Then it looks as if I'm your new landlord." He showed Jenny his driver's license. Hittle, the name was. A. James Hittle.

"Is the A for Asphodemus?" she asked with her heart in her mouth.

"Almost. Actually, it's for Amadeus, my mother was a Mozart freak. What made you ask?"

"I had to know. Then this must be Asphodemus." She took the kitten from him. "Do come in. And make yourself at home, both of you."

She didn't have to say that, they already were. As Mrs. Hittle had promised, it was going to be all right.

Joyce Carol Oates

THE WHITE CAT

There was a gentleman of independent means who, at about the age of fifty-six, conceived of a passionate hatred for his much-younger wife's white Persian cat.

His hatred for the cat was all the more ironic, and puzzling, in that he himself had given the cat to his wife as a kitten, years ago, when they were first married. And he himself had named her—Miranda—after his favorite Shakespearean heroine.

It was ironic, too, in that he was hardly a man given to irrational sweeps of emotion. Except for his wife (whom he'd married late—his first marriage, her second) he did not love anyone very much, and would have thought it beneath his dignity to hate anyone. For whom should he take that seriously? Being a gentleman of independent means allowed him that independence of spirit unknown to the majority of men.

Julius Muir was of slender build, with deep-set somber eyes of no distinctive color; thinning, graying, baby-fine hair; and a narrow, lined face to which the adjective *lapidary* had once been applied, with no vulgar intention of mere flattery. Being of old American stock he was susceptible to none of the fashionable tugs and sways of "identity": He knew who he was, who his ancestors were, and thought the subject of no great interest. His studies both in America and abroad had been undertaken with a dilettante's rather than a scholar's pleasure, but he would not have wished to make too much of them. Life, after all, is a man's primary study.

Fluent in several languages, Mr. Muir had a habit of phrasing his words with inordinate care, as if he were translating them into a common vernacular. He carried himself with an air of discreet self-consciousness that had nothing in it of vanity, or pride, yet did not bespeak a pointless humility. He was a collector (primarily of rare books and coins), but he was certainly not an obsessive collector; he looked upon the fanaticism of certain of his fellows with a bemused disdain. So his quickly blossoming hatred for his wife's beautiful white cat surprised him, and for a time amused him. Or did it frighten him? Certainly he didn't know what to make of it!

The animosity began as an innocent sort of domestic irritation, a half-conscious sense that being so respected in public—so recognized as the person of quality and importance he assuredly was—he should warrant that sort of treatment at home. Not that he was naively ignorant of the fact that cats have a way of making their preferences known that lacks the subtlety and tact devised by human beings. But as the cat grew older and more spoiled and ever more choosy it became evident that she did not, for affection, choose *him*. Alissa was her favorite, of course; then one or another of the help; but it was not uncommon for a stranger, visiting the Muirs for the first time, to win or to appear to win Miranda's capricious heart. "Miranda! Come here!" Mr. Muir might call—gently enough, yet forcibly, treating the animal in fact with a silly sort of deference—but at such times Miranda was likely to regard him with indifferent, unblinking eyes and make no move in his direction. What a fool, she seemed to be saying, to court someone who cares so little for you!

If he tried to lift her in his arms—if he tried, with a show of playfulness, to subdue her—in true cat fashion she struggled to get down with as much violence as if a stranger had seized her. Once as she squirmed out of his grasp, she accidentally raked the back of his hand and drew blood that left a faint stain on the sleeve of his dinner jacket. "Julius, dear, are you hurt?" Alissa asked. "Not at all," Mr. Muir said, dabbing at the scratches with a handkerchief. "I think Miranda is excited because of the company," Alissa said. "You know how sensitive she is." "Indeed I do," Mr. Muir said mildly, winking at their guests. But a pulse beat hard in his head and he was thinking he would like to strangle the cat with his bare hands—were he the kind of man who was capable of such an act.

More annoying still was the routine nature of the cat's aversion to him. When he and Alissa sat together in the evening, reading, each at an end of their sofa, Miranda would frequently leap unbidden into Alissa's lap—but shrink fastidiously from Mr. Muir's very touch. He professed to be hurt. He professed to be amused. "I'm afraid Miranda doesn't like me any longer," he said sadly. (Though in truth he could no longer remember if there'd been a time the creature *had* liked him. When she'd been a kitten, perhaps, and utterly indiscriminate in her affections?) Alissa laughed and said apologetically, "Of course she likes you, Julius," as the cat purred loudly and sensuously in her lap. "But—you know how cats are."

"Indeed, I am learning," Mr. Muir said with a stiff little smile.

And he felt he *was* learning—something to which he could give no name.

What first gave him the idea—the fancy, really—of killing Miranda, he could not have afterward said. One day, watching her rubbing about the ankles of a director-friend of his wife's, observing how wantonly she presented herself to an admiring little circle of guests (even people with a general aversion to cats could not resist exclaiming over Miranda—petting her, scratching her behind the ears, cooing over her like idiots), Mr. Muir found himself thinking that, as he had brought the cat into his household of his own volition and had paid a fair amount of money for her, she was his to dispose of as he wished. It was true that the full-blooded Persian was one of the prize possessions of the household—a household in which possessions were not acquired casually or cheaply—and it was true that Alissa adored her. But ultimately she belonged to Mr. Muir. And he alone had the power of life or death over her, did he not?

"What a beautiful animal! Is it a male or a female?"

Mr. Muir was being addressed by one of his guests (in truth, one of Alissa's guests; since returning to her theatrical career she had a new, wide, rather promiscuous circle of acquaintances) and for a moment he could not think how to answer. The question lodged deep in him as if it were a riddle: *Is it a male or a female?*

"Female, of course," Mr. Muir said pleasantly. "Its name after all is Miranda."

He wondered: Should he wait until Alissa began rehearsals for her new play—or should he act quickly, before his resolution faded? (Alissa, a minor but well-regarded actress, was to be an understudy for the female lead in a Broadway play opening in September.) And how should he do it? He could not strangle the cat—could not bring himself to act with such direct and unmitigated brutality—nor was it likely that he could run over her, as if accidentally, with the car. (Though *that* would have been fortuitous, indeed.) One midsummer evening when sly, silky Miranda insinuated herself onto the lap of Alissa's new friend Alban (actor, writer, director; his talents were evidently lavish) the conversation turned to notorious murder cases—to poisons—and Mr. Muir thought simply, *Of course. Poison.*

Next morning he poked about in the gardener's shed and found the remains of a ten-pound sack of grainy white "rodent" poison. The previous autumn they'd had a serious problem with mice, and their gardener had set out poison traps in the attic and basement of the house. (With excellent results, Mr. Muir surmised. At any rate, the mice had certainly disappeared.) What was ingenious about the poison was that it induced extreme thirst—so that after having devoured the bait the poisoned creature was driven to seek water, leaving the house and dying outside. Whether the poison was "merciful" or not, Mr. Muir did not know.

He was able to take advantage of the servants' Sunday night off—for as it turned out, though rehearsals for her play had not yet begun, Alissa was spending several days in the city. So Mr. Muir himself fed Miranda in a corner of the kitchen where she customarily ate—having mashed a generous teaspoon of the poison in with her usual food. (How spoiled the creature was! From the very first, when she was a seven-weeks' kitten, Miranda had been fed a special high-protein, high-vitamin cat food, supplemented by raw chopped liver, chicken giblets, and God knows what all else. Though as he ruefully had to admit, Mr. Muir had had a hand in spoiling her, too.)

Miranda ate the food with her usual finicky greed, not at all conscious of, or grateful for, her master's presence. He might have been one of the servants; he might have been no one at all. If she sensed something out of the ordinary—the fact that her water dish was taken away and not returned, for instance—like a true aristocrat she gave no sign. Had there ever been any creature of his acquaintance, human or otherwise, so supremely complacent as this white Persian cat?

Mr. Muir watched Miranda methodically poison herself with an air not of elation as he'd anticipated, not even with a sense of satisfaction in a wrong being righted, in justice being (however ambiguously) exacted—but with an air of profound regret. That the spoiled creature deserved to die he did not doubt; for after all, what incalculable cruelties, over a lifetime, must a cat afflict on birds, mice, rabbits! But it struck him as a melancholy thing, that *he,* Julius Muir—who had paid so much for her, and who in fact had shared in the pride of her—should find himself out of necessity in the role of executioner. But it was something that had to be done, and though he had perhaps forgotten why it had to be done, he knew that he and he alone was destined to do it.

The other evening a number of guests had come to dinner, and as they were seated on the terrace Miranda leapt whitely up out of nowhere to make her way along the garden wall—plumelike tail erect, silky ruff floating about her high-held head, golden eyes gleaming—quite as if on cue, as Alissa said. "This is Miranda, come to say hello to you! *Isn't* she beautiful!" Alissa happily exclaimed. (For she seemed never to tire of remarking upon her cat's beauty—an innocent sort of narcissism, Mr. Muir supposed.) The usual praise, or flattery, was aired; the cat preened herself—fully conscious of being the center of attention—then leapt away with a violent sort of grace and disappeared down the steep stone steps to the river embankment. Mr. Muir thought then that he understood why Miranda was so uncannily *interesting* as a phenomenon: She represented a beauty that was both purposeless and necessary; a beauty that was (considering her pedigree) completely an artifice, and yet (considering she *was* a thing of flesh and blood) completely natural: Nature.

Though was Nature always and invariably—*natural?*

Now, as the white cat finished her meal (leaving a good quarter of it in the dish, as usual), Mr. Muir said aloud, in a tone in which infinite regret and satisfaction were commingled, "But beauty won't save you."

The cat paused to look up at him with her flat, unblinking gaze. He felt an instant's terror: Did she know? Did she know—already? It seemed to him that she had never looked more splendid: fur so purely, silkily white; ruff full as if recently brushed; the petulant pug face; wide, stiff whiskers; finely shaped ears so intelligently erect. And, of course, the eyes . . .

He'd always been fascinated by Miranda's eyes, which were a tawny golden hue, for they had the mysterious capacity to flare up, as if at will. Seen at night, of course—by way of the moon's reflection, or the headlights of the Muirs' own homebound car—they were lustrous as small beams of light. "Is that Miranda, do you think?" Alissa would ask, seeing the twin flashes of light in the tall grass bordering the road. "Possibly," Mr. Muir would say. "Ah, she's waiting for us! Isn't that sweet! She's waiting for us to come home!" Alissa would exclaim with childlike excitement. Mr. Muir—who doubted that the cat had even been aware of their absence, let alone eagerly awaited their return—said nothing.

Another thing about the cat's eyes that had always seemed to Mr. Muir somehow perverse was the fact that, while the human eyeball is uniformly white and the iris colored, a cat eyeball is colored and the iris purely black. Green, yellow, gray, even blue—the entire eyeball! And the iris so magically responsive to gradations of light or excitation, con-

tracting to razor-thin slits, dilating blackly to fill almost the entire eye
. . . As she stared up at him now her eyes were so dilated their color was
nearly eclipsed.

"No, beauty can't save you. It isn't enough," Mr. Muir said quietly.
With trembling fingers he opened the screen door to let the cat out into
the night. As she passed him—perverse creature, indeed!—she rubbed
lightly against his leg as she had not done for many months. Or had it
been years?

Alissa was twenty years Mr. Muir's junior but looked even younger: a
petite woman with very large, very pretty brown eyes; shoulder-length
blond hair; the upbeat if sometimes rather frenetic manner of a well-
practiced ingenue. She was a minor actress with a minor ambition—as she
freely acknowledged—for after all, serious professional acting is brutally
hard work, even if one somehow manages to survive the competition.

"And then, of course, Julius takes such good care of me," she would
say, linking her arm through his or resting her head for a moment against
his shoulder. "I have everything I want, really, right here . . ." By which
she meant the country place Mr. Muir had bought for her when they were
married. (Of course they also kept an apartment in Manhattan, two hours
to the south. But Mr. Muir had grown to dislike the city—it abraded his
nerves like a cat's claws raking against a screen—and rarely made the
journey in any longer.) Under her maiden name, Howth, Alissa had been
employed intermittently for eight years before marrying Mr. Muir; her
first marriage—contracted at the age of nineteen to a well-known (and
notorious) Hollywood actor, since deceased—had been a disaster of which
she cared not to speak in any detail. (Nor did Mr. Muir care to question
her about those years. It was as if, for him, they had not existed.)

At the time of their meeting Alissa was in temporary retreat, as she
called it, from her career. She'd had a small success on Broadway but the
success had not taken hold. And was it worth it, really, to keep going, to
keep trying? Season after season, the grinding round of auditions, the
competition with new faces, "promising" new talents . . . Her first
marriage had ended badly and she'd had a number of love affairs of
varying degrees of worth (precisely how many Mr. Muir was never to

learn), and now perhaps it was time to ease into private life. And there was Julius Muir: not young, not particularly charming, but well-to-do, and well-bred, and besotted with love for her, and—*there*.

Of course Mr. Muir was dazzled by her; and he had the time and the resources to court her more assiduously than any man had ever courted her. He seemed to see in her qualities no one else saw; his imagination, for so reticent and subdued a man, was rich, lively to the point of fever, immensely flattering. And he did not mind, he extravagantly insisted, that he loved her more than she loved him—even as Alissa protested she *did* love him—would she consent to marry him otherwise?

For a few years they spoke vaguely of "starting a family," but nothing came of it. Alissa was too busy, or wasn't in ideal health; or they were traveling; or Mr. Muir worried about the unknown effect a child would have upon their marriage. (Alissa would have less time for him, surely?) As time passed he vexed himself with the thought that he'd have no heir when he died—that is, no child of his own—but there was nothing to be done.

They had a rich social life; they were wonderfully *busy* people. And they had, after all, their gorgeous white Persian cat. "Miranda would be traumatized if there was a baby in the household," Alissa said. "We really couldn't do that to her."

"Indeed we couldn't," Mr. Muir agreed.

And then, abruptly, Alissa decided to return to acting. To her "career" as she gravely called it—as if it were a phenomenon apart from her, a force not to be resisted. And Mr. Muir was happy for her—very happy for her. He took pride in his wife's professionalism, and he wasn't at all jealous of her ever-widening circle of friends, acquaintances, associates. He wasn't jealous of her fellow actors and actresses—Rikka, Mario, Robin, Sibyl, Emile, each in turn—and now Alban of the damp dark shiny eyes and quick sweet smile; nor was he jealous of the time she spent away from home; nor, if home, of the time she spent sequestered away in the room they called her studio, deeply absorbed in her work. In her maturity Alissa Howth had acquired a robust sort of good-heartedness that gave her more stage presence even as it relegated her to certain sorts of roles—the roles inevitable, in any case, for older actresses, regardless of their physical beauty. And she'd become a far better, far more subtle actress—as everyone said.

Indeed, Mr. Muir *was* proud of her, and happy for her. And if he felt, now and then, a faint resentment—or, if not quite resentment, a tinge of regret at the way their life had diverged into lives—he was too much a gentleman to show it.

"Where is Miranda? Have you seen Miranda today?"

It was noon, it was four o'clock, it was nearly dusk, and Miranda had not returned. For much of the day Alissa had been preoccupied with telephone calls—the phone seemed always to be ringing—and only gradually had she become aware of the cat's prolonged absence. She went outside to call her; she sent the servants out to look for her. And Mr. Muir, of course, gave his assistance, wandering about the grounds and for some distance into the woods, his hands cupped to his mouth and his voice high-pitched and tremulous: *"Kitty-kitty-kitty-kitty-kitty! Kitty-kitty-kitty—"* How pathetic, how foolish—how futile! Yet it had to be performed since it was what, in innocent circumstances, *would* be performed. Julius Muir, that most solicitous of husbands, tramping through the underbrush looking for his wife's Persian cat . . .

Poor Alissa! he thought. She'll be heartbroken for days—or would it be weeks?

And he, too, would miss Miranda—as a household presence at the very least. They would have had her, after all, for ten years this autumn.

Dinner that night was subdued, rather leaden. Not simply because Miranda was missing (and Alissa did seem inordinately and genuinely worried), but because Mr. Muir and his wife were dining alone; the table, set for two, seemed almost aesthetically wrong. And how unnatural, the quiet . . . Mr. Muir tried to make conversation but his voice soon trailed off into a guilty silence. Midmeal Alissa rose to accept a telephone call (from Manhattan, of course—her agent, or her director, or Alban, or a female friend—an urgent call, for otherwise Mrs. Muir did not accept calls at this intimate hour) and Mr. Muir—crestfallen, hurt—finished his solitary meal in a kind of trance, tasting nothing. He recalled the night before—the pungent-smelling cat food, the grainy white poison, the way the shrewd animal had looked up at him, and the way she'd brushed against his leg in a belated gesture of . . . was it affection? Reproach? Mockery? He felt a renewed stab of guilt, and an even more powerful stab of visceral satisfaction. Then, glancing up, he chanced to see something white making its careful way along the top of the garden wall . . .

Of course it was Miranda come home.

He stared, appalled. He stared, speechless—waiting for the apparition to vanish.

Slowly, in a daze, he rose to his feet. In a voice meant to be jubilant he called out the news to Alissa in the adjoining room: "Miranda's come home!"

He called out: "Alissa! Darling! Miranda's come home!"

And there Miranda was, indeed; indeed it *was* Miranda, peering into the dining room from the terrace, her eyes glowing tawny gold. Mr. Muir was trembling, but his brain worked swiftly to absorb the fact, and to construe a logic to accommodate it. She'd vomited up the poison, no doubt. Ah, no doubt! Or, after a cold, damp winter in the gardener's shed, the poison had lost its efficacy.

He had yet to bestir himself, to hurry to unlatch the sliding door and let the white cat in, but his voice fairly quavered with excitement: "Alissa! Good news! Miranda's come home!"

Alissa's joy was so extreme and his own initial relief so genuine that Mr. Muir—stroking Miranda's plume of a tail as Alissa hugged the cat ecstatically in her arms—thought he'd acted cruelly, selfishly—certainly he'd acted out of character—and decided that Miranda, having escaped death at her master's hands, should be granted life. He would *not* try another time.

Before his marriage at the age of forty-six Julius Muir, like most never-married men and women of a certain temperament—introverted, self-conscious; observers of life rather than participants—had believed that the marital state was unconditionally *marital;* he'd thought that husband and wife were one flesh in more than merely the metaphorical sense of that term. Yet it happened that his own marriage was a marriage of a decidedly diminished sort. Marital relations had all but ceased, and there seemed little likelihood of their being resumed. He would shortly be fifty-seven years old, after all. (Though sometimes he wondered: Was that truly *old?*)

During the first two or three years of their marriage (when Alissa's theatrical career was, as she called it, in eclipse), they had shared a double bed like any married couple—or so Mr. Muir assumed. (For his own marriage had not enlightened him to what "marriage" in a generic sense meant.) With the passage of time, however, Alissa began to complain gently of being unable to sleep because of Mr. Muir's nocturnal "agitation"—twitching, kicking, thrashing about, exclaiming aloud, sometimes even shouting in terror. Wakened by her he would scarcely know, for a moment or two, where he was; he would then apologize profusely and shamefully, and creep away into another bedroom to sleep, if he could, for the rest of the night. Though unhappy with the situation, Mr. Muir was fully sympathetic with Alissa; he even had reason to believe that the poor woman (whose nerves were unusually sensitive) had suffered many a sleepless night on his account without telling him. It was like her to be so considerate; so loath to hurt another's feelings.

As a consequence they developed a cozy routine in which Mr. Muir spent a half-hour or so with Alissa when they first retired for the night; then, taking care not to disturb her, he would tiptoe quietly away into another room, where he might sleep undisturbed. (If, indeed, his occasional nightmares allowed him undisturbed sleep. He rather thought the worst ones, however, were the ones that failed to wake him.)

Yet a further consequence had developed in recent years: Alissa had acquired the habit of staying awake late—reading in bed, or watching television, or even, from time to time, chatting on the telephone—so it was most practical for Mr. Muir simply to kiss her good-night without getting in bed beside her, and then to go off to his own bedroom. Sometimes in his sleep he imagined Alissa was calling him back—awakened, he would hurry out into the darkened corridor to stand by her door for a minute or two, eager and hopeful. At such times he dared not raise his voice above a whisper: "Alissa? Alissa, dearest? Did you call me?"

Just as unpredictable and capricious as Mr. Muir's bad dreams were the nighttime habits of Miranda, who at times would cozily curl up at the foot of Alissa's bed and sleep peacefully through to dawn, but at other times would insist upon being let outside, no matter that Alissa loved her to sleep on the bed. There was comfort of a kind—childish, Alissa granted—in knowing the white Persian was there through the night, and feeling at her feet the cat's warm, solid weight atop the satin coverlet.

But of course, as Alissa acknowledged, a cat can't be forced to do anything against her will. "It seems almost to be a law of nature," she said solemnly.

A few days after the abortive poisoning Mr. Muir was driving home in the early dusk when, perhaps a mile from his estate, he caught sight of the white cat in the road ahead—motionless in the other lane, as if frozen by the car's headlights. Unbidden, the thought came to him: *This is just to frighten her*—and he turned his wheel and headed in her direction. The golden eyes flared up in a blaze of blank surprise—or perhaps it was terror, or recognition—*This is just to redress the balance,* Mr. Muir thought as he pressed down harder on the accelerator and drove directly at the white Persian—and struck her, just as she started to bolt toward the ditch, with the front left wheel of his car. There was a thud and a cat's yowling, incredulous scream—and it was done.

My God! It *was* done!

Dry mouthed, shaking, Mr. Muir saw in his rearview mirror the broken white form in the road; saw a patch of liquid crimson blossoming out around it. He had not meant to kill Miranda, and yet he had actually done it this time—without premeditation, and therefore without guilt.

And now the deed was done forever.

"And no amount of remorse can undo it," he said in a slow, wondering voice.

Mr. Muir had driven to the village to pick up a prescription for Alissa at the drugstore—she'd been in the city on theater matters; had returned home late on a crowded commuter train and gone at once to lie down with what threatened to be a migraine headache. Now he felt rather a hypocrite, a brute, presenting headache tablets to his wife with the guilty knowledge that if she knew what he'd done, the severity of her migraine would be tenfold. Yet how could he have explained to her that he had not meant to kill Miranda this time, but the steering wheel of his car had seemed to act of its own volition, wresting itself from his grip? For so Mr. Muir—speeding home, still trembling and excited as though he himself had come close to violent death—remembered the incident.

He remembered too the cat's hideous scream, cut off almost at once by the impact of the collision—but not quite at once.

And was there a dent in the fender of the handsome, English-built car? There was not.

And were there bloodstains on the left front tire? There were not.

Was there in fact any sign of a mishap, even of the mildest, most innocent sort? There was not.

"No proof! No proof!" Mr. Muir told himself happily, taking the stairs to Alissa's room two at a time. It was a matter of some relief as well when he raised his hand to knock at the door to hear that Alissa was evidently feeling better. She was on the telephone, talking animatedly with someone; even laughing in her light, silvery way that reminded him of nothing so much as wind chimes on a mild summer's night. His heart swelled with love and gratitude. "Dear Alissa—we will be so happy from now on!"

Then it happened, incredibly, that at about bedtime the white cat showed up again. *She had not died after all.*

Mr. Muir, who was sharing a late-night brandy with Alissa in her bedroom, was the first to see Miranda: She had climbed up onto the roof—by way, probably, of a rose trellis she often climbed for that purpose—and now her pug face appeared at one of the windows in a hideous repetition of the scene some nights ago. Mr. Muir sat paralyzed with shock, and it was Alissa who jumped out of bed to let the cat in.

"Miranda! What a trick! What *are* you up to?"

Certainly the cat had not been missing for any worrisome period of time, yet Alissa greeted her with as much enthusiasm as if she had. And Mr. Muir—his heart pounding in his chest and his very soul convulsed with loathing—was obliged to go along with the charade. He hoped Alissa would not notice the sick terror that surely shone in his eyes.

The cat he'd struck with his car must have been another cat, not Miranda . . . Obviously it had not been Miranda. Another white Persian with tawny eyes, and not his own.

Alissa cooed over the creature, and petted her, and encouraged her to settle down on the bed for the night, but after a few minutes Miranda jumped down and scratched to be let out the door: She'd missed her supper; she was hungry; she'd had enough of her mistress's affection. Not so much as a glance had she given her master, who was staring at her with revulsion. He knew now that he *must* kill her—if only to prove he could do it.

Following this episode the cat shrewdly avoided Mr. Muir—not out of lazy indifference, as in the past, but out of a sharp sense of their altered relations. She could not be conscious, he knew, of the fact that he had tried to kill her—but she must have been able to sense it. Perhaps she had been hiding in the bushes by the road and had seen him aim his car at her unfortunate doppelgänger, and run it down . . .

This was unlikely, Mr. Muir knew. Indeed, it was highly improbable. But how otherwise to account for the creature's behavior in his presence—her demonstration, or simulation, of animal fear? Leaping atop a cabinet when he entered a room, as if to get out of his way; leaping atop a fireplace mantel (and sending, it seemed deliberately, one of his carved jade figurines to the hearth, where it shattered into a dozen pieces); skittering gracelessly through a doorway, her sharp toenails clicking against the hardwood floor. When, without intending to, he approached her out-of-doors, she was likely to scamper noisily up one of the rose trellises, or the grape arbor, or a tree; or run off into the shrubbery like a wild creature. If Alissa happened to be present she was invariably astonished, for the cat's behavior *was* senseless. "Do you think Miranda is ill?" she asked. "Should we take her to the veterinarian?" Mr. Muir said uneasily that he doubted they would be able to catch her for such a purpose—at least, he doubted *he* could.

He had an impulse to confess his crime, or his attempted crime, to Alissa. He had killed the hateful creature—*and she had not died.*

* * *

One night at the very end of August Mr. Muir dreamt of glaring, disembodied eyes. And in their centers those black, black irises like old-fashioned keyholes: slots opening into the Void. He could not move to protect himself. A warm, furry weight settled luxuriantly upon his chest . . . upon his very face! The cat's whiskery white muzzle pressed against his mouth in a hellish kiss and in an instant the breath was being sucked from him . . .

"Oh, no! Save me! Dear God—"

The damp muzzle against his mouth, sucking his life's breath from him, and he could not move to tear it away—his arms, leaden at his sides; his entire body struck dumb, paralyzed . . .

"Save me . . . *save me!*"

His shouting, his panicked thrashing about in the bedclothes, woke him. Though he realized at once it had been only a dream, his breath still came in rapid, shallow gasps, and his heart hammered so violently he was in terror of dying: Had not his doctor only the other week spoken gravely to him of imminent heart disease, the possibility of heart failure? And how mysterious it was, his blood pressure being so very much higher than ever before in his life . . .

Mr. Muir threw himself out of the damp, tangled bedclothes and switched on a lamp with trembling fingers. Thank God he was alone and Alissa had not witnessed this latest display of nerves!

"Miranda?" he whispered. "Are you in here?"

He switched on an overhead light. The bedroom shimmered with shadows and did not seem, for an instant, any room he knew.

"Miranda . . . ?"

The sly, wicked creature! The malevolent beast! To think that cat's muzzle had touched his very lips, the muzzle of an animal that devoured mice, rats—any sort of foul filthy thing out in the woods! Mr. Muir went into his bathroom and rinsed out his mouth even as he told himself calmly that the dream had been only a dream, and the cat only a phantasm, and that of course Miranda was *not* in his room.

Still, she had settled her warm, furry, unmistakable weight on his chest. She had attempted to suck his breath from him, to choke him, suffocate him, stop his poor heart. *It was within her power.* "Only a dream,"

Mr. Muir said aloud, smiling shakily at his reflection in the mirror. (Oh! To think that pale, haggard apparition was indeed *his* . . .) Mr. Muir raised his voice with scholarly precision. "A foolish dream. A child's dream. A woman's dream."

Back in his room he had the fleeting sense that something—a vague white shape—had just now scampered beneath his bed. But when he got down on his hands and knees to look, of course there was nothing.

He did, however, discover in the deep-pile carpet a number of cat hairs. White, rather stiff—quite clearly Miranda's. Ah, quite clearly. "Here's the evidence!" he said excitedly. He found a light scattering of them on the carpet near the door and, nearer his bed, a good deal more— as if the creature had lain there for a while and had even rolled over (as Miranda commonly did out on the terrace in the sun) and stretched her graceful limbs in an attitude of utterly pleasurable abandon. Mr. Muir had often been struck by the cat's remarkable *luxuriance* at such times: a joy of flesh (and fur) he could not begin to imagine. Even before relations between them had deteriorated, he had felt the impulse to hurry to the cat and bring the heel of his shoe down hard on that tender, exposed, pinkish-pale belly . . .

"Miranda? Where are you? Are you still in here?" Mr. Muir said. He was breathless, excited. He'd been squatting on his haunches for some minutes, and when he tried to straighten up his legs ached.

Mr. Muir searched the room, but it was clear that the white cat had gone. He went out onto his balcony, leaned against the railing, blinked into the dimly moonlit darkness, but could see nothing—in his fright he'd forgotten to put on his glasses. For some minutes he breathed in the humid, sluggish night air in an attempt to calm himself, but it soon became apparent that something was wrong. Some vague murmurous undertone of—was it a voice? Voices?

Then he saw it: the ghostly white shape down in the shrubbery. Mr. Muir blinked and stared, but his vision was unreliable. "Miranda . . . ?" A scuttling noise rustled above him and he turned to see another white shape on the sharp-slanted roof making its rapid way over the top. He stood absolutely motionless—whether out of terror or cunning, he could not have said. That there was more than one white cat, more than one white Persian—more, in fact, than *merely one Miranda*—was a possibility he had not considered! "Yet perhaps that explains it," he said. He was badly frightened, but his brain functioned as clearly as ever.

It was not so very late, scarcely 1:00 A.M. The undertone Mr. Muir heard was Alissa's voice, punctuated now and then by her light, silvery laughter. One might almost think there was someone in the bedroom with her—but of course she was merely having a late-night telephone conversation, very likely with Alban—they would be chatting companionably, with an innocent sort of malice, about their co-actors and -actresses, mutual friends and acquaintances. Alissa's balcony opened out onto the same side of the house that Mr. Muir's did, which accounted for her voice (or *was* it voices? Mr. Muir listened, bemused) carrying so clearly. No light irradiated from her room; she must have been having her telephone conversation in the dark.

Mr. Muir waited another few minutes, but the white shape down in the shrubbery had vanished. And the slate-covered roof overhead was empty, reflecting moonlight in dull, uneven patches. He was alone. He decided to go back to bed but before doing so he checked carefully to see that he *was* alone. He locked all the windows, and the door, and slept with the lights on—but so deeply and with such grateful abandon that in the morning, it was Alissa's rapping on the door that woke him. "Julius? Julius? Is something wrong, dear?" she cried. He saw with astonishment that it was *nearly noon:* He'd slept four hours past his usual rising time!

Alissa said good-bye to him hurriedly. A limousine was coming to carry her to the city; she was to be away for several nights in succession; she was concerned about him, about his health, and hoped there was nothing wrong . . . "Of course there is nothing wrong," Mr. Muir said irritably. Having slept so late in the day left him feeling sluggish and confused; it had not at all refreshed him. When Alissa kissed him good-bye he seemed rather to suffer the kiss than to participate in it, and after she had gone he had to resist an impulse to wipe his mouth with the back of his hand.

"God help us!" he whispered.

*   *   *

By degrees, as a consequence of his troubled mind, Mr. Muir had lost interest in collecting. When an antiquarian bookdealer offered him a rare octavo edition of the *Directorium Inquisitorum* he felt only the mildest tinge of excitement, and allowed the treasure to be snatched up by a rival collector. Only a few days afterward he responded with even less enthusiasm when offered the chance to bid on a quarto Gothic edition of Machiavelli's *Belfagor*. "Is something wrong, Mr. Muir?" the dealer asked him. (They had been doing business together for a quarter of a century.) Mr. Muir said ironically, "*Is* something wrong?" and broke off the telephone connection. He was never to speak to the man again.

Yet more decisively, Mr. Muir had lost interest in financial affairs. He would not accept telephone calls from the various Wall Street gentlemen who managed his money; it was quite enough for him to know that the money was there and would always be there. Details regarding it struck him as tiresome and vulgar.

In the third week of September the play in which Alissa was an understudy opened to superlative reviews, which meant a good, long run. Though the female lead was in excellent health and showed little likelihood of ever missing a performance, Alissa felt obliged to remain in the city a good deal, sometimes for a full week at a time. (What she did there, how she busied herself day after day, evening after evening, Mr. Muir did not know and was too proud to ask.) When she invited him to join her for a weekend (why didn't he visit some of his antiquarian dealers, as he used to do with such pleasure?) Mr. Muir said simply, "But why, when I have all I require for happiness here in the country?"

Since the night of the attempted suffocation Mr. Muir and Miranda were yet more keenly aware of each other. No longer did the white cat flee his presence; rather, as if in mockery of him, she held her ground when he entered a room. If he approached her she eluded him only at the last possible instant, often flattening herself close against the floor and scampering, snakelike, away. He cursed her; she bared her teeth and hissed. He laughed loudly to show her how very little he cared; she leapt atop a cabinet, out of his reach, and settled into a cat's blissful sleep. Each evening Alissa called at an appointed hour; each evening she inquired after Miranda, and Mr. Muir would say, "Beautiful and healthy as ever! A pity you can't see her!"

With the passage of time Miranda grew bolder and more reckless—misjudging, perhaps, the quickness of her master's reflexes. She sometimes appeared underfoot, nearly tripping him on the stairs or as he left the house; she dared approach him as he stood with a potential weapon in hand—a carving knife, a poker, a heavy, leatherbound book. Once or twice, as Mr. Muir sat dreaming through one of his solitary meals, she even leapt onto his lap and scampered across the dining room table, upsetting dishes and glasses. "Devil!" he shrieked, swiping in her wake with his fists. "What do you want of me!"

He wondered what tales the servants told of him, whispered backstairs. He wondered if any were being relayed to Alissa in the city.

One night, however, Miranda made a tactical error, and Mr. Muir did catch hold of her. She had slipped into his study—where he sat examining some of his rarest and most valuable coins (Mesopotamian, Etruscan) by lamplight—having calculated, evidently, on making her escape by way of the door. But Mr. Muir, leaping from his chair with extraordinary, almost feline swiftness, managed to kick the door shut. And now what a chase! What a struggle! What a mad frolic! Mr. Muir caught hold of the animal, lost her, caught hold of her again, lost her; she raked him viciously on the backs of both hands and on his face; he managed to catch hold of her again, slamming her against the wall and closing his bleeding fingers around her throat. He squeezed, he squeezed! He had her now and no force on earth could make him release her! As the cat screamed and clawed and kicked and thrashed and seemed to be suffering the convulsions of death, Mr. Muir crouched over her with eyes bulging and mad as her own. The arteries in his forehead visibly throbbed. "Now! Now I have you! Now!" he cried. And at that very moment when, surely, the white Persian was on the verge of extinction, the door to Mr. Muir's study was flung open and one of the servants appeared, white faced and incredulous: "Mr. Muir? What is it? We heard such—" the fool was saying; and of course Miranda slipped from Mr. Muir's loosened grasp and bolted from the room.

After that incident Mr. Muir seemed resigned to the knowledge that he would never have such an opportunity again. The end was swiftly approaching.

It happened quite suddenly, in the second week of November, that Alissa returned home.

She had quit the play; she had quit the "professional stage"; she did not even intend, as she told her husband vehemently, to visit New York City for a long time.

He saw to his astonishment that she'd been crying. Her eyes were unnaturally bright and seemed smaller than he recalled. And her prettiness looked worn, as if another face—harder, of smaller dimensions—were pushing through. Poor Alissa! She had gone away with such hope! When Mr. Muir moved to embrace her, however, meaning to comfort her, she drew away from him; her very nostrils pinched as if she found the smell of him offensive. "Please," she said, not looking him in the eye. "I don't feel well. What I want most is to be alone . . . just to be alone."

She retired to her room, to her bed. For several days she remained sequestered there, admitting only one of the female servants and, of course, her beloved Miranda, when Miranda condescended to visit the house. (To his immense relief Mr. Muir observed that the white cat showed no sign of their recent struggle. His lacerated hands and face were slow to heal, but in her own grief and self-absorption, Alissa seemed not to have noticed.)

In her room, behind her locked door, Alissa made a number of telephone calls to New York City. Often she seemed to be weeping over the phone. But so far as Mr. Muir could determine—being forced, under these special circumstances, to eavesdrop on the line—none of her conversations were with Alban.

Which meant . . . ? He had to confess he had no idea; nor could he ask Alissa. For that would give away the fact that he'd been eavesdropping, and she would be deeply shocked.

Mr. Muir sent small bouquets of autumn flowers to Alissa's sickroom; bought her chocolates and bonbons, slender volumes of poetry, a new diamond bracelet. Several times he presented himself at her door, ever the eager suitor, but she explained that she was not prepared to see him just yet—not just yet. Her voice was shrill and edged with a metallic tone Mr. Muir had not heard before.

"Don't you love me, Alissa?" he cried suddenly.

There was a moment's embarrassed silence. Then: "Of course I do. But please go away and leave me alone."

So worried was Mr. Muir about Alissa that he could no longer sleep for more than an hour or two at a time, and these hours were characterized by tumultuous dreams. The white cat! The hideous smothering weight! Fur in his very mouth! Yet awake he thought only of Alissa and of how, though she had come home to him, it was not in fact to *him.*

He lay alone in his solitary bed, amidst the tangled bedclothes, weeping hoarsely. One morning he stroked his chin and touched bristles: He'd neglected to shave for several days.

From his balcony he chanced to see the white cat preening atop the garden wall, a larger creature than he recalled. She had fully recovered from his attack. (If, indeed, she had been injured by it. If, indeed, the cat on the garden wall was the selfsame cat that had blundered into his study.) Her white fur very nearly blazed in the sun; her eyes were miniature golden-glowing coals set deep in her skull. Mr. Muir felt a mild shock seeing her: What a beautiful creature!

Though in the next instant, of course, he realized what she was.

One rainy, gusty evening in late November Mr. Muir was driving on the narrow blacktop road above the river, Alissa silent at his side—stubbornly silent, he thought. She wore a black cashmere cloak and a hat of soft black felt that fitted her head tightly, covering most of her hair. These were items of clothing Mr. Muir had not seen before, and in their stylish austerity they suggested the growing distance between them. When he had helped her into the car she'd murmured "thank you" in a tone that indicated "Oh! Must you touch me?" And Mr. Muir had made a mocking little bow, standing bareheaded in the rain.

And I had loved you so much.

Now she did not speak. Sat with her lovely profile turned from him. As if she were fascinated by the lashing rain, the river pocked and heaving below, the gusts of wind that rocked the English-built car as Mr. Muir pressed his foot ever harder

on the gas pedal. "It will be better this way, my dear wife," Mr. Muir said
quietly. "Even if you love no other man, it is painfully clear that you do not love
me." At these solemn words Alissa started guiltily, but still would not face him.
"My dear? Do you understand? It will be better this way—do not be frightened."
As Mr. Muir drove faster, as the car rocked more violently in the wind, Alissa
pressed her hands against her mouth as if to stifle any protest; she was staring
transfixed—as Mr. Muir stared transfixed—at the rushing pavement.

Only when Mr. Muir bravely turned the car's front wheels in the direction of
a guardrail did her resolve break: She emitted a series of breathless little screams,
shrinking back against the seat, but made no effort to seize his arm or the wheel.
And in an instant all was over, in any case—the car crashed through the railing,
seemed to spin in midair, dropped to the rock-strewn hillside and bursting into
flame, turned end over end . . .

He was seated in a chair with wheels—a wheeled chair! It seemed to him a
remarkable invention and he wondered whose ingenuity lay behind it.

Though he had not the capacity, being almost totally paralyzed, to
propel it of his own volition.

And, being blind, he had no volition in any case! He was quite
content to stay where he was, so long as it was out of the draft. (The
invisible room in which he now resided was, for the most part, cozily
heated—his wife had seen to that—but there yet remained unpredictable
currents of cold air that assailed him from time to time. His bodily
temperature, he feared, could not maintain its integrity against any sus-
tained onslaught.)

He had forgotten the names for many things and felt no great grief.
Indeed, not knowing *names* relaxes one's desire for the *things* that, ghost-
like, forever unattainable, dwell behind them. And of course his blindness
had much to do with this—for which he was grateful! Quite grateful!

Blind, yet not wholly blind: for he could see (indeed, could not *not*
see) washes of white, gradations of white, astonishing subtleties of white
like rivulets in a stream perpetually breaking and falling about his head,
not distinguished by any form or outline or vulgar suggestion of an object
in space . . .

He had had, evidently, a number of operations. How many he did not know; nor did he care to know. In recent weeks they had spoken earnestly to him of the possibility of yet another operation on his brain, the (hypothetical) object being, if he understood correctly, the restoration of his ability to move some of the toes on his left foot. Had he the capacity to laugh he would have laughed, but perhaps his dignified silence was preferable.

Alissa's sweet voice joined with the others in a chorus of bleak enthusiasm, but so far as he knew the operation had never taken place. Or if it had, it had not been a conspicuous success. The toes of his left foot were as remote and lost to him as all the other parts of his body.

"How lucky you were, Julius, that another car came along! Why, you might have *died!*"

It seemed that Julius Muir had been driving alone in a violent thunderstorm on the narrow River Road, high above the embankment; uncharacteristically, he'd been driving at a high speed; he'd lost control of his car, crashed through the inadequate guardrail, and over the side . . . "miraculously" thrown clear of the burning wreckage. Two-thirds of the bones in his slender body broken, skull severely fractured, spinal column smashed, a lung pierced . . . So the story of how Julius had come to this place, his final resting place, this place of milk-white peace, emerged, in fragments shattered and haphazard as those of a smashed windshield.

"Julius, dear? Are you awake, or—?" The familiar, resolutely cheerful voice came to him out of the mist, and he tried to attach a name to it, *Alissa?* or, no, *Miranda?*—which?

There was talk (sometimes in his very hearing) that, one day, some degree of his vision might be restored. But Julius Muir scarcely heard, or cared. He lived for those days when, waking from a doze, he would feel a certain furry, warm weight lowered into his lap—"Julius, dear, someone very special has come to visit!"—soft, yet surprisingly heavy; heated, yet not disagreeably so; initially a bit restless (as a cat must circle fussily about, trying to determine the ideal position before she settles herself down), yet within a few minutes quite wonderfully relaxed, kneading her claws gently against his limbs and purring as she drifted into a companionable sleep. He would have liked to see, beyond the shimmering water whiteness of his vision, her particular whiteness; certainly he would have liked to feel once again the softness, the astonishing silkiness, of that fur. But he could hear the deep-throated melodic purring. He could feel, to a degree, her warmly pulsing weight, the wonder of her mysterious *livingness* against his—for which he was infinitely grateful.

"My love!"

Robley Wilson, Jr.

CATS

When Kate woke up in the night and felt the warmth of one of the cats against her legs, she could tell which cat it was by reaching out to touch its fur. Cass was sleek, soft as mink or sheared beaver—coats she had touched once when she had gone with Alice Rand to the Lord & Taylor salon—and he was fine-boned, delicate as the yellowed cat skeleton she remembered from her high school biology classroom of nearly thirty years ago. Tibb, who was younger, was also coarser, and his skeleton was both bigger-boned and more compact—a tougher version of cat-ness than Cass—and it was Tibb who was more likely to want to be playful. Where Cass would nuzzle Kate's hand and shift into a new sleep position, Tibb, often as not, would go over on his back and embrace her wrist with the needles of his claws. Sometimes when the two cats were on the bed, one on either side of her, she would lie in the dark and stroke both of them, marveling at the peculiar sensuality of her life.

Lately, after a long time of keeping to herself, she had begun to get involved with a man. His name was Barry, and she had met him at the county clerk's office in June, when she was renewing her driver's license. He stood just behind her in the short line leading to the counter. When she pushed her old license toward the clerk, the man spoke.

"Same birthday," he said.

For a moment she hadn't realized he was talking to her, and then—because no second voice responded—she turned, looked at him.

"We have the same date of birth," he said. "June fifteenth."

"Yes," she said. She smiled at him—a nervous smile, she imagined, for what sort of answer to his flat statement did the man expect? Isn't it a small world. What a funny coincidence. Did he truly think there was something portentous here? "But probably not the same year."

"Nineteen forty-seven," he said.

She shook her head. "No, not quite."

He looked expectant.

She laughed. "You don't really expect me to tell you that I'm older than you, do you?"

Now he was sheepish. "Of course not," he said.

Then it was her turn to be photographed—she wished they could have reused the old picture; it actually looked like her—and she sat on a wooden bench nearby until the new license came out of the laminating machine. The man—tall, trim mustache, exactly thirty-seven years old—sat next to her on the bench.

"I hate to see what it's going to look like," she said. "The picture."

He cocked his head to look at her. "I shouldn't think you'd have to worry about that," he said.

*   *   *

When he asked her to have lunch, she decided to accept. He flattered her, he seemed unthreatening, and if he turned out to be married—well, this was only lunch.

In the restaurant, they sat at a table by a window, where they were surrounded by hanging planters and overlooked the river, so slow-moving at this time of year that it held the shade of the nearest bridge in a perfect inverted arch.

He extended his hand across the table. "Barry Miner," he said.

She took the hand for a moment—it was warm, dry—and released it.

"Kate Eastman."

She was nervous then, and that meant she talked too much. She said far more about herself than she had done, or had the opportunity to do, in the two years since her divorce. She confessed that she was older than he was, by five years, and that she had two grown sons. She told him— brightly, as if it were something she was by now entirely comfortable with—how fortunate she was to have married a man decent enough to stay with her until the boys were sent through college. She told him she had just started working as a paralegal in the office of one of her former husband's friends.

Through all of this he listened intently, never taking his eyes from her face, and finally she tried to encourage *him* to talk. "What is it you do?" she said.

"I'm a psychotherapist. In that clinic across from the courthouse."

"Oh, heavens. I'd better watch what I say." And she wondered what she had already let out that might have marked her in his eyes as a "case."

In the weeks that followed, she became more comfortable with Barry, less compulsive. She learned all over again—such a long time since she had forgotten!—that her own silences could draw a man out, that she did not need to interrogate him. He told her that his mother had recently died of cancer—something he revealed almost apologetically, almost as if the woman had done it because it was popular.

"We all worry about it," Kate said, defending her. "It's a terrible, fearful thing, and women have to deal with it."

He had gone silent then—rebuked, perhaps—and she felt vaguely guilty. That was the first night she went to his apartment, the first time she let him persuade her into bed. Afterward she was flustered by what she had done and woke him long before dawn to tell him that she had to leave, that she couldn't be out all night.

"But you live alone," he said.

"Not exactly," she said. And she told him about Cass and Tibb while she put on her clothes to go home to them.

At first he seemed amused by her fondness for the cats. She realized she had let herself in for a good bit of teasing from him, as if she were an eccentric, tolerable despite her odd behavior.

"Do you talk to them?" he asked her once.

"Certainly," she said. She was in bed with him, the second time— later on she would be chagrined to notice that she could remember each time they went to bed by some curious talk that had passed between them—and he was on one elbow, searching her face for God-knew-what knowledge he thought she was keeping to herself. "Shouldn't I?"

"You don't catch yourself sometimes and feel a little foolish?"

"What for?"

"For talking to animals?"

She pondered, not certain how he expected her to respond. "I'd feel foolish if they answered back," she said. "Is this a real discussion, or are you just filling in the time until you get excited again?"

He laughed then, and hugged her. "I'll have to meet them myself," he said. "The cats."

"They'll think you take the world too seriously."

"I suppose. At least I take you seriously."

"I wonder why. I almost feel as if you're picking me apart."

"I don't know what it is," he said. "I guess it seems to me that women like you live your lives on the edge of your emotions."

"Women like me?"

"Older, living without men." He reached out to touch the wisp of hair that had fallen alongside her right temple. "You're at risk somehow."

"But men without women . . . ?"

"Not the same. Men are more inner-directed."

"You have such piercing blue eyes," Kate said. "I'm glad I'm not one of your clients."

But she was thinking about what he had said, and whether she thought it was true or not. What came immediately to mind was her husband—her ex-husband—and how when he worked on the car, sometimes a bolt would be rusted and immovable, or something would break or get scratched while he was trying to remove it. She remembered how he would come into the kitchen, his hands black with grease and orange with rust, and sit at the kitchen table, putting his head in his dirty hands, and sobbing quietly. How she would stroke his hair, try to console him. How finally he would stop crying, and lift his face to her, and she would smile because the grease and rust had made splotchy patterns on his cheeks.

"So am I," he said.

"So are you what?"

"Glad you're not one of my patients."

I should hope so, she thought; all that fuss over talking to pets.

Less than a week later she invited him to her house to spend the weekend. She imagined things were getting "meaningful," that when a woman began to make a habit of a man, "something should come of it"—a statement she dimly recalled hearing from her mother.

"I think he has me at a real disadvantage," she said once in the midst of a conversation with Alice Rand. "I haven't been courted in twenty-five years. I don't remember what's expected of me, let alone what's expected of him."

"There aren't any expectations anymore" was Alice's response— Alice, who had chosen "career" in place of marriage and thought all men were children; who had finished law school and now, nearly fifty years old, was a partner in the firm. "Maybe you should just enjoy your disadvantage," she said.

Still, Kate had expectations she could not define—Barry was so intense with her, so relentlessly attentive. She appreciated the attentiveness. She waited for it to "come to something."

Saturday after dinner he said, "I don't think it's healthy for you to live in this solitary way. It isn't normal."

"How much time does a therapist spend with 'normal' people?" she said.

"You know what I mean." He sighed in what she imagined to be a professional exasperation. "You should have more contact with the world. Maybe you should entertain, play bridge, give a party once in a while."

"I'm a terrible bridge player. I have no card sense."

"Monopoly, then. Trivial Pursuit."

"And I hate giving parties—running around pouring salt on the carpet where the burgundy got spilled, rubbing Vaseline into the piano to get rid of the rings from wet glasses." She poured more coffee. "The cats are sociable enough, and a lot easier to deal with."

He sat back in the chair and looked at her. "Easier than me, I suppose," he said.

"I don't know," she said. How ought she to respond to that wistful expression on his face? "I truly don't."

"Why don't you find out?" he said.

"How?"

"Live with me."

She set the coffeepot back on the stove. Alice was right: Mother would never have expected that; and she gave the proposition—it certainly wasn't yet a proposal—her careful consideration. Would she give up the solitude? Probably. Could she be married again, to someone like Barry? She thought so; she had imagined it often enough. Would she move in with him? She didn't know. She was distracted all evening, and slept badly all night.

At the breakfast table on Sunday, Barry rattled the comics while she cooked bacon and eggs. Domestic bliss. Sunday had always been the one day of the week when she felt most like a woman, when she could wear a frilly robe without feeling overdressed.

Barry cleared his throat. "What was all that racket at three in the morning?" he said.

"It was my fault," she said.

"No, it was those damned cats—on and off the bed, scratching the box springs, meowing in my ear. What was the matter with them?"

"It took me a while to figure out. I kept thinking they wanted to be let out, but every time I got one of them near a door, he bolted back inside. After I'd gotten out of bed three times—" She stopped, the spatula poised above the frying pan. "How do you like the yolks? Runny? Hard? In between?"

"Between."

"After three times I finally got the message. The cat dish was totally empty, not a grain of Cat Chow to be seen. It's the first time they've ever confronted an empty food dish, and it put them in a tizzy."

"I'll bet," he said.

"Once I'd filled the dish—and the water bowl was low, too—they quieted down."

"What time was all this, actually?"

"I think it began around quarter of three, and I didn't solve the problem until four-fifteen or so. Some mother, aren't I?"

He shook his head. Sadly, she thought.

She turned the eggs and brought two plates down from the cupboard. "I've been thinking about what you said. About moving in with you."

"And?"

"And I've been thinking about some of your favorite words. 'Healthy' is one of them, and 'normal.'" She arranged three strips of bacon on each plate. "But they always seem to be applied to things *I* do. How about you?"

"Am I healthy and normal?"

"I mean, how normal is it to be thirty-seven years old and never married?"

He seemed not to have been offended by the question. Instead, the next time he visited her, he was even more serious toward her. He stood at the living-room window, looking out over her three acres with their cedars and plums and spruce, and talked, solemnly and at great length, about women and his life. He was an only child. His father had died when he was three, he had been raised by his mother and his mother's elder sister, and he had never really known male comradeship—a "male role model." He hadn't owned a dog, or turtles or gerbils or a pony—any of the masculine trappings of conventional boyhood. His aunt had a canary, which sang in a brass cage. He remembered his first day of kindergarten: he hadn't even gone into the school building at the boys' entrance, but instead went in with the girls, holding hands with Betty Jean, the daughter of his mother's best friend, who lived next door. Still, he told Kate, he believed he was well adjusted. Did she really believe he ought to have married? Wasn't that what men expected of women, and didn't women despise the expectation?

Kate had no answer to that. Hers was an opposite experience, she told him: three brothers; a he-man father—duck hunter, fisherman, camper—still robust in his early seventies; the attentions of uncles and boy cousins and, in school, plenty of boyfriends. She had married a man her father approved of, had given birth to two boys, had been surrounded all her married life by males—husband, sons, a succession of male dogs, the two cats. Perhaps she'd been out of line with the marriage comment, but Barry could see, couldn't he, how different her life had been.

"You don't have to apologize," he said.

"I'm not," she said. Good Lord, did he think she was?

A week passed. Kate wondered how long she would put off deciding whether or not to live with him, but she convinced herself that she only wanted to give him time to understand her. For one thing, it seemed important that he accept the cats.

"Sometimes when I get up in the morning, only one of them will be at the porch door," she said to Barry. "If it's Cass, I'll give him his breakfast and then let him out again. 'Go find your brother,' I'll say. And sure enough, in five or ten minutes Tibb appears. And vice-versa."

"If Tibb comes home alone, you send him after Cass?"

"Yes."

He sipped her bitter coffee. "I thought they weren't brothers," he said.

"They aren't, really. But they think they are. It can't do any harm if I let them go on thinking so, can it?" She smiled at him. "As a psychologist, what's your opinion?"

"I think it's all coincidence, of course. The other cat just happens to come back shortly after the first has gotten fed. I think it's all right to be silly over animals, so long as you know you're being silly."

"How can it be silly if it pleases me and doesn't hurt anyone else?"

"I said it's okay, if you know you're doing it."

"But you see," she said, "it isn't coincidence. If it only happened once in a while—that would be coincidence. It happens regularly."

He sighed. "If you say so," he said.

"Do you think I'm crazy?" she said. "Or only neurotic?"

Gradually, Barry began to be impatient. She caught him watching her, one eyebrow raised, as if he expected her to blurt out what he wanted to hear. He sat on the edge of the bed after they made love, his hands folded, his head bent in thought. He made her terribly nervous; she wondered if he wanted her to feel guilty. Guilt he could probably cope with.

"I don't mean to press," he said one day. They were having drinks together, in a bar near the courthouse. "But I wish you'd give me an answer. You know how I feel about you."

She thought she did.

"I realize how much you like living on the outskirts," he said. "But think about the conveniences of living in town. Shopping. Closer to your work. The gas you'll save."

"I think about Cass and Tibb."

He looked away, revolved a sweating tumbler between his hands.

"I know you think I'm foolish," she said. "But I couldn't give them up, and I couldn't ask them to be house cats, never able to go outdoors— to hunt, to have all that freedom."

"They could go outside," he said.

"In all the town traffic," she said. "I'd be worried sick. I'd—" She stopped herself, having at that instant an image of one or the other of the cats—they looked so much alike that in the distance of the image she couldn't tell which it was—stiff and dead in a gutter, gold eyes staring, empty. "What might happen," she said. "I can't even think about it."

"And I suppose that means you can't think about living with me." His eyes were averted; his mouth was petulant.

Indirection, she thought. We reach a place without knowing we were headed toward it.

"I'm sorry," she said. "I suppose it does."

He stopped calling her—which was a kindness, Kate thought. At least it was not sex he wanted from her, or not sex only, and for a while she luxuriated in having reclaimed her bed. She imagined the cats were pleased: they were less restless beside her. And she slept better as well—though one morning she woke out of a nightmare in which Cass appeared in the bedroom with a small rabbit squirming in his jaws. Awake, she couldn't decide whether the rabbit was a gift or a warning.

That evening when she fed both cats and let them out, the disturbance of the dream was forgotten. She talked with them as she held the door, saying to Tibb, "Now you be careful," and to Cass, "You take care of Brother, won't you?"

Later she stood at the kitchen window, putting together a salad for her own supper. The cats were moving down the long driveway—Cass in the lead, purposeful, rarely looking back; Tibb following, stopping, then trotting to catch up. Watching them go, she felt a welling-up of emotion she hadn't known since the days when her sons went off to school together.

That's love, she told herself. *There's nothing foolish about love.*

Mercedes Lackey

SKITTY

:*N*asty,: SKitty complained in Dick's head. She wrapped herself a little closer around his shoulders and licked drops of oily fog from her fur with a faint mew of distaste. :*Smelly.*:

Dick White had to agree. The portside district of Lacu'un was pretty unsavory; the dismal, foggy weather made it look even worse. Shabby, cheap, and ill-used.

Every building here—all twenty of them!—was offworld design; shoddy prefab, mostly painted in shades of peeling gray and industrial green, with garish neon-bright holosigns that were (thank the Spirits of Space!) mostly tuned down to faintly colored ghosts in the daytime. There were six bars, two gambling joints, one chapel run by the neo-Jesuits, one

flophouse run by the Reformed Salvation Army, five government buildings, four stores, and one place better left unnamed. They had all sprung
up, like diseased fungus, in the year since the planet and people of Lacu'un
had been declared Open for trade. There was nothing native here; for that
you had to go outside the Fence—

And to go outside the Fence, Dick reminded himself, *you have to get
permits signed by everybody and his dog.*

:*Cat,*: corrected SKitty.

Okay, okay, he thought back with wry amusement. *Everybody and his
cat. Except they don't have cats here, except on the ships.*

SKitty sniffed disdainfully. :*Fools,*: she replied, smoothing down an
errant bit of damp fur with her tongue, thus dismissing an entire culture
that currently had most of the Companies on their collective knees begging for trading concessions.

Well, we've seen about everything there is to see, Dick thought back at
SKitty, reaching up to scratch her ears as she purred in contentment. *Are
you quite satisfied?*

:*Hunt now?*: she countered hopefully.

*No, you can't hunt. You know that very well. This is a Class Four world;
you have to have permission from the local sapients to hunt, and they haven't given
us permission to even sneeze outside the Fence. And inside the Fence you are valuable
merchandise subject to catnapping, as you very well know. I played shining knight
for you once, furball, and I don't want to repeat the experience.*

SKitty sniffed again. :*Not love me.*:

*Love you too much, pest. Don't want you ending up in the hold of some tramp
freighter.*

SKitty turned up the volume on her purr, and rearranged her coil on
Dick's shoulders until she resembled a lumpy black fur collar on his gray
shipsuit. When she left the ship—and often when she was in the ship—
that was SKitty's perch of choice. Dick had finally prevailed on the purser
to put shoulderpads on all his shipsuits—sometimes SKitty got a little
careless with her claws.

When man had gone to space, cats had followed; they were quickly
proven to be a necessity. For not only did man's old pests, rats and mice,
accompany his trade—there seemed to be equivalent pests on every new

world. But the shipscats were considerably different from their Earth-bound ancestors. The cold reality was that a spacer couldn't afford a pet that had to be cared for—he needed something closer to a partner.

Hence SKitty and her kind; gene-tailored into something more than animals. SKitty was BioTech Type F-021; forepaws like that of a raccoon, more like stubby little hands than paws. Smooth, short hair with no undercoat to shed and clog up air filters. Hunter second to none. Middle-ear tuning so that she not only was not bothered by hyperspace shifts and free-fall, she actually enjoyed them. And last, but by no means least, the enlarged head showing the boosting of her intelligence.

BioTech released the shipscats for adoption when they reached about six months old; when they'd not only been weaned, but trained. Training included maneuvering in free-fall, use of the same sanitary facilities as the crew, and emergency procedures. SKitty had her vacuum suit, just like any other crew member; a transparent hard plex ball rather like a tiny lifeship, with a simple panel of controls inside to seal and pressurize it. She was positively paranoid about having it *with* her; she'd haul it along on its tether, if need be, so that it was always in the same compartment that she was. Dick respected her paranoia; any good spacer would.

Officially she was "Lady Sundancer of Greenfields"; Greenfields be-ing BioTech Station NA-73. In actuality, she was SKitty to the entire crew, and only Dick remembered her real name.

Dick had signed on to the CatsEye Company ship *Brightwing* just after they'd retired their last shipscat to spend his final days with other creaky retirees from the spacetrade in the Tau Epsilon Old Spacers Station. As junior officer, Dick had been sent off to pick up the replacement. SOP was for a BioTech technician to give you two or three candidates to choose among—in actuality, Dick hadn't had any choice. "Lady Sundancer" had taken one look at him and launched herself like a little black rocket from the arms of the tech straight for him; she'd landed on his shoulders, purring at the top of her lungs. When they couldn't pry her off, not without injuring her, the "choice" became moot. And Dick was elevated to the position of Designated Handler.

For the first few days she was "Dick White's Kitty"—the rest of his fellow crewmembers being vastly amused that she had so thoroughly attached herself to him. After a time that was shortened first to "Dick's Kitty" and then to "SKitty," which name finally stuck.

Since telepathy was *not* one of the traits BioTech was supposedly breeding and gene-splicing for, Dick had been more than a little startled when she'd started speaking to him. And since none of the others ever mentioned hearing her, he had long ago come to the conclusion that he was the only one who could. He kept that a secret; at the least, should BioTech come to hear of it, it would mean losing her. BioTech would want to know where *that* particular mutation came from, for fair.

"Pretty gamy," he told Erica Makumba, Legal and Security Officer, who was the current on-watch at the air lock. The dusky woman lounged in her jumpseat with deceptive casualness, both hands behind her curly head—but there was a stun-bracelet on one wrist, and Erica just happened to be the *Brightwing*'s current karate champ.

"Eyeah," she replied with a grimace. "had a look out there last night. Talk about your low-class dives! I'm not real surprised the Lacu'un threw the Fence up around it. Damned if *I'd* want that for neighbors! Hey, we may be getting a break, though; invitation's gone out to about three cap'ns to come make tradetalk. Seems the Lacu'un got themselves a lawyer—"

"So much for the 'unsophisticated primitives,'" Dick laughed. "I thought TriStar was riding for a fall, taking that line."

Erica grinned; a former TriStar employee, she had no great love for her previous employer. "Eyeah. So, lawyer goes and calls up the records on every Company making bids, goes over 'em with a fine-tooth. Seems only three of us came up clean; us, SolarQuest, and UVN. We got invites, rest got bye-byes. Be hearing a buncha ships clearing for space in the next few hours."

"My heart bleeds," Dick replied. "Any chance they can fight it?"

"Ha! Didn't tell you *who* they got for their mouthpiece. Lan Ventris."

Dick whistled. *"Somebody's* been looking out for them!"

"Terran Consul; she was the scout that made first contact. They wouldn't have anybody else, adopted her into the ruling sept, keep her at the palace. Nice lady, shared a beer or three with her. She likes these people, obviously, takes their welfare real personal. Now—you want the quick lowdown on the invites?"

Dick leaned up against the bulkhead, arms folded, taking care not to disturb SKitty. "Say on."

"One—" she held up a solemn finger. "Vena—that's the Consul—says that these folk have a long martial tradition; they're warriors, and admire warriors—but they admire honor and honesty even more. The trappings of primitivism are there, but it's a veneer for considerable sophistication. So whoever goes needs to walk a line between pride and honorable behavior that will be a *lot* like the old Japanese courts of Terra. Two, they are very serious about religion—they give us a certain amount of leeway for being ignorant outlanders, but if you transgress too far, Vena's not sure what the penalties may be. So you want to watch for signals, body language from the priest-caste; that could warn you that you're on dangerous ground. Three—and this is what may give us an edge over the other two—they are very big on their totem animals; the sept totems are actually an important part of sept pride and the religion. So the Cap'n intends to make you and Her Highness there part of the delegation. Vena says that the Lacu'un intend to issue three contracts, so we're all gonna get one, but the folks that impress them the most will be getting first choice."

If Dick hadn't been leaning against the metal of the bulkhead, he might well have staggered. As most junior on the crew, the likelihood that he was going to even go beyond the Fence had been staggeringly low—but that he would be included in the first trade delegation was mind-melting!

SKitty caroled her own excitement all the way back to his cabin, launching herself from his shoulder to land in her own little shock-bunk, bolted to the wall above his.

Dick began digging through his catch-all bin for his dress-insignia; the half-lidded topaz eye for CatsEye Company, the gold wings of the ship's insignia that went beneath it, the three tiny stars signifying the three missions he'd been on so far. . . .

He caught flickers of SKitty's private thoughts then; thoughts of pleasure, thoughts of nesting—

Nesting!

Oh, *no!*

He spun around to meet her wide yellow eyes, to see her treading out her shock-bunk.

Skitty, he pleaded, *please don't tell me you're pregnant—*

:*Kittens,*: she affirmed, very pleased with herself.

You swore to me that you weren't in heat when I let you out to hunt!

She gave the equivalent of a mental shrug. :*I lie.*:

He sat heavily down on his own bunk, all his earlier excitement evaporated. BioTech shipscats were supposed to be sterile—about one in a hundred weren't. And you had to sign an agreement with Biotech that you wouldn't neuter yours if it proved out fertile; they wanted the kittens, wanted the results that came from outbreeding. Or you could sell the kittens to other ships yourself, or keep them; provided a BioTech station wasn't within your ship's current itinerary. But, of course, only BioTech would take them before they were six months old and trained. . . .

That was the rub. Dick sighed. SKitty had already had one litter on him—only two, but it had seemed like twenty-two. There was this problem with kittens in a spaceship; there was a period of time between when they were mobile and when they were about four months old that they had exactly two neurons in those cute, fluffy little heads. One neuron to keep the body moving at warp speed, and one neuron to pick out the situation guaranteed to cause the most trouble.

Everyone in the crew was willing to play with them—but no one was willing to keep them out of trouble. And since SKitty was Dick's responsibility, it was *Dick* who got to clean up the messes, and *Dick* who got to fish the little fluffbrains out of the bridge console, and *Dick* who got to have the anachronistic litter pan in his cabin until SKitty got her babies properly toilet trained.

Securing a litter pan for free-fall was not something he had wanted to have to do again. Ever.

"How could you *do* this to me?" he asked SKitty reproachfully. She just curled her head over the edge of her bunk and trilled prettily.

He sighed. Too late to do anything about it now.

* * *

". . . and you can see the carvings adorn every flat surface," Vena Ferducci, the small, dark-haired woman who was the Terran Consul, said, waving her hand gracefully at the walls. Dick wanted to stand and gawk; this was *incredible!*

The Fence was actually an opaque forcefield, and only *one* of the reasons the Companies wanted to trade with the Lacu'un. Though they did not have spaceflight, there were certain applications of forcefield technologies they *did* have that seemed to be beyond the Terrans' abilities. On the other side of the Fence was literally another world.

These people built to last, in limestone, alabaster, and marble, in the wealthy district, and in cast stone in the outer city. The streets were carefully poured sections of concrete, cleverly given stress-joints to avoid temperature-cracking, and kept clean enough to eat from by a small army of street sweepers. No animals were allowed on the streets themselves, except for housetrained pets. The only vehicles permitted were single or double-being electric carts, that could move no faster than a man could walk. The Lacu'un dressed either in filmy, silken robes, or in more practical, shorter versions of the same garments. They were a handsome race, upright bipeds, skin tones in varying shades of browns and dark golds, faces vaguely avian, with a frill like an iguana's running from the base of the neck to a point between and just above the eyes.

As Vena had pointed out, every wall within sight was heavily carved, the carvings all having to do with the Lacu'un religion.

Most of the carvings were depictions of various processions or ceremonies, and no two were exactly alike.

"That's the Harvest-Gladness," Vena said, pointing, as they walked, to one elaborate wall that ran for yards. "It's particularly appropriate for Kla'dera; he made all his money in agriculture. Most Lacu'un try to have something carved that reflects on their gratitude for 'favors granted.' "

"I think I can guess that one," the Captain, Reginald Singh, said with a smile that showed startlingly white teeth in his dark face. The carving he nodded to was a series of panels; first a celebration involving a veritable kindergarten full of children, then those children—now sex-differentiated and seen to be all female—worshiping at the altar of a very fecund-looking Lacu'un female, and finally the now-maidens looking sweet and demure, each holding various religious objects.

Vena laughed, her brown eyes sparkling with amusement. "No, that one isn't hard. There's a saying, 'as fertile as Gel'vadera's wife.' Every child was a female, too, that made it even better. Between the bride-price he got for the ones that wanted to wed, and the officer's price he got for the ones that went into the armed services, Gel'vadera was a rich man. His FirstDaughter owns the house now."

"Ah—that brings up a question," Captain Singh replied. "Would you explain exactly who and what we'll be meeting? I read the briefing, but I still don't quite understand who fits in where with the government."

"It will help if you think of it as a kind of unholy mating of the British Parlimentary system and the medieval Japanese Shogunates," Vena replied. "You'll be meeting with the 'king'—that's the Lacu'ara—his consort, who has equal powers and represents the priesthood—that's the Lacu'teveras—and his three advisers, who are elected. The advisers represent the military, the bureaucracy, and the economic sector. The military adviser is always female; all officers in the military are female, because the Lacu'un believe that females will not seek glory for themselves, and so will not issue reckless orders. The other two can be either sex. 'Adviser' is not altogether an accurate term to use for them; the Lacu'ara and Lacu'teveras rarely act counter to their advice."

Dick was paying scant attention to this monologue; he'd already picked all this up from the faxes he'd called out of the local library after he'd read the briefing. He was more interested in the carvings, for there was something about them that puzzled him.

All of them featured strange little six-legged creatures scampering about under the feet of the carved Lacu'un. They were about the size of a large mouse, and seemed to Dick to be wearing very smug expressions . . . though, of course, he was surely misinterpreting.

"Excuse me, Consul," he said, when Vena had finished explaining the intricacies of Lacu'un government to Captain Singh's satisfaction. "I can't help wondering what those little lizardlike things are."

"Kreshta," she said, "I would call them pests; you don't see them out on the streets much, but they are the reason the streets are kept so clean. You'll see them soon enough once we get inside. They're like mice, only worse; fast as lightning—they'll steal food right off your plate. The Lacu'un either can't or won't get rid of them, I can't tell you which. When I asked about them once, my host just rolled his eyes heavenward and said what translates to 'it's the will of the gods.' "

"Insh'allah?" Captain Singh asked.

"Very like that, yes. I can't tell if they tolerate the pests because it is the gods' will that they must, or if they tolerate them because the gods favor the little monsters. Inside the Fence we have to close the government buildings down once a month, seal them up, and fumigate. We're just lucky they don't breed very fast."

:Hunt?: SKitty asked hopefully from her perch on Dick's shoulders.

No! Dick replied hastily. *Just look, don't hunt!*

The cat was gaining startled—and Dick thought, appreciative— looks from passersby.

"Just what is the status value of a totemic animal?" Erica asked curiously.

"It's the fact that the animal can be tamed at all. Aside from a handful of domestic herbivores, most animal life on Lacu'un has never been tamed. To be able to take a carnivore and train it to the hand implies that the gods are with you in a very powerful way." Vena dimpled. "I'll let you in on a big secret; frankly, Lan and I preferred the record of the *Brightwing* over the other two ships; you seemed to be more sympathetic to the Lacu'un. That's why we told you about the totemic animals, and why we left you until last."

"It wouldn't have worked without Dick," Captain Singh told her. "SKitty has really bonded to him in a remarkable way; I don't think this presentation would come off half so impressively if he had to keep her on a lead."

"It wouldn't," Vena replied, directing them around a corner. At the end of a short street was a fifteen-foot wall—carved, of course—pierced by an arching entranceway.

"The palace," she said, rather unnecessarily.

* * *

Vena had been right. The kreshta were *everywhere.*

Dick could feel SKitty trembling with the eagerness to hunt, but she was managing to keep herself under control. Only the lashing of her tail betrayed her agitation.

He waited at parade rest, trying not to give in to the temptation to stare, as the Captain and the Negotiator, Grace Vixen, were presented to the five rulers of the Lacu'un in an elaborate ceremony that resembled a stately dance. Behind the low platform holding the five dignitaries in their iridescent robes were five soberly clad retainers, each with one of the "totemic animals." Dick could see now what Vena had meant; the handlers had their creatures under control, but only barely. There was something like a bird; something resembling a small crocodile; something like a snake, but with six very tiny legs; a creature vaguely catlike, but with a feathery coat; and a beast resembling a teddy bear with scales. None of the handlers was actually holding his beast, except the bird-handler. All of the animals were on short chains, and all of them punctuated the ceremony with soft growls and hisses.

So SKitty, perched freely on Dick's shoulders, had drawn no few murmurs of awe from the crowd of Lacu'un in the Audience Hall.

The presentation glided to a conclusion, and the Lacu'teveras whispered something to Vena behind her fan.

"With your permission, Captain, the Lacu'teveras would like to know if your totemic beast is actually as tame as she appears?"

"She is," the Captain replied, speaking directly to the consort, and bowing, exhibiting a charm that had crossed species barriers many times before this.

It worked its magic again. The Lacu'teveras fluttered her fan and trilled something else at Vena. The audience of courtiers gasped.

"Would it be possible, she asks, for her to touch it?"

SKitty? Dick asked quickly, knowing that she was getting the sense of what was going on from his thoughts.

:Nice,: the cat replied, her attention momentarily distracted from the scurrying hints of movement that were all that could be seen of the kreshta. *:Nice lady. Feels good in head, like Dick.:*

Feels good in head? he thought, startled.

"I don't think that there will be any problem, Captain," Dick murmured to Singh, deciding that he could worry about it later. "SKitty seems to like the Lacu'un. Maybe they smell right."

SKitty flowed down off his shoulder and into his arms as he stepped forward to present the cat to the Lacu'teveras. He showed the Lacu'un the cat's favorite spot to be scratched, under the chin. The long talons sported by all Lacu'un were admirably suited to the job of cat-scratching.

The Lacu'teveras reached forward with one lilac-tipped finger, and hesitantly followed Dick's example. The Audience Hall was utterly silent as she did so, as if the entire assemblage was holding its breath, waiting for disaster to strike. The courtiers gasped at her temerity when the cat stretched out her neck—then gasped again, this time with delight, as SKitty's rumbling purr became audible.

SKitty's eyes were almost completely closed in sensual delight; Dick glanced up to see that the Lacu'teveras' amber, slit-pupiled eyes were widened with what he judged was an equal delight. She let her other six fingers join the first, tentative one beneath the cat's chin.

"Such soft—" she said shyly, in musically-accented Standard. "—such nice!"

"Thank you, High Lady," Dick replied with a smile. "We think so."

:*Verrrry nice,*: SKitty seconded. :*Not head-talk like Dick, but feel good in head, like Dick. Nice lady have kitten soon, too.*:

The Lacu'teveras took her hand away with some reluctance, and signed that Dick should return to his place. SKitty slid back up onto his shoulders and started to settle herself.

It was then that everything fell apart.

The next stage in the ceremony called for the rulers to take their seats in their five thrones, and the Captain, Vena, and Grace to assume theirs on stools before the thrones so that each party could present what it wanted out of a possible relationship.

But the Lacu'teveras, her eyes still wistfully on SKitty, was not looking where she placed her hand. And on the armrest of the throne was a kreshta, frozen into an atypical immobility.

The Lacu'teveras put her hand—with all of her weight on it—right on top of the kreshta. The evil-looking thing squealed, squirmed, and bit her as hard as it could.

The Lacu'teveras cried out in pain—the courtiers gasped, the Advisers made warding gestures—and SKitty, roused to sudden and protective rage at this attack by *vermin* on the nice lady who was *with kitten*—leaped.

The kreshta saw her coming, and blurred with speed—but it was not fast enough to evade SKitty, gene-tailored product of one of BioTech's finest labs. Before it could cover even half of the distance between it and safety, SKitty had it. There was a crunch audible all over the Audience Chamber, and the ugly little thing was hanging limp from SKitty's jaws.

Tail high, in a silence that could have been cut up into bricks and used to build a wall, she carried her prize to the feet of the injured Lacu'un and laid it there.

:*Fix him!*: Dick heard in his mind. :*Not hurt nice-one-with-kitten!*:

The Lacu'ara stepped forward, face rigid, every muscle tense.

Spirits of Space! Dick thought, steeling himself for the worst, *that's bloody well torn it—*

But the Lacu'ara, instead of ordering the guards to seize the Terrans, went to one knee and picked up the broken-backed kreshta as if it were a fine jewel.

Then he brandished it over his head while the entire assemblage of Lacu'un burst into cheers—and the Terrans looked at one another in bewilderment.

SKitty preened, accepting the caresses of every Lacu'un that could reach her with the air of one to whom adulation is long due. Whenever an unfortunate kreshta happened to attempt to skitter by, she would turn into a bolt of black lightning, reenacting her kill to the redoubled applause of the Lacu'un.

Vena was translating as fast as she could, with the three Advisers all speaking at once. The Lacu'ara was tenderly bandaging the hand of his consort, but occasionally one or the other of them would put in a word, too.

"Apparently they've never been able to exterminate the kreshta; the natural predators on them *can't* be domesticated and generally take pieces out of anyone trying, traps and poisoned baits don't work because the kreshta won't take them. The only thing they've *ever* been able to do is what we were doing behind the Fence: close up the building and fumigate periodically. And even that has problems—the Lacu'teveras, for instance, is violently allergic to the residue left when the fumigation is done."

Vena paused for breath.

"I take it they'd like to have Skitty around on a permanent basis?" the Captain said, with heavy irony.

"Spirits of Space, Captain—they think SKitty is a sign from the gods, incarnate! I'm not sure they'll let her leave!"

Dick heard that with alarm—in a lot of ways, SKitty was the best friend he had—

To leave her—the thought wasn't bearable!

SKitty whipped about with alarm when she picked up what he was thinking. With an anguished yowl, she scampered across the slippery stone floor and flung herself through the air to land on Dick's shoulders. There she clung, howling her objections at the idea of being separated at top of her lungs.

"What in—" Captain Singh exclaimed, turning to see what could be screaming like a damned soul.

"She doesn't want to leave me, Captain," Dick said defiantly. "And I don't think you're going to be able to get her off my shoulder without breaking her legs or tranking her."

Captain Singh looked stormy. "Damn it then, get a trank—"

"I'm afraid I'll have to veto that one, Captain," Erica interrupted apologetically. "The contract with BioTech clearly states that only the designated handler—and that's Dick—or a BioTech representative can treat a shipscat. And furthermore," she continued, halting the Captain before he could interrupt, "it also states that to leave a shipscat without its designated handler will force BioTech to refuse any more shipscats to *Brightwing* for as long as you are the Captain. Now I don't want to sound like a troublemaker, Captain, but I, for one, will flatly refuse to serve on a ship with no cat. Periodic vacuum purges to kill the vermin do *not* appeal to me."

"Well then, I'll order the boy to—"

"Sir, I *am* the *Brightwing's* legal adviser—I hate to say this, but to order Dick to ground is a clear violation of *his* contract. He hasn't got enough hours spacing yet to qualify him for a ground position."

The Lacu'teveras had taken Vena aside, Dick saw, and was chattering at her at top speed, waving her bandaged hand in the air.

"Captain Singh," she said, turning away from the Lacu'un and tugging at his sleeve, "The Lacu'teveras has figured out that something you said or did is upsetting the cat, and she's not very happy with that—"

Captain Singh looked just about ready to swallow a bucket of heated nails. "Spacer, *will* you get that feline calmed down before they throw me in the local brig?"

"I'll—try, sir—"

Come on, old girl—they won't take you away. Erica and the nice lady won't let them, he coaxed. *You're making the nice lady unhappy, and that might hurt her kitten—*

SKitty subsided, slowly, but continued to cling to Dick's shoulder as if he was the only rock in a flood. *:Not take Dick.:*

Erica won't let them.

:Nice Erica.:

A sudden thought occurred to him. *SKitty-love, how long would it take before you had your new kittens trained to hunt?*

She pondered the question. *:From wean? Three heats,:* she said finally.

About a year, then, from birth to full hunter. "Captain, I may have a solution for you—"

"I would be overjoyed to hear one," the Captain replied dryly.

"SKitty's pregnant again—I'm sorry, sir, I just found out today and I didn't have time to report it—but, sir, this is going to be to our advantage! If the Lacu'un insisted, *we* could handle the whole trade deal, couldn't we, Erica? And it should take something like a year to get everything negotiated and set up, shouldn't it?"

"Up to a year and a half, standard, yes," she confirmed. "And basically, whatever the Lacu'un want, they get, so far as the Company is concerned."

"Once the kittens are a year old, they'll be hunters just as good as SKitty is—so if you could see your way clear to doing all the setup—and sort of wait around for us to get done rearing the kittens—"

Captain Singh burst into laughter. "Boy, do you have any notion just how *many* credits handling the entire trade negotiations would put in *Brightwing*'s account? Do you have any idea what that would do for *my* status?"

"No, sir," he admitted.

"Suffice it to say I *could* retire if I chose. And—Spirits of Space—kittens? Kittens we *could* legally sell to the Lacu'un? I don't suppose you have any notion of how many kittens we can expect this time?"

He sent an inquiring tendril of thought to SKitty. "Uh—I think four, sir."

"Four! And they were offering us *what* for just her?" the Captain asked Vena.

"A more-than-considerable amount," she said dryly. "Exclusive contract on the forcefield applications."

"How would they feel about bargaining for four to be turned over in about a year?"

Vena turned to the rulers and translated. The excited answer she got left no doubts in anyone's mind that the Lacu'un were overjoyed at the prospect.

"Basically, Captain, you've just convinced the Lacu'un that you hung the moon."

"Well—why don't we settle down to a little serious negotiation, hmm?" the Captain said, nobly refraining from rubbing his hands together with glee. "I think that all our problems for the future are about to be solved in one fell swoop! Get over here, spacer. You and that cat have just received a promotion to Junior Negotiator."

:Okay?: SKitty asked anxiously.

Yes, love, Dick replied, taking Erica's place on a negotiator's stool. *Very okay!*

Andre Norton

NOBLE WARRIOR

Emmy squinted at the stitch she had just put in the handkerchief. Ivy had curtained almost half of the window, to leave the room in greenish gloom. Too long, she would have to pick it out. On such a grayish day she wanted a candle. Only even to think of that must be a sin. Miss Wyker was very quick to sniff out sins. Emmy squinted harder. It was awfully easy to sin when one was around Miss Wyker.

Not for the first or not even the hundredth time she puzzled as to why Great-Aunt Amelie had asked Miss Wyker to Hob's Green. Who could be ill without feeling worse to see about that long narrow face with the closed buttonhole of a mouth, and mean little eyes on either side of a long, long nose. Elephant nose! Emmy's hands were still while she thought of elephants, big as Jasper's cottage. Father said that they had great seats large enough to hold several men strapped on their backs and one rode them so to go tiger hunting.

She rubbed her hand across her aching forehead as she thought of father. If he were here, he would send old Wyker packing.

Emmy ran a tongue tip over her lips. She was thirsty—but to leave her task to even get a drink of water might get her into trouble. She gave an impatient jerk and her thread broke. Before she could worry about that, sounds from the graveled drive which ran beyond the window brought her up on her knees to look out. Hardly anyone now used the front entrance drive. This was the trap from the inn, with Jeb. Beside him sat a stranger, a small man with a bushy brown beard.

The trap came to a halt and the small man climbed down from the seat. Jeb handed down a big basket to the man who gave him a short nod before disappearing under the overhang of the doorway. Emmy dropped her sewing on the window seat to run across the room as the knocker sounded. She was cautious about edging open the door of the sitting room to give herself just a crack to see through.

The knocker sounded three times before Jennie the housemaid hurried by, patting down her cap ribbons and looking all a-twitter. It had been so long since anyone had been so bold as to use the knocker. Nobody but Dr. Riggs ever came that way any more, and he only in the morning.

Emmy heard a deep voice, but she could not quite make out the words. Then, as quick as if it were meant as an answer, there sounded a strange cry. Emmy jumped, the door opened a good bit wider than was wise.

At least she could see Jennie show the visitor to the library where Dr. Riggs was always escorted by Miss Wyker to have a ceremonial glass of claret when his visit to his patient was over. The stranger had taken the covered basket with him.

Jennie went hurrying up the stairs to get Miss Wyker. To speed her along she sounded another of those wailing cries.

Emmy pulled the door nearer shut, but her curiosity was fully aroused. Who had come visiting and why? And whatever could be in that basket?

She heard the determined tread of Miss Wyker and saw a stiff back covered with the ugliest of gray dresses also disappear into the parlor. Should she try to cross the hall in hope of seeing more of the visitor? She was so tired of one day being like another—all as gray as Miss Wyker's dress—that this was all very exciting. Before she had quite made up her mind, Jennie came in a hurry, probably called by the bell. She stood just within the library door, then backed out to head for the morning room where Emmy had been isolated for numberless dull hours of the day since Great-Aunt had taken ill.

"You—Miss Emmy," Jennie was breathless as she usually was when Miss Wyker gave orders. "They want to see you—right now—over there—" she jerked a thumb toward the library.

Emmy was across the hall and into the room before Jennie had disappeared back down the hall. As she came in, there sounded once more that startling cry. It had come from the big covered basket which was rocking a little back and forth where it stood on the floor.

"This is the child—" Miss Wyker's sharp voice was plainly disapproving.

The brown-bearded man looked down at Emmy. A big grin split that beard in the middle.

"So—you be th' Cap'n's little maid, be you? Must have grown a sight since he was last a-seein' you. Tol' it as how you was a mite younger."

The Cap'n—that was father. For a moment, forgetting Miss Wyker, Emmy burst out with a question of her own:

"Where is he? Please, did his ship come in? Truly?" There was so much Emmy wanted to say that the words stuck in her throat unable to push out clearly.

"Emmiline—this is Mr. Salbridge—manners, IF you please!"

Emmy swallowed and made a bob of a curtsey, one eye on Miss Wyker, knowing that she would be in for a scold when this visitor left.

"Very pleased to make your acquaintance, sir," she parroted the phrase which had been drilled into her.

Mr. Salbridge bowed in return. "Well, now, Miss Emmy, seems like we should be no strangers. Ain't I heard th' Cap'n talk of you by th' hour? Your servant, Miss Emmy. It does a man good to see as how you is doin' well, all shipshape an' tight along the portholes as it were. You probably ain't heard o' me—but I has been a-sailin' with th' Cap'n for a right many years now—would be there on board th' *Majestic* yet, only I had me a bit o' real luck, which gave me a snug purse, an' was minded to come home along of that there windfall. They's none o' us as young as we once was an' me, I got someone as has been a-waiting for me to come home a longish time.

"Th' Cap'n, he gave me a right hearty good-bye but not afore he asked somethin' o' me an' I'm right proud that he did that. I was to see his little maid an' bring 'er somethin' as was give to him by a princess as heard he had a little daughter to home. He was mighty helpful to her paw an' she was grateful to him in return, give him somethin' th' which nobody here at home as seen—somethin' as has lived in a palace right a'long of her. Look you here, Miss Emmy, what do you think o' this?"

He knelt awkwardly on one knee to open the basket. For a minute nothing happened. Then there jumped out of that carrier the oddest animal Emmy had ever seen. It looked like a cat, only it was not gray striped. Rather its face, legs, and the lower part of its slender back were of a brown as dark as Mr. Salbridge's beard, while the rest of it was near the color of the thick cream Mrs. Goode skimmed off the milk. And its eyes—its eyes were a bright blue!

It stood by the side of the basket, its head slowly moving as it stared at each of them in turn, Mr. Salbridge, Miss Wyker, who had drawn back a pace or two and was frowning darkly, and the longest at Emmy.

"Miss Emmy, this here's Thragun Neklop, that there means Noble Warrior. He's straight out o' th' king's own palace. They thinks a mighty lot o' those like him thereabouts. No one as is common gets to have these here cats a-livin' in their houses. The Cap'n now, he was favored when they said this one might go to be with his little missy back in his own country. Yes, this here is a very special cat—"

The cat opened its mouth and gave a short, sharp cry which was certainly not like the meow which Emmy expected. Then its head turned so that it looked directly and unblinkingly at Miss Wyker and it hissed, its ears flattening a little. Miss Wyker's frown now knotted all her long face together.

Emmy squatted down so that she was nearly face to face with the furred newcomer.

"Thragun Neklop." She tried to say the strange words carefully. The cat turned its head again, to stare boldly at her. There was no hissing this time.

"That there is a power name, Miss Emmy. His paw was guard o' th' king. Them as lives there, they do not take kindly to dogs—that's their religion like. But cats, them they train to be their guards. An' mighty good they be at that, too, if all th' stories they tell is true."

The cat rose and came to Emmy. She put out her hand, not quite daring to lay a finger on that sleek brown head. The cat sniffed her fingers and then bumped his head against her hand.

"Well, now, that do beat all. Never saw him do that 'ceptin' to the princess when she said good-bye," commented Mr. Salbridge. "Maybe he thinks as how you're the princess now. Good that'll be. Now—servant, Mistress, servant, Miss Emmy." He made a short bow. "I needs must be gitting along. Have to catch th' York stage."

"Oh," Emmy was on her feet, "please—thank you! And father—is he coming home, too?"

Mr. Salbridge shook his head. "He's got the voyage to make and the *Majestic* warn't due to raise anchor for maybe two months when I left him. He'll be coming through, jus' as soon as he can—"

"It's such a long time to wait—" Emmy said. "But, oh, please, Mr. Salbridge, I do thank you for bringing Thragun Neklop."

"My pleasure, Miss—" The rest of what he might have said was drowned out by another of those strange wails.

Emmy hurried behind Mr. Salbridge who strode for the door. Miss Wyker made no attempt to see him away, as she did the doctor when he came calling. Emmy followed with more eager questions which he answered cheerfully. Yes, the Cap'n was feeling well and doin' well for hisself, too. An' he would be home again before long. He was jus' glad to be of service.

While he climbed back into the rig and drove off down the drive-way, Emmy waved vigorously. She was startled by a very harsh piercing cry and she ran back to the library.

Miss Wyker, poker in hand, that deep scowl still on her face, was advancing on Thragun. The cat stood his ground; now that scream dropped to a warning growl. His long slender tail was puffed out to twice its usual size and his ears were flattened to his skull.

"Dirty animal!" Miss Wyker's voice was as angry as Thragun's war cry. "Get in there, you filthy beast!" She poked with the iron and Thragun went into a crouch.

"Thragun!" Emmy ran forward, standing between the war ready cat and Miss Wyker.

"Get that foul thing into the basket—at once, do you hear me?"

Emmy had witnessed Miss Wyker's anger a good many times, but never had she made such a scene as this before.

"Don't hit him!" Emmy caught at the cat. A paw flashed out and drew a red stripe across her hand. But in spite of that the little girl grabbed him up and put him into the basket. "He wasn't doing any harm!" she cried out, braver as she spoke up for Thragun than she had ever been for herself.

In answer Miss Wyker used the poker to flip the lid down on the basket.

"Fasten it!" she ordered, already heading toward the bell pull on the wall.

Emmy's hands shook. She had always been afraid of loud angry voices, and lately she jumped at every sound, especially when she was never sure when Miss Wyker was going to come up behind her with some punishment already in mind. She had done so many things wrong ever since Great-Aunt Amelie had taken ill. Emmy never even saw her any more. Nobody seemed to see much of Lady Ashely now. Miss Wyker was always there at the bedroom door, to take the trays cook sent up with the special beef jelly or a new egg done to the way Great-Aunt Amelie always liked them.

Even at night Jennie was not called to sit with her. Miss Wyker had a trundle bed moved into the room and spent her own night hours there. When Jennie or Meggy came to clean, she was always standing there watching them. Meggy said, " 'as 'ow they was goin' to 'urt th' old lady— as iffen anybody ever would!"

"Yes, m'm?" Jennie now stood in the half open door.

"Take this beast out to the stable at once! I do not want to see it about again!"

"No!" Courage which she not been able to summon for herself brought words to Emmy. "Father sent him—to me. He's Thragun Neklop an' a prince! The man said so!" She caught the handle of the big basket in both hands and held it as tightly as she could.

Miss Wyker, her long face very red, laid the poker across the seat of the nearest chair before taking long strides to stand directly over Emmy. Her hand swept up, to come down across Emmy's cheek, the blow so sudden and stinging that the child staggered backward, involuntarily losing her hold on the basket. Miss Wyker had scolded her many times since the first hour when she had arrived and doffed her helmet of a bonnet to take over rulership of Hob's Green. But until this moment she had never touched Emmy.

"Take that beast out to the stable," Miss Wyker repeated, "and be quick about it. Animals are filthy, they have no place in a well-run household. And you," she rounded on Emmy who was standing staring at her, one hand pressed to her cheek where those long fingers had left visible marking, "go to your room instantly, you impudent girl! You are wholly selfish, unbiddable, lazy and a handful! Poor Lady Ashely may have been hastened to her bed of illness by your thoughtless impudence! Poor lady, she has had a great deal to burden her these past years but there will be a good many changes made shortly—and your conduct, Miss, will not be the least of those! Go!"

So sharp and loud was that command that it seemed to sweep Emmy out of the room. She hesitated for one moment on the foot of the stairs to watch Jennie's apron strings and the tail of her skirt vanish toward the end of the hall. The maid had taken the basket. What was going to happen to Thragun Neklop? Emmy's tears spilled over the fingers which still nursed the cheek which was beginning to ache as she went up the stairs slowly, one reluctant foot at a time.

There was a strong smell of horses, but there were other scents which were new. Thragun stretched himself belly down in the basket to look through a spread in the wicker weave which had served him for some time now as a window on a very strange and everchanging world. He saw an expanse of stone paved yard and there was a flutter of pigeons about a trough out of which water was being slopped by a young man whose shirt sleeves were rolled clear to the shoulder. Thragun sniffed—water—never before had he been kept shut up to receive food and water only at the pleasure of another. However, if this must be so for some reason he had not yet discovered, then let those who were to minister to him, as was correct, be brought to attention of their duty.

He voiced a call-cry which in his proper home would have brought at least two maids and perhaps a serving slave of the first rank to answer and make proper apologetic submission, letting him out of this strange litter and treating him as Thragun Neklop should be. Was he not second senior of the Princess Suphorn's own household?

The young man turned his head toward the basket. However, he made no attempt to come and act in the proper fashion. This time Thragun gave a truly angry cry to inform this odd looking servant that his superior wanted full attention to his desires. The young man had filled two buckets with water which sloshed back and forth, wetting the yard stones, as he came. Thragun waited, but the slave made no attempt to approach. Instead, inside this place smelling of horses, he was starting to pass Thragun's cage when there was a voice from the general gloom behind.

"Asa, you lunkhead, you messin' with th' Knight agin?" The voice was drowned out then by the shrill squeal of an aroused stallion. Then there were whinneys and the sound of horses moving restlessly.

Asa moved out of the cat's sight even though Thragun turned in the basket and tried to see through another small opening in the wicker. That was too narrow, even though he had been working on it with explorative claws for several days.

He heard two voices making odd noises, some of which he recognized. So did the grooms soothe and tend their charges in the royal stable. Apparently even in this strange land horses were properly cared for. If that much was known, why were cats not properly attended?

Heavy footsteps came toward the basket. Thragun waited. There was more than just hunger and thirst to mark the change in his life now— there was a strange unpleasant feeling. The hair along his spine and his tail lifted a little, his ears flattened.

He was Thragun Neklop—Noble Warrior, acknowledged guardian of a princess. It had been his duty and his pleasure to patrol palace gardens at night's coming, to make sure that nothing dark or threatening dared venture there. Had he in his first year killed one of the serpent ones who had been about to set fang in the princess' hand when she had reached around the rocks to recover her bracelet? Perhaps he had not sprung on a thief to rip open his throat as had Thai Shan, the mightiest of them all, trusted warrior for the king. But he knew what must be—

"So this 'ere's th' beastie? That there Wyker's got a wicked tongue an' a worse eye, that one! Jennie says that this was brot 'ere special—for Miss Emmy—present from 'er paw. So do we do what that long-nosed witch wants, then what do we say when th' Cap'n comes home an' says where is what 'e sent? An' who, I'm askin', made 'er th' Lady 'ere? M' wage is paid by th' Lady Ashely as 'as been since I was six an' came a-helpin' for m' paw. I takes 'er Ladyship's orders, an' that's th' tight an' right o' it!"

"She's got 'er thing 'bout cats. Th' moggy to th' kitchen disappeared. It showed claw to that one first time it saw 'er when she came down givin' orders right an' left to Cook 'erself. Then come two days past and moggy was gone. Saw 'er a-talkin' to Rog out in th' garden—'im 'as no feeling for beasties. But he 'ad 'im a sixpence down to the Arms that week. An' sixpences don't just grown in that there garden 'e's supposed to be a-planting of."

"So—"

There was a moment of quiet. Thragun's eyes were hardly more than slits, and with his ears so flat he looked almost like one of the big carved stone garden snakes on which he used to sun himself in the old days when all was well with his world.

Something deep in him stirred. Once before he had felt its like and that was when he was shedding the last of his kitten fur to take on the browning of his mask, tail, and four feet. His mother had gathered up her family just at twilight one night—there were the three of them, Rannar, his brother, and Su Li, his sister. They had followed their mother into a far part of the largest garden. There, trees and vines and full formed shrubs had grown so closely together there they had formed a wall and such a one as only the most supple of cats could get through. There was something in the heart of that miniature jungle—a gray stone place fashioned as if two of the Naga Serpents had faced one another before a wall, with another piece of wall above which they supported on their heads. They were very old; there was the green of small growth on their weathered scales.

Mother had seated herself before them, her kittens a little behind her. Then she had called. The sound she made was the sort to stiffen one's back fur, made claws ache to be unsheathed. Something appeared between the serpents, under the roof they supported. Mother had sat in silence. Only they were not alone, cat and kittens. Something had surveyed them with cold eyes, and colder thoughts—yet they remained very still and did not run even though they all smelled the fear which was a part of this meeting.

That which had come, and which they had never seen clearly, went. With mother, the kittens scrambled into the freedom of the real garden again. However, from that moment Thragun knew the stench of fear, and that wrongness which is a part of evil to be ever after sensed by those who had met it. Also, he had learned the warning which came before battle to those born to be fighters and protectors.

These two who stood over his basket now did not radiate that smell. But that female in the house did. Thragun knew that it was of her that they spoke now. He had come to this place because his princess had asked him to do so. She had explained to him that there was a great debt lying on her because the man from the far country had saved her father. She had learned that this man had a daughter, and now she wished Thragun to be to that daughter even as he was to her, a noble warrior to be ever her shield and her defense. Knowing that all debts must be paid, Thragun had come, though there were times when he wished only to sit and wail his loneliness to the world.

The man who had taken him by the princess' orders had always sought him out, if he was near, when those times came upon Thragun. He had talked to him, stroked him, spoken of his daughter and the old house where she lived with a kinswoman, waiting for the day when the man's duty would be fully done and he might return himself to be with them. And Thragun understood—to the man, his daughter was a treasure precious above anything in the king's palace.

Now what he felt was that need to be alert before danger, and behind it there was the faint, bitter smell of evil, sly and cunning evil, which could and did slip through the world like one of the serpents-which-were-not-Nagas. He was a warrior and this was the enemy's country through which he must go as silently as wind, as aware as that which hungers greatly. Now he must seem to be as one who had no daggers on the feet, teeth waiting in his jaws. With his mouth he shaped a cry such as a lost kitten might give.

"Like as th' beastie's hungry, Ralf—"

"No one's tellin' me wot is an' 'tisn't right!"

There was a sudden movement and the basket lid swung up. Thragun sat up, his tail top curled properly over his front toes, his unblinking blue eyes regarding the two of them.

The man beside Asa was short and thin and smelled strongly of horse sweat. With his black hair and dark skin he looked almost like one of the stable slaves back in the land where things were done properly. There was none of the evil odor clinging to him, nor to the boy either.

There was a long drawn noise from the man which was not a word, but plainly an exclamation of surprises. He squatted down on his heels, his face not far above Thragun's own.

"Blue eyes," that was the boy. " 'E don't look like any moggy as I ever saw—"

"Sssssisss—" The man held out his hand and slowly, as if he were dealing with one of his horse charges. "You sure be a different one."

Thragun sniffed at the knuckles of the hand offered him. There were smells in plenty, but none were cold or threatening. He ventured a small sound deep in his throat.

"You be a grand one, ben't you! Asa, get yourself over an' speak up to Missus Cobb. She's already got a hankerin' for moggys an' she'll give you somethin' for this fine fellow."

The boy disappeared. Thragun decided to take a chance. Moving warily, with an eye continually on the man, he jumped out of the basket, still facing the small man.

"Yis—" that almost was a hiss again. "You ain't no common moggy." His eyebrows drew together in a frown. "I thinks as 'ow th' Cap'n, he mustta thought as 'ow you was right for Miss Emmy—she likin' beasties so well. An' th' Cap'n sure ain't goin' to take it calm if you go a-missin'—

Standing up, the man rubbed his bristly chin.

"Trouble is, that ole she-devil up to th' house, she's doin' all th' talkin' these days. We don't git to see our Lady a-tall—jus' tell us, they do—that fine gentlemun o' a doctor, an' Mr. Crisp, th' agent—that our lady can't be bothered by anythin' now she is so bad took. An' Miss Emmy, she ain't got no chance t' say nothin'. Th' Cap'n so far away an' nobody knows when he's coming back agin. It ain't got a good smell 'bout all this, that it ain't. So," he leaned back against the wall of a stall, a proud horse head raised over his shoulder to regard Thragun also.

"Soo—" the man repeated, one hand raised to scratch between the large bright eyes of the horse, "we 'as us a thin' as needs thinkin' on. Now was you," Thragun congratulated himself that he had indeed found a very sensible man here, "to git otta that there basket an' disappear—'ow are you goin' to be found—with these 'ere stables as full of holes and 'idey places as a bit o' cheese. An' out there—" he waved one hand toward the open door, "there's a garden an' beyond that, woods—Our lady, she don't allow no huntin' an' them two what wants to answer fur her—they ain't changed that—yet. So supposin', Rog, 'e comes 'long for t' see t' you an' he finds that there basket busted open an' you gone—might be 'e'd jus' put somethin' in his pocket and say as 'ow 'e did as 'e was told—"

"Now," the man raised his voice and caught up a broom. He aimed a blow at Thragun—well off target and yelled, "Git you out, you many critter, we don't want th' likes of you a hangin' 'round, no ways we don't."

Thragun leaped effortlessly to the top of a stall partition, but he made no effort to go farther for a moment. Then he walked leisurely along that narrow path to a place from which he could jump again, this time to a cross bean. At the same moment Asa returned, a small bundle in his hand.

"Ralf, what you be about—"

The man rounded on him. "Me? I 'as been a-chasin' a beast what 'as no place 'ere. An' don't you forget that, lad."

Asa laughed, then darted into the stall where Thragun had made himself comfortable. Flipping open the handkerchief, Asa turned out a chunk of grayish meat, still dripping from the boiling pan, and a wedge of cheese. He hacked the meat into several large chunks with a knife he took from his pocket and crumbled the cheese, leaving the bounty spread out on the napkin well within reach of Thragun. The cat was already licking the meat inquiringly when Asa returned with a cracked cup in which there was water.

"Couldn' get milk," he said as he set the cup down. "Missus Cobb, she's mad as a cow wot's lost 'er calf. Old Pickle-Face is a-giving' orders agin. No tea for Miss Emmy 'cause she's been a-askin' for th' cat. When Pickle-Face tol' her that 'e was gone for good, she stiffed up an' hit the old besom, then said as 'ow her paw would 'ave th' law on Pickle-Face for gettin' rid o' th' cat. She would not ask pardon, so she's not to 'ave no vittles 'cept dry bread and water 'til she gits down on her two knees an' asks for it."

"I'll be a-thinkin' that little Miss is na goin' to 'ave so 'ard of it," Ralf said. Thragun snarled. He had somehow got another whiff of that evil smell. Though the words these two stable slaves used to each other were totally foreign, he could pick out thoughts like little flashes of pictures. Not all the temple and palace four-footed guards could do that. But to Thragun it had become increasingly easy over the years.

Asa kicked at a handful of bedding straw and reached for the broom.

"Meggy, she says as 'ow she 'as heard '*im* two nights now—"

Ralf stopped, his hand on the latch of the stall, but not yet opening it. His face was suddenly blank. There was a long moment of silence before he spoke. Thragun raised his head from tearing at a lump of meat. Back in the dusky stall his eyes shone, not blue, but faintly reddish.

"Missus Cobb, she put out a milk bowl last night," Asa continued, his eyes on the floor he was mechanically sweeping.

"Sooo—" Ralf swung the latch of the stall up. She's one as can sometimes see moren' most. M' granny was like that."

"There's them what says as 'E ain't 'ere nor never was."

"Look to th' name o' this place, boy. 'Twas '*issen* they say a-fore any folks came 'ere. They also say as 'ow 'E brings luck or fetches it away. Lord Jeffery, 'im as wos master 'ere in m' granny's time, 'e got on th' wrong side o' '*im* an' never took no good of life after that. Died young o' a broken neck when 'is mare stepped in a rabbit 'ole. But 'is lady, she was from right believin' folks an' they say as how she came down by candlelight an' went to '*is* own stone wi' a plate of sugar cakes an' a cup o' true cream. Begged pardon, she did. After that, all wot 'ad been goin' wrong became right agin."

"That were a long time ago—" said Asa.

"Some things there is, boy, wot'll never change. You get a rightful part o' th' land an' do your duty to it an' them wot knew it afor you, will do right by you. But iffen 'E was to come, aye, it would be o' a time like'n this."

He led the horse into the stable yard and Asa fell to cleaning out the stall. Thragun swallowed the last of the food. Not that it was what should be served to Thragun Neklop, but these two had done their best. He washed his whiskers and prepared to explore the stable.

There was a good deal to be examined, sniffed, and stored in memory. Asa and Ralf were in and out on various tasks for the comfort of three horses.

It was very late afternoon before a man came in, Asa with him. He was grinning, wiping his hands on his stained and patched breeches. Thragun's lip curled, but he made no noise. This was evil again—though not as cold and deadly as that he had met when he had confronted that black Khon in the house.

The basket in which he had arrived still sat there, but Asa had dealt with it earlier. There was a break in the bamboo frame door leaving jagged ends pointing outward. Thragun was critical of the work. If he *had* done that, he would have made a neater job of it.

"Us came back," Asa was saying, "an' thar' it was. Th' beast—'e made his own way out."

The other young man spat. "Think you'd better 'ave a better story when th' Missus asks."

Asa shrugged. "We ain't been 'ired, me an' Ralf, to take care o' anythin' 'cept th' 'osses. An' Ralf, 'e ain't really got anythin' to watch 'cept Black Knight. She can't come a-botherin' at us nohow. Why tell 'er? Th' beast's gone, ain't it?"

"An' wot iffen 'e comes back?" demanded the other.

"Then you gits 'im, don't you. Ain't I seen you throw that there sticker o' yourn quicker than Ned Parzon can shoot—take th' 'ead offen a 'en that way?"

"Maybe so." The other kicked the basket, sending it against the wall. "You keep your own mouth shut, do you 'ear?"

"I 'ear, Rog, you a-makin' noise enough to fright m' 'osses." Ralf strode in. "You ain't got no right in 'ere an' you knows it. Now git!"

The younger man scowled and tramped out of the stable. Asa and Ralf stood looking after him.

"That's another who don't 'ave no place 'ere. Were th' Lady 'erself, she'd see that in a flick o' a 'osses tail an' 'ave 'im out on th' road with a flea in 'is ear, she would. Asa," he looked straight at the boy, "I ain't a-likin' wot's goin' on over there—" he nodded toward the house. *"She* an' that lardy doctor 'ave been puttin' 'eads together again. Jennie says as 'ow she was tellin' the doctor something about Miss Emmy being 'ard to manage 'cause she ain't thinkin' straight. They don't know as Jennie was in the little room offen th' hall when they was talkin' together. Little Miss—that ain't no one as would take her part was they tryin' to get 'er shut up or somethin'. The old crow she's always smarmy and soft tongued when any of the Lady's friends come askin'. Oh," he raised his voice into high squeaking note, "Lady Ashely, she's no better, poor dear. I fear we 'ont see her long. Miss Emmy, oh, th' little dear is so sad feelin'. She is too sad for a child. We cannot get her comforted— Now that there I 'eard when Mrs. Bateman came a-calling. Told Mrs. Bateman as how Miss Emmy couldn't go to no picnic 'cause she was so worrit about her aunt. Miss Emmy was up in 'er room were Pickle-Face 'ad sent her to be ashamed of herself because she tried to slip in an' see her aunt that very morning."

"Seems as iffen someone should know—" Asa said.

"Who? Supposin' even Missus Cobb were to get herself over to th' Bateman place an' try to tell them—what 'as she really got to tell? An' Pickle-Face would say as 'ow she is a-lyin'—make it stick, too. There ain't any way as I can see that we can help."

"Tain't right!" exploded Asa.

"Boy, there's a good lot what ain't right in this 'ere world an' not much as can be done to clean it up neither. Come on, we've got to see to that tack."

Thragun's well cultivated guard sense might have been confused by the strange language that these slaves used, but he thought he could fit part of it all together. The little princess to whom *HIS* princess had sent him on his honorable task of protection was under threat from that Khon of full evil. She was now a prisoner somewhere in the house. With a knowledgeable eye he measured the shadows in the stable yard. There was a time of dark fast on its way and dark aided both the evildoer and the guard. His kind, for many lives, had patroled palaces, searched gardens, and knew their own ways of taking care. This was a new place and he knew very little about it. The time was ready not only for him to learn but to be about what was perhaps more important, defending his princess. Thragun's jaws opened upon a soundless snarl and his curved and very sharp claws came momentarily out of the fur screening on his toes.

Emmy huddled behind the curtain, both hands pressed against the small panes of the window as she looked down to the terrace. Rog went clumping by, and she scrunched herself into as small a space as possible. Of course, he was not looking in this direction, and, anyway, he was well below her, but she always felt afraid of Rog. Twice he had come out suddenly from dark places in the garden and stood grinning and laughing at her. Also Miss Wyker liked him. He did errands for her. Emmy had seen him take notes and go out the other way—not passing where anyone could see him unless that one was specially watching. He padded heavy-footed along now and it was near dark. Maybe he was just going back to the hut where he lived—a nasty, evil-smelling place. But the worst of it was those nails hammered into the wall on which hung little bodies, some furred and some feathered—birds and a weasel, and—Emmy rubbed both her wet eyes with her hands.

Her eyes hurt because she had been crying. She tried to see even the edge of the drive to the stable. What had happened out there to Thragun Neklop? Somehow now she thought all a lie, he must be somewhere. She had her own plan, but it might be hours and hours yet before it would be dark enough for her to put it to the test. With her tear-sticky hands she tried again with all her strength to push out one side of the divided panes of the window. Tendrils of ivy waved in the breeze back and forth, but there was no wind enough to make a difference, Emmy thought. This was an idea she had had for some time and she now had a very good reason to try it.

A door away down the hall Jennie tapped, her other hand support-ing a tray with a porringer on it. The nutmeg smell was faint, but she could smell it even though the lid was on the small silver bowl to keep its contents warm. Cook had made this special—a smooth, light custard that she said even a newborn babe could take without any hurt. Jennie gave a slight start and looked back over her shoulder. Old houses had many strange noises in the night time. But this evening—She drew a deep breath. *HIM*—That patter sound all the way up the stairs behind her—like to scare her into falling or take her death from it. She knocked again and with more force.

The door opened so suddenly that she might have skidded right in had she not caught herself.

"What do you mean? All this clamor when she is asleep! You stupid, clumsy girl!" Miss Wyker's voice was like the hiss of a snake and Jennie cringed. Somehow she got the tray and the porringer between them.

"Please, Cook did think as 'ow the poor lady might find this tasty. She used to be quite fond of it—jus' good milk, and eggs from the brown 'en as 'as the best and biggest ever—"

With a snap Miss Wyker had the tray out of her hands and was thrusting before her as if to push Jennie out of the room.

"Cook is impertinent," Miss Wyker scowled, enough, as Jennie said later, to make the flesh fair creep on your bones like. "Lady Ashely's food must be carefully selected to match the diet Dr. Riggs has planned. Get back to the kitchen and don't let me see you above the backstairs again or it will be the worse for you." Jennie had backed well into the hall. Now the door was slammed and she quite clearly heard the sound of a key turning in the lock.

For a moment she just stood there and then she gave a quick turn of the head—facing down the hall. Her own face puckered and she put the knuckles of one hand up to cover her mouth as she turned and ran—ran as far and as fast as she could, to get away from that thin high shriek which seemed somehow to echo in her head more than in her ears.

Him! With *him* loose what could a body expect but trouble? Bad trouble. She'd give notice, that she would! There was no one who was going to make her stay here. Her heavy shoes clattered on the uncarpeted backstairs as she sought the kitchen three stories below.

Emmy got to her feet. She had been down on her knees trying to see through the keyhole. These past weeks she had used every method she could to learn things. How long had it been since she had actually seen Great-Aunt Amelie? Three—maybe four weeks, and then she had only gotten a short peek at her through the door before Miss Wyker had come up and pulled her away, her fingers pinching Emmy sharply to propel the girl toward her bedroom where she had also been locked in. That was another night Emmy might not have had any supper, but Jennie had crept up after dark to bring her some of Cook's sugary rolls and a small plum tart. Emmy had discovered some nights ago that, whether she was being openly punished or not, she was always locked in at night. That was when she first began to explore outside the window. She had awakened from a very queer dream. Emmy had never remembered any other dream so well. This one was different. It made her go all shivery, and yet not so fearful that she was afraid to try what she had done in her dream. Of course, then there had been someone with her—though she never really saw who it was—just knew that the unseen had watched her with approval and that had made her feel better.

Now she stood in the middle of the room and unfastened the buttons of her dress, shrugging it off, so that its full skirt lay in a circle around her. Next came her two petticoats. Gathering up all these, she threw them in an untidy bundle on the bed. Then, stopping to think, she gathered them up to roll into a thick armload which she shoved under the covers, pulling the pillow around so it just might look like a sleeper spent from crying.

Emmy herself was through crying. She went to the bottom drawer of the bureau and opened it. There was her mother's beautiful shawl which she brought home from India when she had come with Emmy to Great-Aunt Amelie's. There were other things mother brought, too, and Emmy jerked out a package from the very bottom, struggling to pull it open. Then she was looking at what had belonged to her brother she had never seen—to remember. He had died in India, that was why mother brought her here as the bad seasons did make so many die.

For only a moment she hesitated. Mother had kept this suit as one of her treasures. What would she think of Emmy wearing it? No, she would understand! It was important, Emmy did not know how she was sure of that, no one had told her—unless it was the person in her dream whom she had never seen.

She pulled on the trousers, and pushed her chemise into the top of them. They were a little too big and she had to tie them on with a hair ribbon.

So readied, she returned to the window. It was dark enough now, of that she was sure. She climbed on the sill and slipped through, her feet finding the ledge which ran along the wall just below the windows. Taking the best grip she could on the ivy, Emmy began to edge along that narrow footway.

Thragun slipped like a shadow from one bit of cover to the next. There were lights in some windows and now and then he heard voices. The slaves were gathered in the largest room along the wall. He heard their coarse, rough voices. But he was more intent upon the fact that the walls before him appeared to be covered with a growth of vines. Of course, they were not the thick, properly stemmed ones which provided such excellent highways in the palace and temple gardens. However, he would test just what good footholds they had to offer. There were strange smells in plenty, but he was not to be turned away from his firm purpose now.

Cook stood with both red hands planted firm upon the much scrubbed table, looking across the board at Jennie. Her face was as red as her hands and she made it quite plain just what she was thinking.

"M' lady eatin' only what that puffed pigeon of a doctor tells 'er, is that it? I say it loud and clear, that wry-faced Madam who thinks to cut 'erself a snug place 'ere is goin' to find out that she ain't the mistress. No she ain't!"

"An' just 'ow, Missus, is you goin' to git 'er to listen to you?" Ralf emptied his beer mug and thudded it down on the table.

For a long moment there was no answer. Suddenly Mrs. Cobb straightened up, her weight making her look someone to be taken seriously. She reached out her hand and drew closer a basin of thick brown crockery. Then she turned, without answering the question, and hefted a jug of the same heavy earthenware. From that she poured a stream of milk into the bowl. The milk was so rich and thick one could almost see flakes of butter swimming in it, striving to be free.

The bowl she filled carefully within an inch of the top, then she put down the jug, and, from under the vast sweep of her apron, she brought out a bunch of jingling keys.

Ralf's eyebrows slid up. "Th' keys? 'Ow ever did that Madam let 'em git outta 'er 'ands, now?"

Cook's lips curled but in a sneer not a smile. "Oh, she got our lady's bunch to rattle a little song with, may that which waits at water medder git 'er for that! But m'lady, she saw long ago as 'ow it was not 'andy for me to go runnin' to ask for this store and that when I was a-cookin'. Nor was she ever one as begrudged me what I 'ad to 'ave. So I've had m' own keys these five years now."

"An' what are you goin' to do wi' that?" Ralf pointed to the bowl.

"Ralf Sommers, you ain't as big of a ninny that you 'as to ask that now, are you? This 'ere," she looked around her, "be Hob's Green. An' it didn't get that name for nothin'."

Ralf frowned. " 'IM? You is goin' to deal with '*im?*"

Mrs. Cobb looked down at the bowl as if for a moment uncertain, and then, her mouth firmed, her chin squared. "I be a-doin' nothin' that ain't been done before under this 'ere roof and on this land!"

She walked past Ralf out of the kitchen and down the passage which led to those very dark descending stairs to the vast network of cellars which no one, even in the daytime, willingly visited or if one must go, it would be hurried, lantern in hand and looking all whichways as one did it.

At the top of the stairs there was another door in the wall, opening into the kitchen garden though no one now used that. Mrs. Cobb placed the bowl carefully on the floor. Selecting a key, she forced it into the doorlock and shoved it open a hand's breadth.

She drew back. The way was dark, so much so that she could hardly see the bowl. She cleared her throat and then she recited, as one who draws every word out of some deep closet of memory:

> "Hob's Hole—Hob's own.
> From th' roasting to th' bone.
> Them as sees, shall not look.
> Them's is blind, they'll be shook.
> Sweep it up an' sweep it down—
> Hob shall clear it all around.
> So mote this be."

Mrs. Cobb turned with surprising speed for such a heavy woman and swept with a whirl of her wide skirts down the passage until she could bang the kitchen door behind her.

Thragun stayed where he was crouched, watching through the slit of the door she had opened. He sniffed delicately. That which was in the bowl attracted him. Squeezing through the narrow door opening, the cat looked up and down the narrow stone paved way. He sniffed in each direction and listened. Now he was inside the house again and no one had seen him. He smelled the contents of the bowl, ventured a lap or two, and then settled down to drink his fill.

He jumped, squalled, and turned all in almost one movement. The painful thud on his haunch was not to be forgiven. Thragun crouched, reading himself for a spring.

Crouching almost as low, and certainly as angrily as he himself was, a gray-brown creature humped right inside the door. Thragun snarled, and then growled. In spite of the heavy gloom of the passage his night sight was clear enough to show him exactly what had so impudently attacked him by driving a pointed foot into his back.

Thragun growled again. His right front paw moved lightning quick to pay for that blow with raking claws. But the paw passed through the creature's arm and shoulder. Its body certainly looked thick and real enough but what he struck at might only be a shadow.

He straightened up. Thewada! So this new place had such shadow walkers and mischief makers as he had been warned about since kittenhood—though he had certainly never seen one himself before.

"A-stealin' o' Hob's own bowl, be ye?" The creature straightened up also. It looked like a man but it was very small, hardly taller than Thragun. Its body was fat and round, but the legs and arms were nearly stick thin, and it was covered completely with gray-brown wrappings. Only a wizened face, with ugly squarish mouth and small green eyes like pinheads on either side of a long sharp pointed nose (like the beak of some rapacious bird) were uncovered. However, the skin was so dark it might have been part of that tight clothing.

"This be Hob's place!" The words bit at Thragun. "Fergit that, you night walker, and Hob'll see you into a toad, so he will!" He stamped one long thin foot on the floor, followed by the other in an angry dance. Now he pointed his two forefingers at the cat and began to mouth strange words which Thragun could not understand.

Thewada could be mischievous and irritating, Thragun had heard, but for the most part they were lacking in power to do any serious harm.

He yawned to show that he was not in the least impressed by the other's show of temper.

"I be Hob!" the dancer screeched. "This be my place, this!" Once more he was stamping hard enough to set his ball body bouncing.

"I am Thragun Neklop—guard of the princess," returned Thragun with quiet dignity. "You are a thewada and you have no place near the princess—"

Hob's face was no longer brown-gray like his clothes, rather it had turned a dusky color, and if he tried to mouth words they were swallowed up by a voice which wanted more to screech.

"The bowl is yours," Thragun continued. "I ask pardon for sampling it. It is a good drink," he continued as if they were on the best of polite terms. "What is it called?"

His attitude seemed to bewilder Hob. The creature halted his jumping dance and thrust his head forward as if to aid his small eyes in examining this furred one who was not afraid of him as all proper inhabitants of this house should be.

"It be cream—cream for Hob!" He shuffled a little to one side so he was now between Thragun and the bowl. "Cream they gives when they calls. An' truly it is time for Hob to come—there be black evil in this house!"

Thragun stood up, his lash of a tail moved from side to side and his ears flattened a little.

"Thewada, you are speaking true. Evil have I smelled, ever since I have come into this place. And I—I am the guard for the princess—What do you know of this evil and where does it lie?"

Hob had grabbed up the bowl in his two hands and thrown back his head so far on his shoulders that it seemed to be like to roll off. He opened a mouth which seemed as wide as half his face and was pouring the cream steadily into that opening.

"Where," asked the cat again, impatient, "is that evil? I must see it does not come near to the little one I have been sent to guard."

Hob swallowed for the last time, smeared the back of his hand across his mouth and smacked his thin lips. Then he pointed to the ceiling over their heads.

"Aloft now, so it be. She has a black heart, she has, and a heavy hand, that one. What she wants," his scowl began growing heavier as he spoke, "is Hob's house. An' sore will that one be iffen she gets it! I say that, and I be Hob, Hob!" Once more he stamped on the stone.

"If this place is yours, why do you let that one take it?" Thragun asked. He was staring up at the ceiling, busy thinking how he might get out of here and up aloft as the thewada said it.

"She works black evil," Hob said slowly. "But the law is with her—"

"What is Law?" asked Thragun in return. "It is the will of the king. Is he one to share this evil?"

Hob shook his head. "Mighty queer have you got it in your head. The Law is of us who have the old magic. Only it will do no harm to that one because she does not believe. There are them who lived here long ago and now walk the halls and strive to set fear in her. But until she believes we can no' drive her out. 'Tis the law—"

"It is not my Law—I have only one duty and that is to guard. And guard I will!" Without another look at Hob, Thragun went into action, flashing away down the hall.

Emmy's fingers were pinched and scraped from the holds she kept on the ivy and she dared not look down, nor back, only to the wall before her as she crept foot width by foot width along the ledge.

She shrank against the wall and hardly dared draw a breath. There was a sound from the next window. The casements banged back against the wall. Then she heard Miss Wyker's voice:

"Miss Emmy, my lady? Alas, I fear that you must be sadly disappointed in her. She is impudent and unfeeling. Why, she has never asked to see you nor how you did."

Emmy began to feel hot in spite of the very cool breeze which rustled the vines around her. Miss Wyker was telling lies about her to Great-Aunt!

"Now, my lady, do you rest a bit and I shall be back presently with the night draught Dr. Riggs has prescribed."

There came an answer, so weak and thin, Emmy could hardly hear it.

"Not tonight, Miss Wyker. I always wake so weak and with an aching head. I felt much better before I began to take that—"

"Now, now, m'lady. The doctor knows best what to give you. You'll be yourself again shortly. I shall be back as soon as I can."

There came the sound of a door closing and Emmy moved, daring to edge faster. Then she was at the open casement to claw and pull her way into the room. There were two candles burning in a small table near the door, but the rest of the room was very gloomy.

"Who—who is there?" Great-Aunt's voice, sounding thin and shivery, came out of all the shadows around the big curtained bed.

"Please," Emmy crossed the end of the room to pick up one of the candles. Going closer to the bed she held it out so she could see Great-Aunt resting back on some pillows, all her pretty white hair hidden away under a night cap, so just thin white face was showing.

The anger which had brought Emmy so swiftly into the room broke free now. "Please, Miss Wyker told you a lie. I did want to see you and I asked and asked, but she said you did not want to be disturbed—that I was too noisy and careless—But it was a lie!"

"Emmy, child, I have wanted to see you, too. Very much— But how did you get here? Surely you did not come through the window."

"I had to," Emmy confessed. "She locked me in my room. And she locks your door, too. See," she crossed the room and tried to open the hall door, but, as she expected, she could not. Turning back to the bed, her eyes caught sight of the tray Jennie had brought with Cook's custard on it.

"Didn't you want this?" She took the tray in one hand and the candle in the other. "Cook make it special—out of the best cream and eggs. She said you always liked it when you were not feeling well before."

"Custard? But, of course, I like Cook's custard. Let me have it, Emmy. Then you sit down and tell me about all this locking of doors and my not wanting to see you."

Lady Ashely ate the custard hungrily, while Emmy's words came pouring out about all the things that had been happening in Hob's Green which she could not understand, ending with the story of how Thragun Neklop had come that very day and how Miss Wyker had acted.

"And father sent him to me—he is a gift from a princess, a real princess. Jennie took him away and I don't know what has happened to him!!" One tear and then another cut into the dust of the vines which had settled on Emmy's round face.

"Emmy, child, can you help me with these pillows, I want to sit up—"

Emmy hurried to pull the pillows together and make a back rest for Great-Aunt.

"Emmy, has Mr. Adkins been here lately?" Emmy was disappointed that Lady Ashely had not mentioned Thragun, but she answered quickly:

"He has come three times. But always Miss Wyker said you were asleep, or it was a day you were feeling poorly, and he went away again." Mr. Adkins was the vicar and Emmy was somewhat shy of him, he was so tall, and he did not smile very much.

"So." Great-Aunt's voice sounded a lot stronger. Emmy, without being told, took the empty bowl on its tray and set it on the chest under the window. "I do not understand, but we must begin to learn—"

"But," Emmy dared to interrupt, "what about Thragun? Jennie said Rog took Cook's kitty away and it never came back."

"Yes, we shall most certainly find out about Thragun and a great many other things, Emmy. Go to my desk over there and find my letter case and pen and ink—bring them here."

However, when Lady Ashely tried to write, her hand trembled and shook and she had to go very slowly. Once she looked up at Emmy and said:

"Child, see that brown bottle over on the mantel-piece? I want you to take that and hide it—perhaps in the big bandbox in the cupboard at the back."

It was when Emmy was returning from that errand that they heard the key turn in the lock. Lady Ashely forced her hand to hold steady for two more words. Then she folded it and wrote Mr. Adkins' name on the fold. Without being told, Emmy seized the letter case with its paper and two pens, one now dribbling ink across the edge of a pillow, and thrust it under the bed, stoppering the small inkwell and sending it after it. Lady Ashely pushed the note toward Emmy and the girl snatched it to tuck into the front of the dusty and torn breeches.

The door opened and Miss Wyker stood there, a lighted candle in her hand. She held that high so that the light reached the bed.

"M'lady," she hissed, "what have you been about? What—"

The light now caught Emmy, and Miss Wyker stopped short. Her face was very white and her eyes were hard and glittered.

"You cruel child! What are you doing here! Shameful, shameful!" Her voice rasped as she put down the candle to bear down on Emmy. She caught one straggling lock of the child's hair and jerked her toward the door. "Be sure you will suffer for this!"

"I think not, Miss Wyker." Lady Ashely did not speak very loudly, but somehow the words cut through. Miss Wyker, in the process of dragging Emmy to the door, looked around, but her expression did not change.

"M'lady, you are taken ill again. This cruel child has upset you. Be sure she will be punished for it—"

"And if I say no?"

"But, m'lady, all know that you are very ill and that you sometimes wander in your wits. Dr. Riggs himself has commented upon how mazed you are at times. You will take his medicine and go peacefully to sleep, and when you wake this will all be a dream. Yes, m'lady, you will be very well looked after, I assure you."

Emmy tried to hold onto a bedpost and then to the back of a chair, but pain from the tugging at her hair made her let go. Great-Aunt was looking at Miss Wyker as if some horrid monster were there. She pressed her fingers to her mouth and Emmy could see that she was frightened, really frightened.

The door to the bedroom was thrown open with a crash and Emmy jerked out into the hall.

"You," Miss Wyker shook her, transferring her hold on Emmy's hair, to bury her fingers in the flesh on the child's shoulders, shaking her back and forth, until Emmy went limp and helpless in her hands. "Down in the cellar for you, my girl. The beetles and rats will give you something else to think about! Come!" Now her fingers sank into the nape of Emmy's neck and she was urged forward at a running pace.

They reached the top of the narrow back staircase the servants used. Up that shot a streak of dark and light fur. It flashed past Emmy. Miss Wyker let go of the child and tried vainly to pull loose from what seemed to be a clutch on her back skirts. Unable to free herself, she tried to turn farther about to see what held her so. Something small and dark crouched there.

Then came a battle scream, answered by a cry of fear from Miss Wyker. Now her hands beat the air, trying to reach the demon who clung with punishing claws to her back. She screamed in terror and torment as a paw reached around from behind her head and used claws on a white face which speedily spouted red. Miss Wyker wheeled about again, fighting to get her hands on the cat. Then she tottered as that shadow hunched before her now at her feet struck out in turn. The woman plunged sidewise with a last cry. Thragun flew through the air in the opposite direction, landing on the hall floor not far from Emmy who had crowded back against the wall, unable even to make the smallest sound.

The cat padded toward her, uttering small cries as if he were talking. That candle which had fallen from Miss Wyker's hand rolled, still alight, down to the stair landing below. Miss Wyker lay there very still. But there was something else, too, something dancing by the side of her body and uttering a high thin whistling sound. Only for a minute had Emmy seen that and then it was gone. Thragun was rubbing back and forth against her legs, purring loudly. Emmy stooped and caught him tight. Though this was hardly a dignified thank you, Noble Warrior allowed it. After all, was he not a guard and one who had done his duty nobly and well, even if a skirt-jerking thewada had had something to do with it? *HIS* princess was safe and that was what counted.

Elizabeth Moon

CLARA'S CAT

The old lady was almost helpless. She had never been large, and her once-red hair had faded to dingy gray. Behind thick glasses, necessary since the surgery for cataracts, her eyes were as colorless as a dead oyster. She had always had a redhead's white skin that freckled first, then burned at the least touch of the sun. Now the duller brown spots of age speckled her knotted hands.

It was going to be easy. Jeannie had a blood-claim—the only claim, she reminded herself. Her mother had been the old lady's niece; the old lady had never had children. So it was simple, and no court could deny it. Besides, she was going to spend a while convincing everyone that she had the old lady's best interests at heart. Of course she did. They knew that already. She had come to take care of dear old Great-aunt Clara, left her job in the city—a pretty good job, too, she had explained to everyone who asked. But blood being thicker than water, and her the old lady's last blood relative, well, of course she had come to help out.

"Did I ever tell you about Snowball?" The soft, insistent voice from the bed broke into her fierce reverie. *Yes,* the old lady had told her about Snowball . . . every white cat in creation was probably called Snowball, at least by senile old ladies like Great-aunt Clara. Jeannie controlled herself; there would be time enough later.

"I think so, Aunt Clara." Just a little dig, that implication of careful patience.

"He was so sweet." A vague sound meant to be a chuckle, Jeannie was sure, then . . . "Did I tell you about the time he clawed Mrs. Minister Jenkins on the ankle, when she scolded me about wearing my skirts too short?"

Oh, god. Jeannie had heard that story on every visit—every reluctant, restless visit—since childhood. It was disgusting, that someone of Great-aunt Clara's age remembered the juicy side of youth, remembered rolling her stockings and flirting with a skirt just a bit short . . . that she could still enjoy the memory of a minister's wife's clawed ankle, that she still thought a stupid cat had defended her. But there were visitors in the house, Clara's friends, people Jeannie had not yet won over completely. Clara's lawyer, Sam Benson, stocky and grave and not quite old enough to fall for any tricks. Clara's old friend Pearl, still up and walking around—though Jeannie thought it was disgusting for anyone her age to wear sleeveless knit shirts and short skirts which left knobby tanned knees all too visible.

Jeannie let out a consciously indulgent laugh. "Was that when you were courting Ben, Aunt Clara?"

Again that feeble attempt at a chuckle. "I wasn't courting *him,* dear; we weren't like you girls today. He was courting me. Very dashing, Ben was. All the girls thought so, too." Clara's eyes shifted to her friend Pearl, and the two of them exchanged fatuous grins. Jeannie could feel the smile stiffening on her own face. *Dashing.* And did this mean Pearl had been one of the girls who thought so, too? Had they been rivals?

"I didn't," said Pearl, in the deep voice Jeannie found so strange. Little old ladies had thin, wispy voices, or high querulous voices, or cross rough voices . . . not this combination of bassoon and cello, like a cat's purr. "I thought he was a lot more than dashing, but you, you minx, you wanted him to play off against Larry."

"Ah . . . Larry." Clara's head shifted on the pillow. "I hadn't thought of him in . . ."

"Five minutes?" Pearl conveyed amusement without malice.

"He was so . . ." Clara's voice trailed off, and a tear slipped down her cheek. Jeannie was quick to blot it away. "The War . . ." said Clara faintly. Pearl nodded. The War they meant was the first of the great wars, the one to end wars, and Jeannie was not entirely sure which century it had been in. History was a bore. Everything before her own birth merged into a confused hash of dates and names she could never untangle, and why bother? The lawyer cleared his throat.

"Clara, I hate to rush you, but . . ."

The old lady stared at him as if she couldn't remember his name or business; Jeannie was just about to remind her when she brightened. "Oh—yes, Sam, of course. The power of attorney. Now what I thought was, since Jeannie's come to stay, and take care of me, that she will need to write checks and things. You know how the bank is these days . . . and the people at the power company and so on don't seem to remember me as well. . . ." What she meant was lost bills, checks she never wrote, and a lifetime's honesty ignored by strangers and their computers. But it had never been her habit to accuse anyone of unfairness. "Jeannie can take care of all that," she said finally.

In the face of the lawyer's obvious doubts, Jeannie's attempt at an expression that would convey absolute honesty, searing self-sacrifice for her nearest relative, and steadfast devotion to duty slipped awry; she could feel her lower lip beginning to pout, and the tension in the muscles of her jaw. Silence held the room for a long moment. Then Pearl, carefully not looking at Jeannie, said, "But Sam's been doing all that, hasn't he, Clara?"

"Well . . . yes. . . ." Clara's voice now was the trembling that meant a lapse into confusion, into dismay and fear, as the edges of her known world crumbled. "I mean . . . I know . . . but he is a lawyer, and lawyers do have to make a living . . . and anyway, Jeannie's *family*. . . ." In that rush of broken phrases, in that soft old voice, the arguments Jeannie had tried to teach her aunt to say sounded as silly and implausible as they might printed on a paper. Jeannie knew—as Clara would remember in a moment, if she calmed down—that Sam had not charged her a penny for managing her money since he'd taken it over. Jeannie thought it was stupid; Clara claimed to know the reason, but would never explain.

The lawyer's face stiffened at the mention of money, and Jeannie wished she had not put those words in her aunt's mouth. Yet that seemed to do what she had wished of the whole conversation; his warm voice chilled, and he said "If that's how you feel, Clara—Mrs. Timmons—then of course there's no question of not doing exactly as you wish. I brought the papers, as you asked." Jeannie left the room on a pretext of making iced tea for everyone, while Clara signed and Pearl witnessed; she was not surprised, when she returned, to find them on the point of leaving. The lawyer's glance raked her up and down like an edged blade, but his voice, in deference to Clara, was gentle.

"I'm quite sure you'll take excellent care of your aunt, Mrs. Becker. She's one of our town's favorites, you know—if you need help, you have only to ask."

"Thank you," said Jeannie softly, in her best manner. Great-aunt Clara must have told him she'd been married. She herself liked the modern fashion of "Ms." which left her marital status handily obscured. Keith had been a mistake, and the divorce had been messy, what with the battle over the kids. He had custody, on account of her drinking—not that she was really an alcoholic, it was just that one time and unlucky for her that the roads were wet. But she could trust Great-aunt Clara not to have told anyone about that; she had too much family pride.

Pearl shook hands with her firmly. "I'll be dropping by every day, you know," she said, with her big old teeth showing in a fierce grin. "If you need a few minutes to go downtown, that kind of thing."

The old lady. Clara. She had a heart condition, for which she was supposed to take two of these little pills (morning and evening) and three of those

(with each meal.) There were pills for the chest pain that came on unex-
pectedly, and pills for the bloating. She could just get out of bed, with
help, to use the toilet and sit for a few minutes while Jeannie changed her
bed. Jeannie was very careful and very conscientious, those first weeks. She
kept the rasping whine out of her voice, the note Keith had told the judge
was his first sign that something was really wrong.

And in return, Great-aunt Clara talked. She had had no full-time
companion for years, not since her last sister died, and she had a life's
stored memories to share. Jeannie gritted her teeth through the intermi-
nable tales of Clara's childhood: the pony her brother had had, the rides in
the buggy, the first automobile, the first electric light in the town. And
endlessly repetitive, the stories of Clara's favorite cat, Snowball.

"He looked *just* like that," Clara would say, waving feebly at the
cheap print of a sentimental painting on the wall, the picture of a huge
fluffy white cat with a blue bow around its neck, sitting beside a pot of
improbable flowers on a stone wall. It was a hideous picture, and Jeannie
was sure Snowball must have been a hideous cat. The picture was not the
only reminder of Snowball. Clara had an old, yellowing photograph of the
animal himself (he looked *nothing* like the cat in the painting . . .
merely a white blur beneath a chair), several white china cats of various
sizes, and a cat-shaped pillow covered with rabbit fur. At least Jeannie
hoped it was rabbit-fur, and not the cat himself, stuffed.

She did not care enough to ask. She was sick and tired of Snowball
stories, from the time he caught the mouse in the kitchen ("And carried it
outside without making any mess on the floor at all. . . .") to the time
he hid in the car and startled Clara's father by leaping on his shoulder as
they were driving to church, and the car swerved, and everyone thought
her father had been . . . indulging, you know . . . until the cat leapt
out. The town had laughed for days. Jeannie felt *she* had been trying to
laugh for days, a stiff grin stretched across a dry mouth.

She wanted a drink. She needed a drink. But she would not drink
yet, not while Pearl came by once a day or more, and the lawyer stopped
her on the street to see how things were coming. First they must see what
good care she took of Clara; first they must believe she was what she
appeared.

Day after dull day passed by. Summer in a small town, to one used to a large city, is largely a matter of endurance. Jeannie didn't know any of the faces that fit the names in Clara's stories. She tried harder to follow them when Pearl was there, but the women had been close for over seventy years, and their talk came in quick, shorthand bursts that meant little to an outsider. Pearl, quick to notice Jeannie's confusion, tried to explain once or twice, but gave it up when Clara insisted "Of course she knows who we mean—she's family." The two women giggled, chattered briefly, giggled, shed tears, and to Jeannie it was all both boring and slightly disgusting. All that had happened years ago—before she herself was born—and what did it matter if some long-dead husband had thought his wife was in love with a Chinese druggest two towns away? Why cry over the death of someone else's child in a fire forty years ago? They should have more dignity, she thought, coming in with the tray of iced tea and cookies to find them giggling again.

Grimly, with a smile pasted to her face, she cooked the old-fashioned food Clara liked, washed the old plates and silver (*real* silver: she didn't mind that), and dusted the innumerable figurines on the shelves that seemed to crawl all over the walls. Not just white china cats, but shepherds and shepherdesses, barking dogs, fat-bellied ponies in lavender and cream, unbearably coy children being bashful with each other in costumes that reminded Jeannie of the more sickening children's books of her past. Blown-glass birds and ships and fish, decorative tiles with flowers hand-painted, Clara explained carefully, by the girls of her senior class. Pearl's tile had a wicked-looking yellow rose, thorns very sharp, on pale green. Jeannie thought it was typical of her . . . sallow and sharp, that's what she was. She dusted the old photographs Clara had on every wall surface not covered by shelves of knickknacks: hand-colored mezzotints of a slender girl in a high-necked blouse with leg-o-mutton sleeves . . . "your great-grandmother, dear" . . . and a class portrait from Clara's high school days. Ben and Larry, the boys Clara and Pearl had loved (or whatever it was) were two stiff, sober-faced lads with slicked-down hair in the upper right and upper left-hand corners. Jeannie tried to imagine them in ordinary clothes and hair, and failed. All the faces were sober, even frightened; it had been the class of '17.

In August, Jeannie first began to notice the smell. No one had ever said Jeannie was slovenly; the one thing she truly prided herself on was cleanliness. She hated the feel of Clara's flesh when she bathed her—that white, loose skin over obscene softness—but she would keep her great-aunt clean until her dying day. The smell of age she found unpleasant, but not as bad as in a nursing home. No, the smell she noticed was another smell, a sharper, acrid smell, which her great aunt tried to tell her was from the bachelor's buttons under the window.

Jeannie did not argue. If she argued, if someone heard her arguing with her great-aunt, it would be hard to present herself as the angel of mercy she knew she was. She did say she thought bachelor's buttons had no smell, but with a wistful questioning intonation that let her aunt explain that *those* bachelor's buttons smelled like that every summer, and she liked the smell because it reminded her of Snowball.

Of course, Jeannie thought, it's a cat. A tomcat smell, the smell of marked territory. Odd that it came through a closed window, in spite of air-conditioning, but smells would do things like that. Since Clara said she liked it, Jeannie tried to endure it, but it was stronger in *her* bedroom, as if the miserable cat had marked the bed itself. She looked, finding no evidence, and vacuumed vigorously.

Outside, on the white clapboard skirting of the old house, she found the marks she sought. Hot sun baked the bachelor's buttons, the cracked soil around them (she had not watered for more than a week), and the streaked places on the skirting that gave off that memorable smell. On the pretext of watering the flowers (they did need watering, and she picked some to arrange inside) she hosed down the offending streaks. And a few days later, dragging the hose around to water another of the flowerbeds (when she had this house, she would forget the flowerbeds), she saw a white blurred shape up near the house, and splashed water at it. A furious streak sped away, yowling, *Gotcha,* thought Jeannie, *that'll teach you,* and forgot about it.

Clara had another small stroke in September, that left her with one drooping eyelid and halting speech, now as ragged as soft. Jeannie had driven her (in Clara's old car) to the hospital in the county seat, and Jeannie drove her home, with a list of instructions for diet and care. In between those two trips, in the hours when the hospital discouraged visitors, she explored Clara's little town. The square with its bandstand had been paved, parking for the stores around it. She remembered, with an unexpected pang of nostalgia, climbing into the empty bandstand and pretending to be a singer. A hardware store had vanished, replaced by a supermarket which had already swallowed a small grocery store the last time she'd visited. The farm supply and implement company had moved out of town, as had the lumberyard; a used car dealer had one lot, and the other was covered with rows of tiny boxlike rental storage units. A few people recognized her; she hurried past the door that opened onto a narrow stair—upstairs was the lawyer's office, with its view over the town square and out back across a vacant lot to the rest of town.

It was stiflingly hot. Jeannie got back in Clara's car and drove out of town toward the county seat and its hospital, well aware of watching eyes. But the county seat had more than a hospital, and it was larger, and she was less known, Clara's car less noticeable. She parked in the big courthouse lot, walked a block to a sign she'd noticed, and glanced around. Midafternoon: the lawyer would be in his office, or in court.

She came out two hours later. Not drunk at all—no one could say she was drunk. A lady, worried to death about her old great-aunt, needing a cool place to spend a few hours before the hospital would let her back in . . . that's all. She knew her limits well, and she knew exactly what she wanted. She had the name and number she had expected to find, and would not need to visit the Blue Suite again.

That night, alone in the house (Clara would be in the hospital another two days, the doctor had said), she lounged in the parlor as she never did when Clara was there. She had remembered to call Pearl, had said she didn't need any help with anything, and now she relaxed, safe, wearing the short lacy nightshirt she'd bought in the county seat, enjoying the first cold beer she'd ever had in this house. She smirked up at the shelves of figurines. Clara's monthly allowance wouldn't exactly cover what she wanted, but she knew there were places to sell some of this trash, and if Clara were bedfast she'd never know.

Clara came home more fragile than before. She never left the bedroom now, and rarely managed to sit up in the armchair; Jeannie had to learn to make the bed with her in it. She had to learn other, more intimate services when Clara could not get out of bed at all. But she persisted, through the rest of September and October, until even thorny Pearl admitted (to the supermarket clerk, from whom Jeannie heard it) that she seemed to be genuinely fond of Clara, and taking excellent care of her. When the first November storm slashed the town with cold rain and wind, Pearl called to apologize for not visiting that day. Jeannie answered the phone in the hall.

"It's all right," she told Pearl. "Do you want me to wake her, so you can talk?"

"Not if she's sleeping," said Pearl. "Just tell her."

"She sleeps a lot more now," said Jeannie, in a voice that she hoped conveyed delicate sadness.

Clara was not asleep, but her voice no longer had the resonance to carry from room to room . . . and certainly not enough to be overheard on the phone. "Who was it, dear?" she asked when Jeannie came back to her.

"Nothing," said Jeannie. She knew Clara's hearing was going. "Some salesman about aluminum siding." She felt a rising excitement; it had taken months, but here was her chance. A day or so without Pearl, another inevitable stroke—it would work. It would be easy. "Do you think Pearl will try to come out in this storm?"

Clara moved her head a little on the pillow. "I hope not . . . but she'll call. Tell me if she calls, dear, won't you?"

"Of course."

Two days later, it was possible to tell Pearl that Clara had forgotten being told—of course she had told her about the calls, but since this latest stroke, and with the new medications . . . Jeannie delivered this information in a low voice, just inside the front door. Pearl herself looked sick, her wisps of white hair standing out in disarray, her deep voice more hoarse than musical. If Jeannie had been capable of it, she would have felt pity for Pearl then—she knew she ought to, an old woman whose oldest friend was fading into senility—but what she felt was coarse triumphant glee. *Old cow,* she thought, *I should try you next.* Pearl was nodding, showing no suspicion; perhaps she was too tired.

She left them alone, and went to fix them tea; she could just hear Pearl's deep voice, and a wisp of plaintive trembling treble that must be Clara. When she came in with the tray, Clara's hands were shaking so that she could not hold the cup.

"Are you *sure* you told me, dear?" she asked Jeannie. "You couldn't have forgotten?"

"I'm sure, Aunt Clara. I'm sorry—maybe you were still sleepy, or maybe the medicine . . ." She held the cup to Clara's lips, waited for her to slurp a little—no longer so ladylike in her sips—and set it down.

Pearl, leaning back in her chair, suddenly sniffed. Jeannie stiffened; she had bathed Clara carefully *(that* duty she would always perform) and instantly suspected Pearl of trying to make her feel inferior. But Pearl merely looked puzzled.

"Do you have a cat again, Clara?" she asked. Jeannie relaxed, relieved. She answered for her aunt.

"No, but there's a stray, and he . . . uh . . . he . . . *you* know."

"He sprays the house? It must be, to smell that strong on a chilly day. I thought perhaps indoors—"

"Did I ever tell you about the time Snowball clawed the minister's wife?" asked Clara brightly. Jeannie glanced at Pearl, and met a wistful and knowing glance. She accepted that silent offer of alliance as silently, and told her aunt no.

After that it was as easy as she'd hoped. November continued cold and damp; Clara's friends came rarely, and readily believed Jeannie's excuses on the telephone. Once or twice she let a call go through, when Clara was drowsy with medicine and not making much sense. Soon the calls dwindled, except on sunny bright days when they asked if they could come see her. This Jeannie always encouraged so eagerly that everyone knew how hard it was on her, poor dear, all alone with dying Clara.

When they came, Clara would be exquisitely clean and neat, arrayed in her best bedjacket; Jeannie, in something somber and workmanlike. They never smelled alcohol on her breath; they never saw bottles or cans in the house. They never came without calling, because, as Jeannie had explained, "Sometimes I'm up most of the night with her, you know, and I do nap in the day sometimes. . . ." That was only fair; no one could fault her for that, or wanted to bring her out, sleepy and rumpled, to answer the doorbell.

It was true that Clara's monthly allowance from the trust would not buy Jeannie what she wanted. She began in the cedar chests which were full of a long lifetime's accumulation: old handpainted china tea sets, antique dolls and doll clothes, handmade quilts and crocheted afghans. She would not risk the county seat, but it was less than fifty miles to the big city, where no one knew anyone else, and handcrafted items brought a good price.

Gradually, week by week, she pilfered more: an old microscope that had belonged to Clara's dead husband, a set of ruby glass that they never used, a pair of silver candlesticks she found in the bottom cupboard in the dining room. Clara had jewelry that had been her mother's and her older sisters', jumbled together in a collection of old jewelry boxes, white and red and green padded leather, hidden in bureau drawers all over the house, under linens and stationery and faded nightgowns from Clara's youth and brief marriage. With one eye on the bed, where Clara lay dozing, Jeannie plucked first one then another of the salable items: a ruby ring, a gold brooch, a platinum ring with diamond chips, a pair of delicate gold filigree earrings.

Autumn passed into winter, a gray, nasty December followed by a bleak and bitter January. Jeannie felt the cold less, with her secret cache of favorite beverages and pills. Pearl came once a week or so, on good days, but Jeannie always had plenty of warning . . . and Clara now knew better than to complain. Jeannie had used no force (she had read about it), but threats of the nursing home sufficed. And it was not like real cruelty. As she'd told Clara, "What if it does take me a little while sometimes . . . at least you got a nurse to yourself, on call day and night, and that's more than you'd get there. They let people like you lie in a wet bed . . . they don't come running. You ought to be glad you've got me to take care of you—because you don't have no place else." She felt good about that, really, even using bad grammar on purpose. The world was not the bright, shiny gold ring Clara had told her about when she was a child; using good grammar didn't get you anywhere she wanted to go.

She intended it to be over before spring. She could not possibly stand another summer in this dump. But picking a time, and a precise method—that was harder. Clara slept most of the day now, helped by liberal doses of medicine; the doctor was understanding when Jeannie explained that she needed her own sleep, and couldn't be up and down all the time when her aunt was agitated. Jeannie watched her, half-hoping she'd quit breathing on her own. But the old lady kept breathing, kept opening her eyes every morning and several times a day, kept wanting to talk, in that breathy and staggering voice, about the old days.

And especially, to Jeannie's disgust, about cats. Snowball, of course, first and always. But she sent Jeannie out to find and bring into the bedroom the other cats, the china ones and glass ones and the elegant woodcarving of a Siamese that Jeannie had not noticed in a corner cabinet until Clara told her which shelf. Clara not only talked about cats, she seemed to talk *to* them: to the picture ("Snowball, you beauty, you dear . . .") and the china cats ("You're so sleek, so darling . . .") It made Jeannie gag. So did the tang of tomcat, which remained even in cold weather. Had the cat hit a hot-water pipe, Jeannie wondered? Was it living under the house, in the crawl space?

In the middle of January, Pearl came one day without calling first. Jeannie wakened suddenly in midmorning, aware of the doorbell's dying twang. Her mouth was furry and tasted horrible; she knew her eyes were bleary. She popped two breath mints, put on her hooded robe, and peered out the spyhole. Pearl, muffled in layers of brilliant knitting, stood hunched over a walker on the front porch, holding a folded newspaper in her hand. Jeannie opened the door, backing quickly away from the gust of cold air. "Sorry," she said vaguely. "I've had a sort of cold, and I was up last night. . . ."

"That's all right, dear, and I won't disturb Clara—" Pearl handed her the paper. "I just thought you should know, to break it gently—our other classmate, May, died yesterday in the nursing home."

"Oh, how terrible." She knew what to say, but felt the morning after lassitude dragging at her mind. "Sit down?"

"No." Pearl glanced at Clara's shut bedroom door. "I don't think I—I mean, I might cry . . . I *would* cry . . . and she'd be more upset. Pick your time, dear." And shaking her head to Jeannie's offers of a cup of tea or a few minutes of rest, she edged her way back out and down the walk in careful steps behind the walker. Jeannie watched through the window, then glanced at the paper. "May Ellen Freeman, graduated high school in '17, one of the last few . . ." The newspaper writer had let herself go, wallowing in sentimentality.

It was, in fact, the perfect excuse. Everyone knew that old people were more fragile, could fall apart when their friends died. Pearl was using a walker—Pearl, who two weeks ago had climbed the front steps on her own. So if she told Clara, and Clara's heart stopped, who would question it? And she would choose her time carefully.

Clara, of course, was awake, and had heard the doorbell. Another mistake, Jeannie told her. She hurried Clara though the morning routine—after all, they were late—rushing her through the bedpan part, bathing her as quickly as she could, changing the bed with quick, jerking tugs at the sheets. She even apologized, with the vague feeling that she ought to be polite to someone she was going to kill in a few minutes, for being late. She'd felt a cold coming on, she'd had a headache last night, she'd taken more aspirin than she should. Clara said nothing; her tiny face had crumpled even further.

"I'll get your breakfast," said Jeannie, carrying away the used bed linens. Her head was beginning to pound with the effort of thought. She glanced at the clock as she pushed the sheets into the washer. After ten already! Suppose they did an autopsy . . . Clara would have nothing in her stomach, and she should have had breakfast. Could Jeannie say she had refused her breakfast? Sometimes she did. A snack now? The thought of cooking turned Jeannie's stomach, but she put a kettle on the stove and turned on the back burner. Tea, perhaps, and something warmed in the microwave. She went to her room and brushed her hair vigorously, slapped her face to get the color in it. In her mind she was explaining to the doctor how Clara had seemed weaker that morning, hadn't eaten, and she'd taken her a roll, wondering whether to tell her yet, and Clara had

. . . had what? Should Clara eat the roll first, and then be told, or . . . the kettle whistled to her.

Rolls, cups of tea, the pretty enameled tray she might sell at the flea market for a few dollars. She carried it into Clara's bedroom with a bright smile, and said, "Here you are, dear."

"Wish I could have eggs." Clara fumbled for one of the rolls, and Jeannie helped her. It was stupid, the doctor saying she couldn't have eggs, when she was over ninety and couldn't live long anyway, but it saved Jeannie from having to smell them cooking when she had a hangover. She sipped tea from her own cup, meditatively, wondering just when to do it. She felt someone staring at her, that unmistakable feeling, and turned around to see nothing at the window at all. No one could see through the blinds and curtains anyway. Her neck itched. She glared at the picture on the wall, the fake fluffy cat Clara called Snowball. Two glowing golden eyes stared back at her, brighter than she remembered. Hangover, she told herself firmly; comes from mixing pills and booze. So did the stench of tomcat.

What it really did was remind her of the perfect method. She cleared away the tray, gently wiped Clara's streaked chin and brushed away the crumbs, then carried the tray to the kitchen. She was a little hungry now, and fixed herself a bowl of Clara's cereal. The right bowl would be in the sink, later, if anyone looked. They would look; it was that kind of town.

Then she carried in the morning paper, and the white cat-shaped pillow, fixing her face in its fake smile for the last time. She would have a fake sad look later, but this was the last fake smile, and that thought almost made it real.

"I'm sorry, Aunt Clara," she said, as sorrowfully as she could. "I've got bad news—"

"Pearl?" Clara's face went white; she was staring at the paper. Jeannie almost wished she'd thought of that lie. It would have done the trick. But in her own way she was honest. She shook her head.

"No," she said gently. "May Ellen." Clara's face flushed pink again.

"Law! You scared me!" Her breath came fast and shallow. "May's been loony this five years—I expected *her*—" But her chin had started to tremble, and her voice shook even more than usual.

"I thought you'd be upset," said Jeannie, holding out the cat pillow, as if for comfort. "Pearl said—"

Clara's good eye looked remarkably alive this morning, a clear unclouded gray. "I thought I heard you two whispering out there. She here?"

"No, Aunt Clara. She didn't want to disturb you, and she said she'd start crying—"

"S'pose she would. May was her maid of honor, after all." Jeannie had not realized that Pearl had ever been married. Clara's voice faded again. "It was a long time ago. . . ." Now she was crying, grabbing for the cat-shaped pillow as Jeannie had hoped she would, burying her face in that white fur, her swollen knuckles locked onto it. Weak sobs shook her body, as disorganized as her speech.

"There, there," Jeannie said, as soothingly as if she expected it to go on tape. "There, there." She slipped an arm under Clara's head, cradling her, and pushed the pillow more firmly onto her face. It didn't take long, and the bony hands clung to the pillow, as if to help.

Jeannie "discovered" her an hour later. By then she had bathed, dressed, downed two cups of strong coffee, and made her own bed. She checked her appearance in the mirror. Slightly reddened eyes and nose could be grief; she left off her usual makeup. When she called the doctor, he was unsurprised, and quickly agreed to sign the certificate. She let her own voice tremble when she admitted she'd told Clara of May's death. He soothed her, insisted it was not her fault. "But it's so awful!" she heard herself say. "She started crying, into that old fur pillow . . . she wanted to be left alone, she said, so I went to take my bath, and she's . . . it's like she's holding it to her—" Sounding a little bored, the doctor asked if she wanted him to come by and see . . . she could tell he thought it was silly: old ladies do not commit suicide by smothering themselves with fur pillows. "I guess not," she said, hoping he hadn't overdone it.

"You're all right yourself?" he asked, more briskly.

"Yes . . . I'll be fine."

"Call if you want a sedative later," he said.

Jeannie removed the pillow from Clara's face, unclenching the dead fingers, surprised to feel nothing much at all when she touched that cooling flesh. Clara's face looked normal, as normal as a dead face could look. Jeannie called the funeral home Clara had always said she wanted ("give the condemned their choice"), and then, nervous as she was, called Pearl. It was a replay of the doctor's reaction. Jeannie lashed herself with guilt, admitted she had chosen the time badly, explained at length why it had seemed safe, and let Pearl comfort her. The irony of it almost made her lose character and laugh—that Pearl, now twice bereft, and sole survivor, would comfort the murderer—but she managed to choke instead. Pearl wanted to come, right away, and Jeannie agreed—even asked her to call Mr. Benson, the lawyer. "I feel so guilty," she finished, and Pearl replied, wearily enough, "You mustn't."

Everything went according to plan. Pearl arrived just before the funeral home men; she had her moment alone with Clara, and came out saying how peaceful Clara looked. She herself looked exhausted and sick, and Jeannie insisted on giving her a cup of tea and a roll. The funeral home men were swift and efficient, swathing Clara's body in dark blue velvet, and removing it discreetly by the back door, rather than wheeling the gurney past Pearl in the living room. "So thoughtful," Jeannie murmured, signing the forms they handed her, and they murmured soothing phrases in return. She wondered if they would be so soothing to someone who felt real grief. The lawyer arrived; she sensed a renewed alertness in his glance around the living room, but she had been careful. None of the conspicuous ornaments was missing. He murmured about the will filed in his office; Jeannie tried to look exhausted and confused.

"Will? I don't suppose she has much, does she? I thought—if I can just stay here a week or so, I'll go back to my job in the city—" In point of fact, Clara had to have been rich; she'd been married to a rich man—or so Jeannie had always been told—and he'd left her everything. And Mr. Benson had always spoken of her monthly income as allowance from a trust; trusts were for rich people. Jeannie had not come to a small town to work herself to the bone for nothing. But she knew she must not say so. The lawyer relaxed slightly.

"Of course you're free to stay here as long as you need; we all know you've put a lot into nursing Clara. The funeral, now—?"

"I thought Tuesday," said Jeannie.

"Excellent. We'll talk about the will afterward."

A steady stream of visitors came by that afternoon; Jeannie had no time for the relaxing drink she desperately wanted. Someone middle-aged stripped the bed, made it from linens taken from a bureau drawer. The woman seemed to know Jeannie, and where everything was, which made Jeannie very nervous, but the woman said nothing. She slipped away after restoring Clara's bedroom to perfect order. Several people brought food: a ham, a bean casserole, two cakes, and a pie. Two of the women walked into the kitchen as if they owned it, and put the food away in the refrigerator without asking Jeannie anything. But she survived it all, and at last they left. She was alone, and safe, and about to be richer than she'd ever been in her life.

She was also deadly tired. She thought of pouring herself a drink, but it seemed like too much trouble. Her own bed beckoned, a bed from which she need not rise until she felt like it. No more answering Clara's bell (in her memory, already blurring, she had always answered Clara's bell). No more getting up each morning to help an old lady use a bedpan and give her a bath. No more cooking tasteless food for a sick old fool. She stretched, feeling the ease of a house empty of anyone else's needs, with plenty to satisfy her own, and settled into her bed with a tired grunt. Beside her, the bedside table held what she needed if she woke suddenly: the pills, the flat-sided bottle that would send her straight back to lovely oblivion. She turned out the light, and yawned, and fell heavily asleep in the midst of it.

She woke with stabbing pains in her legs: literally stabbing as if someone had stuck hatpins into her. Before her eyes were open, she was aware of the rank smell of tomcat somewhere nearby. She kicked out, finding nothing, and reached down under the bedclothes to feel her legs. Something clinked, across the room, in the darkness. It sounded like beercans. The rattle came again, followed by the unmistakable sound of someone rummaging through tightly packed bottles.

Something was in the room with her, and had found her cache, her secret store of liquor hidden in the back of her closet. Furious, she reached for the bedside table lamp. Something raked her arm, painfully. *Claws* she thought, as her hand found the switch and light sprang out, blinding her. A waifish ginger kitten crouched on the bedside table, one paw extended. Its wistful eyes were pale gray, an unusual color she had never seen on any cat. A dull clank came from the closet, and the smell of whiskey joined the smell of tomcat. A yowl, and another clank and the tinkle of broken glass. Something white streaked across the floor; Jeannie shivered. It slowed, stopped, turned to look at her. A small, sleek, white cat, hardly larger than the china cats on the shelf in Clara's bedroom. Her stomach roiled. Another small white cat joined the first, just enough larger to look like one of a set.

She wanted to scream, to say that this was impossible, but no sound came when she tried. She stared at the open door, where an impossibly fluffy white tail showed now, as an enormous white cat, a blue satin bow tied around its neck, backed out of the closet with something in its mouth. A beer can, one of the silver ones. Her mind chattered crazily, reminding her that cats are not dogs; they do not fetch things that way. The cat turned, gave her a long yellow stare, and dropped the beer can, which rolled across the floor. The two small white cats batted it with their paws as it went by.

Her voice returned enough for her to ask, "Snowball. . . ?"

The white cat grinned at her, showing many sharp teeth, and ran its claws out and in. It was as big as the cat-shaped pillow, as big as the cat in the painting. She felt something land on the bed, and looked to see the ginger kitten bound across to jump off the far side and go to the big white cat. They touched noses, rubbed cheeks, and then sat down facing her.

Her mind went blank for a few minutes. It could not be what it looked like, yet she had seen pictures of young Clara, a slight ginger-haired girl with wide, waifish gray eyes. And in the huge white—tomcat, it must be—she saw the protective stance of the acknowledged mate. *Cats aren't like that,* she told herself, as both of them jumped onto the bed, as the sleek smaller cats jumped onto the bed, as she batted helplessly at mouths full of sharp teeth and paws edged with sharp claws, as the massive white fur body of the tomcat settled over her face, and the light went out. *Snowball* she could hear Clara saying in a meditative tone *was not just an ordinary cat.* Jeannie had time to worry about what the broken whiskey bottles, the rolling beer cans, the unmarked packet of pills, would say to those who found her, before she realized that she didn't have to worry about that after all.

Susan Shwartz

ASKING MR. BIGELOW

They'll *think you're crazy.* It was the same tape that always played in her head. Lisa had spent a lifetime cringing when she heard those words from parents or friends, never daring to ask them to stop. She dodged a suit, a street person, and a stroller that seemed determined to pass right through where she was standing and headed down into the station.

As she fished her sunglasses out of her purse and thrust them on with shaking hands, she nearly jabbed herself in the eye. You were allowed to wince if you poked yourself in the eye, weren't you? You were even allowed to cry.

People cried all the time on the subway. Discreetly, like secretaries who'd just gotten laid off so their bosses could have bigger bonuses. Noisily, like toddlers who had the good sense to hate the E train. Unabashedly, like the teenagers who'd just broken up. Or wildly, like the crazies who could turn hysteria into a great way to get a seat at rush hour.

No one noticed. Not the poke in the eye, not the red sunglasses she had bought to make herself look more cheerful, and certainly not Lisa herself.

You'd think someone would ask "what's wrong?" She even had her answer all ready. "I've got the mother of all migraines," she'd say. Brave, perky, guaranteed to win a smile. If Dana at work said that, people would be pulling Advil and Excedrin out of their purses, practically dragging her to the nurse, and sending her home in a taxi. (Last time Lisa was sick, with a bad back, they had heaped her desk with everyone else's least-favorite projects. "Who's your backup?" the cockiest of the secretaries had asked. "My back's fine," she had replied, touched that someone had bothered. "That isn't what I asked. You weren't here, and I needed those memos." Seething, Lisa had apologized and fetched the memos.)

No one asked. No one ever asked. And she was proud of herself: she didn't actually cry.

You don't want people to think you're weird, the usual self-help tape in her head came on. No, she didn't. She was armored against it, not just in the sunglasses, but in concealment that, over the years, had become solitary confinement. And she had avoided it so successfully that people barely thought of her at all. Especially not for promotions at work. Her fingers caressed the yellow envelope of the card she held—a picture of a black and white cat holding a salmon skeleton, with the message inside: *Better luck next time.* It wasn't losing the promotion and the raise; it was the unexpected kindness that made her glad that the red sunglasses were so big.

The younger woman who got the job—no one said she was weird. Or scared her for making a dumb mistake. Or assumed that of course she'd be in the office the day after Thanksgiving just the way she always had. Or that she wouldn't mind covering while all the people the next

level up went to lunch with the new Senior Vice President. Dana would
go now, too. Of course.

Also, of course, Dana had gotten cards congratulating her; hard to
believe that there were that many dancing-cat cards in the world. *You don't
want them to think you're a sore loser.* So Lisa had stopped by the party Dana's
friends had thrown, made herself smile, sip the sweet cheap champagne,
and even eat a bite of chocolate mousse cake. She had even meant congrat-
ulations. You couldn't help but like Dana, especially when she smiled.

But still . . . but still, Lisa kept waiting for it to be her turn. She
worked hard and got good performance reviews. She tried hard. She had
always tried hard and never taken a cent from anyone. And she'd succeeded after a fashion. *Nice life, for a rough draft.*

You try too hard, she had always been told. People could go crazy
between not trying and trying too hard, yet that was the place she'd lived
her whole life.

"*Ask* for the job as executive assistant," a coworker had urged her.
She liked mothering Lisa, worrying over her and giving her advice and
didn't even get mad at the "yes buts" that were all Lisa could muster in
the way of reply.

"It's not like a secretary—more an assistant manager. You're quali-
fied. And it's still posted. You could get it. But you have to ask."

The post called for someone to be right-hand man—or woman—to
the new senior VP, who was so new that no one knew his name. Or her
name, though Lisa was betting on it being a "him." Lisa's stomach
clenched. Her usual way of dealing with senior management was to duck
her head and ask someone else to bring in whatever material had been
asked for. If she got this job—assuming it didn't go to someone with
more flair—she would have to work directly with vice presidents, and
maybe worse. Besides, she would have to *ask,* risk being turned down, risk
being scolded for thinking of herself, risk—worst of all—being laughed
at. *You actually think we'd give anything that good to you?*

Real people didn't ask. *Real* people didn't have to. She could still
hear other people, lucky, entitled people saying "It just happened!" and
laughing over the good fortune that meant opportunities simply dropped
into her lap. *That's not really the way it is, you know,* the tapes in her head

told her. But those messages clashed with all the other ones that *nice people wait to be asked.*

Was a raise worth all that worry? Maybe not a raise, but a career, a life. Yet what if she failed?

Damned if you do, damned if you don't. And if not damned, stalled. Paralyzed, unable to move, let alone to climb. As indeed she was.

Lisa fixed her eyes on the Purina Cat Chow poster with its pampered ginger cat across the subway car from her and wished that this could have been one of the cars with the broken lights. Even if those weren't safe. No one noticed her. It stood to reason, a mugger wouldn't either.

The E train lurched out of World Trade. The Purina Cat Chow poster cat seemed to be dancing . . . chow chow chow . . . in and out of focus, a cha-cha in exact rhythm with the pounding in her temples. Her stomach ached. Her hands were cold, but the rest of her was sweating. Good thing she had the bench to herself. She hadn't even lied about the "mother of all migraines," but it was coming true.

By Canal Street, she could practically hear the cat on the poster. "Purina Cat Chow . . . chow chow chowwww," it chanted at her.

By Spring Street, she knew for sure that the mousse cake and champagne had been a *bad* idea. But if she'd turned them down, she'd have been a bad sport. She swallowed hard, wanting to cough, but knowing better. Damn air-conditioner seemed to have stopped working.

"Purina Cat Chow . . . chow chow chow . . ." mewed the poster cat. *When had it gone from being a red cat to a big, fat black and white like the cat on her card?* The train pulled into the West Fourth Street Station and jolted sickeningly to a stop. More commuters erupted into the car.

Chow chow chowwwww! The idea of food, let alone cat food—! Just as the doors were sliding shut, Lisa thrust past three briefcases and a baby carriage and onto the overheated platform. Her eyes were squeezing shut, and she avoided the bad exit, the one that smelled like a catbox, in favor of the one by the bank. With any luck, she could get a cab, one with air-conditioning. If things got really bad, she'd make it take her straight to an Emergency Ward. *With all the druggies. They'll think you're crazy.* Damned tapes—every reprimand she'd ever had (and she'd had plenty, despite a rather timid life) seemed to replay in her mind, scolding her at every step—she wished she could turn them off.

They had all meant well, from her parents and older sister, to her roommates to coworkers. Everyone saw her as a source for all their second-hand advice. *It's because we care. Would you rather be left all alone? What would happen to you then?*

I'd manage. Don't care, she had retorted once. The aftershocks had gone on for years. And she had had to eat her words.

They felt as if they were coming back up on her.

The broken concrete stairs tripped her up three-quarters of the way up. Something darted by her feet—was it a street cat? She teetered backward with a despairing cry, imagining every bump down to the concrete and, probably, broken bones and lying there while muggers stole her purse and her wristwatch. A rough hand caught her arm and pulled her up.

"Thanks," she muttered.

When she saw who had caught her, she managed—but only just—not to recoil. One of the panhandlers who worked this staircase, the one with the ski jacket and the dreadlocks. But he had crumpled the stained coffee cup he used for donations in his haste to rescue her, and he steadied her on her feet as carefully as if he were sane, and she were well, and they were normal people together.

She fumbled with her wallet. She might not have gotten the promotion, but she could give him a buck. Maybe five. Let somebody be happy.

He took the money on his palm, admiring the crisp bill. "Lady, you in bad shape. You better go ask Mr. Bigelow." It came out as "axe." She wondered if he really meant her to turn axe-murderer, but he pointed to a sign. *(Illegible Old English Initials) Bigelow, Chemist Since 1838.*

Dwayne Reed or Rite-Aid aren't good enough for you? A real drugstore with antique jars of colored water in the windows. It would be as pricey as Caswell-Massey. But it would have aspirin. It would have tissues. It would even have a pharmacist, maybe the second or third Mr. Bigelow to run the place, and he might help her.

"Thanks," she said again. "I'll ask him."

And tried not to weave like a drunk as she walked past the hot dog stand on the corner, the noisy electronics store, and what looked like an S&M version of Frederick's of Hollywood, and into the drugstore—no, it was classier than that. Into the chemist's.

It smelled of expensive violet soaps and cool, clean air, with a hint of antiseptic: a high, clean room with glossy, weathered paneling and glassed shelves built in to protect the perfumes, the costume jewelry, and the fancy velvet bows. She might have liked to hold one, even buy it, but *You can just imagine the markup on that junk,* the usual censors told her.

The pharmacist's counter was at the back of the store. She hoped there wouldn't be a long line of people waiting for their prescriptions, people tapping their feet and clicking their tongues at her as she blurted out what she needed. He'd probably say, "I'm not your doctor, lady."

Here were the over-the-counter remedies. She'd save everyone the trouble. She bent down, squinting to read the labels, bracing herself against a heavy cardboard box some fool had left in the aisle. . . .

And just what do you think you're doing? Like the "don't-be-weird, don't-be-crazy" scripts in her usual tapes, the voice filled her mind.

Lisa saved herself from sprawling in the aisle, crowded with natural sponges, $9.00 for the small size, by a twist that sent pain shooting through her temples.

I've lost it this time, Lisa thought. If she had lost her mind, she wouldn't have to worry about promotions. Everybody knew crazy people lost their jobs, their friends, their homes, and they wound up . . . *maybe I can get handouts from people by telling them 'Ask Mr. Bigelow.' Maybe I should ask him where the Thorazine is. Now.*

"Sorry," she muttered and started to lever herself up.

Owwwww, that was a bad one. Sorry to hurt you when you're hurting already.

None of her voices had ever bothered to apologize to her before, not in all her life. A cold nose nudged at her knee, and Lisa nearly leapt for the ceiling.

Easy, kitling. She had the sense of a kind of purring amusement.

She looked at the carton she had been ready to shove aside. On its lid was taped an index card: THIS BOX AND ITS CONTENTS ARE THE

PROPERTY OF MR. BIGELOW, with an arrow pointing downward. Someone had cut open the carton and fitted it with a square of carpet and a towel, a comfortable bed for the large, fat, black and white cat who stared at her, then yawned.

"You're Mr. Bigelow?" she whispered.

You were maybe expecting Bustopher Jones? Again, the purry amusement.

"Well, you look like him," she retorted, chuckling a little herself at the black and white, portly clubcat from *Cats.* She had loved Eliot's poems. And even though she'd been out of work at the time, she'd managed to see the musical—standing room at a matinee at the Winter Garden on Broadway, wishing she had had the nerve to move down into an empty seat; wishing especially that she were the lucky woman in the front row whom the lithe, sinister RumTumTugger pulled onstage for a wild dance in the first act.

I am Mr. Bigelow. At your service. You might scratch my left ear. . . .

Lisa obeyed before she thought. The cat leaned into her fingers.

"I was told to ask Mr. Bigelow . . ."

The big cat raised his head with supreme assurance. Lisa had never been what *she* would have called "cat people." If the truth be known, she envied cats more than she liked them: their sleek, bored looks; their ability to do any damned thing they wanted with complete confidence; the way people were charmed by anything they did. For example, here she was, talking to a cat. Did anyone at all think that was strange?

The big cat heaved himself to his paws and rubbed against Lisa's legs. She rubbed his back, then scratched his ears again. *Gentle hands,* the cat approved. *Your eyes don't look good. Your nose looks warm. If you were a kit, I would show you which plants are the right ones to eat when you don't feel well. All these humans and their hairballs. . . .* The cat's mental voice seemed to sigh like an exasperated physician. *What you need, though . . .*

He nudged Lisa down the aisle.

"You've made a friend," said one of the salesclerks. One or two of the customers smiled at the cat with its latest human in tow. Some of the smile went to Lisa, too, and she dared to smile back. No one thought it was weird to be following the cat.

Not those things, he growled in her mind when she looked at the shelves of pills in sealed bottles. *Those are for foolish humans. This should help you.*

Lisa bought and paid for a tiny round vial, brave in red paper, gold foil, and Chinese lettering, with "Tiger Balm" stamped across the top.

Then Mr. Bigelow herded Lisa toward a chair in a secluded corner of the store, across from an ancient clock.

Down, ordered the cat. She sat and, at the autocrat's next mental order, she opened the tiger balm. She sniffed, sneezed at the aromatic, even pungent scent, then rubbed it on her temples. Heat filled her sinuses, and the headache dissipated, as if some vein had been tapped in a volcano and the magma drained.

Better, eh? Mr. Bigelow jumped on her lap, sniffed at her, nose to nose, said "huuuuu" aloud, then yawned.

"Much better," said Lisa through a yawn at least as wide. With her headache going, all she wanted to do was sleep. But the cat lay on her lap, it would be rude to dislodge it . . . *him,* corrected the voice in her mind.

She yawned again and shut her eyes. The Muzak from the loud-speakers, the absence of pain, and the purring warmth in her lap reassured her. For once, she was glad that no one ever seemed to notice her. She would rest here for just a minute where it was quiet and sweet-smelling and with the comfort of a living creature who didn't see her presence as a reason to make demands.

She let her clutch on her tote bag drop and stroked Mr. Bigelow's soft fur with both hands. The big cat started to purr. Sound and vibrations passed into her until her hands went slack on his warm back, and the room darkened about her.

Lisa's eyelids snapped open, and her stomach chilled. *Oh. My. God.* Across from her the big clock, lit by one or two orange lights, showed 10:30 p.m. She'd been right that no one would notice her. They'd gone and closed the store around her.

She'd be late for work. Then a second, and more frightening thought struck her. Bigelow's Pharmacy had to have burglar alarms. Burglar alarms were keyed to an electric eye—probably one of the little lights that picked out details of door or glass case or shelf. Sooner or later, she was going to have to get up and move. She couldn't cower in this chair all night. The alarms would go off; the cops would come. That's *one* way of getting out of here, she thought wryly.

Promotion? She'd be lucky to keep her job if the pharmacy prosecuted for trespassing.

Let's have that again, miss. You say you fell asleep in that chair with a big cat purring on your lap. Right.

Now she'd have been glad to lose three promotions, if that would have meant her standing outside the pharmacy. What was she going to do?

Ask Mr. Bigelow. The tape inside her mind replayed to show her what a fool she had been.

Then she opened her eyes. What did she have to lose?

"Okay, what now, cat?" Even her whisper was absurdly loud in the empty store.

Mr. Bigelow rose on all fours. Standing on her lap, he stretched and yawned. *We have had a good nap,* he announced. *So we will be right. Or almost right. Hmmmmm.* The purr sounded so thoughtful that she almost laughed.

Wait here.

The cat jumped off her lap and padded off into the shadows, which promptly magnified themselves and began to dance in a way that reminded Lisa of the horror film she had seen as a result of "you pick the movie; I really don't care." *Next time, I am* going *to care,* she told herself.

One by one, white and orange lights at knee height flicked off. Did Bigelow know how to turn off alarms? Some cats, she knew, could open doors, flush toilets, and raid cabinets: why not this one?

A cold nose brushed her knee and she nearly jumped ceiling-high again.

Follow me, said the cat. She could have sworn he sounded amused.

He led her behind the foremost glass case, the one with all the elaborate headbands and bows stored in it.

You must look right.

Lisa stuck her hands in her pockets. Her suit was serviceable and of good quality, and that was about all you could say about it. Still, she hadn't charged it; it had years of wear in it; and if she touched anything in that case—even if she could get it unlocked, they'd probably find her fingerprints. What a spoiled cat this spoiled cat was if he thought he could turn her into as big a thief as he probably was. She just bet they had to lock up the catfood and anything else edible around here.

Mr. Bigelow made a *humphing* noise, as if aggravated by her thoughts.

He nudged with his nose, and a cardboard box slid out from beneath the counter. A shimmer of metallic thread and rhinestones met her eyes.

They were going to throw it out, said the cat. *You take it. Wear it.*

Fine, Lisa thought. *I've got a cat as a wardrobe consultant. Well, it worked in* Puss in Boots.

Rhinestones and glitter were never her thing; they made her too conspicuous and weren't worth the money. Still, she found herself putting the bright headband in her hair, like a punk tiara.

Come on! Bigelow urged her. He rubbed against her legs, then darted toward the door leading downstairs to the storage basement. Reluctantly, Lisa followed. This was New York. God only knew what kind of rats . . .

You have *to be kidding to think I would permit* rats. *This is my home,* Bigelow told her. *Come* on. *Unless you need the . . .* discreetly, he let his mental voice trail away.

It was tempting to find out a cat's view of human litterboxes. But Bigelow's urgency was contagious. Stifling her fear, Lisa followed the cat downstairs, past case after case of diapers and perfumes and canes and goodness knows what all else. Past supplies to a side door, Bigelow led her, and out the door into the darkness.

Come on, he said. *What are you afraid of* this *time?*

"I'm not afraid *of* anything," Lisa said. Strangely enough, it was true for a change. "I'm afraid for you. You're too small to be walking around alone late at night."

Bigelow fluffed and arched his back.

"And much too cute," she tried flattery as a ploy. *"Anyone* seeing you would want to take you home; and you'd never see your store again. But I have an idea."

She held out her arms. Mr. Bigelow swarmed up into them, to perch heavily on her shoulder. People were always walking around Greenwich Village "wearing" cats and, in the process, getting lots of attention. *Making themselves conspicuous. You wouldn't want to do that,* the tapes admonished her. But making herself conspicuous, even making herself ridiculous, was better than risking a cat's life, Lisa reasoned as the fifth person in one block approached and rubbed Mr. Bigelow's ears. He took it with the grace of a corpulent prince whose loyal subjects approach at his levee to kiss his hand. Some of the smiles rubbed off on her, too.

Head east, would you? asked the cat. Was she imagining it, or was he reluctant to break away from his "public"?

"We have to go now," she told people who wanted just one last ear-rub from the cat. "I think he's getting nervous." He hid his head demurely against Lisa, and she almost choked.

Past Second. Past First Avenue. Into Alphabetland where the wild things—and wilder clubs—are and onto Saint Mark's Place.

"Bigelow," Lisa murmured, the cat's whiskers brushing her cheek, "if we get any farther east, we could be in big trouble."

Over there. You'll know it when you see it.

Lisa found herself staring at a sign, splashed with graffiti.

"Bigelow, that's a rehab center."

Don't you remember the Electric Circus?

"Ohhh." The summer she was 18, she had come to New York. It had been the greatest adventure of her life. She had seen *2001*—maybe not stoned, but she had seen it and gotten through the light show without falling asleep. She had gotten her ears pierced, and they hadn't gotten infected. She had helped drink her first bottle of wine (she had never let anyone throw out the straw-covered Bardolino bottle, which still held silk flowers). And, carefully togged out in her cousin's least-freaky gear, she had gone to the Electric Circus.

I wanted to have fun. The years fell away, and she saw the careful, cautiously pretty girl she had been. Oh, granted, she danced. She raised her hands above her head; she closed her eyes; she whooped with the music (half a beat behind everyone else to make sure it was all right). As the strobes flashed on and off, she watched herself in the mirrors. Amazing: she looked like everyone else. She, too, looked like magic—but she knew the truth: it was a magic she saw, but somehow couldn't quite break through to share. She closed her eyes, threw herself into the music and the lights and the comforting press of bodies, and almost—a man with long hair tied back with a ribbon reached out for her hand, to pull her further into the crowd . . . *and maybe after the show, we'd wander in Washington Square* . . . but she was afraid, and hung back for an instant.

And then the house lights came up. The sleek young man disappeared, the music died, and the moment was gone.

She moaned with everyone else, then left the Circus and hung up her borrowed beads and satins. The next day, she had left New York, not to return for years. And her pierced ears had turned infected. *That'll teach you to let your damn fool cousin lead you around by the ears.*

And that was the closest she had ever come to breaking through to touch the magic she sensed all about her.

She had failed to reach it at the Circus, but, even so, she had mourned just a little when the Circus had closed. Whether she could share it or not, there was too little wonder in the world.

What do you call this? demanded Mr. Bigelow. *Nothing good is ever lost. Around back, here. Follow your ears.*

Follow her nose was more like it. She'd bet there were a lot of street cats around here. She tightened her arms around Mr. Bigelow. Maybe he talked to her, mind to mind; but he was still a cat and he might decide to fight or give chase. Claws pricked at her. *Okay, so I'm stupid,* she retorted silently. *I'm sneaking around a building in Alphabetland. You just bet I'm stupid.*

Feral cats rubbed against her ankles, meowing a welcome—not to her, but to Bigelow. *Bigelow, it's dark here. Those cats may have Fe-Luke, feline leukemia. And there may be muggers.*

I've had my shots. Trust the guides, said the cat.

The street cats steered her toward a low door, marked with garish paint. "I'm not going in there," Lisa muttered. But three of the cats reared up and pushed with their forepaws against the door. It gaped open, and other cats pushed at her legs, urging her forward as if she faced an opened refrigerator, crammed full of cream and chopped meat and tuna, and all for them, if she'd only get it down from the shelves.

The image in her mind was so strong when she ventured through the door that she expected to feel cold and hear a refrigerator hum.

Instead, LIGHTS, MUSIC, ACTION! just the way an old-time director might shout before the cameras rolled struck her. She stepped back, but only for a moment. The cats urged her forward, the door shut behind her, and she was inside.

"Ohhhhh." She forgot her fear and touched wonder. Her memories came alive. And the old heartache of loss and failure dissipated.

It *was* the old Electric Circus, complete with bands and records screaming, strobes catching the crowded dancers in infinite freezeframes, and mirrored balls flashing on the high ceiling. The projection screens on the walls glowed with bright life, just as they had when Lisa was 18. She remembered being dazzled by the rainbow colors and caparisons of merry-go-round horses, dancing up and down on the screens in rhythm with the dancers on the floor. Now, instead of horses, she saw cats, leaping and writhing and pouncing on the screens overhead. Cats of all colors, shapes, and sizes—though black and white cats like Bigelow predominated.

Unafraid of the dancers, the cats who had brought her inside darted into the crowd. An instant later, Lisa saw them on the overhead screens, too.

Bigelow gave a happy little meow. *We're here. I told you so. Nothing good is ever lost.*

"You want down, boy?" Lisa said. She plucked him off her shoulder and held him, despite his girth and dignity, in front of her face. In his glowing eyes, she saw her own, kindling with an astonished surmise.

"Bigelow, have you brought me to the Jellicle Ball?" Beneath the calls and drums and songs of the band whose old T-shirts read Cats Laughing came the rollicking electronics of Eliot's poems, set to Andrew Lloyd Webber's music. " 'Jellicle cats come out tonight.' "

The Jellicle moon *had* been shining overhead. And Bigelow had brought her to the Jellicle Ball. She had seen *Cats* in the Winter Garden. Here, there wasn't a recreation of an alley, with giant replicas of discarded boots, milk cartons, or spare tires. Here, she had found the old Electric

Circus, before psychedelics and the world had turned dark, and she had lost . . . she had lost something, she knew; and she had lost it here.

Nothing good is ever lost, said Mr. Bigelow.

So, here she was at the Jellicle Ball. Turn, swing around, raise your arms, sing with the chorus, stamp, commanded the music; and she did. Astonishing that she could. And even more so that she could enjoy it.

At the end of the Ball, sometimes, someone was selected to go to the Heavyside Lair and be reborn. *I could use a miracle,* she told herself, as she told herself every day.

You two-legs worry too much. You are warm, you are fed, you do not hurt. Dance!

Bigelow leapt from her arms like a kitten, and she saw his image, capering on the screens, touching noses with a hundred other cats, who greeted him with ceremonious feline respect before tumbling in a playful heap.

A hand caught her hand and drew her into the mass of human dancers. Guitars, electric keyboards, and voices swelled and twanged. For now, this was her miracle. So Lisa danced. She saw bodies moving and freezing as the lights flashed on and off—fast, graceful, strong, and free. Her own motions, mirrored on screens and in the dancers' eyes, were as sure and as happy. And when the set ended and the band paused, throwing back their long hair, wiping their foreheads, and saluting the humans dancing on the floor, the cats dancing in an inner ring at the center, she cheered and clapped, hands above her head.

Lights rose about her. Faces grinned into her own. The girl she had been, who mimicked the dancers rather than become one with them, had been afraid. Eyes would have closed against her, and people would have drawn back. But this Lisa, despite her grown woman's knowledge of muggers and AIDS and a thousand other fears *plus* the warning tapes of a lifetime's fears and reprimands, laughed and danced and hugged the people around her. Like a wraith in an empty house, the girl she had been flickered briefly in her mind, then vanished into the colors and the shouts.

My night, she thought exultantly.

Bigelow's image grinned down at her from the projection screens.

Cats and humans danced. Lisa remembered the story line from the musical; at the end of the Ball, someone would be chosen at the Ball to ascend to the Heavyside Lair and be reborn into a new, Jellicle life.

Maybe me? I could do with a future. A future that was young, free of tapes, and free of fears. Where she could ask for what she needed, where she could dream, where she could dance without feeling foolish. Ever again.

Maybe, said the cats' enigmatic, moonlight eyes.

Maybe, blared the music.

Yes, flashed the strobes. *No,* flashed the strobes. *Maybe.*

Lisa peeled off her crumpled jacket and threw it onto a chair. She abandoned her shoulder bag. She kicked off her shoes. A young man with long hair and a gypsy vest drew her further into the room. At the center of the dance floor, fenced off by glass, was a sunken area where the cats danced, safe from humans' clumsy feet, and where they paid respect to a huge, white-muzzled cat. *Old Deuteronomy?* Lisa thought. She pushed closer to meet the cat, to show him . . . *am I actually going to ask a cat for a second chance?*

She was not eighteen anymore. She had earned the right to not think, to not listen to the tapes. She had earned her magic.

The cat looked up and met her eyes.

Ask.

Lisa felt herself kindling into wonder. Had it been that simple, all her life?

She laughed, pointed to the big cat, shouted something to her partner, and pressed against the partition separating human from cats. He laughed back and gestured.

Go ahead.

There was a door in the partition. She had only to push it open, go down there, and ask the big cat for what she wanted: rebirth, a new life, freedom.

"Hey!" Lisa yelped in pain as claws raked down her leg.

Mr. Bigelow leapt back, tail held protectively high against the stamping feet of the dancers.

Tears of shock and disappointment filled Lisa's eyes. She had trusted Bigelow. He had led her here. Why, at the moment when she was about to try . . . ? *never mind, if you had been* meant *to have it,* the tapes told her . . . even he betrayed her.

Look over there! came the cat's voice in her head.

Lisa looked. Her purse and jacket lay on a table, not on the chair where she had stashed them. A young girl was sitting on the chair watching the dancers. From time to time, she put out her hands, as if dancing in place, rapt with delight at the sight of the dancing cats.

A boy emerged from the crowd and asked her to dance. She shook her head.

Me as a girl? Lisa asked Bigelow in her mind. But she had learned her lessons, and now she was dancing.

She turned back to the glass partition. She had learned. So would this girl.

Bigelow stood between her and the doorway. His back arched, and he glared at her.

Why did you bring me here? It seemed so unfair.

Unfair? asked the black and white cat. *Look!*

Lisa edged in for a closer look, her dance partner with her. She owed Bigelow that much, at least. One good look, and then she would ask Old Deuteronomy for a second chance.

The boy had persisted, holding out his hand to the girl who sat, as if guarding Lisa's jacket and bag. He took her hand where it rested on the table and tugged.

The girl shook her head. Splotches of color, feverish in the off/on of the strobes appeared on her face. Her eyes glistened with—that was *anger,* Lisa realized. She pushed away from table, from the dancers—and almost fell. Her chair wobbled and started to overturn.

In an instant, Lisa and her partner had leapt forward, were steadying her, righting the chair.

The girl glared at them and drew the checkered tablecloth across her lap, hiding her legs, the left so much shorter than the right. Then she grasped Lisa's jacket and covered her face with it.

She doesn't dance because she can't.

Lisa waited for the tapes to begin. She could just imagine what they'd reproach her with this time: selfishness would be the least of it. But the tapes were silent. So was the entire room.

She backed away, allowing the girl what scraps of privacy she could. It was all she could give her.

Oh, it is, is it? asked Bigelow.

In a moment, the music would begin. She might even make it to see Old Deuteronomy at the center of the dance floor and ask for her new life, and they would all dance again.

Not all of us, Lisa thought.

All she had to do was ask. Ask, and she'd have it all: youth, fearlessness, a chance to live her life over without the fear and the tapes. And that girl would still be sitting there in the midst of wonder, weeping into a borrowed jacket.

What sort of second chance was it at *that* price?

Ask Mr. Bigelow. Just ask. She had never been a person to ask. But she would now.

She walked across the floor to the glass partition, opened the waist-high gate, and stepped down toward the biggest and oldest of the cats in their sunken dancing ground. She knelt and held out her hand to him, and he sniffed it—imperial permission rather than Bigelow's mere princely graciousness.

Then she pointed—straight at the girl who had set down her jacket and was trying frantically to smooth her face into some semblance of party manners.

Bigelow purred and rubbed against Lisa's legs. Old Deuteronomy leaned forward and touched noses with her, as if she had been promoted to feline status. Then he rose, stalked over to the girl, and rubbed, first against her straight right leg, then against the withered left one and its black leather brace.

All you have to do is ask.

Lisa squeezed her eyes until red and black lights flashed inside her eyelashes. With all her heart, she concentrated on asking: *let the girl dance. Let* her *be reborn.*

The strobes flashed. When the lights came on again, the chair was empty, except for Lisa's jacket, slightly tearstained. The leather brace lay unstrapped by its side.

Old Deuteronomy was back in his place, and all around him, the cats were dancing. Lisa looked around for Mr. Bigelow. He wasn't next to her, and she wouldn't have had him there, to be stepped on. There he was, on the screens, clasped in the arms of a young woman whose face shone as she danced, shone as if she had been reborn.

Lisa's smile of joy hurt, and she wiped tears from her eyes as she raised her hands on the upbeats, dancing, still dancing.

Lisa glanced back at the leather brace. The second chance she had longed for with all her heart—she had asked for it to be given to someone else whose need—and whose heartbreak—were greater. So her chance was gone, her rebirth was gone, and, judging from the way Mr. Bigelow clung to his new friend, so was Mr. Bigelow.

Look what you threw away, the tapes reproached her.

Look what I got, she answered. *Now shut up. I'm dancing.*

Her feet had never felt so light or so much attuned to the music. She *was* the music and the lights. And, seeing herself in her partner's eyes, she knew she was the magic, too.

And then the house lights flashed on.

The crowd of dancers groaned. Shielding her eyes from the glare, Lisa hugged her partner, then released him. He was magic, too, and if she never saw him again, it did not matter. It wasn't as if the Circus were real. She knew a Rehab center occupied this building here and now. And in another way, it was the most real place she had ever been. Bless it; bless them all.

Nothing good is ever lost, the big cat had said. It wasn't. It was inside her now.

Retrieving her jacket, Lisa stumbled past the discarded leg brace— so that much was *true* change, she thought with satisfaction and a total lack of surprise. She looked around for Mr. Bigelow, but the cat was gone, probably riding home in triumph on the healed girl's shoulder. She smiled at the thought and waited for the tapes to tell her what a sap she'd been.

Silence, except for a line of a ballad. *And I awoke and found me on the cold hillside.* The silver and rhinestone band Bigelow had made her wear tumbled from her sweaty hair. *What? I thought fairy treasure disappeared at dawn.* Maybe things were different in New York than Under the Hill. She tucked the bauble away in her bag, to be treasured forever. And maybe she'd wear it again—next time she went dancing.

A street beggar, his hair in dreadlocks, ambled past, not even asking for a handout. "Are you lost, miss?" a man asked, standing at a distance so she wouldn't be startled.

She surprised both of them with a wide smile. "I was," she said. "But not any more."

She had had her night of magic, and she would always have it—and the memory of the joy on the girl's face as she realized that she would not be trapped forever in a body tied to a clumsy brace. They were both free— and she had freed them.

She smiled at a pair of entwined students, and when a yellow cab prowled by, she hailed it and went home. Maybe later this week, she'd stop by the drugstore with a tin of catfood for Mr. Bigelow, but now she was tired, she had dreaming to do, tomorrow was work—and there was something she needed to ask for.

In the morning, she dressed with care, sailing past even the senior recep- tionist (whom everyone whispered reported people's comings and goings to management) with her head up and her smile sparkling. She waved at Dana, already ensconced in her new office, and Dana waved back. Maybe a friend, if what Lisa had in mind worked out. . . .

"Lisa! Where were you last night?" Her coworker's hands and voice reached out to ensnare her, attracting the attention of half the room. "I tried to reach you." Then, in a carefully pitched whisper, "I was worried. How *are* you?"

Lisa studied the woman. Yes, there was actually concern there under the theatricality.

"I went dancing," Lisa said. And managed not to laugh at the woman's stunned face. *A promotion lost and she went* dancing? Easy to see the sort of tapes running through *her* mind. She heard whispers from the secretaries who had gathered to see how she had gotten through the night. Admiring whispers. *Did you hear that? Lost out on a job, and she went* dancing. *I'd be home crying my eyes out, and she went partying without a care in the world.*

The respect hit her blood like brandy.

Ignoring requests that sounded like demands for details, Lisa went to her workstation, printed out her resume, fished her performance reviews out of her files, and went back to her friend's desk. "Do you have the specs on that executive assistant job?" she asked.

The woman flushed.

After all that nagging, she hadn't even bothered with the job description. She must have been very sure that Lisa would back out.

"Well," said Lisa, "I guess I'll have to ask personnel about that. Or maybe ask the new VP what he has in mind. Do you know where he sits?"

Stupid question; he had to have a corner office, and only one of them was vacant. "By the way," Lisa said as she headed down the hall, "do you know his name?"

The answer made her laugh. She was laughing when she knocked on the door with its shining brass nameplate, **M. BIGELOW**, and when she was asked to enter.

A tall man, no longer young, was rising from behind his desk. His polite "business" mask changed into a genuine smile.

"I heard you laughing. Nice to know that someone here has a sense of humor. What can I do for you?" he asked.

"I'm here," said Lisa, "to ask what I can do for you. I'd like to apply for that position as your assistant."

He spread out his hands in a gesture of frustration. "They have these headhunters out beating the jungle for an assistant for me, but . . ."

"Headhunters are expensive," Lisa cut in as smoothly as if she had rehearsed it. "So I thought I'd ask. After all, if you don't ask . . ."

". . . you don't get. Sit down, please," said Mr. Bigelow. Would he be pleased by her resume? Did he like her? Just as important, did he seem to be the sort of person she could work with?

Maybe she wouldn't get the job. It was a risk she took.

Maybe she wouldn't get a *lot* of what she asked for. But she had to ask. Somewhere in the city, there was a woman who could walk and dance because Lisa had cared to, dared to ask.

Do you really think you're ready for this kind of responsibility? What if he thinks you're out of line for asking? came the voices in her head.

I thought I'd shut you up at the Electric Circus. Now go away! she told them. You didn't ask the tapes, apparently: you told. There was a lot she'd have to learn. But, for the rest of her life—all she had to do was ask about it.

Now that she had turned off the tapes, her mind was quiet of any thoughts but her own. Still, she distinctly thought she heard a big cat purr with satisfaction as the man across the desk turned back to her with a smile.

Ask Mr. Bigelow indeed!

Carole Nelson Douglas

THE MALTESE DOUBLE CROSS

"You are good," I tell her in my best Bogart growl. "You are very good."

Sassafras brushes against my shoulder and purrs like a puma on catnip.

She is a long, lean lady in a two-tone autumn haze coat with cara-mel-colored eyes. She is also my secretary, occasional nurse and gal Friday. And sometimes more than that.

Right now she has just given me the rundown on a new client: sleek number in foreign furs. Might be money in it. Said she was a Miss Wonder Leigh.

I am the unofficial house dick at the Crystal Phoenix Hotel and Casino, the most tasteful joint in Las Vegas. Tasty, too. I keep a private office under the calla lilies out back by the carp pond. The fish add a touch of class to my waiting room, and divert clients while Sassy and I confer. Watching fish can be fascinating, although I prefer catching them. I always was an outdoor dude, when I am not acting as an inside man.

In a moment the lady in question struts in. She is a wonder, all right. Sleek smoke gray fur from head to toe. Legs that do not know the meaning of the word "stop." Limpid eyes as hot blue as Lake Mead at high noon in July. Lake Mead is also quite a haven for carp, did I mention that? I am very fond of carp.

"Oh, Mr. Midnight," this little doll begins in a nervous, high trill, "I do so hope you can help me."

"Have a seat and we will see," say I.

She settles herself delicately upon the base of a nearby birdbath—I like a room with a view—and pats at her little ears and her little mouth. This doll has a case of nerves laudanum could not cure.

"Mr. Midnight, I am so worried about my sister. She is from the East Coast, where she met this most unsuitable gentleman. Now they have come to Las Vegas, and I have not heard from Whimsy for weeks. I fear that this cad might hurt her."

"Description?"

"My sister's or that of her gentleman friend?"

I eye her sleek, languid length. Inside she might be a nervous Nellie, but outside she is a long velvet glove. I am your ordinary American domestic of immigrant stock, but I recognize breeding when I see it.

"Your sister would of course be your twin," I point out. "It is the looks of the dude in question that are a mystery."

She stretches her lovely neck and tilts her head. "Why, Mr. Midnight, however did you know that my sister and I were twins?"

"Easy. I could see right off that you were not from these parts. Where do you hail from?"

She simpers happily. Every dame likes to think that she is exotic, although this babe definitely proves to have a claim to fame in that department. "Malta."

"Malta? Heard of it. That would make you Maltese, then?"

She shrugs with exquisite indifference, the silver-tipped blue gray fur casually draped over her shoulders shifting as subtly as sand in a dune. I had always thought a Maltese was a breed of dog, but no one in his right mind would apply such a noun to this lady. It crosses my mind to wonder whether Miss Wonder's affections are otherwise engaged.

"Now what does this bad-boyfriend of your sister's look like?" I ask instead.

"He goes by the name of Thursday. I have only seen him once since I arrived. A rude-looking bounder who dresses cheaply. Three colors," she sniffs, "and his shirts are none too white. He frequents the Araby Motel."

I wrinkle my nose at the address, a dive a dog would not touch for sanitary purposes. Things look bad for lost Little Miss Malta.

"Thursday, huh?" An odd name for a lowbrow Romeo, but I cannot fault it. Once in my dimmest youth I was called Friday in honor of my antecedents and my black hair by a little doll in anklets interested in keeping me, but I ran out on that dame. She was more than somewhat underage. Now they call me what I tell them. Usually my friends call me Midnight Louie, though I admit I require a professional pseudonym now and then.

"And where do you hang your collar?" I ask, purely for professional reasons.

"The Cattnipp Inn."

"All right, Miss Leigh." I rise and yawn to indicate the interview is over. "I will have my leg man look into it."

On cue Manny slinks from around a palm tree. He is a cobby tailless dude with an untidy set of whiskers, and his interest in legs is close up and personal. While he is eyeballing Miss Leigh's silken gray hose and generally cozying up to my client, I maintain a businesslike distance. She finally tumbles to my fixed stare and offers me a fistful of legal tender— Tender Vittles coupons.

After she leaves, Manny drools over the cash as well. I tell him to tail this Thursday dude and find out where the sister is. Simple enough. Even a Manx could handle it. Then I go home.

I room with a classy redhead named Miss Temple Barr at the Circle Ritz condominium, a fifties establishment long on vintage charm and short on residents of my particular persuasion. I like to stand out, except when I do not wish to be seen while working, and then I am virtually invisible, especially at night.

Miss Temple Barr and I have a very modern arrangement: she provides room and board, I am free to come and go and see whom I will. At two A.M. a scratching on the French door to the patio wakes me from visions of sugarpusses kicking in a chorus.

When I pry open the door, I am hit with a blast of hot air and the news from a snitch of mine that Manny has bought a oneway ticket to Cat Heaven, found dead as a dormouse outside the Araby Motel. Hit and run. I tell my informant to find Sassy and have her look in on the unfortunate widow. Then I go to the scene of the crime. An acquaintance of mine, Detective Sergeant Doghouse, is on the case. Below the embankment I see Manny sprawled on his side, legs askew. I do not hang around.

I am in not too good a mood at the office the next day (sure, I can always grab a catnap, but I need my beauty sleep). Then Mrs. Manx trots in, sides heaving and blue eyes large and limpid. She is a white-hot platinum blonde, but a bit on the neurotic side.

That happens to be the side that is all over me before Sassy can make a discreet exit. The widow's long nails clutch my shoulders, putting a crimp in my tailoring.

"Oh, Louie," says she. "You have heard?"

I discourage the Saran Wrap act, peeling free before she can cause any permanent damage. The scene is delicate. Iva Manx and I have been known to share a midnight rendezvous in more ways than one, both before and after she linked up with Manny.

"Be kind to me, Louie," she whimpers, wriggling her rear.

I disengage as gently as possible and tell her to go home until the murderer is caught. She seems less interested in my investigative schedule than in my off-hours plans. I give her a lick and a promise and escort her to the reception room.

After her exit, Sassy looks up with one amber peeper halfcocked and says, "Wherever she has been, it was not at home. They lived under a desert bungalow, and the cupboard was bare—not even a mouse, much less the lady of the house—when I got there at three A.M."

Sassy has never liked Iva, but then Sassy has a distate for flashy blondes from exotic climes like Turkey. And maybe Malta, too.

This is troubling news. Iva would not be the first dame to hurry hubby off the planet under the mistaken impression that some other dude—say a business associate of the same spouse—might take her for a stroll under the orange blossom were she free. I would not take Iva for better or worse if she were even $2.98.

Next I report to Miss Wonder Leigh. The Cattnip Inn, however, reports a vacancy at the room number—2001—given me by the lady in question. I look it over anyway, and who should ankle into the landscaping out front but the missing Miss Leigh.

"Oh, Mr. Midnight," says she, widening her azure eyes until her pupils are thin vertical slits and I think I am in blue heaven.

I tell her the news, at which she waxes the usual distraught: much pacing, pausing every now and then to chew her nails. She admits she has taken the room under a false name: Blanche White. Given her coloring, I tell her, Griselda Gray would have been better.

She whines a bit about poor dead Mr. Manx.

I tell her to save the sobs, that Manny had a prepaid plot at Smokerise Farm, no kits, and a wife that would not so much as clean his stockings.

"Oh, be generous, Mr. Midnight," she wheedles, all the while wrapping that soft gray fur around me. "You are so brave, so strong. Help me."

"You are good," I tell her. "You are so good I believe that I can get you a job in the soaps. Especially when you get that little catch in your purr."

"Oh, I deserve that," says she, casting herself away. "I have not been straight with you. My sister is not missing at all."

"Never figured that she was. You cannot hide a Maltese dame in Las Vegas. So are you going to tell me the truth now, Miss White?"

"My name is not White. It is really . . . Blue. Babette Blue."

"And Thursday's your, er, pal?"

"My . . . partner. I met him in Hong Kong. He was escorting a shipment of Siamese back to the States for clandestine breeding purposes. I needed protection—"

"Like Schwarzenegger," I interjected, and she flashes me a pleading look that could wring a filet mignon from a vegetarian.

"It is not what you think. Thursday was big and mean. He had come to Hong Kong as bodyguard for a gambler who had to leave the States. He was always ready for action. He even slept with kitty litter around his bed so no one or nothing could creep up on him. Sometimes he . . . he knocked me around. I was afraid of him, Mr. Midnight, that is all. I thought you and Mr. Manx could scare him off. And now Mr. Manx is dead and—"

"And now we get to the nitty gritty, speaking of kitty litter. Who are you so afraid of, that you would hook up with an ugly customer like Thursday?"

"Oh, Mr. Midnight, I cannot tell you."

I rise to go.

"Please, you must help me. It is a matter of life or death."

"More like death, Miss Blue." I examine the dirt at the base of an oleander bush. "This is not an act. I really have to go."

"You are right; I cannot expect a stranger to risk life and limb on my behalf. Go, then. I do not blame you."

I pause to scratch my neck. I do not wish to walk out on a lady at a critical moment, even if it is my own. "Listen. I can look into this without knowing everything, but I need some filthy lucre to fling around if you expect me to keep you out of Thursday's death. How much you got lying around?"

She fluffs her furs and goes huffy, but finally produces a fistful of cash from the kitty. "What will I live on?"

"Got any jewelry?"

"Some . . . genuine faux diamond dollars."

"Hock 'em," say I, giving her back a few coupons for snacks. "Now I really got to go."

After I leave, I check out the facilities behind the azaleas, then I check with a business acquaintance. In such instances it is necessary to consort with the sorry dogs who run the law and order game in this town. It turns out that they are looking for me. Doghouse, the sergeant and my sometimes pal, is all right, but Lieutenant Dandy is a typically tight Scotsman. The pair collar me and tell me that Thursday has been found dead. Did I do it in revenge for Manny? Might have, say I, but did not get around to it. I talk them out of hanging the rap on me and go where I was heading when so crudely interrupted, my lawyer's office. At least I know a legal beagle who knows how to keep his tongue rolled up like a red carpet and his nose relatively snot-free.

I spread most of Miss Blue's kitty litter coupons around—there is a black market in this stuff; apparently people find it conducive to growing seedlings. Then I go back to the office at the Crystal Phoenix.

It has not moved, and Sassy is out front straightening the seams on her stripes. I head for the desk and a short snooze, seeing as how my slumber has been as fitful as that of the fairytale princess forced to recline on an illegally concealed legume.

Sassy soon rounds the calla lily curtain marking my inner sanctum and poses artfully. "Mr. Puss-in-Boots to see you, boss." Her pet name is no compliment to the forthcoming visitor.

She admits a stranger broadcasting a distinct odor of baby powder, a fussy sort born to give basic black a bad name. He accessorizes his fine black coat with pristine white gloves and spats. A precious little spot of pure white like a pearl stickpin nestles in his black cravat. Not my type, believe it.

He gives his name as Jewel Thebes. I cannot tell if he is announcing his profession but is lisping, or if he is indeed of Egyptian ancestry. I can certainly picture him mummified.

First he consoles me on Manny's death. Then he announces with the softest of purrs that he is prepared to pay five thousand Fancy Feast coupons with no expiration date for an item, merely ornamental, says he, that he believes I know the whereabouts of: "the black bird."

I cannot quarrel with the quality of the color, nor the amount of the reward: five thousand mackerels is nothing to sniff at. Nor am I normally adverse to a little bird hunting. While I am distracted by the sight of Sassy swaying off to lunch under an archway of calla lily leaves, Thebes pulls a pretty little piece from a discreet pocket and asserts that he is about to search my office.

Go ahead, say I, putting my mitts up. As he is searching me, I pinion his white bootie with my rear foot, pounce, and knock the weapon halfway to the birdbath. One good five-finger exercise on that dainty jaw, and Mr. Thebes is seeing the bluebirds of happiness.

I steel myself and search the dude. A flowered pouch of catnip, a fat wallet and a ticket to *Cats!* is about it. Thebes recovers in time to pout at my inroads upon his person, which also enables him to fork over two hundred clams via my intervention. Clams are not carp, but I remain fond of seafood in all forms. I also choke out of him that the lively Miss Blue is now in Room 635 of the Belle Chat Hotel.

When I get outside the Crystal Phoenix, though, I discover that some alley cat is tailing me, so I hop a ride on a motor scooter and head over to the hotel.

She may no longer be owning up to the name "Wonder," but this gray lady still manages to amaze. When I mention Thursday's death and my visit from Thebes, she goes down on all fours and lifts a dainty paw to her worried brow.

"I have not lived a good life," she confides with a tremor. "I have been bad."

To Midnight Louie this is not necessarily a detriment. I remind her that I find her theatrics good, very good. This is a favorite saying of mine. The ladies like it, yet it leaves me room to be cynical, not to mention mysterious.

"If only," wails she, "I had something to give you. What can I bribe you with?"

I manage a quick pass of the kisser that makes the answer painfully evident. The notion does not seem to dismay her, but then the girl is good. All right, bad.

She also comes clean about the black bird. It will be hers within the week, she says. The late Thursday hid it.

What, I ask, really happened to that late unlamented partner?

"The Fat Cat," says she, employing a thrilling tone.

I am not impressed. I weigh in at eighteen pounds on a good day.

Then who should show up but Thebes, still packing that pretty little piece. We three are at a standoff, when who should arrive but my police pals, Doghouse and Dandy. It is hard to take two guys whose names sound like the title of a television cop show seriously.

They take me into the hall to give me trouble. Now they are thinking I might have killed Manny as well as Thursday. Were Iva and I involved? Nope, say I. I only lie in defense of a lady. And was she trying to divorce Manny, but he was against it? Manny, I say, was not against anything, including fur coats.

A commotion erupts inside. We three burst in and what have we but Jewel Thebes sporting a slash above the right eye and lovely Miss Blue holding the decorative gat on the little Egyptian.

"Please," this Thebes dude whines to the police, "do not leave me or these two will kill me when you go."

Nothing gets the police's goat so much as death threats, and the dogged pair settle in for an inquiry. I turn it all into a joke, for by now both the ex-Miss Wonder and the sniveling Thebes have figured out that the one thing neither of them wants is the police involved in the hunt for this black bird. None of us three is particularly big on sharing with the force.

Things do get ugly, though, and Lieutenant Dandy squeezes up his ugly Scottish mug and wipes my face with a big black-gloved paw.

I hold my temper, mainly because there is a reputed lady present. Doghouse finally herds his inferior superior officer out of the room, along with Thebes.

Babette eyes me with her long mascara-black lashes half-lowered. "You are the most persistent pussycat I have ever known," she coos, stroking an agile extremity over my jaw. "So wild and unpredictable."

I never turn down a compliment, but point out that a little accurate information would soothe my wounded kisser more than this rub-and-tickle game.

So she comes across. Babette, Thursday and Thebes stole the black bird from the dude who owned it because the Fat Cat offered five hundred pounds of prime Venezuelan catnip for it. But Thebes planned to ditch the duo and elope with the black bird on his lonesome, so Babette and

Thursday teamed up to do to Thebes what he would have done to them before he could do it. That is what a life of crime will do to your grammar.

Then, she confides, she found Thursday was planning to ditch her and keep the bird all to himself.

"What does this desirable bird look like?" I ask.

Big, she says. So high, and shiny. Has feathers. She only saw it once for a few minutes. I gaze deep into those baby blues and tell her she is a liar.

"I have always been a liar," she purrs.

I suggest that she should find something new to brag about.

"Oh, Louie, I am so tired," she says, leaning listlessly against my shoulder. "I am so tired of lying and not knowing what is a lie and what is true. I wish—"

Well, there is only one way to shut up a lady bent on confessing her sins, and I take it. I could tell you that this is the end of that scene, but you were not born yesterday. Let us just say that talk is cheap after that point.

The Belvedere Hotel, when I get there, is cheesy as usual. I spot several rats on the fringes. I also find Thebes fresh from a long interrogation with Doghouse and Dandy. He looks as if he had been mauled by a rat terrier, but claims he told the cops nothing. He also rags me about my association with Babette, but I tell him I had to throw in with her.

Back at the office, Sassy is full of bad news. A Mr. Spongecake called, says she, and Babette is waiting for me. I am surprised to see her so soon again, but the lady is more ruffled than ever, and it has nothing to do with our private matters.

"Oh, Louie," she says, "my place was mussed up when I returned and I am scared."

I stash her where I always stash disheveled dames, at my gal Sassy's place, which is not too bad. It has a great view on the alley behind Sing Ho's Singapore restaurant. No sooner are the two dames on the way there, but my calla lilies part and Iva Manx pads in. Has a dude no privacy?

She admits that she sent the police to my place.

I reply by asking where she was when Manny was given his fatal shove.

This encourages her to leave in a hurry and brings my first peace of the day, which is interrupted by a call on the blower from this Fat Cat, Spongecake. He is in Room 713 of the Crystal Phoenix and wants the black bird.

There is nothing to say but that I got it and we can talk. Like Miss Blue, I am a liar, too, but purely for professional reasons.

When I arrive I realize that the Fat Cat has great taste. He has taken the ghost suite at the Crystal Phoenix. These rooms feature the same forties decor as when Jersey Joe Jackson lived at the hotel, then known as the Joshua Tree. Some say Jersey Joe still lives there. The rooms are never rented, but we law-bending dudes are not against arranging a private powwow on the premises. As for Jersey Joe, he had proclivities of a criminal nature, to hear tell. If he objecst to some larcenous company, he is the last to say so.

The Fat Cat is an oversize bewhiskered gent in a brown striped suit with full sideburns and a stomach pouch that would make the spreading chestnut tree look like a bonsai bush. I have heard this particular breed called a Maine Coon, and he is indeed big enough to pass for a raccoon, or perhaps the state of Maine itself.

An anonymous, almost albino gunsel is hunched in the corner with his eyes hooded. I pay him no mind.

"Are you here, sir, as Miss Blue's representative," says Spongecake, who tends to talk like a preacher addressing the millionaires' club, "or Mr. Thebes's?"

I pull a pussycat face. "There is me," I say modestly.

The bushy eyebrows frosting Spongecake's fat face lift. "She did not tell you what it is, did she?"

"Thebes offered me ten thousand for it," I return, upping the ante to keep things interesting.

Spongecake arranges himself more comfortably in his chair, which is a green satin upholstered job with wine fringe. There is a lot of Spongecake to rearrange. He offers some coffee for my cup of cream, which I accept. A dash of caffeine adds spice to my day and Spongie is big on formalities.

"Let me tell you about the bird," Spongecake begins, his yellow eyes slit with greed and nostalgia. "It is a songbird of sorts," says he, "but not in the usual sense. It wears a glossy black coat somewhat like your own. I like," he adds, "a gentleman who maintains his grooming. This legendary bird dates from the mid-eighteenth century. Eighteen forty-five, to be precise."

I get the impression that Spongecake is nothing if not precise.

"After a circuitous history beginning in the States, the black bird finally arrived in the possession of a gent of antiquarian nature, a Russian blue, in Istanbul. A general. Then, sir," Spongie adds, "I sent agents to acquire it. They did."

"What can one bird be worth?" I ask.

"That depends upon the buyer. I confess that this globe hosts certain . . . collectors, shall we say? Such individuals would be willing to pay dearly for a rare bird of the proper vintage, much as others would kill for a bottle of Napoleon brandy. Reputedly this bird's craw is crammed with diamonds." Spongie leans back to look down his flowing white cravat. "I can offer you, sir, twenty-five thousand in whatever currency you prefer, or one-quarter of what I realize from the sale, which might be a hundred thousand, or even a quarter of a million."

This is not an insignificant amount of nip. Plans for this pile of affluence are dancing in my head, along with something of a chemical character. It occurs to me that the caffeine I have imbibed is having an effect reminiscent of valium.

The room blurs, which is disturbing. Spongecake blurs, which is an improvement. I rise and spar briefly with the furniture, then conk out on the floor.

I wake to the sound of four-and-twenty blackbirds piping in a pie. They flock away like cobwebs. I find myself alone in the Jersey Joe Jackson suite. Whenever I find myself alone, I make good use of the opportunity, but first I lurch to the nearest mirror, which requires a staggering bound atop a console table covered in snakeskin. Speaking of which, it seems one of the dear recently departed—Spongecake, Thebes or the pale gunsel in the corner—has given my head a parting shot. Four slashes decorate my temple. I clean up by rubbing a wet mitt over them, then search the premises. I find little or nothing, but I feel better.

One of the little nothings I find is yesterday's newspaper listing the schedule of charter flights to Las Vegas. La Paloma Airlines is flying in a raft of eager gamblers from Hong Kong, I read. Those of an Oriental persuasion have a fondness for gaming that is exceeded only by my taste for carp, but I find the name of the charter suggestive. According to a hot-tempered hoofer of my acquaintance, "paloma" means dove in Spanish.

Such irony as a white bird flying in a black bird cannot be merely accidental, but it *is* Occidental: the port of departure is in the right quarter of the globe. I recall that the lovely Babette was definite about needing a week to get her paws on the bird.

By the time I return to the office, the sidewalk has stopped playing spin the bottle. Babette is not there, but Sassy says the lady has called and is now at the Wellington Hotel. That lady changes hotels more frequently than a sheepdog rotates fleas.

So I am sitting at my desk nursing my noggin, which requires me to add a little milk to the Scotch I keep in my drawer, when the calla lily leaves part dramatically. I prepare myself for the entrance of another foxy lady. Instead, a wizened Siamese staggers in, dragging a parcel almost as big as he is wrapped in burlap.

The old dude falls over, and a quick check finds him pumped full of birdshot. Sassy is not amused. She does not do cleanup work.

"Do not blame the poor sap for keeling over on our turf," say I. "He has just come in on a long intercontinental flight."

I pat him down and find his identification tag. "Captain Jack." No doubt his last assignment was the La Paloma.

Sassy agrees to tidy the place.

"You are a good man, sister," I tell her, then take the burlap bundle and scram. I deposit it in one of my favorite stashes, which I am not about to divulge, save that it is under a blackjack table in the Crystal Phoenix. I take a hike to the address of the Wellington, and find a vacant lot. I am not surprised. Napoleon did not do well with Wellington, either. So I return to home, sweet homicide.

Guess who is waiting at my place? It could be the police, but it is Miss Babette, looking, as usual, ravishing.

Unfortunately, she is accompanied by Spongecake and Thebes, neither of whom look ravishing, although Thebes always looks as if he would be amenable to the idea. The nondescript gunsel is in the corner, looking threatening.

Spongie wastes no time.

"You are a most headstrong individual, sir. I see we will have to cut you in on ten thousand for your trouble."

"No trouble," I reply. "I want a much bigger cut than that. What say we feed the gunsel to the police dogs? After all, he did shoot Thursday and Captain Jack."

Here Spongie gets apoplectic, which he reveals by twitching his whiskers. "You cannot have Wilmar. Wilmar is a particular pet of mine."

I cannot say much for Miss Babette's associates; they all appear to have unnatural attachments. Well, say I, give them Mr. Thebes then.

The dude in question's pouty little peke-face whitens before my eyes.

Wilmar erupts from the corner to spit in my face, the whites of his eyes forming a neat circle around his putty-colored orbs. As far as whisker-twitching goes, he has Big Daddy Spongecake beat by a hairsbreadth.

Poor Wilmar is so wrought up that the beauteous Babette slinks up and disarms the poor sap with one practiced swipe of her pretty paw.

Wilmar belly-crawls into the corner in a funk.

"So, Mr. Midnight," Sponge demands affably, which does not fool me a bit. The only thing affable about Spongecake is his vocabulary. "Where is the bird?"

"It will be delivered here. Shortly. Meanwhile, we might as well entertain ourselves. Let me see if I have the playbill down pat. You," I tell Spongie, "killed Thursday because he was in cahoots with Babette. What about Captain Jack?"

"Oh," says Sponge, "that was Wilmar's doing, as was Thursday. I do not descend to dirty work. And it all really was Miss Babette's fault. She had given Captain Jack the bird in Hong Kong, to deliver it to her here.

Wilmar—whom I had, er, picked up in the East—and I called upon Thursday and Miss Blue in Malta. I was to pay Babette for the bird when they snatched it. While I went to get the payment, she and Thursday got away. Wilmar and I traced them to Hong Kong, then here. After La Paloma landed, we followed Captain Jack to Babette's apartment. Captain Jack ran with the bird. Wilmar shot him on the fire escape, but the captain managed to get away. That is when I . . . persuaded Babette to call you and say she was at the Wellington. I wanted to search your office."

"Find anything I been missing?"

Spongecake glowers, then pats his enormous stomach until he withdraws ten one-dollar Whiskas coupons.

I take the cash, look it over, and say I want fifteen.

Spongecake and I dance around some more on price. When I hand back the ten, he says I kept one coupon. No, say I, you padded it. In fact it is crumpled tighter than a love note between his front fingernails.

"A word of advice, Mr. Midnight." Sponge narrows his bland yellow eyes. "Be careful." He jerks his head in Babette's direction. It takes a crook to predict another crook. "Now, where is the bird?"

I manage to dial Sassy's number on the vintage rotary phone and tell her to withdraw the bundle from my favorite storage facility. Not much later the ever-efficient Sassy drops off the burlap-wrapped object of all our affections.

Spongecake is so pleased he hyperventilates as he claws away the wrappings. What we see is one large, black bird, its scrawny feet tied with some sort of leather anklet. Over its head is a leather hood like you see on fancy hunting birds like falcons.

Spongecake's long nails tremble as they pluck the bag away.

The big bird is somewhat disoriented, which—given its port of departure—is understandable.

"Hawwwk," this creature declares.

Spongecake recoils as if scratched, and indeed the sound is crude enough to scar the most senstive ear.

"Fraud," Spongecake declares, still incensed at the idea of criminal doings. "Fakery. This is a genuine, live bird!" he snarls at Babette. "I

235

expected a stuffed specimen—stuffed with diamonds. A live bird could not harbor such treasure for long."

Babette shakes her pretty head. "I did not know—"

"You cheated me," Thebes screams at Spongecake, bristling until his hair stands up all over, even on his white-socked feet. "You promised me riches beyond counting!"

I turn to Babette. "You must have known."

"No, Louie, I did not!" She curls sharply filed fingernails into my lapels. "I never saw the bird for more than a few moments—"

"Peacock feathers!"

"I want my ten coupons back." Spongecake pokes me crudely on the shoulder.

I shrug. "Too bad."

Thebes and Spongecake depart, arguing. Spongecake is threatening to find the Russian blue who pulled the switch in Malta. Thebes is threatening to go along for the ride. That is what you call company that loves misery. No one notices Wilmar hunched quietly in the corner.

I turn to Babette, who is looking nervous.

"All right, baby, time to talk turkey. What exactly is this here bird?"

"I do not know, Louie, truly I do not," she says, barely casting the creature a glance.

"What about Manny?"

"What *about* Manny?" She runs light nails up and down my spine.

"You warned Thursday that he was being followed, hoping he would confront Manny and force him to kill Thursday for you. When that did not work, and Manny went up the alley, just doing his job, you pushed him into the path of an oncoming Brinks truck. You knew the Crystal Phoenix transports the casino take at that hour along that route. So did I. You set Manny up. You killed him."

"Why, why, Louie? Why would I do it?"

"Because you are bad, sweetheart; you said it yourself. And you figured that I would go after Thursday to avenge Manny. You were right, only Wilmar got there first. Do not fret, pet; maybe someone will bail you out of stir. You still have your long legs and eyelashes. They say there is a sucker born every minute. You are a pretty swell-looking purebred, after all, both you *and* your sister."

"S-sister?" She swishes past me nervously, twitching her tail in a way that is not a come-on. "I have no sister, I told you. That was a lie."

"Sure you do." I nod at the subdued gunsel everybody has overlooked. "In that corner, we have Wilma Leigh, aka Whimsy. And here, weighing in at seven pounds soaking wet, is her sister Wonder, aka Babette. No wonder you disarmed 'Wilmar' so easily just now. How long did your sister work for the Fat Cat by posing as a pansy?"

"Louie . . . what are you saying?"

"You gave it away yourself. Came from Malta, you said. Could not help bragging about your exotic origins. That was about the only honest thing you said. See, there is this small oddity about certain types of purebreds that gave you away. If you had not snagged the black bird, your sister would have been around to collect it off Spongecake and Thebes when they got it. She was your ace in the hole. Either way, Midnight Louie would have been out in the cold wailing Dixie, and I do not play the patsy for any dame."

Wilma is ankling over, shaking herself out of the nondescript tan trenchcoat that hid her natural coat of creamy blonde fur. Once Wilma doffs her macho demeanor she proves to be a nubile lady with eyelashes as extenuated as the gams on a daddy-longlegs.

"You are both the unacknowledged daughters of the general, the Russian blue from Malta who owned the bird," I tell them. "There is something called the Maltese dilution in cat-breeding circles, with which I am not normally intimate, I admit.

"In the Maltese dilution, a coat that is black dilutes to blue, and one that is yellow dilutes to cream. The Russian blue was already one watered-down dude. You two came from the same litter—twin sisters, only one of you came out cream, and the other gray. It is a Maltese peculiarity. You remember when I met you, angel? I said I had heard of Malta. As it happens, the dilution is the solution."

"Will you turn us in, Louie?" Babette pouts, pressing her warm soft body close to mine.

"I should."

Wilma presses close to my other side, giving me the eye but no lip.

"Naw," I decide. "The bird is a family heirloom of sorts. But I will never turn my back on you two."

As the evening turns out, such a maneuver is not in the least necessary. I must say that these Maltese dilutions lack for nothing when it comes to nocturnal gymnastics.

As for the bird, the twins insist that it is valuable to their esteemed daddy for reasons relating not to diamonds, but to dinner. Some gourmands, they claim, would kill to consume a rare bird of proper vintage, much as other individuals would sell their souls for a bottle of Napoleon brandy. I tell the Maltese sisters that I wish to keep the black bird for a while as a souvenir, and they can hardly object.

The next morning—late—I take it over to a friend of mine who runs a used musical instrument shop off the Strip. This dude can play a riff on a piano that would have a shar-pei tapping its tail, and that particular breed is notoriously tone-deaf. My pal is also something of a feather fancier. His moniker is Earl E. Bird. He shares the same sophisticated coloring I do, only he happens to be short on hair, long on skin and as bald as an eight ball on top of it.

I show him the bird.

He jerks off the hood and smiles until he exposes what look like all fifty-two ivories in his mouth.

"Say, Louie, my man! Where did you get this? This here bird is a genuine mynah, or maybe a raven. Or possibly a crow."

Some expert. "Do these mynahs, ravens and crows live for a long time?"

"Some parrots can reach a hundred."

I would whistle if I could; most dudes I know do not make much more than twelve. "I had in mind about a hundred and fifty years."

Earl E. shrugs. "I do not know how well these black birds age, but I know this one to be a mellow fellow, and an oracle of old. Talks, if you know what to say to it. What is the word, bird? Tell me your name. Where are the seven keys to Baldpate? When will the Cubs win the World Series?"

Earl E. can go on like this indefinitely, but at this interrogation the bird finally perks up, cocks its head, flashes a beady eye about the premises and intones, "Nevermore."

I wish that I could say what this means, since I have a feeling that it expresses the dark, brooding soul of mystery itself. But I am a practical dude, not a poet. At that pivotal moment I find the room spinning as if I had imbibed another shot-glass of Spongecake's spiked Coffeemate.

The bird starts flapping its wings and squawking "Nevermores." Brass instruments glitter past like a carousel. Must have been something Maltese I had for dinner the night before.

As my vision clears, I find myself alone in Miss Temple Barr's comfy condominium, stretched out on her batik pillows with one mitt on the televison remote control.

Some black-and-white film of days gone by is reeling off the screen. I breathe a sigh of relief. For a moment, in my mental fog, I thought that this vintage classic had been colorized. As anyone of any taste whatsoever knows, the only classic colors in film and real life are black with a dash of white around the whiskers and the incisors.

I still cannot figure out how the bird lasted almost a hundred and fifty years, or who would pay big dough to consume such a senior citizen. I do know one thing: if Midnight Louie keeps snoozing in front of the television set, the Bogeyman will get him.

J. A. Jance

THE DUEL

Howard was nothing if not dependable. Living up to his reputation for constant vigilance, he was at his assigned post and standing guard, carefully studying the parade of homebound cars that tooled down the rainy, winter-darkened street. He examined each pair of fuzzy, rain-softened headlights, waiting for the one, all-important pair which would slice away from the others and turn onto the graveled driveway.

The atmosphere in the room was charged with floating particles of waiting while the graceful old Seth Thomas clock on the mantel ticked hollowly away. Every fifteen minutes it gave sonorous voice to each quarter-hour interval. The only other sounds in the chilly and ominously expectant house came from a single person playing cards. The cards slapped down angrily on the faded finish of the rosewood table where Anna played her ever-present game of solitaire.

The hands of the clock marched slowly, inevitably past the delicate Roman numerals on the mother-of-pearl clock face. It was late and getting later and still Edgar wasn't home. With each passing moment, Anna's playing grew more impassioned and frenetic. The cards hit the table with increasing force and urgency. The periodic shuffles were like threatening claps of thunder preceding an approaching storm.

"Any sign of him?" Anna asked without looking up.

Howard didn't move, and he didn't answer, either. That was to be expected. Howard never had been the talkative kind, nor was he particularly sociable. He seldom remained in the same room with them once Edgar arrived home. As soon as the Lord and Master stepped inside the front door—Lord and Master was the nickname Anna and Howard called Edgar behind his back—as soon as L&M came home, Howard would stalk off upstairs, leaving Anna to fend for herself, to deal with her husband on her own. Howard's position was that Edgar was Anna's problem.

Up to a point, that was true. But now, thank God and Federal Express, the two of them were evenly matched. Edgar no longer had her outgunned, as it were.

Her use of the word *outgunned* made her smile in spite of herself. Pausing briefly from her game of cards, Anna slipped one hand into the deep pocket of her heavy, terrycloth robe and let her fingers close tentatively around the rough grip of the still-almost-new Lady Smith and Wesson she kept concealed there. She touched the gun because it was there for the touching. She touched it for reassurance, and perhaps even for luck. Stroking the cool metal of the short barrel, she wondered if the confrontation would come tonight. If so, it would finally be over and done with, once and for all.

Anna Whalen no longer cared so much what the ultimate outcome would be. She just wanted out of limbo. Whatever the cost, she wanted the awful waiting to end.

And how long had she been waiting? Forever, it seemed, although it was probably only a matter of months since the situation had become really intolerable. Howard, ever observant, was the one who had first pointed Edgar's dalliance out to her. He was also the one who had realized and warned her that Edgar might try poison.

Initially, the idea of Edgar's poisoning her had seemed like a wildly farfetched idea, a preposterous, nightmarish joke. Anna had laughed it off, but later, the more she thought about it and the more she observed Edgar's increasingly suspicious behavior, the more it had made sense. After all, he was the only one in the house who did any cooking, such as it was. Eventually she realized that it would be a simple thing for him to slip some kind of death-inducing substance into her food.

Faced with this possibility, Anna and Howard had wisely hit upon a countermeasure. True friend that he was, Howard had generously agreed to taste whatever food appeared on Anna's plate. Howard tried everything first—everything that is, except green beans and snow peas. Howard despised green vegetables. Unfortunately, the frozen-dinner people were very big on snow peas this year. Friend or not, when servings of suspicious green things turned up on Anna's tray, Howard wouldn't touch them.

If she hadn't been cagey about it, green vegetables might well have been Anna's undoing, her Achilles heel. Instead, she carefully slipped the offending green things off her plate and surreptitiously stuffed them behind the cushion of her recliner whenever Edgar wasn't watching. Every morning, as soon as the Lord and Master was safely out of the house, she'd return to the chair and dispose of the previous evening's incriminating evidence. So far, so good.

Outside a passing car slowed, but it turned left into the Mossbecks' driveway across the street. Anna still called it Mossbecks' although the Mossbecks hadn't lived there in fifteen years. She had no idea who lived there now—some nameless, childless young couple who both had important, well-paying jobs in the city. Why someone like that needed a house as big as the Mossbecks' Anna couldn't imagine.

But then, to be fair, she and Edgar didn't need such a big house, either. They lived in only four of the downstairs rooms in Grandmother Adams's gnarled old house. Edgar was too tight to heat the rest of it. He claimed they couldn't afford it. He slept on a day bed in what had once been Cook's room off the kitchen. Anna's ornate bedroom suite had been moved downstairs into what had once been her grandmother's parlor. For years, no one but Howard had ventured upstairs, but he had assured Anna that he didn't mind the cold. In fact, he preferred it.

Actually, the escalating warfare between Edgar and Howard was what had finally alerted Anna to her own danger and to the possibility that another woman might be the root cause of all the trouble. Most of it anyhow. For at least six months now, Edgar had been coming home late on Tuesday nights, and only on Tuesdays. Howard, whose nose was particularly sensitive to such things, had detected a hint of very feminine perfume, the same scent every time, lingering on Edgar's clothing on each of those selfsame Tuesday nights. Anna had racked her brain to figure out who this perfume-drenched homewrecker might be.

Anna's forty-year marriage to Edgar had never been an especially happy one, but then neither one of them had been brought up to believe in happy marriages. Marriages lasted, of course, because that was expected. How one functioned inside those lasting marriages was left to the good grace and wit of the individuals involved.

Part of the problem was due to the fact that there had been certain misunderstandings from the very beginning which were traceable to parental meddling and mismanagement on both sides. Edgar had been touted to Anna's family as having "good breeding and good prospects" although the chief touter, mainly his widowed mother, should have been somewhat suspect as a source of reliable information. But then Anna's family wasn't entirely blameless when it came to stretching the truth either.

Edgar had presumably married for money without realizing that Anna's father, Bertram Quincy Adams III, had done an excellent job of concealing his own foolhardy squandering of the family fortunes. By the time Edgar discovered his wife was practically penniless, except for her grandmother's house and a small trust fund, he himself was far too committed to the gentlemanly lifestyle.

Anna Quincy Adams Whalen wasn't rich, but her pedigree opened doors that otherwise would have been closed to her husband on his own. Constitutionally unfit for regular work, Edgar shamelessly used Adams family connections to procure himself a couple of corporate directorships and a private school trusteeship. The small income from those combined with minimal Social Security checks kept the wolf from the door and paid the property taxes, but that was about it. They lived on the right side of town with a fashionable address but behind a closed door which carefully concealed their genteel poverty. To Anna's way of thinking there was nothing genteel about it.

She looked around the chilly room. What had once been a large, elegant dining room had been forced into the mold of dining and living room both. The extra leaves had long since disappeared from the rosewood table. Grandmother Adams's remaining furniture, quality once but now faded and dingy, had been pushed up against the walls to make room for a monster television set and two La-Z-Boy recliners which Anna found ungainly and uncomfortable both, but that was where she and her husband sat, night after night, matching bookends in their matching chairs, eating frozen dinners on TV trays while CNN droned on and on.

It would have been nice, every once in a while, to watch a sitcom or even one of those dreadful made-for-television police-dramas, but Edgar was the keeper of the remote control, and he liked to watch the news. When he was there they watched what he wanted. When he was gone, the television stayed off completely because Anna found the push-button controls far too complicated to understand.

Naturally, Edgar had bought the set without consulting her which may have been one reason why Anna hated it. The first she had known anything about it was when the delivery man rang the doorbell and asked her where she wanted him to set it up. Oh well, she had gotten even. Anna had made an unauthorized purchase of her own. The mail-order Smith and Wesson had come to the house less than five days after she phoned in her order. She had intercepted the VISA card bill for three months in a row, paying it herself out of her own paltry Social Security check until she had gotten the balance down low enough that Edgar hadn't questioned it.

Just then headlights flashed across the rain-splashed window. Tires crunched in the driveway. Edgar was home.

Howard got up at once. "Please don't leave me alone with him tonight," Anna begged, but Howard only shook his head and wouldn't stay. She resented it that he could so callously abandon her and leave her to face Edgar alone, but that was just the way Howard was. Over the years, it seemed as though she would have gotten used to it.

Edgar came into the room, set down his briefcase and grocery bag, and immediately closed the drapes. "How many times do I have to tell you to close the drapes in the winter? You're letting all the heat out."

"I forgot," Anna said, and continued to play her game of solitaire with diligent concentration.

Edgar went over to the television set and picked up the remote control. For a moment he stood staring down at the small electronic device on top of the set.

"Have you let the damn cat sit up on the cable box again? You let it wreck the last one. That's what the guy said, you know, that the insides were all plugged full of cat hair."

"Maybe it keeps his feet warm," Anna offered.

"Don't start with that 'the house is too cold' stuff again," Edgar said irritably. "If the house is too cold, close the damn drapes. Are you hungry?"

She wasn't, but Edgar liked to eat as soon as he got home so he could watch the news for the rest of the night without any unnecessary interruptions. "Yes," Anna said. "I could eat a horse."

"It's chicken," he said, picking up the groceries and carrying them into the kitchen. "Fried chicken, mashed potatoes, and corn."

Good, Anna thought. Howard liked corn. She listened to the familiar sounds from the kitchen—the tiny bleatings of the control on the microwave, ice tinkling into a glass, something, gin probably, being poured over the ice. Suddenly Anna found herself feeling sorry that it was corn instead of snow peas. She had wanted it to be tonight. She had wanted to end the uncertainty and get it over with.

The swinging door to the kitchen banged open. She knew without looking that Edgar was standing behind her, staring down over her shoulder at the cards scattered across the smooth surface of the table.

"Did you win today?" he asked.

"No."

Anna played a complicated, two-deck kind of solitaire which she won only once every year or so. If she had cheated, she probably would have won more often, but she was always scrupulously honest. She didn't like it when Edgar looked over her shoulder, though. Having him watch made her nervous, and she missed plays she could have made.

"Why don't you try a different game?" Edgar asked.

"I like this one," she replied.

The beeper on the microwave went off. Edgar returned to the kitchen. As soon as he left, Anna could see that she had missed putting the six of spades on the descending spades pile for at least three turns. Damn him. She threw down her cards in disgust and went to set the table.

That's what they called it, setting the table, although it was really nothing more than setting up the two TV trays. Edgar always brought the silverware and napkins in with him from the kitchen, but he liked to have the trays set up by the time he got there so he didn't have to stand there with his hands full and wait for her to do her part of the job.

The microwave was going again, and the door to the kitchen was shut. Edgar couldn't hear her.

"Howard," Anna called softly. "Howard. You come back down here. I need you." But for some strange reason, Howard didn't appear.

"Where's Howard?" Anna asked when Edgar brought the food in from the kitchen.

Edgar shrugged. "Beats me," he said. "I haven't seen him since I got home."

Anna waited, but still there was no sign of Howard. She didn't dare make a fuss or call to him again. Edgar was soon eating away, his eyes glued to the television set. Only when there was a station break did he turn to look at her.

"You're not eating your dinner," he said accusingly. "I thought you said you were hungry."

She was hungry, now. The smell of the food, the look of it, had made her hungry, but without Howard there to try it for her, she didn't dare eat any of it, and she was afraid to stuff the chicken, bones and all, down behind the cushion.

This must be it, she was thinking. He must have locked Howard away somewhere, so he can't help me. She slipped her hand into her pocket and screwed up her courage.

"Why are you doing this?"

He looked over at her, surprised. "Doing what? Watching television? I always watch television. You know that."

Her fingers closed around the grip of the pistol, but she didn't take it out of her pocket. Not yet. She didn't want to give everything away at once.

"Why are you trying to poison me?" she asked.

Edgar choked quite convincingly on a piece of chicken. "Me? Trying to poison you? Anna, you've got to be kidding! You've been reading too many books."

"There's another woman, isn't there, Edgar," she continued. Anna kept her voice low and even. She didn't want him to think she was just being hysterical. "You've been seeing another woman on the side for some time now, and the two of you are trying to get rid of me."

"My God, Anna, that's the wildest thing I've ever heard. Wherever did you come up with such a crazy, cockamamie idea?"

"Tuesdays," she answered. "It's because of Tuesdays. You're late coming home every single Tuesday without fail."

He looked relieved. "Oh, that," he said. "I've been seeing a counselor, trying to sort some things out in my own mind. And it's been helping more than you know. Maybe you should try it, see if it wouldn't help you as well. I could come home early enough to pick you up, and we could go see the counselor together. What would you think of that?"

The story about the counselor sounded vaguely possible, but she wasn't about to fall for it. "I don't believe you," she said, and pulled the gun.

Edgar's eyes filled with shocked disbelief. "My God, Anna! Where did you get that thing? Is it loaded?"

Of course it was loaded. What would be the point of carrying a gun that wasn't? Edgar started to get up, but she shot him square in the chest before he ever made it to his feet. The force of the blow flung him back into the chair which shifted automatically into the reclining position, leaving him with his feet jutting into the air like a helpless, overturned turtle. He lay there for some time, groaning and clutching his chest.

Anna watched him curiously. If he had tried to get up, she would have shot him again, but he didn't. Eventually he stopped groaning. His hands fell limply to his sides. Meanwhile, the news droned on and on, talking about something that was going on in the Middle East again . . . still. Anna didn't pay much attention. She wasn't particularly interested in world affairs.

After a while, though, when they started talking about a nationally known murder case, a trial that had been in process for several months and was just now going to the jury, she got interested in the program. Forgetting her customary caution, she began to eat her dinner. Anna was so interested in what the lady news commentator was saying, she barely noticed the funny almond taste of the corn.

Howard did, though. Much later, thinking Anna and Edgar must have fallen asleep in front of the droning television set, he finally crept back down from upstairs. The big yellow cat sniffed disdainfully at what was left of the corn on Anna's plate, but he had sense enough not to eat it. Howard's nose was far too sensitive for that.

Sharyn McCrumb

NINE LIVES TO LIVE

It had seemed like a good idea at the time. Of course, Philip Danby had only been joking, but he had said it in a serious tone in order to humor those idiot New Age clients who actually seemed to believe in the stuff. "I want to come back as a cat," he'd said, smiling facetiously into the candlelight at the Eskeridge dinner table. He had to hold his breath to keep from laughing as the others babbled about reincarnation. The women wanted to come back blonder and thinner, and the men wanted to be everything from Dallas Cowboys to oak trees. *Oak trees?* And he had to keep a straight face through it all, hoping these dodos would give the firm some business.

The things he had to put up with to humor clients. His partner, Giles Eskeridge, seemed to have no difficulties in that quarter, however. Giles often said that rich and crazy went together; therefore, architects who wanted a lucrative business had to be prepared to put up with eccentrics. They also had to put up with long hours, obstinate building contractors, and capricious zoning boards. Perhaps that was why Danby had plumped for life as a cat next time. As he had explained to his dinner companions that night, "Cats are independent. They don't have to kowtow to anybody; they sleep sixteen hours a day; and yet they get fed and sheltered and even loved—just for being their contrary little selves. It sounds like a good deal to me."

Julie Eskeridge tapped him playfully on the cheek. "You'd better take care to be a pretty, pedigreed kitty, Philip," she laughed. "Because life isn't so pleasant for an ugly old alley cat!"

"I'll keep that in mind," he told her. "In fifty years or so."

It had been more like fifty days. The fact that Giles had wanted to come back as a shark should have tipped him off. When they found out that they'd just built a three-million-dollar building on top of a toxic landfill, the contractor was happy to keep his mouth shut about it for a mere ten grand, and Giles was perfectly prepared to bury the evidence to protect the firm from lawsuits and EPA fines. Looking back on it, Danby realized that he should not have insisted that they report the landfill to the authorities. In particular, he should not have insisted on it at 6:00 P.M. at the building site with no one present but himself and Giles. That was literally a fatal error. Before you could say "philosophical differences," Giles had picked up a shovel lying near the offending trench, and with one brisk swing, he had sent the matter to a higher court. As he pitched headlong into the reeking evidence, Danby's last thought was a flicker of cold anger at the injustice of it all.

His next thought was that he was watching a black-and-white movie, while his brain seemed intent upon sorting out a flood of olfactory sensations. *Furniture polish . . . stale coffee . . . sweaty socks . . . Prell Shampoo . . . potting soil . . .* He shook his head, trying to clear his thoughts. Where was he? The apparent answer to that was: lying on a gray sofa inside the black-and-white movie, because everywhere he looked he saw the same colorless vista. A concussion, maybe? The memory of Giles Eskeridge swinging a shovel came back in a flash. Danby decided to call the police before Giles turned up to try again. He stood up, and promptly fell off the sofa.

Of course, he landed on his feet.

All four of them.

Idly, to keep from thinking anything more ominous for the moment, Danby wondered what *else* the New Age clients had been right about. Was Stonehenge a flying saucer landing pad? Did crystals lower cholesterol? He was in no position to doubt anything just now. He sat twitching his plume of a tail and wishing he hadn't been so flippant about the afterlife at the Eskeridge dinner party. He didn't even particularly like cats. He also wished that he could get his paws on Giles in retribution for the shovel incident. First he would bite Giles's neck, snapping his spine, and then he would let him escape for a few seconds. Then he'd sneak up behind him and pounce. Then bat him into a corner. Danby began to purr in happy contemplation.

The sight of a coffee table looming a foot above his head brought the problem into perspective. At present Danby weighed approximately fifteen furry pounds, and he was unsure of his exact whereabouts. Under those circumstances avenging his murder would be difficult. On the other hand, he didn't have any other pressing business, apart from an eight-hour nap which he felt in need of. First things first, though. Danby wanted to know what he looked like, and then he needed to find out where the kitchen was, and whether Sweaty Socks and Prell Shampoo had left anything edible on the counter tops. There would be time enough for philosophical thoughts and revenge plans when he was cleaning his whiskers.

The living room was enough to make an architect shudder. Clunky early American sofas and clutter. He was glad he couldn't see the color scheme. There was a mirror above the sofa, though, and he hopped up on the cheap upholstery to take a look at his new self. The face that looked back at him was definitely feline, and so malevolent that Danby wondered how anyone could mistake cats for pets. The yellow (or possibly green) almond eyes glowered at him from a massive triangular face, tiger-striped, and surrounded by a ruff of gray-brown fur. Just visible beneath the ruff was a dark leather collar equipped with a little brass bell. That would explain the ringing in his ears. The rest of his body seemed massive, even allowing for the fur, and the great plumed tail swayed rhythmically as he watched. He resisted a silly urge to swat at the reflected movement. So he was a tortoiseshell, or tabby, or whatever they called those brown striped cats, and his hair was long. And he was still male. He didn't need to check beneath his tail to confirm that. Besides, the reek of ammonia in the vicinity of the sofa suggested that he was not shy about proclaiming his masculinity in various corners of his domain.

No doubt it would have interested those New Age clowns to learn that he was not a kitten, but a fully-grown cat. Apparently the arrival had been instantaneous as well. He had always been given to understand that the afterlife would provide some kind of preliminary orientation before assigning him a new identity. A deity resembling John Denver, in rimless glasses and a Sierra Club tee shirt, should have been on hand with some paperwork regarding his case, and in a nonthreatening conference, they would decide what his karma entitled him to become. At least, that's what the New Agers had led him to believe. But it hadn't been like that at all. One minute he had been tumbling into a sewage pit, and the next: he had a craving for Meow Mix. Just like that. He wondered what sort of consciousness had been flickering inside that narrow skull prior to his arrival. Probably not much. A brain with the wattage of a lightning bug could control most of the items on the feline agenda: eat, sleep, snack, doze, dine, nap, and so on. Speaking of eating . . .

He made it to the floor in two moderate bounds, and jingled toward the kitchen, conveniently signposted by the smell of lemon-scented dishwashing soap and stale coffee. The floor could do with a good sweeping, too, he thought, noting with distaste the gritty feel of tracked-in dirt on his velvet paws.

The cat dish, tucked in a corner beside the sink cabinet, confirmed his worst fears about the inhabitants' instinct for tackiness. Two plastic bowls were inserted into a plywood cat model, painted white, and decorated with a cartoonish cat-face. If his food hadn't been at stake, Danby would have sprayed *that* as an indication of his professional judgment. As it was, he summoned a regal sneer, and bent down to inspect the offering. The water wasn't fresh; there were bits of dry cat food floating in it. Did they expect him to drink *that?* Perhaps he ought to dump it out so that they'd take the hint. And the dry cat food hadn't been stored in an airtight container, either. He sniffed contemptuously: the cheap brand, mostly cereal. He supposed he'd have to go out and kill something just to keep his ribs from crashing together. Better check out the counters for other options. It took considerable force to launch his bulk from floor to counter top, and for a moment he teetered on the edge of the sink, fighting to regain his balance, while his bell tolled ominously, but once he righted himself, he strolled onto the counter with an expression of nonchalance suggesting that his dignity had never been imperiled. He found two breakfast plates stacked in the sink. The top one was a trove of congealing egg yolk and bits of buttered toast. He finished it off, licking off every scrap of egg with his rough tongue, and thinking what a favor he was doing the people by cleaning the plate for them.

While he was on the sink, he peeked out the kitchen window to see if he could figure out where he was. The lawn outside was thick and luxurious, and a spreading oak tree grew beside a low stone wall. Well, it wasn't Albuquerque. Probably not California, either, considering the healthy appearance of the grass. Maybe he was still in Maryland. It certainly looked like home. Perhaps the transmigration of souls has a limited geographic range, like AM radio stations. After a few moments consideration, while he washed an offending forepaw, it occurred to Danby to look at the wall phone above the counter. The numbers made sense to him, so apparently he hadn't lost the ability to read. Sure enough, the telephone area code was 301. He wasn't far from where he started. Theoretically, at least, Giles was within reach. He must mull that over, from the vantage point of the window sill, where the afternoon sun was marvelously warm, and soothing . . . zzzzz.

Danby awakened several hours later to a braying female voice calling out, "Tigger! Get down from there this minute! Are you glad Mommy's home, sweetie?"

Danby opened one eye, and regarded the woman with an insolent stare. *Tigger?* Was there no limit to the indignities he must bear? A fresh wave of Prell Shampoo told him that the self-proclaimed "Mommy" was chatelaine of this bourgeois bungalow. And didn't she look the part, too, with her polyester pants suit and her cascading chins! She set a grocery bag and a stack of letters on the counter top, and held out her arms to him. "And is my snook-ums ready for din-din?" she cooed.

He favored her with an extravagant yawn, followed by his most forbidding Mongol glare, but his hostility was wasted on the besotted Mrs. . . . (he glanced down at the pile of letters) . . . Sherrod. She continued to beam at him as if he had fawned at her feet. As it was, he was so busy studying the address on the Sherrod junk mail that he barely glanced at her. He hadn't left town! His tail twitched triumphantly. Morning Glory Lane was not familiar to him, but he'd be willing to bet that it was a street in Sussex Garden Estates, just off the by-pass. That was a couple of miles from Giles Eskeridge's mock-Tudor monstrosity, but with a little luck and some common sense about traffic he could walk there in a couple of hours. If he cut through the fields, he might be able to score a mouse or two on the way.

Spurred on by the thought of a fresh, tasty dinner that would beg for its life, Danby/Tigger trotted to the back door and began to meow piteously, putting his forepaws as far up the screen door as he could reach.

"Now, Tigger!" said Mrs. Sherrod in her most arch tone. "You know perfectly well that there's a litter box in the bathroom. You just want to get outdoors so that you can tomcat around, don't you?" With that she began to put away groceries, humming tunelessly to herself.

Danby fixed a venomous stare at her retreating figure, and then turned his attention back to the problem at hand. Or rather, at paw. That was just the trouble: Look, Ma, no hands! Still, he thought, there ought to be a way. Because it was warm outside, the outer door was open, leaving only the metal storm door between himself and freedom. Its latch was the straight-handled kind that you pushed down to open the door. Danby considered the factors: door handle three feet above floor; latch opens on downward pressure; one fifteen-pound cat intent upon going out. With a vertical bound that Michael Jordan would have envied, Danby catapulted himself upward and caught onto the handle, which obligingly twisted downward, as the door swung open at the weight of the feline cannonball. By the time gravity took over and returned him to the ground, he was claw-deep in scratchy, sweet-smelling grass.

As he loped off toward the street, he could hear a plaintive voice wailing, "Ti-iii-ggerr!" It almost drowned out the jingling of that damned little bell around his neck.

Twenty minutes later Danby was sunning himself on a rock in an abandoned field, recovering from the exertion of moving faster than a stroll. In the distance he could hear the drone of cars from the interstate, as the smell of gasoline wafted in on a gentle breeze. As he had trotted through the neighborhood, he'd read street signs, so he had a better idea of his whereabouts now. Windsor Forest, that pretentious little suburb that Giles called home, was only a few miles away, and once he crossed the interstate, he could take a short cut through the woods. He hoped that La Sherrod wouldn't put out an all-points bulletin for her missing kitty. He didn't want any SPCA interruptions once he reached his destination. He ought to ditch the collar as well, he thought. He couldn't very well pose as a stray with a little bell under his chin.

Fortunately, the collar was loose, probably because the ruff around his head made his neck look twice as large. Once he determined that, it took only a few minutes of concentrated effort to work the collar forward with his paws until it slipped over his ears. After that, a shake of the head—jingle! jingle!—rid him of Tigger's identity. He wondered how many pets who "just disappeared one day" had acquired new identities and went off on more pressing business.

He managed to reach the by-pass before five o'clock, thus avoiding the commuter traffic of rush hour. Since he understood automobiles, it was a relatively simple matter for Danby to cross the highway during a lull between cars. He didn't see what the possums found so difficult about road crossing. Sure enough, there was a ripe gray corpse on the white line, a mute testimony to the dangers of indecision on highways. He took a perfunctory sniff, but the roadkill was too far gone to interest anything except the buzzards.

Once across the road, Danby stuck to the fields, making sure that he paralleled the road that led to Windsor Forest. His attention was occasionally diverted by a flock of birds overhead, or an enticing rustle in the grass that might have been a field mouse, but he kept going. If he didn't reach the Eskeridge house by nightfall, he would have to wait until morning to get himself noticed.

In order to get at Giles, Danby reasoned that he would first have to charm Julie Eskeridge. He wondered if she were susceptible to needy animals. He couldn't remember whether they had a cat or not. An unspayed female would be nice, he thought; a Siamese, perhaps, with big blue eyes and a sexy voice.

Danby reasoned that he wouldn't have too much trouble finding Giles's house. He had been there often enough as a guest. Besides, the firm had designed and built several of the overwrought mansions in the spacious subdivision. Danby had once suggested that they buy Palladian windows by the gross, since every nouveau riche homebuilder insisted on having a brace of them, no matter what style of house he had commissioned. Giles had not been amused by Danby's observation. He seldom was. What Giles lacked in humor, he also lacked in scruples and moral restraint, but he compensated for these deficiencies with a highly-developed instinct for making and holding onto money. While he'd lacked Danby's talent in design and execution, he had a genius for turning up wealthy clients, and for persuading these tasteless yobbos to spend a fortune on their showpiece homes. Danby did draw the line at carving up antique Sheraton sideboards to use as bathroom sink cabinets, though. When he also drew the line at environmental crime, Giles had apparently found his conscience an expensive luxury that the firm could not afford. Hence, the shallow grave at the new construction site, and Danby's new lease on life. It was really quite unfair of Giles, Danby reflected. They'd been friends since college, and after Danby's parents died, he had left a will leaving his share of the business to Giles. And how had Giles repaid this friendship? With the blunt end of a shovel. Danby stopped to sharpen his claws on the bark of a handy pine tree. Really, he thought, Giles deserved no mercy whatsoever. Which was just as well, because, catlike, Danby possessed none.

The sun was low behind the surrounding pines by the time Danby arrived at the Eskeridges' mock-Tudor home. He had been delayed en route by the scent of another cat, a neutered orange male. (Even to his color-blind eyes, an orange cat was recognizable. It might be the shade of gray, or the configuration of white at the throat and chest.) He had hunted up this fellow feline, and made considerable efforts to communicate, but as far as he could tell, there was no higher intelligence flickering behind its blank green eyes. There was no intelligence at all, as far as Danby was concerned; he'd as soon try talking to a shrub. Finally tiring of the eunuch's unblinking stare, he'd stalked off, forgoing more social experiments in favor of his mission.

He sat for a long time under the forsythia hedge in Giles's front yard, studying the house for signs of life. He refused to be distracted by a cluster of sparrows cavorting on the birdbath, but he realized that unless a meal was forthcoming soon, he would be reduced to foraging. The idea of hurling his bulk at a few ounces of twittering songbird made his scowl even more forbidding than usual. He licked a front paw and glowered at the silent house.

After twenty minutes or so, he heard the distant hum of a car engine, and smelled gasoline fumes. Danby peered out from the hedge in time to see Julie Eskeridge's Mercedes rounding the corner from Windsor Way. With a few hasty licks to smooth down his ruff, Danby sauntered toward the driveway, just as the car pulled in. Now for the hard part; how do you impress Julie Eskeridge without a checkbook?

He had never noticed before how much Giles's wife resembled a giraffe. He blinked at the sight of her huge feet swinging out of the car perilously close to his nose. They were followed by two replicas of the Alaska pipeline, both encased in nylon. Better not jump up on her; one claw on the stockings, and he'd have an enemy for life. Julie was one of those people who air-kissed because she couldn't bear to spoil her make-up. Instead of trying to attract her attention at the car (where she could have skewered him with one spike heel), Danby loped to the steps of the side porch, and began meowing piteously. As Julie approached the steps, he looked up at her with wide-eyed supplication, waiting to be admired.

"Shoo, cat!" said Julie, nudging him aside with her foot.

As the door slammed in his face, Danby realized that he had badly miscalculated. He had also neglected to devise a backup plan. A fine mess he was in now. It wasn't enough that he was murdered, and reassigned to cathood—now he was also homeless.

He was still hanging around the steps twenty minutes later when Giles came home, mainly because he couldn't think of an alternate plan just yet. When he saw Giles's black sports car pull up behind Julie's Mercedes, Danby's first impulse was to run, but then he realized that, while Giles might see him, he certainly wouldn't recognize him as his old business partner. Besides, he was curious to see how an uncaught murderer looked. Would Giles be haggard with grief and remorse? Furtive, as he listened for police sirens in the distance?

Giles Eskeridge was whistling. He climbed out of his car, suntanned and smiling, with his lips pursed in a cheerfully tuneless whistle. Danby trotted forward to confront his murderer with his haughtiest scowl of indignation. The reaction was not quite what he expected.

Giles saw the huge, fluffy cat, and immediately knelt down, calling, "Here, kitty, kitty!"

Danby looked at him as if he had been propositioned.

"Aren't you a beauty!" said Giles, holding out his hand to the strange cat. "I'll bet you're a pedigreed animal, aren't you, fella? Are you lost, boy?"

Much as it pained him to associate with a remorseless killer, Danby sidled over to the outstretched hand, and allowed his ears to be scratched. He reasoned that Giles's interest in him was his one chance to gain entry to the house. It was obvious that Julie wasn't a cat fancier. Who would have taken heartless old Giles for an animal lover? Probably similarity of temperament, Danby decided.

He allowed himself to be picked up, and carried into the house, while Giles stroked his back and told him what a pretty fellow he was.

This was an indignity, but still an improvement over Giles's behavior toward him during their last encounter. Once inside, Giles called out to Julie, "Look what I've got, honey!"

She came in from the kitchen, scowling. "That nasty cat!" she said. "Put him right back outside!"

At this point Danby concentrated all his energies toward making himself purr. It was something like snoring, he decided, but it had the desired effect on his intended victim, for at once Giles made for his den, and plumped down in an armchair, arranging Danby in his lap, with more petting and praise. "He's a wonderful cat, Julie," Giles told his wife. "I'll bet he's a purebred Maine Coon. Probably worth a couple of hundred bucks."

"So are my wool carpets," Mrs. Eskeridge replied. "So are my new sofas! And who's going to clean up his messes?"

That was Danby's cue. He had already thought out the piece de resistance in his campaign of endearment. With a trill that meant "This way, folks!", Danby hopped off his ex-partner's lap, and trotted to the downstairs bathroom. He had used it often enough at dinner parties, and he knew that the door was left ajar. He had been saving up for this moment. With Giles and his missus watching from the doorway, Danby hopped up on the toilet seat, twitched his elegant plumed tail, and proceeded to use the toilet in the correct manner.

He felt a strange tingling in his paws, and he longed to scratch at something and cover it up, but he ignored these urges, and basked instead in the effusive praise from his self-appointed champion. Why couldn't Giles have been that enthusiastic over his design for the Jenner building? Danby thought resentfully. Some people's sense of values were so warped. Meanwhile, though, he might as well savor the Eskeridges' transports of joy over his bowel control; there weren't too many ways for cats to demonstrate superior intelligence. He couldn't quote a little Shakespeare or identify the dinner wine. Fortunately, among felines toilet training passed for genius, and even Julie was impressed with his accomplishments. After that, there was no question of Giles turning him out into the cruel world. Instead, they carried him back to the kitchen, and opened a can of tuna fish for his dining pleasure. He had to eat it in a bowl on the floor, but the bowl was Royal Doulton, which was some consolation. And while he ate, he could still hear Giles in the background, raving about what a wonderful cat he was. He was in.

"No collar, Julie. Someone must have abandoned him on the highway. What shall we call him?"

"Varmint," his wife suggested. She was a hard sell.

Giles ignored her lack of enthusiasm for his newfound prodigy. "I think I'll call him Merlin. He's a wizard of a cat."

Merlin? Danby looked up with a mouthful of tuna. Oh well, he thought, Merlin and tuna were better than Tigger and cheap dry cat food. You couldn't have everything.

After that, he quickly became a full-fledged member of the household, with a newly-purchased plastic feeding bowl, a catnip mouse toy, and another little collar with another damned bell. Danby resisted the urge to bite Giles's thumb off while he was attaching this loathsome neckpiece over his ruff, but he restrained himself. By now he was accustomed to the accompaniment of a maniacal jingling with every step he took. What was it with human beings and bells?

Of course, that spoiled his plans for songbird hunting outdoors. He'd have to travel faster than the speed of sound to catch a sparrow now. Not that he got out much, anyhow. Giles seemed to think that he might wander off again, so he was generally careful to keep Danby housebound.

That was all right with Danby, though. It gave him an excellent opportunity to become familiar with the house, and with the routine of its inhabitants—all useful information for someone planning revenge. So far he (the old Danby, that is) had not been mentioned in the Eskeridge conversations. He wondered what story Giles was giving out about his disappearance. Apparently the body had not been found. It was up to him to punish the guilty, then.

Danby welcomed the days when both Giles and Julie left the house. Then he would forgo his morning, mid-morning, and early afternoon naps in order to investigate each room of his domain, looking for lethal opportunities: medicine bottles, perhaps, or perhaps a small electrical appliance that he could push into the bathtub.

So far, though, he had not attempted to stage any accidents, for fear that the wrong Eskeridge would fall victim to his snare. He didn't like Julie any more than she liked him, but he had no reason to kill her. The whole business needed careful study. He could afford to take his time analyzing the opportunities for revenge. The food was good, the job of house cat was undemanding, and he rather enjoyed the irony of being doted on by his intended victim. Giles was certainly better as an owner than he was as a partner.

An evening conversation between Giles and Julie convinced him that he must accelerate his efforts. They were sitting in the den, after a meal of baked chicken. They wouldn't give him the bones, though. Giles kept insisting that they'd splinter in his stomach and kill him. Danby was lying on the hearth rug, pretending to be asleep until they forgot about him, at which time he would sneak back into the kitchen and raid the garbage. He'd given up smoking, hadn't he? And although he'd lapped up a bit of Giles's Scotch one night, he seemed to have lost the taste for it. How much prudence could he stand?

"If you're absolutely set on keeping this cat, Giles," said Julie Eskeridge, examining her newly-polished talons, "I suppose I'll have to be the one to take him to the vet."

"The vet. I hadn't thought about it. Of course, he'll have to have shots, won't he?" murmured Giles, still studying the newspaper. "Rabies, and so on."

"And while we're at it, we might as well have him neutered," said Julie. "Otherwise, he'll start spraying the drapes and all."

Danby rocketed to full alert. To keep them from suspecting his comprehension, he centered his attention on the cleaning of a perfectly tidy front paw. It was time to step up the pace on his plans for revenge, or he'd be meowing in soprano. And forget the scruples about innocent bystanders: now it was a matter of self-defense.

That night he waited until the house was dark and quiet. Giles and Julie usually went to bed about eleven-thirty, turning off all the lights, which didn't faze him in the least. He rather enjoyed skulking about the silent house using his infrared vision, although he rather missed late-night television. He had once considered turning the set on with his paw, but that seemed too precocious, even for a cat named Merlin. Danby didn't want to end up in somebody's behavior lab with wires coming out of his head.

He examined his collection of cat toys, stowed by Julie in his cat basket, because she hated clutter. He had a mouse-shaped catnip toy, a rubber fish, and a little red ball. Giles bought the ball under the ludicrous impression that Danby could be induced to play catch. When he'd rolled it across the floor, Danby lay down and gave him an insolent stare. He had enjoyed the next quarter of an hour, watching Giles on his hands and knees, batting the ball, and trying to teach Danby to fetch, but finally Giles gave up, and the ball had been tucked in the cat basket ever since. Danby picked it up with his teeth, and carried it upstairs. Giles and Julie came down the right side of the staircase, didn't they? That's where the banister was. He set the ball carefully on the third step, in the approximate place that a human foot would touch the stair. A tripwire would be more reliable, but Danby couldn't manage the technology involved.

What else could he devise for the Eskeridges' peril? He couldn't poison their food, and since they'd provided him with a flea collar, he couldn't even hope to get bubonic plague started in the household. Attacking them with tooth and claw seemed foolhardy, even if they were sleeping. The one he wasn't biting could always fight him off, and a fifteen-pound cat can be killed with relative ease by any human determined to do it. Even if they didn't kill him on the spot, they'd get rid of him immediately, and then he'd lose his chance forever. It was too risky.

It had to be stealth, then. Danby inspected the house, looking for lethal opportunities. There weren't any electrical appliances close to the bathtub, and besides, Giles took showers. In another life Danby might have been able to rewire the electric razor to shock its user, but such a feat was well beyond his present level of dexterity. No wonder human beings had taken over the earth; they were so damned hard to kill.

Even his efforts to enlist help in the task had proved fruitless. On one of his rare excursions out of the house (Giles went golfing, and he slipped out without Julie's noticing), Danby had roamed the neighborhood, looking for . . . well . . . pussy. Instead he'd found dimwitted tomcats, and a Doberman pinscher, who was definitely Somebody. Danby had kept conversation to a minimum, not quite liking the look of the beast's prominent fangs. Danby suspected that the Doberman had previously been an IRS agent. Of course, the dog had *said* that it had been a serial killer, but that was just to lull Danby into a false sense of security. Anyhow, much as the dog approved of Danby's plan to kill his humans, he wasn't interested in forming a conspiracy. Why should he go to the gas chamber to solve someone else's problem?

Danby himself had similar qualms about doing anything too drastic—such as setting fire to the house. He didn't want to stage an accident that would include himself among the victims. After puttering about the darkened house for a wearying few hours, he stretched out on the sofa in the den to take a quick nap before resuming his plotting. He'd be able to think better after he rested.

The next thing Danby felt was a ruthless grip on his collar, dragging him forward. He opened his eyes to find that it was morning, and that the hand at his throat belonged to Julie Eskeridge, who was trying to stuff him into a metal cat carrier. He tried to dig his claws into the sofa, but it was too late. Before he could blink, he had been hoisted along by his tail, and shoved into the box. He barely got his tail out of the way before the door slammed shut behind him. Danby crouched in the plastic carrier, peeking out the side slits, and trying to figure out what to do next. Obviously the rubber ball on the steps had been a dismal failure as a murder weapon. Why couldn't he have come back as a mountain lion?

Danby fumed about the slings and arrows of outrageous fortune all the way out to the car. It didn't help to remember where he was going, and what was scheduled to be done with him shortly thereafter. Julie Eskeridge set the cat carrier on the back seat and slammed the door. When she started the car, Danby howled in protest.

"Be quiet back there!" Julie called out. "There's nothing you can do about it."

We'll see about that, thought Danby, turning to peer out the door of his cage. The steel bars of the door were about an inch apart, and there was no mesh or other obstruction between them. He found that he could easily slide one paw sideways out of the cage. Now, if he could just get a look at the workings of the latch, there was a slight chance that he could extricate himself. He lay down on his side and squinted up at the metal catch. It seemed to be a glorified bolt. To lock the carrier, a metal bar was slid into a socket and then rotated downward to latch. If he could push the bar back up and then slide it back . . .

It wasn't easy to maneuver with the car changing speed and turning corners. Danby felt himself getting quite dizzy with the effort of concentrating as the carrier gently rocked. But finally, when the car reached the interstate and sped along smoothly, he succeeded in positioning his paw at the right place on the bar, and easing it upward. Another three minutes of tense probing allowed him to slide the bar a fraction of an inch, and then another. The bolt was now clear of the latch. There was no getting out of the car, of course. Julie had rolled up the windows, and they were going sixty miles an hour. Danby spent a full minute pondering the implications of his dilemma. But no matter which way he looked at the problem, the alternative was always the same: do something desperate or go under the knife. It wasn't as if dying had been such a big deal, after all. There was always next time.

Quickly, before the fear could stop him, Danby hurled his furry bulk against the door of the cat carrier, landing in the floor of the backseat with a solid thump. He sprang back up on the seat, and launched himself into the air with a heartfelt snarl, landing precariously on Julie Eskeridge's right shoulder, and digging his claws in to keep from falling.

The last things he remembered were Julie's screams and the feel of the car swerving out of control.

When Danby opened his eyes, the world was still playing in black and white. He could hear muffled voices, and smell a jumble of scents: blood, gasoline, smoke. He struggled to get up, and found that he was still less than a foot off the ground. Still furry. Still the Eskeridges' cat. In the distance he could see the crumpled wreckage of Julie's car.

A familiar voice was droning on above him. "He must have been thrown free of the cat carrier during the wreck, Officer. That's definitely Merlin, though. My poor wife was taking him to the vet."

A burly policeman was standing next to Giles, nodding sympathetically. "I guess it's true what they say about cats, sir. Having nine lives, I mean. I'm very sorry about your wife. She wasn't so lucky."

Giles hung his head. "No. It's been a great strain. First my business partner disappears, and now I lose my wife." He stooped and picked up Danby. "At least I have my beautiful kitty-cat for consolation. Come on, boy. Let's go home."

Danby's malevolent yellow stare did not waver. He allowed himself to be carried away to Giles's waiting car without protest. He could wait. Cats were good at waiting. And life with Giles wasn't so bad, now that Julie wouldn't be around to harass him. Danby would enjoy a spell of being doted on by an indulgent human; fed gourmet cat food; and given the run of the house. Meanwhile, he could continue to leave the occasional ball on the stairs, and think of other ways to toy with Giles, while he waited to see if the police ever turned up to ask Giles about his missing partner. If not, Danby could work on more ways to kill humans. Sooner or later he would succeed. Cats are endlessly patient at stalking their prey.

"It's just you and me, now, fella," said Giles, placing his cat on the seat beside him.

And after he killed Giles, perhaps he could go in search of the building contractor that Giles bribed to keep his dirty secret. He certainly deserved to die. And that nasty woman Danby used to live next door to, who used to complain about his stereo and his crabgrass. And perhaps the surly headwaiter at *Chantage*. Stray cats can turn up anywhere.

Danby began to purr.

Nancy Pickard

FAT CAT

"Zeke, have a heart. How would it *look?"*

My friend, the Mt. Floresta chief of police, Jamison Grant, screwed up his face into what he apparently thought was a pleading expression. The effect produced among the deep, tanned wrinkles of his fifty-six years was unnervingly grotesque.

"So that's how you get criminals to confess." I grimaced back at him. Not the same effect, though, me being thirty years younger. "No need to beat it out of them. Just pull a face like that and they'll say anything."

Having thrown himself on my mercy and found it wanting, Jamison resorted to his own particular brand of subtlety. "Now listen, you harebrain." He sucked in his stomach behind his massive brass belt buckle and pulled his gargantuan frame upward until his face hovered several inches above my own six feet. From up there, like a great blue bald-headed eagle, he loomed. I was not intimidated. Insulted, maybe, but not intimidated. The legal eagle squawked: "Now this may be a small town, and we may not get reams of rapes and murders to keep us busy, but that does not mean I am free to go chasing some old lady's damn cat!"

"It's more than one cat and more than one old lady," I informed him. "And they're not all old. The ladies, I mean. I can name you at least one who's young and pretty."

"Do not interrupt me when I am being officious," Jamison said sternly. He grabbed a sheaf of paperwork from the in-basket on his desk and fanned the air in front of my nose with it. "Do you see these papers? *All* these papers? If you were to examine them closely, you would see there are blanks on them. I have to fill out those blanks, Zeke. And I have two thefts to investigate, one mayor to meet, the owner of a health spa to placate, three trials to attend in Gunnison, and a hell of a lot of other *important* work to do."

"The cats are important to their owners," I protested.

As owner, manager and general runabout for our town's animal shelter, I know a priority when I see one. It was quickly evident, however, that my priorities were not necessarily those of the Mt. Floresta, Colorado, police force.

"I don't even *like* cats," the bald eagle reminded me. Under the fluorescent light, his shiny pate gleamed. "Cats are sneaky, like thieves in the night and some young friends I could mention."

I decided it was the better part of caution not to argue with him. When you're an animal freak, as I am, sometimes you forget all the world does not love a cat. So I said in my best martyr's tone, "Okay, okay. I don't know what's become of the police in this town. Used to be they'd come help you get a kitten out of a tree, just one little kitten—"

"That was the firemen, Ezekiel."

"But now—" I waved my arms to encompass the entire one-room police station. "But now, I can't even get your attention when fifteen cats vanish."

"You exaggerate."

"No way, Jamison. I swear to God, fifteen cats have disappeared from this town in the last two months. And there may be more, for all I know."

"They got run over."

"Nope. No bodies, no squashed cat bodies lying around the streets. And don't tell me they ran away from home. These are pets, gorgeous cats, mamma's little darlings."

"Zeke." Jamison's voice dripped compassion. "Old pal, friend of my own son, I would love to help you. You know I'd do anything if I could—"

"Yeah, right!"

"—but you are a fanatic when it comes to animals. And fanatics cannot see the forest for the aspens, the glacier for the ice. Just trust me on this one. There is no mystery. There is no problem. Cats come, cats go. Like tourists. And, like tourists, not soon enough, in my opinion."

I squinted my eyes like an angry tom. "You forgetting the cat lobby, Jamison?"

"The what?" He looked suspiciously on the verge of laughing.

I yelled at my friend the political appointee, "Cat owners vote, you know!" I let the door slam behind me when I stomped out of the station.

Outside, the crisp mountain air cooled me off as it always does. There's something about living in the mountains, at 10,000 feet above sea level, that puts things in perspective, or so the tourists say. I wouldn't know. Having lived in Mt. Floresta all my life, I have no perspective on that. Maybe Jamison was right, I thought, maybe I have blown this out of proportion. I snapped my ski vest shut against the fall wind and hiked up my jeans. Worry makes me lose weight, and I'd been getting real concerned about the increasing number of lost-cat reports coming into my office from distraught cat owners.

"Mr. Ezekiel Leonard?" That's how many of the calls began. The really older ladies called me by my full name and mister. It made me feel older than my twenty-six years, and smarter, which is possibly what they hoped I was. Like most of the cat owners, they sounded nervous, timorous, hesitant to bother me, and sad. "Mr. Leonard," they'd say, "my Snowflake has disappeared." Or Big Boy or Thomasina or Annabelle. "He's (she's) never done this before, and I just don't know what to think. I've looked everywhere, and I've asked everybody I know. But nobody has seen my Big Boy (or Thomasina or Snowflake) since Tuesday."

At first, I didn't attach any significance to the calls. I just searched our pens for a feline of the right description and then assured the caller I'd keep an eye out for kitty. Then I'd add kitty's name and phone number to my "missing" list.

It took me a while to notice how long that list was getting. And how few names I was crossing off. Oh, I found Mrs. McCarty's Siamese and returned him. And I had to break the news to Bobby Henderson after I saw his calico lying by the side of the highway. But by the end of September, the obvious was becoming just that: seventeen pet cats had been declared missing since August and I'd found only two of them. I was sure somebody was stealing them. But what the hell would somebody want with fifteen very spoiled cats? There wasn't any animal experimentation lab in the county, or anywhere else nearby that I knew of. And I made it my business to know such things. I just couldn't figure it out.

I broke off my reverie on the steps of the police station and headed down Silverado Street toward the office of the *Lode,* which passes for a newspaper in our town. "Get a Lode of This!" is their motto, which actually appears above the masthead. I guess everything's a lot more casual up here in the mountains, where everybody wears blue jeans and nobody ever wears a suit, except maybe visiting bank examiners.

Mt. Floresta is an old mining center turned chic: we're about as "in" as a ski resort can get and still stand itself. We have your restored Victorian buildings, we have your ugly new condos, we have your charming gas streetlights and your café au laits, we have your lift tickets and your gourmet restaurants, we have your drunk tourists and your inflated prices. We also have a lot of great big dogs—Malamutes, Samoyeds, huskies, and the like—that people who move here think they just have to have along with a nice cat to sit by the fire at their rental hearth. And then, when they move out after getting a taste of one whole cold long snowy winter season, they sometimes abandon those poor creatures, and that's where I come in, at the Mt. Floresta Animal Shelter located on the edge of town just around the corner of the closest mountain.

As I walked, I ducked my head, but not against the wind or the tourists. The longer I went without finding those cats, the harder it was to face the cat lovers in town. I knew if I encountered the lugubrious eyes of Miss Emily Parson one more time I'd go jump in Spirit Lake. Miss Parson's great black Angora, Puddy, was among the missing.

I was so intent on making like a turtle that I nearly collided with the current love of my life.

"Hello, Atlas," she said. "World a little heavy on those shoulders?"

"Hi, Abby." I leaned down and kissed her cheek, which was soft and downy and well shaped like the rest of her. Abigail Frances, late of New York, was by far the best of the current crop of easterners to have fallen in love with our town and decided to grace us with their permanent presence. If I sound cynical, it's because in a resort town, *permanent* has a shelf life of about nine months. I've gotten leery of making new friends and weary of farewell parties.

"No luck with the police?"

There was sympathy in her soft voice, but I thought I detected an edge to it that had nothing to do with her New York accent. If I was a fanatic, Abby was a flaming zealot when it came to cats and, as I knew only too well, she was one of the grieving and aggrieved cat owners whose baby was missing. In fact, she and I had met over the report of her lost cat, a magnificent—to judge by the pictures she showed me—Himalayan, name of Fantasia.

Like Atlas, I shrugged. But I didn't feel any burdens roll off.

I took Abby's arm and turned her around.

"Come spend your lunch hour with me," I said. Abby, who didn't need the money, worked hard at the gift shop she bought when she moved to Mt. Floresta. "We're going to give the *Lode* a front-page story."

* * *

"Classifieds, Zeke, that's where missing cats go."

"But, Ginny," I protested to my friend, the editor of the *Lode,* "that's where they've been going for two months! Aren't your classifieds getting a little full by now? I'll bet you've got more missing cats than you do skis for sale—"

"I doubt *that.*"

"Well, I'm telling you this is a bona-fide front-page story, a *scoop.*"

Ginny Pursell cast her navy-blue eyes skyward. "Dear Ezekiel, darling Zeke, whom I have loved more or less like a brother since grade school, in your business you may know all there is to know about *scoops.* But let me tell you a thing or two about front-page stories."

By my side, Abby cracked a knuckle ominously. It's a disgusting habit she likes to indulge in when she really wants to annoy somebody—like a local who makes it clear who is the newcomer to town and who is not. I did think Ginny's comment about grade school was a shade gratuitous.

"A front-page story," she lectured us, "is our cretinous mayor making an ass of himself in front of the White House in a protest against oil-shale development. No," Ginny held up a foresalling hand, "we shall not argue politics. I have my editorial stance and I shall keep it. What's good for oil-shale development is good for Mt. Floresta."

More knuckles. Mine. I am about as much in favor of digging into our mountains as I am of vivisection. Besides, the mayor's also a friend of mine. But Ginny's an anomaly—a conservative Republican journalist in a liberal Democratic county. As a newspaper editor and publisher, she's the only game in town, however, so we have to swallow her opinions along with the news.

"A front-page story is the hassle I'm getting from Larry Fremont—"

"You too?" I recalled the chief's gripe about having to "placate" the owner of a health spa. "Hell, I never thought ol' Larry would give this town anything, not even so much as a hassle or a hard time."

"What do you mean, 'you too'?"

"I think he's bugging Jamison Grant about something."

"Oh, lord." Ginny groaned. "He'll try anything to keep my story out of print." Like Jamison before her, she picked up some papers and waved them at me. I was rapidly tiring of the gesture. "I had this article practically written. All about trash disposal and what we're going to do about it in the future. It's a major problem, you know, because we need places to toss our garbage and the environmentalists won't let us put a dump near any place that's practical or economical."

"Like right beside Spirit Lake? Good for them."

"Who's Larry Fremont?" Abby asked, bravely asserting her ignorance.

Ginny threw me a knowing look, local-to-local, as it were, whereupon Abby's knuckles cracked resoundingly. I hurried to explain. Larry, I told her, was a local boy made good. So good he wouldn't have anything to do with us anymore. He was the founder of La Floresta, the combination health spa/dude ranch down in the valley. It was one of those resorts where rich ladies paid thousands of dollars to get a few pounds beaten and starved out of them.

"They all look the same to me when they come out," said Ginny, who has nothing to worry about herself when it comes to the slim-and-trim department. She also has lots of curly black hair—like a standard poodle, I tell her, which always makes her reach for a comb immediately, to my regret—and one of those tanned mountain faces in which blue eyes stand out like beacons. "Except they look like they go in fat and unhappy and they come out fat and happy."

At first *everybody* was happy about Larry's success, I told Abby, particularly since he was generous with jobs. But in the last year he'd started firing everybody from around here. Not that he made it so obvious; it happened little by little, person by person. Before we knew it, there wasn't one person from Mt. Floresta left on his payroll. Instead, he was hiring folks from further down the valley. And he took on a lot of college kids looking for resort work.

"Since then," I said, "nobody from Mt. Floresta cares much for Larry Fremont. We call him Fremont the Freeloader. He trades on our famous name without giving anything back to our economy. The S.O.B. even banks in Denver." I turned to Ginny. Her office cat, a stray she'd picked up from my shelter, jumped on her desk and made pet-me sounds. "What if Tiger was one of the cats that was missing?" I reached over to stroke his ugly yellow head. "Then how would you feel?"

"Why is Fremont hassling you about trash dumps?" Abby asked. She sticks to a subject better than I do.

"Because La Floresta sits on a landfill," Ginny told her. "Remember, Zeke? That was the old county dump for fifty years. God knows how many secrets are buried there. They filled it in just before Larry bought the land and built his spa.

"And he doesn't want me to say so in my article," she went on. "I have to mention it because it's such a good example of a landfill. Shows how the land can be reclaimed successfully. But he's afraid for his image. Can you believe it? He doesn't want his precious customers to know La Floresta sits on a trash heap!" Ginny shook her head in apparent dismay over the sorry state of progressive conservatives in the United States. "So I can't help you, Zeke. I've got more on my mind than cats. If you want a front-page story, give me something with blood and guts. Like a good juicy murder."

She smirked. We left.

Knowing Ginny, I'm sure she regretted that smirk the next day when she had to write the story of Rooney Bowers' death. OIL SHALE ENGINEER VICTIM OF HIT AND RUN, her headline told me. The story said that Rooney Bowers, associate professor of petroleum engineering at the university, had been bowled down in front of his house in the frosty hours of the morning. Whatever hit him threw him fifty feet across Mabel Langdon's holly hedge and into her front yard. Mabel found him a few hours later when she went out to get the paper.

"It was awful," she allowed herself to be quoted as saying. "There he was dead as a smelt and him such a nice quiet neighbor and all." Mabel sometimes has a colorful way of putting things.

I called Chief Jamison Grant immediately.

"It's Zeke." I got right to the point. "Where is Rooney Bowers' cat?"

"Honest to God, Ezekiel, you have the most one-track mind of anyone I ever knew." Jamison sounded harried. "The man gets killed and all you can think of is his damn cat. I don't know where it is. Maybe the neighbors have it, maybe—"

"It's a long-haired silver tabby. It wasn't in the house when you got there?"

"No, it wasn't in the house or around the house and I didn't even know Rooney had a cat and will you please stop bugging me about cats? Look, we'll get the cat to you. You know we will. Nobody's going to let the darned thing starve. But I got a hit-and-run to solve, Zeke. The cat's got to wait."

"Wait, Jamison, listen to me. I know Rooney pretty well, I mean, I knew him. We used to get together for a beer, he and the mayor and I, and we'd argue about oil shale."

"Zeke, please—"

"But the last time we didn't talk about oil, Jamison. We talked about cats. I told them all about the missing cats and how I thought somebody was stealing them."

"So?"

"So Rooney always gets—got—up real early to start his research. About four in the morning. And that's when he let his cat out, Jamison. He used to joke about it. Said his Tom was the only one he ever knew who liked it better in the morning than at night. Like some women he knew, he said."

"I repeat: so?"

"So . . ." Suddenly I knew how foolish I sounded. "So maybe it's got something to do with his death, that's all. I mean maybe all the missing cats are some kind of clue or something." It has been pointed out to me more than once that the less I know the more inarticulate I get.

"Thank you so much, Zeke," Jamison said heavily. "I'll certainly think on it."

I hung up quickly while we were still friends.

Abby thought I was crazy, too.

"But what if somebody was stealing Rooney's cat and Rooney saw him do it?" I said, expressing my theory in the sparsity of its fullness.

"Well, I seriously doubt they'd kill him over it," she said. We were sitting in my office trying to talk over the cacophony coming from the pens. I'd just put a new dog out there and he was getting quite a greeting. "I mean, don't you think you're being just a bit melodramatic? I'm as upset as you about the cats, but still—murder?"

She took a careful sip of the truly awful coffee I had brewed in my brand-new machine. "You know, if you put a lot of sugar in this, you might cover the taste of the plastic."

"Sugar rots teeth," I said righteously.

"These missing cats are rotting your brain. Zeke, I've shown cats before. I know that competition at cat shows is killing, and there are a few cat owners I could easily have murdered when their mangy beasts placed higher than my own Fantasia. But that's all hyperbole. We wouldn't really kill each other. We love our cats, but not that much."

"So?" I demanded in good cop form.

"So I can't believe anybody wants these cats badly enough to kill for them."

She had me there. I love cats, too, but murder?

I tried it from another angle: "Okay, then where is Rooney's cat? What if it doesn't show up? Will you say that's just coincidence, just another missing cat?"

"It'll show up," my lady love assured me. When she thought I wasn't looking, she poured her coffee into the litter box I keep in the corner.

It didn't show up, not hide nor long hair of it.

Abby drove out to my office on the Saturday morning after the hit-and-run, which was still unsolved.

"Wake up, Zeke!" She lifted one cat off my stomach, pushed another aside and sat down beside my sleeping body on the overstuffed couch I keep for the convenience of visitors, human and un-. *"I believe!"* she said, like one born again. "Rooney's missing cat is one too many coincidences, I agree. Let's talk." She tickled my ear with a strand of her long silky blonde hair. I loved the hair, hated the technique. Like a cranky old dog, I barked at her: "Dammit, Abigail, don't do that! Can't a man get a little catnap?"

Her lovely gray eyes widened. Her delicate jaw dropped. She looked like a woman who's seen the truth. I panicked, shot up in bed, grabbed and hugged her. "Abby! I'm sorry! I'm a grouch in the—"

"Catnap," she said breathily into my left ear, so that it sent nice little electric shivers down my side, and I didn't for a moment catch on that she wasn't whispering sweet nothings to me. "That's it, Zeke! Cat-nap, catnip, *kidnap*—that's how we need to think about this business. Like a kidnapping!"

Distracted as I was by kissing her neck, I said, "What?"

She pushed me away. "What if it weren't cats that were missing?" she enunciated with a clarity that was just this side of insulting. "What if they were *people?*"

I leaned toward her. "Um?"

"Well, how would the police investigate their disappearances? However *they'd* do it, that's how *we* should do it."

"How would they do it?"

"Oh, honestly, Zeke. Well, let's think about it. I mean, wouldn't they want to figure out why these particular people were kidnapped?"

"Yeah." Finally, I got excited about something besides her proximity. "What do these people—cats—have in common that might attract a kidnapper?"

"Good, Zeke!" She was no longer condescending. Unfortunately, she was also no longer within reach, having stood up and started to pace. "Maybe they'd look at the times and days the kidnappings took place."

"And where, to see if that had anything to do with it."

"And method."

"And motive." I picked up a cat and tucked him under my arm. "Come on, Abs, let's look at my list of missing cats."

We looked.

"So what *do* they have in common?" Abby demanded. "I don't know them, and you do."

I squinted at the list until something hit me.

"Geez, Abby, they're all long-hairs."

"Really?" She was excited, too. "What does that mean?"

"I don't know," I confessed.

We stared at each other in frustration.

"Find me another clue," she demanded.

I did, but it took a while. First we considered the ages of the cats, but that was no good because they ranged from a few months to seventeen years. Sex was no good, either, so to speak, as they were males, females and "other." Nor could we find any common denominators in their owners, other than the fact that they all lived around Mt. Floresta and they were mighty upset with my lack of efficiency. But then Abby raised the question of breeds. And it turned out that all but two were purebreds—Angora, Himalayan, Persian and other classy cats. There were two mixed breeds, which stumped us until Abby asked me if they *looked* like purebreds.

"Yes," I decided. "If you didn't know cats, you'd think they were Persians."

"So maybe our catnapper doesn't know cats?"

"Maybe." I was doubtful. "But he knows them well enough to know he wants only long-haired cats that are purebreds or look as if they are."

As I summed up, Abby jotted down key words on the chalkboard I use for messages. She scrawled *long hair* and *purebred.* Then she added *elegant* and *beautiful.*

"Maybe that doesn't have anything to do with it," she said defensively in the face of my skepticism. "But those are other qualities all the cats share. What if a lot of women were kidnapped, and they all happened to be young and beautiful? Don't you think the police would call that a clue?"

I guessed so. But then we ran up against the problem of motive. People kidnap other people for money, sex, revenge, power or leverage. Why cats? It obviously wasn't for ransom, since none had been demanded. And Abby didn't think the catnapper was selling them, because if he were he'd have snatched some valuable short-hairs, as well. I'd already eliminated lab experiments, I told Abby, unless she wanted to consider the possibility of a mad scientist working in a secret mountain cave, conducting weird tests on long cat hair. She thought we were pretty safe in eliminating that.

"Maybe the tourists are taking them," I offered.

"Have you ever tried to get a cat in a suitcase?" But then, as though inspired, she pronounced: "Oil shale! Maybe they didn't kill Rooney because he saw them take the cat. Maybe they killed him and took the cats because of something to do with the oil-shale controversy."

"Come on, Abby." I felt tired and crabby again. "What do you think, that they've discovered a way to get oil out of cats?"

She withdrew into a dignified and injured silence to my coffee pot. I knew she must be really mad if she was going to drink that stuff, but I was too frustrated to be contrite.

"Maybe we're getting the wrong answers because we're asking the wrong questions," I said into the chilly silence.

Being of a basically forgiving nature, she looked at me with interest.

"Maybe we're getting too fancy by asking what's the motive," I suggested. "Maybe the question is real simple. Like, what's a cat for?"

"Rats!" said my lady love, and I knew it wasn't because she'd spilled the coffee. "*Rats,* Zeke!"

My legs being longer than hers, by all rights I should have beat her to the car. But she was already in the driver's seat by the time I got in and slammed the door.

"So sorry, but only guests are admitted to La Floresta."

We got that maddening response at two out of the three gates of the walled compound of the health spa. Having raced five miles as fast as Abby's specially-calibrated-for-high-altitude Jag would scream, and gotten ourselves wound to a fever pitch of resolve, it was infuriating to be so easily halted by an upturned hand.

A snooty upturned hand.

"Maybe it's me," I suggested, humbly, after the second rejection. "Maybe I don't look the part. You try it alone next time. You look like trust funds."

"So kind," she said through gritted teeth. She didn't like to be reminded of her inherited wealth. I always told her if she felt so guilty about it, she could assuage that guilt by sharing the loot with poor folks like me. "The only reason you don't look the part is because you've let yourself get so skinny. On the other hand, as it were, if you let your fingernails grow, maybe they'd think you were Howard Hughes."

"Touché," I said, wounded. I'm told I can dish it out, but I can't take it, a piece of criticism I resent very much. "I mean it, though. I'll stay back in the bushes, and you try the next gate by yourself."

It didn't work. Abby's name wasn't on their list and she didn't have the gold membership card they so tactfully demanded. Perhaps the young lady would like to call and make a reservation? Perhaps they'd like to go to hell, the young lady said to me upon arriving back at my bush.

We thought it best to wait until dark before launching our assault on the elegant buff walls. When we left Mt. Floresta the second time, we packed a ladder into Abby's precious Jaguar. "You scratch that paint and I'll kill you," she said sweetly. I'd heard that Jags get something like seventeen hundred coats of hand-rubbed lacquer on them. I told her she would never miss one little coat of paint in one little spot. "I won't miss *you,* either," she said. I took the hint and stowed the ladder without damage to the car or the relationship.

So getting in was no problem.

"It's awfully dark," she said, as we crouched on our respective haunches in the well-pruned shrubbery. In the dark, the bushes looked like fat ladies squatting.

"It's awfully big," I rejoined. Across a lawn like a cemetery, the administration building rose white against the night. All around in the darkness we could hear the sounds of guests moving from their cabins to other parts of the compound. A splash to the right alerted us to the location of one of the swimming pools, presumably heated for cold fall nights like this one. Like spies in a B movie, we scuttled across the grass to the shelter of an enormous fir tree.

"Zeke, I just thought of something." Abby sounded less sure of herself than usual.

"I wish you wouldn't say things like that at a time like this," I whined.

"No, listen," she whispered. "I've been thinking about how Rooney Bowers died. If you're letting your cat out of the house, all you do is open the door, right? And the same thing when you let him in. I mean, you don't have to step outside with him. You don't *walk* a cat."

"Few do."

"Yes, well, how come Rooney was out there in the street where he could get hit? Zeke, I think he opened the door to call his cat in, and that's when he saw somebody grab the cat. If it were you, what would you do?"

"I'd go chasing and yelling after the son of a—"

"Right, and that would put you in the street. But, Ezekiel, if somebody were stealing a cat, they'd have to slow down to do it. So when Rooney saw them, they couldn't have been going fast enough to hit him as hard as they did."

"Oh, God." Gooseflesh crawled down my arms.

"Yes," Abby whispered in a curiously vibrating voice. "And that means they saw *him* when he saw *them*. So they came back around to kill him. They had to speed up to do it."

We stared at each other.

Premeditated murder? Even if it was only premeditated by a few seconds?

We stared at Larry Fremont's million-dollar administration building.

"What is important enough for premeditated murder?" I asked, appalled at the idea we had formed. A hit-and-run was one thing, and plenty bad enough, but this . . . "Abby, we should go back out the way we came in. We should drive back to town and call Jamison."

She told me what she thought of those cowardly ideas by scooting across the lawn to a stand of pines further inside the compound. I thought of all the times my mother told me not to cross the street without looking both ways, and I ran after her. She had slipped into the shadows, so I couldn't see her, when she suddenly called my name. Just as I was ready to shush her, she grasped my elbow. Or, at least I thought she did. I was certainly surprised when the person attached to that grasp turned out to be good ol' Larry Fremont himself.

* * *

"Zeke Leonard," he said in a less-than-welcoming tone of voice. In the years since the high school football team, Zeke had not lost muscle, he'd added it—on his fancy spa weight-lifting equipment, no doubt. If he'd looked then like he looked now, we'd have won every game for the Mt. Floresta Mountain Lions. "And friend."

"Long time no see, Larry," I babbled. "I'd like you to meet my good friend Tanya Smith. Tanya is staying up at Mt. Floresta and she indicated an interest in your beautiful place, so I said, well, Tanya, I'll take you down and introduce you to ol' Larry himself."

Ol' Larry himself proved there is such a thing as a cold smile.

Abby moved out of the shadows and looked at me as if I were the resident fool of the mountains.

"That's thoughtful of you, Zeke," he said. "And I'd show your friend, uh, Tanya, around, but as you can see, it's rather dark for show and tell. So I think I'll just escort you to the gate."

Instead of releasing my elbow, he added another to his collection. From Abby's wince, I could tell his grip of her was every bit as firm as the one he had on me. But it wasn't so strong I couldn't break away when I saw a black cat stroll by about three steps ahead of me.

"Zeke, it's Fantas—" Abby cried.

I didn't look to find out why her last syllables were cut off. I just threw myself on the bundle of soft fur as if it were an opposing lineman, and held on for dear life. The cat, unclear as to my intentions, returned my embrace—with claws. I swore loudly. Which is probably why I didn't know Larry had come up behind me until his head hit me in the middle of the small of my back. In high school, he and I had played on the same team, so I never knew how much damage he could do with his famous illegal tackles. As I collapsed, the cat jumped over my shoulder, landing with all four clawed paws on Larry's head. His attention having been thus nicely distracted, I turned and threw a tackle of my own. I didn't grieve when his head hit an imitation Greek sculpture like a football hitting a goal post.

Fremont the Freeloader lay on the ground, out cold.

But the hollering from cats and people had switched on a lot of lights in the compound. I sat on Larry and took the petrified cat in my arms. He held still, probably paralyzed by fright, like me.

"Zeke, Zeke, are you okay?" Abby ran up out of the dark where Larry had thrown her into the bushes in his chase after me. "Zeke, is it Fantasia? Is it my Fantasia?"

Her voice was full of tears and hope.

"No," I said gently. "It's not."

She sank to her knees. I saw the light go out of her face.

"It's not Fantasia," I said quickly. "It's Puddy! It's Miss Emily Parson's cat, Puddy."

Hope returned to Abby's eyes just as the guests and employees merged on our mangled scene.

"Call the police!" someone yelled.

"Yes," I agreed, "do that. Ask for the chief. Tell him I told him so."

"We smell more than a rat," Jamison told us the next day in his office. "Larry confessed to Rooney's hit-and-run. When Rooney saw him grab the cat, he went racing out to Larry's car, accusing him of stealing all those other cats. And that was enough to panic Larry. He knew if that got out, everything else would too."

"*What* else?" Abby looked up from a chair in the corner where her hands were occupied in petting Fantasia. The Himalayan purred and blinked smugly at me as if to re-establish squatter's rights to that lovely blue-jeaned lap.

"Fraud," Jamison announced. "All kinds of consumer fraud." He glanced at the intrepid editor busily scribbling notes. "Ready, Ginny?"

"Go," she commanded, pencil poised.

"It's almost funny." Jamison was seated on a corner of his desk, and now he folded his arms over his stomach. "It seems that Larry got himself financially overextended, so he started cutting corners to save money. For one thing, the food at La Floresta is not exactly what their menus say it is. They've been altering the recipes with cheaper, more fattening ingredients—using starches for fillers and sugar for taste, for instance, instead of all those expensive herbs and spices they advertise."

"But don't the guests get weighed?" I asked.

"They fixed the scales!" Jamison hooted with laughter. "And they made sure the guests got plenty of exercise to burn up some of those calories they didn't know they were eating. Plus, nobody stayed long enough to gain much. Most of them just went out weighing the same as when they went in. Gives a whole new meaning to the phrase, 'fat farm,' wouldn't you say?"

"But they'd find out the truth when they got home," Ginny said.

"Nope." The bald eagle preened on his exclusive information. "Larry told them they could expect to gain back some water weight as soon as they started to eat regularly again."

"Diabolical," Abby hissed. "Not to mention mean and lousy."

Jamison said, "It wasn't just the food, either. The doctor was a quack, the physical therapists were phonies, the dietitian was just an amateur cook, and the European chefs were ordinary restaurant cooks from Denver; not even the aerobics instructors had the experience the advertising says they did. Almost nobody was quite what they claimed to be, and so they could be paid a lot less. It was all a joke to most of them, but it meant serious money in the bank to Larry. Now we know why he fired everybody from Mt. Floresta. His original employees from up here knew how things were supposed to be. They wouldn't have stood for his cheating."

"He didn't want any of us to know." I shook my head over the greed of my old teammate. "I bet that's why he took all his business away. It was safer to deal with out-of-town banks and suppliers. They weren't close enough to catch him at his shell game."

"But the cats," Ginny interrupted. "Why the cats?"

Abby and I traded supercilious smiles.

"Remember your story about landfills?" I asked Ginny. "The one Larry didn't want you to run? That was our best clue. We thought of all the reasons somebody might want a cat and came up with the oldest reason of all: to kill rats. And where in this wide valley might there be a problem with rats?"

"At a landfill over a garbage dump!" Ginny exclaimed.

"Right. Larry saw big fat ugly rats invading his precious gold mine. He had to get rid of them. Poison was dangerous because some of the guests bring their dogs to stay with them. And dead dogs are bad for business. Live cats was the answer."

"But not just any cats." Abby giggled and held Fantasia aloft. "They had to fit the 'ambiance.' They had to be beautiful, elegant cats, so the guests would not object."

"And they had to be long-haired," I added. "Because Larry wasn't going to feed them much. He wanted them hungry so they'd kill rats. And a long-haired cat always looks fatter than a short-hair. So nobody would notice if the cats lost weight."

"But why so many?" Ginny persisted.

"It's a big place," was my simple explanation.

"Beast," Abby said, and she didn't mean cats.

"It was all a matter of appearances," I continued, taking the opportunity to philosophize grandly. The others exchanged tolerant glances, but I ignored them. "That's what La Floresta was all about anyway, wasn't it? Appearances. Larry stole the cats and killed Rooney to keep up appearances."

I stood up and streched carefully. My kidneys still hurt where Larry's head had dented them. "Glad to be of help, Jamison," I said graciously. "But Abby and I must be off. Miss Emily Parson is serving tea in our honor."

I looked into his amused, craggy face.

"You wanna come, too?"

"A cop having tea?" He recoiled in mock horror. "Have a heart, Zeke. How would it *look?*"

Bruce Holland Rogers

ENDURING AS DUST

I drive past the Department of Agriculture every morning on my way to work, and every morning I slow to a crawl so that I can absorb the safe and solid feel of that building as I go by. The north side of Agriculture stretches for two uninterrupted city blocks. The massive walls look as thick as any castle's. Inside, the place is a warren of offices and suboffices, a cozy organizational hierarchy set in stone. I've often thought to myself that if an H-bomb went off right over the Mall, then the White House, the Capitol, the memorials and the reflecting pools would all be blown to ash and steam, but in the midst of the wreckage and the settling dust, there would stand the Department of Agriculture, and the work inside its walls would go securely on.

I don't have that kind of security. The building that houses the Coordinating Administration for Productivity is smaller than our agency's name. The roof leaks. The walls are thin and haven't been painted since the Great Depression.

That I am here is my own fault. Twenty years ago, when I worked for the Bureau of Reclamation, I realized that the glory days of public dam building were over. I imagined that a big RIF wave was coming to the bureau, and I was afraid that I'd be one of those drowned in the Reduction In Force. So I went looking for another agency.

When I found the Coordinating Administration for Productivity, I thought I had found the safest place in Washington to park my career. I'd ask CAP staffers what their agency did.

"We advise other agencies," they would say.

"We coordinate private and public concerns."

"We review productivity."

"We revise strategies."

"We provide oversight."

"But clearly, clearly, we could always do more."

In other words, nobody knew. From the top down, no one could tell me precisely what the administrative mission was. And I thought to myself, I want to be a part of this. No one will ever be able to suggest that we are no longer needed, that it's time for all of us to clear out our desks, that our job is done, because no one knows what our job *is.*

But I was wrong about the Bureau of Reclamation. It hasn't had a major project for two decades, doesn't have any planned, and yet endures, and will continue to endure, through fiscal year after fiscal year, time without end. It is too big to die.

The Coordinating Administration for Productivity, on the other hand, employs just thirty civil servants. We're always on the bubble. With a stroke of the pen, we could vanish from next year's budget. All it would take is for someone to notice us long enough to erase us. And so, as I soon learned, there was an administrative mission statement after all: Don't Get Noticed.

That's why we never complained to GSA about the condition of our building, why we turned the other cheek when FDA employees started parking in our lot and eventually took it over. That's also why no one ever confronted the secretaries about the cats named Dust. And above all, that is why I was so nervous on the morning that our chief administrator called an "urgent meeting."

I sat waiting outside of the administrator's office with Susana de Vega, the assistant administrator, and Tom Willis, Susana's deputy. "I don't like this," Tom said. "I don't like this one damn bit."

Susana hissed at him and looked at the administrator's secretary. But Roxie wasn't listening to us. She was talking, through an open window, to the cat on the fire escape. The cat was a gray tom with the tattered ears of a streetfighter. He backed up warily as Roxie put the food bowl down. "Relax, Dust," she said. "I'm not going to hurt you."

It was January, a few days before the presidential inauguration, and the air coming in through the window was cold, but nobody asked Roxie to close it.

"When has Cooper ever called an *urgent* meeting?" Tom continued in a lower voice. "Hell, how many times has he called a meeting of any damn kind? He's up to something. He's got to throw his goddam Schedule-C weight around while he still has it to throw."

Throwing his weight around didn't sound like Bill Cooper, but I didn't bother to say so. After all, Cooper was a political appointee on his way out, so whether he threw his weight around or not, Tom's underlying point was correct: Cooper was a loose cannon. He had nothing to lose. Intentionally or not, he might blow us up.

Roxie waited to see if the cat would consent to having his chin scratched, but Dust held his ground until the window was closed. Even then, he approached the food warily, as if checking for booby traps.

Susana told Tom to relax. "Two weeks," she reminded him. "Three at the outside."

"And then god only knows what we'll be getting," Tom said, pulling at his chin. "I hate politics."

Roxie's intercom buzzed, and without turning away from the cat she told us, "You can go in now."

I followed Susana and Tom in, and found Cooper nestled deeply in his executive chair, looking as friendly and harmless as he ever had. His slightly drooping eyelids made him seem, as always, half asleep. He waved us into our seats, and as I sat down, I realized how little he had done to personalize his office in the twelve years of his tenure. Everything in the room was government issue. There weren't any family pictures or the usual paperweights made by children or grandchildren. In fact, there wasn't anything on the surface of his desk at all. It was as if Cooper had been anticipating, from the day he moved in, the day when he would have to move out.

There was *some* decoration in the room, a pen and ink drawing on the wall behind Cooper, but that had been there for as long as I had been with the CAP. It showed an Oriental-looking wooden building next to a plot of empty ground, and I knew from having looked once, maybe fifteen years ago, that the drawing wasn't just hung on the wall. The frame had been nailed into the paneling, making it a permanent installation.

"People," Cooper said from deep inside his chair, "we have a problem." He let that last word hang in the air as he searched for what to say next.

Susana, Tom and I leaned forward in our chairs.

"An impropriety," he went on.

We leaned a little more.

"A mystery."

We watched expectantly as Cooper opened his desk drawer and took out a sheet of paper. He studied it for a long time, and then said, "You people know my management style. I've been hands-off. I've always let you people handle the details," by which he meant that he didn't know what we did all day and didn't care, so long as we told him that everything was running smoothly. He tapped the sheet of paper and said, "But here is something that demands my attention, and I want it cleared up while I'm still in charge."

And then he read from the letter in his hand. The writer represented something called the Five-State Cotton Consortium, and he had come to Washington to get advice on federal funding for his organization. He had taken an employee of the Coordinating Administration for Productivity to lunch, picking her brain about the special appropriations process as well as various grant sources. The woman had been very helpful, and the letter writer just wanted Cooper to know that at least one member of his staff was really on the ball. The helpful staffer's name was Kim Semper.

At the sound of that name, I felt ice form in the pit of my stomach. I stared straight ahead, keeping my expression as plain as I could manage. I knew some of what Cooper was going to say next, but I tried to look genuinely surprised when he told us what had happened after he received the letter.

"I wanted to touch base with Ms. Semper and make sure that the citizen hadn't actually paid for her lunch. You people know as well as I do that we don't want any conflict of interest cases."

"Of course not," said Susana. "But I don't see how there could be any such conflict. We don't actually make funding decisions."

"We don't?" Cooper said, and then he recovered to say, "No, of course not. But you people will agree that we wouldn't want even the *appearance* of impropriety. And anyway, that doesn't matter. What matters is that in my search for Kim Semper, I came up empty. We don't have an employee by that name."

Trying to sound more convincing than I felt, I said, "Maybe it's a mistake, Bill. Maybe the letter writer had the name wrong, or sent the letter to the wrong agency."

"Hell, yes!" Tom said with too much enthusiasm. "It's just some damn case of mistaken identity!"

But Cooper wasn't going to be turned easily. "I called the citizen," he told us. "No mistake. Someone is posing as an officer of our agency, a criminal offense."

I said, "Doesn't there have to be intent to defraud for this to be a crime?"

Cooper frowned. "The citizen did buy lunch for this Kim Semper. She benefitted materially." He shook the letter at me. "This is a serious matter."

"And one we'll get to the bottom of," Susana promised.

"I want it done before my departure," Cooper said. "I don't want to saddle my successor with any difficulties," by which he meant that he didn't want to leave behind any dirty laundry that might embarrass him when he was no longer in a position to have it covered up.

Susana said again, "We'll get to the bottom of it."

Cooper nodded at Tom. "I want a single point of responsibility on this, so the personnel director will head up the investigation."

With Cooper still looking at him, Tom looked at me expectantly, and I felt compelled to speak up. "That would be me," I said. "Tom's your deputy assistant."

"Of course," Cooper said, covering. He turned to me. "And you'll report to him." Then he added, "You aren't too busy to take care of this matter, I assume."

"It'll be tight," I said, thinking of the Russian novel I'd been wading through for the last week, "but I'll squeeze it in."

Outside of Cooper's office, Susana patted Tom's shoulder, then mine, and said with complete ambiguity, "You know what to do." Then she disappeared down the hall, into her own office.

Roxie's cat was gone, but Roxie had something else to distract her now. She was reading a GPO publication called, *Small Business Administration Seed Projects: Program Announcement and Guidelines.* She didn't even look up when Tom hissed at me, "Sit on it!"

"What?"

"You know damn well what I mean," Tom said through his teeth. "I don't know what this Kim Semper thing is all about, and I don't want to know! This is just the kind of problem that could blow us out of the goddam water!"

I said, "Are you telling me to ignore an assignment from the chief administrator?"

I could see in Tom's eyes the recognition that he had already been too specific. "Not at all," he said in a normal voice, loud enough for Roxie to overhear if she were listening. "I'm telling you to handle this in the most appropriate fashion." Then he, too, bailed out, heading for his own office.

I found my secretary, Vera, trying to type with a calico cat in her lap. The cat was purring and affectionately digging its claws into Vera's knee.

"Damn it, Vera," I said, surprising myself, "the memo specifies feeding only. Everybody knows that. You are not supposed to have the cat inside the building!"

"You hear that, Dust?" Vera said as she rubbed behind the cat's ears. "It's back out into the cold with you." But she made no move to get up.

"Hold my calls," I growled. I went into my office and closed the door, wishing that I had a copy of the legendary memo so that I could read chapter and verse to Vera. It was bad enough that the secretaries had distorted the wording of the memo, issued well over twenty years ago, that had allowed them to feed a stray cat named Dust, "and only a cat named Dust." It seemed like every so often, they had to push beyond even the most liberal limits of that allowance, and no manager was willing to make an issue of it, lest it turn into a civil service grievance that would bring an OPM investigation crashing down around our ears.

I didn't stew about the cat for long. I still had Kim Semper on my mind. It took me a few minutes to find the key to my file cabinet, but once I had the drawer open, there weren't many folders to search through before I found what I wanted. I untaped the file folder marked PRIVATE and pulled out the letter. It was addressed to me and sported an eleven-year-old date. "After failing to determine just who her supervisor is," the text began, "I have decided to write to you, the Director of Personnel, to commend one of your administrators, Miss Kim Semper." The story from there was pretty much the same: a citizen had come to Washington looking for information, had stumbled across the Coordinating Administration for Productivity, and had ended up buying Semper's lunch in exchange for her insights on the intricacies of doing business in the Beltway. Though he had been unable to contact her subsequently, her advice had been a big help to him.

After checking the personnel files, I had called the letter writer to tell him that he'd been mistaken, that there was no Kim Semper here at the CAP. Maybe, I suggested, he had gone to some other agency and confused the names? But he was sure that it was the CAP that he had consulted, and he described our building right down to the tiny, nearly unreadable gray lettering that announced the agency's name on the front door.

In a government agency, a mystery, any mystery, is a potential bomb. If you're not sure of what something is, then you assume that it's going to blow up in your face if you mess with it. At the CAP, where everything was uncertain and shaky to begin with, the unknown seemed even more dangerous. So I had buried the letter.

Now maybe it was coming back to haunt me. I wondered if I should cover my tail by Xeroxing my letter and bringing Cooper a copy right now. "Hey, Bill. I had to check my files on this, to make sure, but would you believe . . ." Maybe that would be good damage control.

But maybe not. After all, Cooper seemed to think this was an urgent matter. I had known about it for eleven years and done nothing. And my letter was so old that I probably didn't have to worry about it hurting me if I didn't bring up its existence. By now, the writer himself might not even remember sending it to me. Perhaps the man was even dead. If I kept my mouth shut, it was just possible that no one would ever know about my Kim Semper letter. And if that was what I wanted, then it would help my cause to do just what Tom had urged: To sit on the investigation, to ignore Kim Semper until the executive branch resignations worked their way down, layer by layer, from the new president's cabinet to our agency, and Cooper was on his way.

Either option, hiding the letter or revealing it, had its dangers. No matter how I played it out in my mind, I couldn't see the safe bet. I returned to what I'd been doing before the meeting with Cooper, and I should have been able to concentrate on it. Napoleon was watching this Polish general, who wanted to impress him, trying to swim some cavalry across a Russian river, but the horses were drowning and everything was a mess. It was exciting, but it didn't hold my attention. I read the same page over and over, distracted with worry.

At the end of the day, there was no cat in Vera's lap, but there was a skinny little tabby begging on the fire escape. At her desk, Vera was pouring some cat food into a bowl labeled, "Dust."

"Sorry I snapped earlier," I said.

"Bad day?" Vera said, opening the window.

"The worst," I told her, noticing the stack of outgoing mail on her desk. "Is that something I asked you to do?"

"Oh, I'm just getting some information for the staff library," she said.

I nodded, trying to think of something managerial to say. "You're self-directed, Vera. I like to see that."

"Oh, I've always been that way," she told me. "I can't stand to be idle." She opened the window to feed the cat and said, "Here you go, Dust."

Cooper called another meeting for Thursday of the next week. It was the day after the inauguration, and he must have felt the ticking clock. Before the meeting, Tom called me.

"How's your investigation coming?" he said.

"Slowly."

"Good. That's damn good. See you in the old man's office."

For once there wasn't a cat on Roxie's fire escape. Cooper's door was open, and I walked right in. Susana and Tom were already there, and Cooper motioned me to a seat. Cooper didn't waste any time.

"What have you got?"

I opened my notebook. "First, I double-checked the personnel files, not just the current ones, but going back twenty-five years." I looked at cooper grimly. "No one by the name of Kim Semper has *ever* worked for the Coordinating Administration for Productivity."

"Yes, yes," Cooper said. "What else?"

"I called over to the Office of Personnel Management. There is not now, nor has there ever been, anywhere in the civil service system, an employee named Kim Semper." I closed the notebook and put on the face of a man who has done his job well.

Cooper stared at me. I pretended to look back at him earnestly, but my focus was actually on the framed pen and ink behind him. If I had to give it a title, I decided, it would be, "Japanese Shed With Empty Lot."

At last Cooper said, "Is that all?"

"Well, Bill, I haven't been able to give this my full attention."

"It's been a week, a *week* since I brought this up to you people."

"And a hellish week it's been," I said, looking to Tom for help.

"That's true," Tom jumped in. "The inauguration has stirred things up. We've had an unusually, ah, unusually heavy run of requests." Cooper frowned, and I could see Tom's hands tighten on the side of his chair. He was hoping, I knew, that Cooper wouldn't say, "Requests for what? From whom?"

Susana saved us both by saying, "I'm ashamed of the two of you! Don't you have any sense of priorities? And, Tom, you're supposed to be supervising this investigation. That means staying on top of it, making sure it's progressing." She turned to Cooper. "We'll have something substantial next week, Bill."

"I don't know, people," Cooper said. "Realistically, something like this is out of your purview. Maybe it calls for an outside investigator."

Cooper was almost certainly bluffing. Any dirt at the bottom of this would cling to him like tar if we brought in the consul general's office. He wanted to keep this internal as much as we did.

Even so, Susana paled. She played it cool, but it was a strain on her. "Why don't you see what we come up with in seven working days? Then you can decide."

Minutes later, in the hallway, Tom said, "So what now?"

"Don't look at me," Susana told him without breaking stride. "I pulled your bacon out of the fire, boys. Don't ask me to think for you, too." Then over her shoulder, she added, "You'd just better appear to be making progress by our next little get-together."

Before he left me standing alone in the hallway, Tom said, "You heard the lady, Ace. Let's see some goddam action."

In my office, with the door closed behind me, I finished another chapter of the Russian novel and then got right on the case. I cleared space on the floor and laid out the personnel files for the last eleven years. It made sense to assume that "Kim Semper" was an insider, or had an inside confederate who could arrange her lunchtime meetings. And I knew that Ms. Semper had been working this free-lunch scam since at least the date of my letter. I figured that I could at least narrow down my suspect pool by weeding out anyone who hadn't been with the CAP for that long.

Unfortunately, this didn't narrow things much. Even Cooper, by virtue of three straight presidential victories for his party, had been with the CAP for longer than that.

So what did I really have to go on? Just two letters of praise for Kim Semper, dated eleven years apart. The letter writers themselves had met Kim Semper, but there were good reasons for not calling them for more information. After all, I wanted to keep my letter buried to preserve my plausible deniability. And Cooper's letter writer had already been contacted once about Kim Semper. If I called again and grilled him, he might resent it, and I could use up his good will before I even knew what questions to ask. Also, he might get the impression that the Coordinating Administration for Productivity didn't have its act together, and who knew where that could lead? I didn't want a citizen complaining to his congressional rep.

What I needed was another source, but there wasn't one.

Or was there?

I arranged the personnel files on the floor to look like an organizational hierarchy. If someone were to send a letter praising an employee of the CAP, where might that letter go?

To the top, of course. That was Cooper.

And to the Director of Personnel. That was me.

But what about the space between these two? What about the Assistant Administrator and her Deputy? That is, what about Susana and Tom?

Outside of Susana's office, her administrative assistant, Peter, was preparing to feed a black cat on the fire escape. Almost as soon as he opened the window, Peter sneezed.

"Susana in?"

"Yes," Peter said, "but she's unavailable." He set the cat bowl down and closed the window. Then he sneezed again.

"If you're so allergic," I said, "how come you're feeding the kitty?"

"Oh, I like cats, even if they do make my eyes swell shut." He laughed. "Anyway, feeding Dust is the corporate culture around here, right? When in Rome . . ."

From the other side of Susana's door, I could hear the steady beat of music.

I watched the stray cat as it ate. "I'm surprised, with all the cats on our fire escapes, that it isn't just one continuous cat fight out there."

"They're smart animals," Peter said. "Once they have a routine, they stay out of each other's way."

I nodded, but I wasn't really paying attention. Over the beat of the music, I could hear a female voice that wasn't Susana's counting *one-and-two-and-three-and—*

I went to her door and put my hand on the knob.

"I told you," Peter said. "Susana's unavailable. If you want to make an appointment . . ."

"This can't wait," I said. I opened the door.

Susana was in a leotard, and I caught her in the middle of a leg lift. She froze while the three women on the workout tape kept on exercising and counting without her.

"I told Peter I wasn't to be disturbed," she said, still holding her leg up like some varicolored flamingo.

"This won't take but a minute," I said. "In fact, you can go right on with your important government business while we talk."

She stopped the tape and glared at me. "What do you want?"

"To get to the bottom of this Kim Semper thing. And if that's what you really want too, then you can't be throwing me curve balls."

"What are you talking about?" She pushed the audiovisual cart between two file cabinets and threw a dust cover over it.

"I'm talking, Susana, about sitting on information. Or call it withholding evidence. I want your correspondence file on Kim Semper."

Susana circled behind her desk and sat down. Ordinarily, that would have been a good gesture, a way of reminding me that she was, after all, the assistant admin, and this was her turf I had invaded. But it was a hard move to pull off in a leotard. "Just what makes you think I even have such a file?"

That was practically a confession. I fought down a smile. "I'm on your side," I reminded her. "But we've got to show some progress on this. Cooper is on his last official breath. Dying men are unpredictable. But if we hold all the cards, how dangerous can he be?"

She stared over my head, no doubt thinking the same thoughts I had about my own Kim Semper letter. How would Cooper react to knowing that she'd had these letters in her files all along?

"You've got the file where, Susana? In your desk? In one of those cabinets? If I close my eyes," I said, closing them, "then I'll be able to honestly tell Cooper that I don't know *exactly* where my information came from. It was just sort of dropped into my lap."

It took her a minute of rummaging, and then a folder fell into my hands. I opened my eyes. The three letters ranged from two to ten years old.

"Read them in your own office," she said. "And next time, knock."

On my way out, I noticed that Peter was reading something called *America's Industrial Future: A Report of the Presidential Colloquium on U.S. Manufacturing Productivity for the Year 2020 and Beyond.* A thing like that wouldn't ordinarily stick in my mind, except that Tom's secretary, Janet, was reading the same report. She was also holding a mottled white and tan cat in her lap. I didn't bother to confront her about it—that was Tom's fight, if he wanted to fight it. I just knocked on Tom's door and stepped into his office.

He swept a magazine from his desk and into a drawer, but he wasn't fast enough to keep me from noting the cover feature: THE GIRLS OF THE PAC TEN. "What the hell do you want?" he growled.

"A hell of a lot more than I'm getting," I barked back. "Damn little you've done to help this investigation along, Willis. Enough bullshit. I'm up to here with bullshit. I want your goddam Kim Semper correspondence file."

"Like hell." Tom glowered, but a little quiver of uncertainty ran across his lowered eyebrows. He wasn't used to being on the receiving end of such bluster.

"Cut the crap, Tom. This goddam Semper bullshit will toss us all on our asses if we don't give Cooper something to chew on. So give."

A little timidly, he said, "I don't know what you're . . ."

"Like hell," I said, waving de Vega's letters. "Susana came across, and I'd sure as hell hate to tell Cooper that you're the one stalling his goddam investigation."

He bit his lip and took a file cabinet key from his desk drawer. "Jesus," he said. "I've never seen you like this."

"You better hope like hell you never see it again," I said, which was probably overdoing things, but I was on a roll.

As I read it in my office, the first of Tom's letters cheered me considerably. One was twenty years old, which altered my suspect list quite a bit. From my array of files on the floor, I removed anyone who hadn't been with the CAP for the last two decades. That left just myself, Tom Willis, and Tom's secretary Janet. I picked up Janet's file and smiled. Kim Semper, I thought, you have met your match.

And then I read Tom's other letter, the most recent one of all, excepting Cooper's. It praised Mr. Kim Semper, for *his* dedication to public service.

No, I thought. This can't be right.

Unless there was more than one Kim Semper.

I sat down behind my desk. Hard. And I thought about the cat named Dust, who came in a dozen variations, but who, by long tradition, was always Dust, was always considered to be the same cat, because the ancient memo had allowed for the feeding of a cat named Dust, "and only a cat named Dust."

I picked up the phone and dialed the number of the man who had written to praise Mr. Semper. "Mr. Davis," I said when I had him on the line, "one of our employees is in line for a service award, and I just want to make sure it's going to the right person. You wrote a letter to us about a Mr. Kim Semper. Now, we've got a Kim Semple on our staff, and a Tim Kemper, but no Kim Semper. Could you do me the favor of describing the man who was so helpful?"

As lame stories go, this one worked pretty well. It sounded plausible, and it didn't make the CAP look bad. And it brought results. Davis was only happy to make sure Semper or Semple or Kemper got his due. The description fit Peter to a T.

I tried the next most recent letter, but the number had been disconnected. The next one back from that—I changed Tim Kemper to Lynn— brought me a good description of Roxie. The third call, the one that cinched it, paid off with a description that could only be my own Vera.

That's when I buzzed Vera into my office.

"I want a copy of the cat memo," I told her.

"The cat memo?"

"Don't fence with me. If you don't have a copy of it yourself, you know how to get one. I want it within the hour." Then I lowered my voice conspiratorially. "Vera, I don't have anything against cats. Trust me on that."

She had a copy in my hands in five minutes. When I looked at the date, I whistled. Dust the cat had been on this officially sanctioned meal ticket for more than forty years, much longer than I had supposed. The memo also named the secretary who had first started feeding Dust. After a phone call to OPM, I was on my way to Silver Spring, Maryland.

The house I stopped in front of was modest, but nonetheless stood out from all the other clapboard houses on that street. There were abstract, Oriental-looking sculptures in the garden. The white stones around the plum trees had been raked into tidy rows, and there was a fountain bubbling near the walkway to the front door.

A white-haired woman holding a gravel rake came around the side of the house, moving with a grace that belied her eighty years.

"Mrs. Taida?" I said. She looked up and waved me impatiently into the garden. As I opened the gate, I said, "I'm the one who called you, Mrs. Taida. From the Coordinating Administration for Productivity."

"Yes, of course," she said. As I approached, she riveted me with her gaze. Her eyes were blue as arctic ice.

"You are Janet Taida, yes?"

"You expected me to look more Japanese," she said. "Taida was my husband's name. Sakutaro Taida. The artist." She waved at the sculptures.

"I see," I said, then reached into my pocket for the photocopied memo. "Mrs. Taida, I want to talk to you about the cat named Dust."

"Of course you do," she said. "Come inside and I'll make some tea."

The house was furnished in the traditional Japanese style, with furniture that was close to the floor. While Mrs. Taida started the water boiling in the kitchen, I looked at the artwork hanging on the walls. There were paintings and drawings that seemed vaguely familiar, some- how, but it wasn't until I saw the big pen and ink on the far wall that I knew what I was looking at.

"There's a drawing like this in the administrator's office," I said when Mrs. Taida came into the room with the teapot.

"A drawing *almost* like that one," Mrs. Taida said. She waved toward a cushion. "Won't you sit down?" she commanded. She poured the tea. "That's a Shinto temple. It has two parts, two buildings. But only one stands at a time. Every twenty years, one is torn down and the other is rebuilt. They are both present, always. But the manifestation changes."

"The drawing at work shows the other phase," I said, "when the other building is standing and this one has been torn down."

Mrs. Taida nodded. A white long-haired cat padded into the room. "Dust?" I said.

Taking up her teacup, Mrs. Taida shook her head. "No, there's only one Dust."

I laughed. "But like the temple, many manifestations." I unfolded the memo. "This memo, the Dust memo, mentions you by name, Mrs. Taida. You started it, didn't you? You were the administrator's secretary when the secretaries received their sanction to keep caring for, as it says here, 'a cat named Dust.' "

"Once we began to feed one, it was very hard to turn the others away. So I read the memo very carefully."

"Mrs. Taida, cats are one thing, but . . ."

"I know. Cats are one thing, but Kim Semper is far more serious, right?" She lowered her teacup. "Let me explain something to you," she said. "The Coordinating Administration for Productivity was commissioned over fifty years ago. They had a clear wartime purpose, which they completed, and then the agency began to drift. Your tea is getting cold."

She waited until I had picked it up and taken a sip.

"A government agency develops a culture, and it attracts people who are comfortable with that culture. After its wartime years the CAP attracted ostriches."

I opened my mouth, but she held up her hand.

"You can't deny it," she said. "For forty years, the CAP has been managed by men and women who wanted to rule over a quiet little fiefdom where nothing much happened."

She sipped her own tea.

"Do you have any idea what it's like to be a secretary under conditions like that?" She shook her head. "Nothing happens. There's too little to do, and the day just crawls by. You can't have any idea how hard it was, at the end of the war and with a Japanese husband, to get a government job. And then to have to sit on my hands all day, doing nothing . . ."

"Mrs. Taida . . ."

"I am not finished speaking," she said with authority, and I felt my face flush. "As I was saying, working at the CAP was like being a sailor on a rudderless ship. Have some more tea."

I held out my cup, as commanded.

"What endures in a government agency?" she asked as she poured again. "The management? The support staff? Job titles shift. Duties change. But the culture remains. It's like the tradition of a secretary feeding a stray cat at ten in the morning. The secretary may retire, but another will come, and if there's a tradition of feeding the stray cat at ten, then the person who takes the job will likely be someone who likes cats anyway. The cat may die or move on, but another will appear before long. The feeding goes on, even if who is fed and by whom changes over time."

She put the teapot down. "Administrators come and go, but the culture endures. And Kim Semper endures. When a citizen calls the agency for help, he isn't referred to management. No one at that level knows anything. No, the citizen is referred to Kim Semper. And for the pleasure of the work itself, of knowing things and being helpful, the secretaries do the job of the Coordinating Administration for Productivity. And they do a very good job. How many of those people who are helped by Kim Semper bother to write letters, do you suppose? And how many of the letters that are written actually end up in the hands of CAP administrators? Kim Semper provides good answers to hard questions about productivity and legislative action. I gave the CAP a rudder, you see. It operates from the galley, not the bridge."

"There's the question of ethics," I said. "There's the matter of lunches paid for by citizens, of benefit derived by fraud."

She looked at me long and hard. It was a look that said everything there was to say about collecting a GS-13 salary working for an agency where the managers were fuzzy about how they should fill their days. She didn't have to say a word.

"Well, what am I supposed to do then?" I said. "Now that I know the truth, what do I say when the administrator asks for my report?"

"You didn't get to where you are today without knowing how to stall," Mrs. Taida said. "You do what you do best, and let the secretaries do what *they* do best."

"What about *after* Cooper is gone?" I said. "This is a bomb just waiting to go off. This is the kind of thing that can sink a little agency like ours."

"The Coordinating Administration for Productivity is a fifty-year-old bureaucracy," Mrs. Taida said, "with a little secret that no one has discovered for forty years. You're the only one who threatens the status quo." She picked up our teacups and the pot. "If you don't rock the boat, I'm sure the CAP, along with Dust and Kim Semper, will endure for time without end. And now, if you don't mind, I have things to do."

I drove back to the office slowly. I knew what I had to do, but I didn't know exactly how to get it done. At least, not until I got as far as the Department of Agriculture. There, I pulled into the right lane and slowed to a crawl.

Size, I thought. The thing that comforts me about the Department of Agriculture is its size. It is big and white and easy to get lost in. That's what safety is.

I drove back and got right to work. It was a big job. I enlisted Vera and Roxie, along with Janet, Peter, and some of the secretaries from downstairs. I didn't explain in great detail what we were doing or why it was important. They understood. In a week, we had generated the very thing that Bill Cooper had called for.

"Results," I announced, shouldering between Susana and Tom to drop my report onto Cooper's desk. It landed with a thud. Cooper blinked slowly, then opened the heavy white binding to the first page. *A Report on Personnel and Operational Dislocation at the Coordinating Administration for Productivity,* it read. "Everything you need to know about Kim Semper is in there."

Cooper nodded. "It's, ah, impressive. You people really knocked yourselves out."

"Yes, sir," I said. "I can't take all the credit. Susana and Tom were instrumental, really."

Neither of them looked up. They were still staring at the report.

Cooper began to scan the executive summary, but his eyes began to glaze when he got to the paragraph about operational location as a time- and institution-based function not contingent upon the identity of the individual operator. "So can you summarize the contents for me?"

"Well," I said, "it's a bit involved. But you can get the gist of it in the summary that you're reading."

Cooper kept thumbing through the summary. It went on for ninety-three pages.

"To really get a complete sense of the situation," I said, "you'll need to read the complete report. Right, Susana?"

She nodded. "Of course."

"Tom?"

"You bet your ass. It's all there, though. Every damn bit of it." He said it with pride, as though he really had made some contribution.

"It took a thousand pages to get it said, Bill. And it really takes a thousand to make sense of it all. So, you see, I can't just give it to you in a sentence."

"I see," Cooper said, nodding, and he was still nodding, still looking at the four-inch volume, when Susana and Tom and I left the room.

"You're a goddam genius is what you are," Tom said. And Susana told me, "Good work."

And when Cooper cleared out for good, he left the report behind. It's there still, taking up space on his successor's desk. Sometimes when I see it sitting there, I think to myself that a bomb could go off in that room, and everything would be blown to hell but that plastic-bound, metal-spined, ten-pound volume of unreadable prose. It wouldn't suffer so much as a singed page.

It gives me a safe and solid feeling.

Bill Crider

HOW I FOUND A CAT, LOST TRUE LOVE AND BROKE THE BANK AT MONTE CARLO

1

Actually, the cat found me.

I was in the market section of Monaco, between the hills that support the royal palace on the one hand and the casino section of Monte Carlo on the other. It was a lovely day in early fall, the kind you read about in tourist manuals. The sun was bright, and the sky was a hard, brilliant blue.

The market was so crowded that I could hardly move. Flower vendors offered red and yellow and white blossoms that overflowed their paper cones, while food vendors hawked fish and vegetables, fruit and pastries. Shoppers swirled around me, and the street was packed with cars and vans.

The smells of roses and freshly caught seafood mingled with the odor of coffee from the sidewalk cafés, and I was thinking about having a cup of mocha when the cat ran up my leg, digging its claws into my jeans and hoisting itself right up to my waist.

For some reason I've never understood, cats find me attractive.

I settled my glasses on my nose, gently pried the cat loose, and held her in my arms. She was mostly black, with a white streak on her nose, a white badge on her chest, and white socks on her legs. Her eyes were emerald green and her heart was pounding as if she were frightened, but in that mob it was hard to tell what might be scaring her.

"What's the matter, cat?" I asked. Maybe that's why cats like me. I treat them as if their brains were larger than walnuts, though they aren't.

The cat of course didn't answer, but she did seem to relax a bit. Then a dog barked somewhere nearby and the cat tensed up, sliding her claws out and through my shirt, into the skin of my chest.

"It's all right," I said, squirming a little. "I won't let the dog get you."

The cat looked wide-eyed out over the heads of the crowd for the source of the barking. There was no dog in evidence, and though the cat didn't appear entirely convinced of my ability to protect her, she withdrew her claws from my shirt.

I hadn't come to Monaco to adopt a cat, as attractive as that idea might seem, so I looked around for someone to take her off my hands.

That's when I saw the woman.

She wasn't just any woman. She was *the* woman. Even in that crowd of the rich and beautiful, she stood out. She was tall and lithe. Her hair was midnight black under a pink sunhat, and her eyes were as deeply green as those of the cat I held in my arms. And she was walking straight toward me.

I was in love.

I opened my mouth, but nothing came out. Truly beautiful women affect my nervous system. They might not often be attracted to me, but I was certainly attracted to them.

"Hello," she said in English. She had that unidentifiable continental accent that I'd heard a lot in the last few days, but somehow it seemed much more charming from her than it had from anyone else. "Are you American?"

I managed to get my mouth to work. "How did you know?"

She laughed, though it was more like music to me than laughter. "You Americans are all alike. There is such an innocence about you."

She reached for the cat and rubbed a white hand along its dark coat. The cat began purring.

"That is why animals trust you," she said. "They can sense the innocence."

"I wondered about that," I told her.

"I'm sure that you did. True innocence never knows itself."

She took the cat from me. It went quite willingly and settled into her arms as if it belonged there.

"I thank you very much for rescuing Michelle. My uncle and I came to the market for fish, and she escaped my car when I opened the door to leave. There was a dog nearby, and I suspect that his barking may have frightened her."

"We heard him," I said.

She started to turn away, which is usually the case with women I meet. But then something unusual happened. She turned back.

"Would you like a cup of coffee, perhaps? Michelle would like to repay you for the rescue."

"What about your uncle?" I asked. Somehow I managed it without stuttering. "Won't he be worried about the cat?"

"He won't mind. He'll find us, I'm sure."

"I'd love some coffee," I said.

It was just as noisy at the small table where we sat under a striped umbrella as it had been in the market, but somehow we seemed isolated in an island of quiet where the only sounds were our two voices, along with the occasional mew from Michelle, who sat on a chair beside her owner, whose name was Antoinette Sagan. Tony to her friends, of which I was now officially one.

I had already told her to call me Mike.

"And what are you doing here in Monaco?" Tony asked me as she sipped her coffee.

"I came to break the bank at the casino," I said, pushing up my glasses.

Tony set her cup down and laughed. "As so many have. And how do you plan to do so?"

"Roulette," I said. "I have a system."

Tony winked at the cat. "Do you hear that, Michelle? The American has a system."

Michelle wasn't interested. She was watching some kind of bug that was crawling along the walk just beneath her chair.

Tony looked back at me and smiled. The green of her eyes was amazing. I think my heart fibrillated.

"Everyone has a system," she said. "For cards, for dice, for roulette. They come to Monaco daily. But no one has ever broken the bank."

"You'd never know if someone did," I said. "They'd never tell, and the banks here know how to keep a secret. Anyway, I don't have to break the bank, not really. I'd settle for a few million dollars."

Michelle had lost interest in the bug. She stepped up on the table and walked across it to me. She climbed into my lap, turned in a circle, and lay down, purring loudly.

"I believe you've made a conquest," Tony said. "And what is your system, if I may ask? Or is it a secret?"

I told her it wasn't a secret. I took one of my pens out of my pocket protector and pulled a napkin across the table.

"Do you know the game?" I asked.

Tony shrugged. The white shirt moved in interesting places, but I tried to ignore that.

"Of course," she said.

"Then you know the odds favoring the house." I jotted them on the napkin. "In American roulette, the house edge is five-point-two-six percent; in the European version it's two-point-seven-oh percent because there's no double zero on the wheel."

"So of course you'll be playing the European version."

"Of course. Now. Have you ever heard of the Martingale system?"

Tony made a comic frown. "Who has not? Many millions of francs have been lost with it. You make your bet. If you win, you take your winnings and begin again. If you lose, you double the bet. Lose again, double again." She took the pen from my hand and began scribbling on the napkin. "Say that your bet is one hundred francs on red. Seven times in a row the wheel comes up black. That means that your next bet will be twelve thousand eight hundred francs, but you will have already lost twelve thousand seven hundred francs. Should you win, you win one hundred francs, should you lose . . ." She shrugged again. "The croupier will be overjoyed to have you at his table."

Her figures were correct, and of course the house odds defeat everyone in the long run. I was going to beat the odds.

I told Tony that I was a math teacher at a community college in the States. That I'd always been fascinated with odds and statistics. And that I'd recently won fifty thousand dollars in the state lottery.

"Winning such a large amount was very lucky," she said. "And you have come to Monaco to lose it all at the roulette table? That does not seem practical."

"I'm not practical, and I don't think I'm going to lose."

I tried to elaborate on my system, which I explained was an elegant variation on the Martingale, involving shifting the bet to different locations, avoiding the low payoffs like red or black while never trying for the larger payoffs like the single number bet, and even dropping out of the betting occasionally.

"And if all else fails," I said, "maybe I'll get lucky."

"It has happened," she said.

"Right. About eighty years ago, black came up seventeen times in a row on one table. Anyone starting out with a dollar and leaving it on black would have won over, let's see . . ." I worked it out on the napkin. "One hundred thirty-one thousand seventy-two dollars. It could happen to me."

She looked at the cat, which was still lying comfortably in my lap. "You seem like a nice man, Mike. I hope it does happen to you, and that you pick up your money before the eighteenth spin of the wheel."

Her smile made my knees weak.

"I could share it with you if it happens that way," I said, hardly caring that her answer could pose a real problem for me if it was the one I wanted to hear.

She opened her mouth to say something, but I never found out what it was. She saw someone behind me, and her eyes darkened. She closed her mouth.

I looked around. A very large man stood there. He wore a white shirt and dark slacks, and he had a dark face that was pitted like volcanic rock. I suppose you could call him ruggedly handsome if you liked the type.

Tony said, "Hello, André. This is Mike. He has found Michelle."

I picked up the cat in my left arm and began to turn. Michelle growled low in her throat, and the hair ridged along her back.

"Stupid cat," André said. His voice was like Michelle's growl.

"André is my uncle," Tony explained. "He and Michelle are not mutual admirers."

I could see that much. I could also see that André was not at all interested in meeting me, much less in shaking hands. I dropped the hand that I had been about to extend.

Tony came around the table and took Michelle, who had stopped growling, though she didn't look very happy.

"Thank you so much, Mike," Tony said. "André and I are both grateful."

Sure they were. André had already turned his back and was walking away. He was wide as a billboard.

"I hope you win at the casino," Tony said over her shoulder as she turned to follow André.

I watched them move through the crowd. André didn't look like anyone's uncle to me, and I wondered if Tony had lied. I suppose that it didn't make any difference.

Besides, if she had lied, we were even. After all, I hadn't won the lottery. I wasn't even a math teacher.

2

Cammie was waiting for me in a little café not far from the market. She was drinking black coffee and smoking a Players. She knew I didn't like cigarettes, but she didn't bother to snuff it out when I sat down. No one else minded. It wasn't like an American café. There were lots of smokers.

It was a little after noon, and I ordered a sandwich. Cammie didn't want one. She was too wired to eat.

"You look really dorky in those glasses," she said. Her voice was low and slightly husky, a quality I attributed to the cigarettes. "And where on earth did you get the pocket protector? Elmer's Plumbing? Give me a break."

"I thought it was nice touch," I told her.

She took a deep swallow of coffee. "You probably think that stupid part in your hair's a nice touch, too, but it isn't."

"It should fool the croupier," I said. "He won't know he's seen me before."

"I guess. If you want to risk it."

"I'm willing. What did you find out?"

She blew a spiral of smoke and looked around. No one appeared interested in us.

"I think you were right," she said, grinning.

She looked good with a grin. Short blonde hair, blue eyes, a small mouth and nose. Sort of the gamine look. Not that she looked as good as Tony, but she looked pretty good.

And like me, she could look quite different when the occasion called for it, as it had lately. Yesterday she'd looked like a fashion model on vacation, and the day before that she'd looked like a harassed mother who'd misplaced her three kids.

We'd been watching the wheels in Monte Carlo's famous casino for four days, and a couple of days earlier we'd settled on the one at table four. My theory was that a system wasn't good enough. It would help if you could find a wheel that was just slightly out of balance.

It didn't need to be out of balance much. Hardly any, in fact, and the odds against finding one were quite high in themselves. Casinos generally go to a lot of trouble to make sure that everything is perfect, but now and then someone slips up. It doesn't happen often. Hardly ever, in fact. But it does happen.

We'd been looking for weeks. Monte Carlo wasn't our first stop, and it wouldn't have been our last had we not found the right wheel. It looked as if we had.

All we needed was a wheel that turned up one number more often than any other. To be sure that we'd found one, we had to watch it for at least twenty-four hours. We'd been watching for forty-eight, spread out over three days, in our various disguises. Cammie had just come off the final shift.

"So it's the five?" I said.

She crushed out the cigarette. "It's the five, all right. Table four."

The odds of any single number coming up are one in thirty-seven. The red five was coming up more often than that, more like one time in thirty. That was more than often enough to offset the house odds on a single zero wheel.

"So if they don't adjust the wheel before tonight, we use the system on the five," she said. "At table four. And you're the player."

"That's me. Joe Nerd."

"You're not going to wear that get-up. Not really."

I told her that I wasn't going to change much, and that I had a good reason. When I told her why, she wasn't happy with me.

"You idiot! You actually *told* someone we had a system?"

"Not *we*. I told her that *I* had a system. She doesn't know about you. And I didn't tell her anything at all about the wheel. So don't worry."

Cammie showed instant suspicion, one of her less attractive qualities. "I should have known it was a woman. You always talk too much to women. What does she look like?"

The waiter brought my sandwich, and I took a bite to avoid answering. After I'd finished chewing, I said, "She looks good. But not great."

Cammie narrowed her eyes. I could tell she didn't trust me, not that I blamed her.

Cammie and I had met two years earlier in Las Vegas, where she'd been dealing blackjack. I'd made a bundle at her table, and we'd gotten out of town just before anyone figured out how I was doing it, a little matter of a trick that involved her help and that was in violation of every casino rule in the book. We'd made a little money since, here and there, enough so that I had a pretty good stake, and then I'd come up with the idea of finding a roulette wheel that was just slightly out of whack. I'd never expected to find it in Monte Carlo, really, but I was just as happy that we had.

"So why did you tell her?" Cammie asked. "I thought you were nervous around women."

She knew me pretty well. I'd been nervous around her too, at first, and talked too much, though if I hadn't had a drink or three too many, I'd never have tried to con her into helping me with the blackjack scam. As it turned out, she didn't need conning. She was eager to help.

"I found her cat," I said. I told her all about Tony, the cat, and Uncle André.

"Uncle, my Aunt Fanny," she said. She got out a Players and lit it with a disposable lighter from her purse. "You should've kept your mouth shut."

"Not really," I rationalized. "That's the beauty of it. She seems to know her way around here, and when word gets out that some geek broke the bank, she'll remember me and tell people about my supposed system. People will think I got lucky. No one will ever know we had a fixed wheel."

"It isn't fixed. It's just a little out of balance."

"You're absolutely right. And they certainly can't blame us for that."

She blew a smoke ring and stuck her finger through it. "Describe this André for me again."

I did.

"Dark hair?"

For some reason I don't usually notice men's hair, but now that she mentioned it, I remembered.

"Yes," I said. "And a little curly."

"I think I've seen him around the casino. Do you think he could be security?"

He was certainly big enough, but I didn't think they'd use anyone that obvious.

"Probably just another gambler," I said. "And remember what we just discussed. It's not our fault if the wheel's out of balance."

She took a deep drag from the cigarette and turned to blow the smoke away from me. Or maybe she just didn't want me to see her face.

"I'll remember," she said.

3

I went to the casino just as night was falling. I had to walk, because parking in the crush of automobiles there is almost impossible, but I didn't mind. The casino is an impressive sight, worth looking at as you approach it from nearly any angle, especially at night when the floodlights are on.

The floodlights brighten the ornate casino facade and throw into obscurity the high-rises that suffocate the area around it. Once Monte Carlo must have been a beautiful place, but now it looks a lot like any city anywhere.

Across from the casino, boats lined the harbor, and there was just the faintest tinge of azure still in the sky where it met the dark sea.

I had on my thick-rimmed glasses, and I was wearing a dark three-piece suit that was about four years out of style, loafers with tassels, and a paisley tie. I was worth a second glance from the man who checked my passport, but no more than that. He didn't care how I dressed as long as I had on a tie.

He returned my passport, and I walked into the American Room, which is filled with tourists who seem to want to lose their money fast. The smoky air was noisy with the sound of the 120 slot machines and the balls clacking around the American-style roulette wheels.

I walked right on through, with only a glance into the Pink Salon, the bar where Cammie would be waiting for me. The ceiling was painted with floating women, most of whom were nude and most of whom were smoking. I didn't see Cammie.

As I paid my fee to enter the European Room, I had a qualm or two about the tie and about the tassels on the loafers; the standards here were somewhat higher than for the first room in the casino. But apparently I passed muster. I was allowed to enter.

Besides being classier, the European Room was much quieter than the American Room. Nearly everyone was better-dressed than I was, and everyone looked quite serious about the business at hand, which was gambling. The *chefs* watched the tables from tall wooden chairs, their eyes bright and alert for any sign of trouble.

I wasn't going to be any trouble. I was just there to win a large sum of money. I exchanged a huge wad of francs for chips and walked up to the table, which was set up a bit differently from an American table. There are layouts for betting on both sides of the table, and in this room there were padded rails not far away so that onlookers could lean at their ease and get a few vicarious thrills by watching the real gamblers.

I approached the table and put five hundred francs down on the black ten. I thought I might as well lose a little to begin with.

Almost as soon as the money was down, one of the croupiers said, *"Rien ne va plus."* The *tourneur* spun the wheel and dropped the silver ball, which whirred and bounced and clicked. I took a deep breath and waited for it to drop.

I don't know when Tony arrived. I noticed her about two hours into the game, standing at the rail directly across the table from me. She smiled when I looked up, and my concentration broke for a moment.

That was all right. I needed a little break. I was almost fifty thousand francs in the hole. It wasn't as bad as it sounds at first, since a dollar is worth five francs, but ten thousand dollars is still a lot of money. In fact it was about a third of my stake. Things weren't working out exactly as I'd planned.

The five hadn't been coming up, not often enough and certainly not when I had money on it. My real plan—as opposed to the one I'd told Tony about—had been to move the money around at first, putting a little on the red five now and then so that no one would be suspicious when I started playing the five exclusively. I'd win a little, lose a little, then get hot and break the bank.

It had seemed like a good plan when I thought of it, but obviously it wasn't working out. I was losing more than I was winning. Maybe the wheel wasn't out of balance after all. Or maybe I was just unlucky.

There was a TV commercial in the States when I left, something about never letting them see you sweat. Well, I was sweating, and if something good didn't happen soon, they were going to see me doing it.

The break was over. I wondered if Tony's appearance at the rail might not be an omen. What the hell, I thought. I shoved all the rest of my chips out on the table, onto the five.

The *tourneur* gave the wheel a practiced spin and flipped the ball in the opposite direction. Time suddenly slowed down. The ball glided like mercury on tile, and then it began bouncing. Every time that it bounced, it seemed to hang in the air for several seconds before striking the wheel again.

I looked at Tony. She was still smiling; it was as if she hadn't moved at all.

I glanced back at the wheel, and things suddenly snapped back to normal. The ball bounced once, twice, three times, and landed in the five.

As the croupier called out the number, I let out a breath that I hadn't even known I was holding. I'd put nearly twenty-five thousand francs on the number, at odds of thirty-five to one. That meant I'd won almost one hundred seventy-five thousand dollars in one spin of the wheel.

I straightened my glasses. "Let it ride," I said. It was time to go with the flow.

The croupier called to someone, and a man dressed better than most of the gamblers came over to the table. There was a whispered conversation.

I thought about the time all those years ago when the ball had landed in the black seventeen times in a row. I didn't need seventeen times in a row. I just needed to hit one more time. The odds against it happening were huge, but not as bad as you might think. The wheel didn't know that the red five had just come up. I had the same chance of hitting it again that I'd had the first time. And if the wheel really was out of balance, maybe the chance was better than it should be.

The croupier was looking at me as the well-dressed man whispered to him. I tried to keep my voice level and repeated, "Let it ride."

The man was finished with the croupier. Now he wanted to talk to me. I didn't blame him. If I hit, I was going to win something like six and a quarter million dollars. I was sweating a lot more now than I'd been when I was losing.

The man was very polite, and he didn't appear to be as nervous as I was. Probably he dealt with large sums of money more often than I did.

"Are you enjoying yourself, *monsieur?*" he asked.

"Very much," I said, taking off my glasses and cleaning them with a tissue from my suit pocket. My heart was about to jump out of my chest, but my hands didn't tremble. Much.

"Do you realize the value of your bet?" His voice was as calm as if he were discussing the beautiful autumn weather we were having.

"I believe I do," I said, settling the glasses on my nose and returning the tissue to my pocket. I patted my hair just to the right of the part and smiled at him.

"You have won quite a sum of money already. Are you sure that you want to risk it all on one spin of the wheel?"

I shrugged. Casual Joe Nerd. "Easy come, easy go."

He mumbled something then that might have been a reference to "stupid Americans," but I didn't quite catch it. I wasn't meant to.

I looked around at the crowd. There were a lot more people watching now than there had been only moments before. All of them were observing us expectantly, Tony among them. She licked her lips in anticipation, and my heart beat even faster.

"Everyone's waiting," I said. "I hope the casino won't let them down."

The man didn't bother to look at the crowd. For that matter, he didn't bother to look at me. Six million dollars wasn't really that much money, not to him and the house. It wouldn't break the bank, though it would come close enough to satisfy me.

The man nodded to the croupier, who said, *"Rien ne va plus."* The room became as silent as an empty cathedral.

When the *tourneur* spun the wheel, it seemed to roar like a jet plane on takeoff. The ball zipped around like an Indy racer, and when it bounced it sounded like a skull ricocheting inside a marble cavern.

I couldn't watch. I closed my eyes. I may even have crossed my fingers.

About ten years later, I heard the croupier.

"Rouge." There was a pause of nearly a century, and I could hear the blood pounding in my head. Then he said, quite calmly, *"Cinq."*

I opened my eyes. There was a clamoring and shouting like you might hear when an underdog wins the Superbowl. Men were pounding me on the back and women were trying to kiss me. My knees were weak, but I was rapidly gaining strength.

I craned my neck above the sea of heads, trying to find Tony, but she was gone. I didn't wonder about her for long. Instead I looked back at the wheel and the silvery ball nestling in the five.

I'll admit it. There was an instant when I actually thought about saying, "Let it ride." If I hit again, I'd win over 214 million dollars. I really would break the bank at Monte Carlo, or come very close.

Would the well-dressed man have let me take the chance? Probably, in the hope that I'd lose; the odds were certainly against me, unbalanced wheel or not. Or maybe he'd hustle me outside, unwilling to allow me the opportunity to win.

It didn't matter. I told them to cash me in.

"Follow me, *monsieur*," the well-dressed man said. I did, after making sure that the croupiers and the *tourneur* had nice tips. I could afford to be generous.

I couldn't resist looking back, though, to see where the ball landed on the next spin.

In the black, thirty-two.

It was just as well I'd stopped.

4

Cammie was in the bar when I arrived carrying a black leather case.

"My God," she said. "You won."

I nodded.

She crushed out the cigarette she had been smoking, a sure sign that she was excited. "How much?" She didn't wait for an answer. "Was that cheering I heard in there for you? I thought it might be, but I couldn't bear to go in and find out."

I said that the cheering had been for me.

"Oh my God! I can't believe it! How much?"

I told her.

She stared at the leather bag. "And it's all in there?"

"Not all of it. They don't keep that much on hand, or if they do, they don't give it out to guys like me. But there's a lot. I told them I'd take a check for the rest."

"My God." She fumbled in her purse for her cigarettes, then gave it up. She looked back at the bag. "Everyone in that room knows you won. How are we going to get it to the hotel without being robbed?"

I turned and gestured toward the doorway. There were two large men in tight suits standing there.

"The casino was kind enough to provide an escort. No one wants to see a lucky gambler lose his winnings to a footpad."

"A footpad?"

"Cutpurse, mugger, what-have-you."

"You talk funny when you're excited."

"If you think I'm excited now, wait until we get to the hotel. I've always wanted to play Scrooge McDuck. You know. Throw it up and let it hit me on the head. Burrow through it like a gopher."

"Now's your chance," she said. She hooked an arm through mine. "Let's go."

5

We arrived at the hotel without incident, and the bodyguards left us without a word, except to thank me for the tip. I was about to have the bag put in the hotel vault when Cammie stopped me.

"Scrooge McDuck," she said. "Remember?"

I didn't suppose it would hurt anything. She deserved to see the money. And the check. We went up to the room.

When we opened the door, we got quite a surprise.

Tony was sitting in an armchair, waiting for us. So was Michelle, who was curled in Tony's lap, asleep.

And so, unfortunately, was Uncle André, who was holding a very ugly pistol in his right hand. A Glock 17, ugly but very accurate, or so I've heard.

"Shit," Cammie said, glaring at me. I didn't blame her.

"Close the door," André said, moving the pistol barrel just slightly.

I did what he said.

"Who's your friend, Mike?" Tony asked.

"Inspector Lestrade, Scotland Yard," I said, but no one laughed.

"You're a very lucky man, Mike," Tony said, stroking Michelle's back. The cat began to purr so loudly that I could hear her across the room. "Didn't I tell you he seemed lucky, André?"

"If I were lucky, you wouldn't be here," I said, thinking that it was really too bad. She was such a beautiful woman, and I'd been halfway in love with her. If she'd asked me nicely, I might have given her the money; after all, in a way, she'd helped me win it. Then again, maybe I wouldn't have.

André didn't seem to care one way or the other. "Give me the bag," he said.

"It won't do you any good," Cammie said. "There's no money. It's a check."

"I'm afraid we don't believe that," Tony said. "You see, we've been waiting around for days for someone like you, Mike. André is a terrible

319

gambler, and I am not much better, but I could tell this morning that you were different. Did I not say so, André?"

André said nothing. He just stared at me with eyes like black glass.

"I had to ask André to wait. He wanted to take you for a little ride this morning and relieve you of your stake, but I told him to wait. I told him I had faith in you. Is that not true, André?"

André didn't answer the question. "Give me the bag," he told me, "or I will shoot your woman."

Cammie was furious. With me, for having told Tony I had a system, and with André for calling her my woman.

"He won't shoot," she said. "If he does, half the hotel will come running to this room."

"That is true," Tony said.

She got up, carrying the cat along with her, and walked to the bed. She picked up one of the pillows and took it to André.

"Use this," she said.

André muffled the pistol with the pillow. "Give me the bag."

I tensed just a little.

"And don't throw it," André said. "I'll shoot your woman."

"Shoot me then, you son of a bitch," Cammie said, throwing her purse at him.

When she did, I swung the bag as hard as I could at Tony. I hated to mess up her beautiful face, but I didn't hate it as much as I hated the thought of giving them any of my money.

The bag hit Tony at just about the same time the pistol went off, and made just about as much noise.

Even noisier than the pistol was the cat, which had jumped from Tony's arms and was yowling in the middle of the floor, its back arched, its tail puffed to three times its normal size. The air was filled with feathers from the pillow. I couldn't see Cammie. Maybe she had taken cover in the bathroom.

Tony had fallen back across the bed. Her nose was bleeding, but I wasn't worried about her. I was worried about André, who had started toward me. He wouldn't need the pistol. He could break me in half with his bare hands if he wanted to.

He might have done it, but he made one mistake. He didn't watch out for the cat. Maybe he didn't see her because of the feathers.

Michelle didn't like him anyway, and when he ran into her, she fastened herself to his right leg, sinking her claws into his calf and trying to bite through his pants.

He was hopping on his left leg and pointing the pistol at her when I let him have it with the bag. His face was one I didn't mind messing up.

I connected solidly, and André staggered backward. Michelle released him and ran under the bed, which was just as well. When I hit André again, he wobbled against the french doors that led to a tiny balcony.

The doors weren't locked, and they hardly slowed him down. Neither did the low railing outside. I have to give him credit. He didn't yell as he went over, or even on the way down. I heard him crash into some patio furniture.

I went outside and looked down. André was sprawled atop the remains of a metal table. Our room was on the third floor, not so great a distance from the ground. Maybe he'd even survive.

I heard a noise and turned back to the room. Tony was still on the bed, but now Cammie was sitting on top of her, straddling her waist. Tony was struggling to get up, but Cammie had pinned her arms and all she could do was thrash around.

"Let her go," I said. "She won't bother us without André around."

Cammie got off Tony, though I could tell she wanted to do a little more damage first. She stood beside the bed, disheveled and glowering. Her nose was no longer bleeding, however.

"Are you all right?" I asked Tony.

"You brogue my dose, you sud of a bitch."

Cammie, either because she felt sorry for Tony or because she didn't like the sight of blood, got her purse from the floor and dug around until she found a couple of tissues. She handed them to Tony.

"Sorry about your nose," I said. "You were trying to rob me, after all. Is that what you and André do for a living? Rob innocent tourists?"

She crumpled the tissues. "Iddocedt? Whod's iddocedt, you sud of a—"

"Never mind," I said. "And you don't have to call us names. We're not going to turn you in."

"We're not?" Cammie said.

"We don't want to cause any trouble. We just want to go on our way and enjoy our money. And we have lots to enjoy."

Tony sat up. She was wearing a white blouse, and there was a lot of blood on it. I wondered what the hotel staff would make of that, but I decided I didn't care.

"I cad go?" she said.

"Sure. Don't let us keep you. And you might want to check on your friend. I'm not sure, but I thought I saw him moving."

She stalked across the room. When her hand touched the doorknob, Cammie said, "Don't forget your cat."

"André has never liked Michelle," Tony said. "I do not think he will want to see her again."

And then she was out the door and gone.

Cammie took a deep breath. "You always talk too much to women," she said.

"And you smoke too much. I'll try to quit talking too much to women if you'll try to stop smoking."

I still had the bag in my hand. I walked over and put it on the chair. I thought it would be a good idea to put the money in the hotel safe now. I was no longer in the mood to play Scrooge McDuck.

"Why all the sudden concern about my smoking?" Cammie asked.

Michelle came halfway out from under the bed and stared at us. After a second or two she walked over and started rubbing against my leg and purring.

"Secondhand smoke," I said, reaching down to stroke Michelle's head. She began to purr even louder. Cats like me, all right. "It's bad for the cat."

Ambrose Bierce

A CARGO OF CAT

On the 16th day of June, 1874, the ship *Mary Jane* sailed from Malta, heavily laden with cat. This cargo gave us a good deal of trouble. It was not in bales, but had been dumped into the hold loose. Captain Doble, who had once commanded a ship that carried coals, said he had found that plan the best. When the hold was full of cat the hatch was battened down and we felt good. Unfortunately the mate, thinking the cats would be thirsty, introduced a hose into one of the hatches and pumped in a considerable quantity of water, and the cats of the lower levels were all drowned.

You have seen a dead cat in a pond: you remember its circumference at the waist. Water multiplies the magnitude of a dead cat by ten. On the first day out, it was observed that the ship was much strained. She was three feet wider than usual and as much as ten feet shorter. The convexity of her deck was visibly augmented fore and aft, but she turned up at both ends. Her rudder was clean out of water and she would answer the helm only when running directly against a strong breeze: the rudder, when perverted to one side, would rub against the wind and slew her around; and then she wouldn't steer any more. Owing to the curvature of the keel, the masts came together at the top, and a sailor who had gone up the foremast got bewildered, came down the mizzenmast, looked out over the stern at the receding shores of Malta and shouted: "Land, ho!" The ship's fastenings were all giving way; the water on each side was lashed into foam by the tempest of flying bolts that she shed at every pulsation of the cargo. She was quietly wrecking herself without assistance from wind or wave, by the sheer internal energy of feline expansion.

I went to the skipper about it. He was in his favorite position, sitting on the deck, supporting his back against the binnacle, making a V of his legs, and smoking.

"Captain Doble," I said, respectfully touching my hat, which was really not worthy of respect, "this floating palace is afflicted with curvature of the spine and is likewise greatly swollen."

Without raising his eyes he courteously acknowledged my presence by knocking the ashes from his pipe.

"Permit me, Captain," I said, with simple dignity, "to repeat that this ship is much swollen."

"If that is true," said the gallant mariner, reaching for his tobacco pouch, "I think it would be as well to swab her down with liniment. There's a bottle of it in my cabin. Better suggest it to the mate."

"But, Captain, there is no time for empirical treatment; some of the planks at the water line have started."

The skipper rose and looked out over the stern, toward the land; he fixed his eyes on the foaming wake; he gazed into the water to starboard and to port. Then he said:

"My friend, the whole darned thing has started."

Sadly and silently I turned from that obdurate man and walked forward. Suddenly "there was a burst of thunder sound!" The hatch that had held down the cargo was flung whirling into space and sailed in the air like a blown leaf. Pushing upward through the hatchway was a smooth, square column of cat. Grandly and impressively it grew—slowly, serenely, majestically it rose toward the welkin, the relaxing keel parting the mastheads to give it a fair chance. I have stood at Naples and seen Vesuvius painting the town red—from Catania have marked afar, upon the flanks of Ætna, the lava's awful pursuit of the astonished rooster and the despairing pig. The fiery flow from Kilauea's crater, thrusting itself into the forests and licking the entire country clean, is as familiar to me as my mother-tongue. I have seen glaciers, a thousand years old and quite bald, heading for a valley full of tourists at the rate of an inch a month. I have seen a saturated solution of mining camp going down a mountain river, to make a sociable call on the valley farmers. I have stood behind a tree on the battle-field and seen a compact square mile of armed men moving with irresistible momentum to the rear. Whenever anything grand in magnitude or motion is billed to appear I commonly manage to beat my way into the show, and in reporting it I am a man of unscrupulous veracity; but I have seldom observed anything like that solid gray column of Maltese cat!

It is unnecessary to explain, I suppose, that each individual grimalkin in the outfit, with that readiness of resource which distinguishes the species, had grappled with tooth and nail as many others as it could hook on to. This preserved the formation. It made the column so stiff that when the ship rolled (and the *Mary Jane* was a devil to roll) it swayed from side to side like a mast, and the Mate said if it grew much taller he would have to order it cut away or it would capsize us.

Some of the sailors went to work at the pumps, but these discharged nothing but fur. Captain Doble raised his eyes from his toes and shouted: "Let go the anchor!" but being assured that nobody was touching it, apologized and resumed his revery. The chaplain said if there were no objections he would like to offer up a prayer, and a gambler from Chicago, producing a pack of cards, proposed to throw round for the first jack. The parson's plan was adopted, and as he uttered the final "amen," the cats struck up a hymn.

All the living ones were now above deck, and every mother's son of them sang. Each had a pretty fair voice, but no ear. Nearly all their notes in the upper register were more or less cracked and disobedient. The remarkable thing about the voices was their range. In that crowd were cats of seventeen octaves, and the average could not have been less than twelve.

Number of cats, as per invoice 127,000
Estimated number dead swellers 6,000
Total songsters 121,000
Average number octaves per cat 12
Total octaves 1,452,000

It was a great concert. It lasted three days and nights, or, counting each night as seven days, twenty-four days altogether, and we could not go below for provisions. At the end of that time the cook came for'd shaking up some beans in a hat, and holding a large knife.

"Shipmates," said he, "we have done all that mortals can do. Let us now draw lots."

We were blindfolded in turn, and drew, but just as the cook was forcing the fatal black bean upon the fattest man, the concert closed with a suddenness that waked the man on the lookout. A moment later every grimalkin relaxed his hold on his neighbors, the column lost its cohesion and, with 121,000 dull, sickening thuds that beat as one, the whole business fell to the deck. Then with a wild farewell wail that feline host sprang spitting into the sea and struck out southward for the African shore!

The southern extension of Italy, as every schoolboy knows, resembles in shape an enormous boot. We had drifted within sight of it. The cats in the fabric had spied it, and their alert imaginations were instantly affected with a lively sense of the size, weight and probably momentum of its flung boot-jack.

Théophile Gautier

THE WHITE AND BLACK DYNASTIES

A cat brought from Havana by Mademoiselle Aïta de la Penuela, a young Spanish artist whose studies of white angoras may still be seen gracing the printsellers' windows, produced the daintiest little kitten imaginable. It was just like a swan's-down powder-puff, and on account of its immaculate whiteness it received the name of Pierrot. When it grew big this was lengthened to Don Pierrot de Navarre as being more grandiose and majestic.

Don Pierrot, like all animals which are spoilt and made much of, developed a charming amiability of character. He shared the life of the household with all the pleasure which cats find in the intimacy of the domestic hearth. Seated in his usual place near the fire, he really appeared to understand what was being said, and to take an interest in it.

His eyes followed the speakers, and from time to time he would utter little sounds, as though he too wanted to make remarks and give his opinion on literature, which was our usual topic of conversation. He was very fond of books, and when he found one open on a table he would lie on it, look at the page attentively, and turn over the leaves with his paw; then he would end by going to sleep, for all the world as if he were reading a fashionable novel.

Directly I took up a pen he would jump on my writing-desk and with deep attention watch the steel nib tracing black spider-legs on the expanse of white paper, and his head would turn each time I began a new line. Sometimes he tried to take part in the work, and would attempt to pull the pen out of my hand, no doubt in order to write himself, for he was an aesthetic cat, like Hoffman's Murr, and I strongly suspect him of having scribbled his memoirs at night on some house-top by the light of his phosphorescent eyes. Unfortunately these lucubrations have been lost.

Don Pierrot never went to bed until I came in. He waited for me inside the door, and as I entered the hall he would rub himself against my legs and arch his back, purring joyfully all the time. Then he proceeded to walk in front of me like a page, and if I had asked him, he would certainly have carried the candle for me. In this fashion he escorted me to my room and waited while I undressed; then he would jump on the bed, put his paws round my neck, rub noses with me, and lick me with his rasping little pink tongue, while giving vent to soft inarticulate cries, which clearly expressed how pleased he was to see me again. Then when his transports of affection had subsided, and the hour for repose had come, he would balance himself on the rail of the bedstead and sleep there like a bird perched on a bough. When I woke in the morning he would come and lie near me until it was time to get up. Twelve o'clock was the hour at which I was supposed to come in. On this subject Pierrot had all the notions of a concierge.

At that time we had instituted little evening gatherings among a few friends, and had formed a small society, which we called the Four Candles Club, the room in which we met being, as it happened, lit by four candles in silver candlesticks, which were placed at the corners of the table.

Sometimes the conversation became so lively that I forgot the time, at the risk of finding, like Cinderella, my carriage turned into a pumpkin and my coachman into a rat.

Pierrot waited for me several times until two o'clock in the morning, but in the end my conduct displeased him, and he went to bed without me. This mute protest against my innocent dissipation touched me so much that ever after I came home regularly at midnight. But it was a long time before Pierrot forgave me. He wanted to be sure that it was not a sham repentance; but when he was convinced of the sincerity of my conversion, he deigned to take me into favour again, and he resumed his nightly post in the entrancehall.

To gain the friendship of a cat is not an easy thing. It is a philosophic, well-regulated, tranquil animal, a creature of habit and a lover of order and cleanliness. It does not give its affections indiscriminately. It will consent to be your friend if you are worthy of the honour, but it will not be your slave. With all its affection, it preserves its freedom of judgment, and it will not do anything for you which it considers unreasonable; but once it has given its love, what absolute confidence, what fidelity of affection! It will make itself the companion of your hours of work, of loneliness, or of sadness. It will lie the whole evening on your knee, purring and happy in your society, and leaving the company of creatures of its own kind to be with you. In vain the sound of caterwauling reverberates from the house-tops, inviting it to one of those cats' evening parties where essence of red-herring takes the place of tea. It will not be tempted, but continues to keep its vigil with you. If you put it down it climbs up again quickly, with a sort of crooning noise, which is like a gentle reproach. Sometimes, when seated in front of you, it gazes at you with such soft, melting eyes, such a human and caressing look, that you are almost awed, for it seems impossible that reason can be absent from it.

Don Pierrot had a companion of the same race as himself, and no less white. All the imaginable snowy comparisons it were possible to pile up would not suffice to give an idea of that immaculate fur, which would have made ermine look yellow.

I called her Seraphita, in memory of Balzac's Swedenborgian romance. The heroine of that wonderful story, when she climbed the snow peaks of the Falberg with Minna, never shone with a more pure white radiance. Seraphita had a dreamy and pensive character. She would lie motionless on a cushion for hours, not asleep, but with eyes fixed in rapt attention on scenes invisible to ordinary mortals.

Caresses were agreeable to her, but she responded to them with great reserve, and only to those of people whom she favoured with her esteem, which it was not easy to gain. She liked luxury, and it was always in the newest armchair or on the piece of furniture best calculated to show off her swan-like beauty, that she was to be found. Her toilette took an immense time. She would carefully smooth her entire coat every morning, and wash her face with her paw, and every hair on her body shone like new silver when brushed by her pink tongue. If anyone touched her she would immediately efface all traces of the contact, for she could not endure being ruffled. Her elegance and distinction gave one an idea of aristocratic birth, and among her own kind she must have been at least a duchess. She had a passion for scents. She would plunge her nose into bouquets, and nibble a perfumed handkerchief with little paroxysms of delight. She would walk about on the dressing-table sniffing the stoppers of the scent-bottles, and she would have loved to use the violet powder if she had been allowed.

Such was Seraphita, and never was a cat more worthy of a poetic name.

Don Pierrot de Navarre, being a native of Havana, needed a hothouse temperature. This he found indoors, but the house was surrounded by large gardens, divided up by palings through which a cat could easily slip, and planted with big trees in which hosts of birds twittered and sang; and sometimes Pierrot, taking advantage of an open door, would go out hunting of an evening and run over the dewy grass and flowers. He would then have to wait till morning to be let in again, for although he might come mewing under the windows, his appeal did not always wake the sleepers inside.

He had a delicate chest, and one colder night than usual he took a chill which soon developed into consumption. Poor Pierrot, after a year of coughing, became wasted and thin, and his coat, which formerly boasted such a snowy gloss, now put one in mind of the lustreless white of a shroud. His great limpid eyes looked enormous in his attenuated face. His pink nose had grown pale, and he would walk sadly along the sunny wall with slow steps, and watch the yellow autumn leaves whirling up in spirals. He looked as though he were reciting Millevoye's elegy.

There is nothing more touching than a sick animal; it submits to suffering with such gentle, pathetic resignation.

Everything possible was done to try and save Pierrot. He had a very clever doctor who sounded him and felt his pulse. He ordered him asses' milk, which the poor creature drank willingly enough out of his little china saucer. He lay for hours on my knee like the ghost of a sphinx, and I could feel the bones of his spine like the beads of a rosary under my fingers. He tried to respond to my caresses with a feeble purr which was like a death rattle.

When he was dying he lay panting on his side, but with a supreme effort he raised himself and came to me with dilated eyes in which there was a look of intense supplication. This look seemed to say: "Cannot you save me, you who are a man?" Then he staggered a short way with eyes already glazing, and fell down with such a lamentable cry, so full of despair and anguish, that I was pierced with silent horror.

He was buried at the bottom of the garden under a white rosebush which still marks his grave.

Seraphita died two or three years later of diphtheria, against which no science could prevail.

She rests not far from Pierrot. With her the white dynasty became extinct, but not the family. To this snow-white pair were born three kittens as black as ink.

Let him explain this mystery who can.

Just at that time Victor Hugo's *Misérables* was in great vogue, and the names of the characters in the novel were on everyone's lips. I called the two male kittens Enjolras and Gavroche, while the little female received the name of Eponine.

They were perfectly charming in their youth. I trained them like dogs to fetch and carry a bit of paper crumpled into a ball, which I threw for them. In time they learnt to fetch it from the tops of cupboards, from behind chests or from the bottom of tall vases, out of which they would pull it very cleverly with their paws. When they grew up they disdained such frivolous games, and acquired that calm philosophic temperament which is the true nature of cats.

To people landing in America in a slave colony all negroes are negroes, and indistinguishable from one another. In the same way, to careless eyes, three black cats are three black cats; but attentive observers make no such mistake. Animal physiognomy varies as much as that of men, and I could distinguish perfectly between those faces, all three as black as Harlequin's mask, and illuminated by emerald disks shot with gold.

Enjolras was by far the handsomest of the three. He was remarkable for his great leonine head and big ruff, his powerful shoulders, long back and splendid feathery tail. There was something theatrical about him, and he seemed to be always posing like a popular actor who knows he is being admired. His movements were slow, undulating and majestic. He put each foot down with as much circumspection as if he were walking on a table covered with Chinese bric-à-brac or Venetian glass. As to his character, he was by no means a stoic, and he showed a love of eating which that virtuous and sober young man, his namesake, would certainly have disapproved. Enjolras would undoubtedly have said to him, like the angel to Swedenborg: "You eat too much."

I humoured this gluttony, which was as amusing as a gastronomic monkey's, and Enjolras attained a size and weight seldom reached by the domestic cat. It occurred to me to have him shaved poodle-fashion, so as to give the finishing touch to his resemblance to a lion.

We left him his mane and a big tuft at the end of his tail, and I would not swear that we did not give him mutton-chop whiskers on his haunches like those Munito wore. Thus tricked out, it must be confessed he was much more like a Japanese monster than an African lion. Never was a more fantastic whim carved out of a living animal. His shaven skin took odd blue tints, which contrasted strangely with his black mane.

Gavroche, as though desirous of calling to mind his namesake in the novel, was a cat with an arch and crafty expression of countenance. He was smaller than Enjolras, and his movements were comically quick and brusque. In him absurd capers and ludicrous postures took the place of the banter and slang of the Parisian gamin. It must be confessed that Gavroche had vulgar tastes. He seized every possible occasion to leave the drawing-room in order to go and make up parties in the backyard, or even in the street, with stray cats,

"De naissance quelconque et de sang peu prouvé,"

in which doubtful company he completely forgot his dignity as cat of Havana, son of Don Pierrot de Navarre, grandee of Spain of the first order, and of the aristocratic and haughty Doña Seraphita.

Sometimes in his truant wanderings he picked up emaciated comrades, lean with hunger, and brought them to his plate of food to give them a treat in his good-natured, lordly way. The poor creatures, with ears laid back and watchful side-glances, in fear of being interrupted in their free meal by the broom of the housemaid, swallowed double, triple, and quadruple mouthfuls, and, like the famous dog, Siete-Aguas (seven waters) of Spanish *posadas* (inns), they licked the plate as clean as if it had been washed and polished by one of Gerard Dow's or Mieris's Dutch housewives.

Seeing Gavroche's friends reminded me of a phrase which illustrates one of Gavarni's drawings, "Ils sont jolis les amis dont vous êtes susceptible d'aller avec!" ("Pretty kind of friends you like to associate with!")

But that only proved what a good heart Gavroche had, for he could easily have eaten all the food himself.

The cat named after the interesting Eponine was more delicate and slender than her brothers. Her nose was rather long, and her eyes slightly oblique, and green as those of Pallas Athene, to whom Homer always applied the epithet of γλαυχῶπιζ. Her nose was of velvety black, with the grain of a fine Périgord truffle; her whiskers were in a perpetual state of agitation, all of which gave her a peculiarly expressive countenance. Her superb black coat was always in motion, and was watered and shot with shadowy markings. Never was there a more sensitive, nervous, electric

333

animal. If one stroked her two or three times in the dark, blue sparks would fly crackling out of her fur.

Eponine attached herself particularly to me, like the Eponine of the novel to Marius, but I, being less taken up with Cosette than that handsome young man, could accept the affection of this gentle and devoted cat, who still shares the pleasure of my suburban retreat and is the inseparable companion of my hours of work.

She comes running up when she hears the front-door bell, receives the visitors, conducts them to the drawing-room, talks to them—yes, talks to them—with little chirruping sounds, that do not in the least resemble the language cats use in talking to their own kind, but which simulate the articulate speech of man. What does she say? She says in the clearest way, "Will you be good enough to wait till monsieur comes down? Please look at the pictures, or chat with me in the meantime, if that will amuse you." Then when I come in she discreetly retires to an armchair or a corner of the piano, like a wellbred animal who knows what is correct in good society. Pretty little Eponine gave so many proofs of intelligence, good disposition and sociability, that by common consent she was raised to the dignity of a *person,* for it was quite evident that she was possessed of higher reasoning power than mere instinct. This dignity conferred on her the privilege of eating at table like a person instead of out of a saucer in a corner of the room like an animal.

So Eponine had a chair next to me at breakfast and dinner, but on account of her small size she was allowed to rest her two front paws on the edge of the table. Her place was laid, without spoon or fork, but she had her glass. She went right through dinner dish by dish, from soup to dessert, waiting for her turn to be helped, and behaving with such propriety and nice manners as one would like to see in many children. She made her appearance at the first sound of the bell, and on going into the dining-room one found her already in her place, sitting up in her chair with her paws resting on the edge of the tablecloth, and seeming to offer you her little face to kiss, like a well-brought-up little girl who is affectionately polite towards her parents and elders.

As one finds flaws in diamonds, spots on the sun, and shadows on perfection itself, so Eponine, it must be confessed, had a passion for fish.

She shared this in common with all other cats. Contrary to the Latin proverb,

"Catus amat pisces, sed non vult tingere plantas,"

she would willingly have dipped her paw into the water if by so doing she could have pulled out a trout or a young carp. She became nearly frantic over fish, and, like a child who is filled with the expectation of dessert, she sometimes rebelled at her soup when she knew (from previous investigations in the kitchen) that fish was coming. When this happened she was not helped, and I would say to her coldly: "Mademoiselle, a person who is not hungry for soup cannot be hungry for fish," and the dish would be pitilessly carried away from under her nose. Convinced that matters were serious, greedy Eponine would swallow her soup in all haste, down to the last drop, polishing off the last crumb of bread or bit of macaroni, and would then turn round and look at me with pride, like someone who has conscientiously done his duty. She was then given her portion, which she consumed with great satisfaction, and after tasting of every dish in turn, she would finish up by drinking a third of a glass of water.

When I am expecting friends to dinner Eponine knows there is going to be a party before she sees the guests. She looks at her place, and if she sees a knife and fork by her plate she decamps at once and seats herself on a music-stool, which is her refuge on these occasions.

Let those who deny reasoning powers to animals explain if they can this little fact, apparently so simple, but which contains a whole series of inductions. From the presence near her plate of those implements which man alone can use, this observant and reflective cat concludes that she will have to give up her place for that day to a guest, and promptly proceeds to do so. She never makes a mistake; but when she knows the visitor well she climbs on his knee and tries to coax a tit-bit out of him by her pretty caressing ways.

Susan Fromberg Schaeffer

CHICAGO AND THE CAT

Sometime during the night, the huge wooden clockwork in back of the sky ticked, moved once, and now the weather changed. The heat was gone and the humidity with it. A crisp wind blew in the hopsacking curtains his girlfriend Marie had made for him. He refused to call her his *significant other*. The phrase was ludicrous, and he never knew how significant she was, or how other. In conversation she remained, therefore, his girlfriend, although the phrase seemed, among his friends, antique, as did his habit, in spite of his training, of attributing human purpose and intent to events in the mechanistic world. The world might well be a tapestry knotted together by intersecting forces and vectors, but when he was not in the laboratory, he preferred to

336

see everything as if it were animate and full of purpose, so that each unpredictable thing might, at any moment, decide to alter its nature, and perhaps in so doing, change the significance of the entire design.

The wind blew the navy blue curtains into the room so that, for an instant, they floated up toward the ceiling like the last long, thready clouds of the night, and then dropped down, every thread in the fabric visible. There was a sharpness to the air that smelled like apples, and the wind rustled dryly in the oak leaves, a sound that reminded him of his mother's taffeta slip as she dressed for a wedding one night, in the winter, long ago, in New York. Summer was gone. Autumn had come for it, plunged its sharp teeth through its sluggish, long throat and carried it off. He looked with regret at Marie, who sat on the blue couch, pressed against the armrest, in the same position she'd been in for hours, weeping without sound, occasionally lifting her hand holding a handkerchief to her nose, then lowering her arm and letting it rest once more across her stomach. She was wearing jeans and a peach-colored brassiere, and over it she wore her white chenille bathrobe. He must have interrupted her, she must have been doing something, getting ready for something, when she asked him, "Do you still love me?" and he said, he said it immediately, because he had been asking himself the same question for months, for almost a year, "We never meant this to last forever." She put down her mascara and began weeping, put her bathrobe on over her jeans and brassiere, and sat down on the couch where she wept still.

He was curiously unmoved by the sight. He thought odd things. When she moves out, will she take the curtains? She was entitled to them. She had made them, but he loved them more than she did. He saw the morning light coming through the fabric's rough weave, and thought, Once we were like those threads, so close, and now we are not. Will she take Figaro, our small black-and-white cat? He had been her cat, but now the cat cared only for him. Figaro was nowhere to be seen, probably asleep on the dining room table in the back room. He had an image, so vivid as to be a hallucination, of two people, himself and Marie, coming into an empty laboratory. Each of them carried a white bakery box tied with string. The string had been made by twisting together red and white strands of thread. In each box was the love each one felt for the other. The love itself, its substance, was ensconced in the box, and rested on a white paper doily cut to look like lace; it resembled a cake. Its substance was crystalline and it was very clear, but it was sticky to the touch and somehow unformed. It reminded him of sap on the bark of a tree, sap that had not yet hardened. Except for a huge black table, the room was empty. At each end of the black table was a gold scale, and he knew immediately that they were to take their boxes and weigh them, thus settling once and for all the question of who loved whom more. Outside, the wind had picked up strength, and blew the curtains in and up once again. They rose suddenly, like a flock of startled pigeons. Perhaps if pigeons were deep blue, not battleship gray, people might love them more. He turned his attention to the gold scales. Each placed his box on the scale, and as Marie looked at her scale, and then her box, she began to weep. Did her box weigh more or less than she had hoped? It occurred to him that he was so tired he was dreaming with his eyes open. He waited for her to say, "You never loved me." Once she uttered those words, this scene would come to an end. She would stop weeping. Either they would begin to discuss what came next, or one of them would fall asleep, but in any case, Marie would move, get up, decide whether she wanted to be dressed for day or for night; they would not be frozen in their poses forever. Or, he thought, she might try to kill me. She was looking at him now out of narrowed eyes. The eyes of snakes, he thought, must look like that. "You never loved me," she said. In the laboratory, the bakery boxes turned into pigeons—or perhaps they were doves, they were so white—flew up from the scales and out of sight. The laboratory had no roof.

He smiled at Marie. He was always pleased when events confirmed his expectations. It was a satisfactory outcome, as when an experiment confirmed a hypothesis. Next she would say, "Why are you smiling?" and she was beginning to say something when the phone rang. "I'll get it," she said, jumping up to answer the telephone, as if to say, I'm still of some use here. Once I'm gone, you'll have to answer your own phone and make your own excuses. You better think twice. She always covered the phone with her hand and whispered the name of the caller so that, should he so desire, he could shake his head, and she would say that he had not yet come in, was asleep, would call back later, but now she stood still, her

white robe over her jeans, the receiver of the telephone thrust out in front
of her. She had become inanimate.

He took the receiver from her. His mother's voice came through the
small holes. What was she saying? He felt Marie's hand on his arm. With
her other hand, she was vigorously drying her eyes. "Dead?" he said aloud.
"Dead?" His mother was saying disconnected words, *sudden, no pain, a
blessing,* and then parts of sentences, "so sudden he didn't have time to ask
for you," "tomorrow, someone will pick you up at the airport, just tell me
what flight you're taking, he wants to be buried in Florida. That's where
he lived," and he thought, Why not Chicago? It's colder in Chicago. He'll
last longer. He said some things. They must have been satisfactory because his mother let him hang up. "I'll go with you to the funeral," Marie
said.

"No," he said. "I'll go alone."

"Oh," she said. "You'll go alone." She knew his dread of death. She
sat down on the couch. Not again, he thought. We're not starting that
again. "So," she said, "if it's over, you'll want me to move out." She
watched him. "I'll start packing," she said. When he nodded, she shook
her head. "You bastard," she said, getting up and going into the bedroom,
from which, in seconds, issued the sounds of drawers yanked open. He
knew, without getting up, that the bed was now covered with her possessions. He lay down on the couch, on his back, looking at the cracks in the
ceiling. "The trouble with you," his mother used to say, "is that you're
too sensitive. You're too sensitive and too fussy. You have to compromise.
You can't be such a perfectionist." He didn't know if he was sensitive or if
he was a perfectionist, but in that instant, he knew there was something
wrong with him, something missing.

"I'm sorry about your father," Marie said, standing over him.

"Mmmmm," he said. The higher the sun rose, the colder it became.

"Oh, well," Marie said.

"So that," he told his mother, "was the end of Marie." He thought his
mother would do more than smile or nod; she had liked Marie, but Marie
was not Jewish and was therefore unacceptable. He looked at his mother,
disappointed, but then reminded himself that his father had just died and

that his mother was now a widow. Who knew how widows reacted to anything? And this might not be the best time to tell his mother about Marie, not while they sat in the second seat of the black limousine driving to the cemetery. His mother's hot, dry hand rested on his wrist. She stared straight ahead. He looked out the window and thought how ugly it was here in Florida, flat and green and hot, the frying pan of the country, while in Chicago it was cold and at night frost nipped at the earth. If his father had to die, then he had died at a good time. The semester had not yet begun, there were no exams or papers. His father's death had rescued him from Marie. She could not very well ask him to stay with her and miss his father's funeral. Altogether, his father had picked a most convenient time to expire. He suspected his mother did not think so, but then she seemed calm. All her conversation had, so far, concerned finances, although she had said that she intended to stay in Florida because she had built a life here. Built a life! What was she, a mason? But then his mother always tended to talk in cliches. *Don't throw out the dirty water until you have new.* Of course it was not right to be annoyed at his mother, who was now a widow. When she stopped being a widow, then he could become annoyed at her. But did people ever stop being widows? It occurred to him he was not thinking properly.

The cemetery shocked him. Proper cemeteries had headstones that stood at right angles to the ground, mausoleums, statuary, winged angels carved from marble; they resembled little cities, had, from the highway, silhouettes of great cities. A cemetery seen from the highway defied your sense of scale, or at least disturbed it. This cemetery had stones set in the earth, a name and a date carved on each; flat, shiny gray stones he at first mistook for paving stones so that he tried to walk on them to avoid the muddy earth. It must have rained the night before. He hadn't noticed. His mother, who saw him stepping on the stones, jumping from one to another, said nothing, as if she saw nothing odd in his behavior. Perhaps she thought this was the way sons behaved whose fathers had just died.

The rabbi was saying something, but then rabbis always said something and in any event, he couldn't hear him. He felt the pressure and heat of his mother's hand on his arm, and he began to see a line of people coming in to a low gray granite cottage where a dead man was laid out on a large oval mahogany table. "Sorry for your trouble," said each visitor as they passed the widow and her daughters. "Sorry for your trouble," until it became a chant, and watching, he was outraged. "Sorry for your trouble," as if the visitors were commenting on a toothache rather than a death. When his mother tugged at his arm, he understood the funeral was over and that they were to return to the car, and as they walked, he wondered why he had just attended a funeral in Ireland, one that someone had described to him some months back, instead of his own father's funeral, at which he had been, as anyone who could read minds would know at once, absent.

His mother was regarding him, smiling sadly. "It hasn't hit you yet," she said.

"It hasn't?"

"It hasn't hit me either."

"I think it's hit you," he said.

He didn't like the way she looked at him now. "If it doesn't hit you, you'll be sorry," she said. Wasn't that wrong? Wasn't she supposed to say, "If it hits you, you'll be sorry?" The heat had unhinged him, the heat and these stepping stones. His mother would be all right. She was one tough cookie.

Marie had gone. There was no trace of her. It was as if she had viciously scoured herself from the apartment. She had, however, left the curtains, and Figaro was asleep in the middle of the bed waiting for him. The neighbor had fed him in his absence. He sat down on the bed and contemplated Figaro.

He had never had a pet before Figaro. His mother, who often boasted that her kitchen floor was so clean that a brain surgeon could operate upon it, and whose tragedy, in his opinion, was that no such surgeon had ever come to her door saying he had an emergency and needed a sterile kitchen floor, had feared dust, germs, animal hair, the sharp claws of animals shredding the beautiful tapestry fabric of her chairs. He had once brought home a parrot, and for the few weeks it lasted in the house, he had sat next to its cage, trying to teach it to say, "Hello, Daddy," so that, when his father came home from work, the parrot could greet him. He knew his father well enough to understand that a bird with a kind word for him at the end of the day would have a permanent place beneath their roof. However, the bird did not learn quickly, and after several weeks, his mother read an article about a recent outburst of parrot fever in Jamaica, and the bird was returned to the store.

Figaro had arrived with Marie, the Mother Teresa of cats. She found him when she took her cat into the veterinarian's to be put to sleep. "This is a wonderful kitten," the vet said, bringing out a black kitten he held by the neck. The cat hissed and spit and struggled while Marie inspected him. He had an asymmetrical streak of white fur which bisected his face and cut across his nose. He looked, as everyone noted, demented. Marie picked up the cat and he walked across her arm, used his nose as a wedge to lift her coat, and went to sleep above her breast just beneath her shoulder. She had decided to take the cat when the vet reminded the receptionist that the woman who had brought in the kitten and who had paid its bills had asked to approve the person who would adopt it. The woman was duly called and within fifteen minutes came in, brushing snow from the collar and chest of her coat.

"Where is the cat?" she asked.

Marie opened her coat. Only the cat's rear end and tail were visible. At the sound of the woman's voice, the cat turned, peered out from the depths of Marie's coat, and then retreated.

"Oh, well, he loves you already," the woman said.

"I love cats," said Marie.

"Her cat just died," said the receptionist. "Of diabetes."

"Diabetes?" the woman said. "I didn't know cats got diabetes."

"They do," said Marie. The kitten was absentmindedly chewing on one of her fingers.

"You know why he's here?" the woman said. "There's this gray cat who leaves her kittens in our boiler room. We found him down there. He was sneezing, his eyes were gummy, he was a mess, so we started feeding him. We wanted to bring him in here but he wouldn't let us near him. So we waited until his eyes stuck together and we dropped a carton on him. We got him here just in time."

"Just in time," said the receptionist. "He had pneumonia."

"So he's not such a friendly cat," the woman said. "I mean, first it was a boiler room, and boxes dropped on him, and then it was a cage and things stuck in his rear end and needles through his skin. You know."

"A survivor, that cat," said the receptionist. "If you see what I mean."

Marie took the cat home. For the first week, it hid beneath her legal bookcase, coming out to eat when she left the room. Then it began to lie down on the living room rug, as far from her as possible. She always spoke to the cat, said hello when she came in, told the cat she would be back soon when she left. Occasionally, she read aloud to the cat. One morning when she awakened, she was surprised to find the cat wedged into her side, asleep on its back. When she tried to scratch its stomach, the cat attacked her wrist and she walked around the Mercurochrome stains and Band-Aids for a week. She named the cat Figaro.

He met Marie when the cat had begun to sit, cautiously and suspiciously, on the couch with her. Its fur was now so shiny the light reflected from it and the fleas that had bitten Marie so hungrily were long gone. It was no longer a kitten, but neither was it a cat. It was thin and long and leggy and its only interest, as he saw it, was in food. When they fed the cat, it would eat until the plate was clean and then cry for more. They fed the cat incessantly and ignored its cries only when the cat's stomach bulged ominously. At such times, the cat looked as if it had swallowed a shoe box.

"*Can* cats explode?" he asked Marie.

"Don't give it any more," she said.

Marie usually fed the cat, although he often stood over Figaro and watched him eat. Still, he was the one the cat followed, the one onto whose lap the cat jumped, the one of whom Figaro was jealous. If he read a book, he had to hold it high in the air so that the cat could not lie down on it, and when he held it up, tiring his arms, the cat would stand up on his hind legs and pull the book down with his front paw. When he went to bed, the cat came with him. When it was cold, the cat tunneled under the covers and slept on his ankle. If he went into the bathroom, the cat scratched at the door until he let him in.

"Why me?" he asked.

343

"It's love," Marie said.

"I don't love him," he said.

"But you will," she said.

He looked at Figaro, lying on the bed. He had come to adore the cat. The cat seemed to him, in its calm surveillance of all that occurred, almost omniscient. Its green glass eyes, so clear and transparent, were like pools of the purest water, so deep that, when he looked into them, he thought he could almost see into the brain that perceived the world. When he spoke to the cat, he believed there was nothing the cat could not understand. When he gave the cat commands, it obeyed them. If he told the cat to flip over on its back, the cat did, waving its paws in the air, waiting for its stomach to be scratched. If he held his hand over the cat's head and said, "Stand up," the cat stood up and held onto his fingers. He explained his experiments to the cat and the cat understood them. He knew the cat was a pure soul. He knew beyond a shadow of a doubt that the cat loved him. Once Marie had pretended to hit him with a newspaper and the cat had jumped on her leg and begun to rake at her skin with its back claws.

As he stroked the cat, it seemed to him that the cat did not look well. He tried to remember: Was it feed a fever, starve a cold? Starve a fever, feed a cold? Until the cat seemed healthier, he would not feed it. Figaro stretched, yawned, and as if approving of his decision, climbed onto his lap. He lay back on the bed and the cat crept onto his stomach, rising and falling as he breathed.

When he came home from the lab the next day, the cat seemed better but more nervous. Figaro flew around the room. He crept into the paper bag he put down on the floor and sprang out waving his front paws. He would crouch down in the middle of the rug and then run madly around the room, his wide, round eyes on him. He thought, He is more playful because he feels better. He considered feeding the cat, but decided that, to be on the safe side, he would wait until morning.

In the morning, Figaro once again seemed unwell. He decided that his lab assistants had the experiment he was running well under control. He would stay home with the cat. As the days went by, he read book after book. For the first few days, the cat protested, as was his habit, either lying on the book or standing up to drag it down, but eventually, the cat grew resigned and lay across his legs without disturbing him. By the end of the week, he had to carry the cat over to his dish of water, and as Figaro drank, he would look up at him from the floor, reproach in his eyes. His lab assistant called and said things were going well. He decided to remain at home with the cat until he was better.

"You have your whole life ahead of you," said his mother. "I have nothing. All I have left of him are his golf clubs. You could call more often. I'm always here."

"What's the weather like?" he asked his mother.

"What's the weather like?" his mother asked, her voice rising to a shriek. "This is Florida! What should the weather be like? It's hot! It's always hot!"

"No hurricanes?" he asked.

His mother hung up. He stared at the receiver in disbelief. He was making conversation. She always liked to talk about the weather. Why did she only have his father's golf clubs? What had she done with his clothes? If she'd given away his clothes, why didn't she give away his golf clubs and make a clean sweep of it? But then she was a widow. He didn't understand widows.

"I'm not a widow!" his mother shouted at him when he next called her. "I'm still your mother!"

"You're a widow and you're my mother," he said. Widows, apparently, were irrational. His mother hung up. Perhaps widows did that— lost their tempers, hung up on their sons.

Figaro, meanwhile, absorbed all his attention. The cat was listless. His ribs showed through his fur. When he pulled back the cat's lower lip, his gums looked pale. When he went into the kitchen or to the bathroom, the cat sighed and got down from the couch, following him, but when he first landed on the floor, his legs seemed to wobble beneath him. Lately, he seemed to stagger as he walked. He took to picking up the cat and carrying him wherever he went. When he lay on the bed, the cat sucked at his fingers or licked his skin. Occasionally, the cat, as if apologizing for his weakened state, reached out to pat his arm.

"Why can't you come down for Christmas?" his mother demanded. "All the other children are coming down for Christmas. It's not as if these are normal circumstances!" His mother, he believed, kept actuarial tables of the number of visits children made to their parents in Florida. He said something to that effect and the line went dead. When she ceased being a widow, he thought, she would cease hanging up.

When it became apparent to him that the cat was going to die, he spent every moment with the cat. He no longer read or watched television. He watched the cat. He wanted to observe the exact instant when it ceased to breathe. He wanted to know when the cat went from being something living and warm to something dead and cold. He began drinking cup after cup of coffee in order to stay awake. The cat now slept most of the time. When it awakened, it would look around, turning its head from side to side, but not lifting it, to see where he was. Then the cat would stretch out its small hot paw and rest its paw on his arm. He stroked the cat rhythmically and incessantly, and softly, because the cat's ribs now showed so prominently through its fur. He imagined the full weight of his hand on the cat would be painful and so, when he touched the cat, he did so lightly and carefully.

The doorbell rang one day and when he opened the door he saw Marie standing on the landing. She waited, expecting him to invite her in, and he thought, Figaro was her cat, too; I should let her see the cat, but then he thought, The cat is so weak the excitement would kill him immediately. He muttered something about having someone in the apartment, but if she'd wait a minute everyone would be decent. Marie flushed and said she had better be leaving. He went back in to the cat. Figaro had managed to pick up his head and was staring fixedly at the door as if were hoping for rescue, but of course had been too weak to go to the door. Figaro had no choice. That was what it meant to be dying, he thought. The dying had few choices and then they grew weaker and had no choices. They wanted to live and they struggled to live but they could not choose to live. "She's gone," he told the cat, and the cat lowered his head and lay still. He was still breathing. He lay down next to the cat and fell asleep. When he awakened, the cat was still breathing.

As it happened, he was awake when the cat ceased to breathe. He pressed his ear to the cat's chest and could not hear his heartbeat. He saw that the eyes of the cat no longer focused. Still, the cat moved, odd, convulsive movements. Wake up, he told the cat. Get up. I'll give you something to eat. But the cat did not wake up and he understood the cat had died. As he stroked the cat's stiffening body, he began to cry, and he sat on the edge of the bed through the night, stroking the cat and weeping. In the morning, he put Figaro in a carton and took him to the lab where he would be cremated.

When he went home, he called his mother and said perhaps he might come to Florida for Christmas after all. He asked his mother whether or not she still had his father's golf clubs, and if so, could he use them. As he talked to her, his eyes wandered to the almost-full carton of cat food next to the refrigerator. How long had it been since he'd fed the cat? Almost two weeks. It was astonishing to him that an animal could go that long without food.

"So," said his mother, "it's finally hit you."

"What's hit me?" he asked.

"Look, I don't want to talk," his mother said. But she did not hang up.

He thought of this now because he was staying for the weekend with friends in Maine. They had a huge fieldstone house and when he had driven up to it, his two children fighting in the backseat, his wife still reading the directions scribbled on the back of an envelope, a black cat had been sitting on the front step. A lightning-like stripe zig-zagged from its nose to its chin and when he saw the cat he felt a surge of joy that rose like a warm tide from his stomach and flooded his chest. He helped the children unload their suitcases and he carried in the golf clubs in their old red leather golf bag—the leather had cracked and had the texture of old, weatherbeaten skin—and then went back for the boxes of cake his wife had baked, but his attention was fastened to the cat. As soon as everyone was inside, he announced that he had a headache and asked if anyone would mind if he went up to bed. No one minded. The children were running down the road to the ocean and his wife was running after them. The cat was standing in front of him, and he swooped down upon the cat and carried it with him to the bedroom his hostess had pointed out. He took the cat inside and closed the door. He put the cat down on the braided rug and lay down. He pulled the brass bed's feather comforter over him. Milky white light poured in through the curtainless window. He lay on his back, his hands folded beneath his head. Eventually the cat jumped up on the bed and lay down on his chest, staring into his eyes, just as he had known it would.

"It's you," he said to the cat. "You're back."

The cat purred and flexed his claws. "My mother died," he told the cat. "Not long ago, but long enough." The cat crept forward until his cold nose touched his own. He began to stroke the cat, and as he did, he began to weep. "I'm sorry," he told the cat. "You're not angry?" The cat reached out, touched his cheek, and flexed his claws. He tapped the cat's paw gently and the cat, purring louder, retracted his claws. "She's been dead eight weeks," he said, and the sound of the cat's purr, ever louder, made him sob, so loudly he had to turn on his side and bury his face in the pillow. It seemed to him that the least thing made him cry, and he remembered his mother saying, not long before her death, that when he was younger he never cried and she had worried what would become of him. She was old; she spoke in non sequiturs. *You look like your father,* she said. The cat, as if he were walking on a rolling log, managed to stay on, settling on his hip. He thought, as he wept, that from a sufficient distance he might look like a grave covered in snow, and the cat the carving on top of the stone. It is because of Figaro that I have anything, he thought, poor Figaro, who starved to death, and as he thought that, he felt sleep settling on him, erasing him, and he understood the fog wanting to erase him, as he understood how the houses, the lawns, and the sea would feel when the fog gathered its strength, thickened, and erased them all.

Merrill Joan Gerber

TOUCHING IS GOOD FOR LIVING CREATURES

"Can't you put in mayonnaise?" Myra asked. "The baby birds won't like it that dry."

"Do you think birds eat mayonnaise in the wild?" Janet asked, mashing away. Bits of egg were flying out of the bowl and landing in the clean glasses in the cabinet.

"Well, they don't eat hard-boiled egg in the wild either."

"All right," Janet said. "Put in mayonnaise. Put in ketchup. Put in sautéed mushrooms, for all I care. Here—you mash."

"I don't have time. I have to catch the school bus."

"But *I* have time?"

"You're home all day, Mom," Myra said. "It stands to reason." She wiped her hands on a dish towel and hurried down the hall to the bathroom. Janet heard her turn the barrette box upside down on the counter. Of course she would leave the box open. She would leave it there with ribbons and rubber bands and colored combs strewn about and Janet would have to put it away.

The baby birds must have heard her unscrew the top of the mayonnaise jar. *"Beep-beep! Beep-beep!"* They were craning their skinny little necks over the top of the shoe box, crowding together under the bulb of the gooseneck lamp for warmth and pleading to be fed.

"They're hungry again, Mom," Myra called down the hall. She appeared with her book bag over her shoulder, her hair held back with a red, white, and blue ribbon. "Be sure to feed them every hour. Don't give them bread—it expands in their stomachs. And stroke them so they can move their bowels."

"Anything else?" Janet asked. "Anything else you want me to do for you while I'm just home all day?"

"Would you feed the bunny?" Myra said. "And Creamy? I forgot to feed him. And the kitty too."

"The *kitty?* Is he still around? Didn't Daddy say not to encourage him? You *know* how Daddy feels about two cats. One is too many, as far as he's concerned."

"You gave the kitty milk last night, Mom. I *saw* you."

"Only because I don't want him dying on my doorstep. But Daddy doesn't want anyone feeding him. He'll be ours forever then."

"Yeah," Myra said. "Wouldn't that be super?"

"We *can't,* Myra. We're overextended. The vet bills, the cat food, the carrots, the eggs!" For emphasis, Janet tossed a spoonful of mashed egg in the air, and it landed in a clump on the floor. *"Me!"*

"You don't cost anything," Myra said. *"Luckily."*

They heard the brakes of the school bus squeaking down the hill.

"I've got to go. Would you open the door for me? I have to carry this poster to school."

Janet opened the front door for Myra, and leaned over to kiss her good-bye. Myra turned her head away.

"Hey," Janet said, "I just want a good-bye kiss. Touching is good for living creatures. You always tell me that when you spend hours petting Creamy."

"That's okay," Myra said. "You kissed me yesterday. And you touched me enough when I was a baby. . . ." She dashed out the door, running on her skinny long legs toward the bus stop.

As soon as the bus was out of sight, Janet pulled up a stool to the kitchen counter and began to croon to the baby birds. "Yes, little ones, food is coming. Be patient." She dipped her eyebrow tweezers into the mashed egg, pinching a morsel with the silver tongs. The babies peeped and screamed, reaching their open beaks in desperation toward her hand. Each beak, huge in proportion to the bird's frail body, was outlined in fluorescent yellow. "Bull's-eye," Janet whispered, poking food into one eager beak and then the other. "Yes, you love it, don't you?" The birds chirped and gobbled, vibrating the tweezers in her hand with the enthusiasm of their hunger. "One for you. Now one for you. Now your turn, now yours." The birds were like teaspoonfuls of life, all beak and fine new feathers, hollow bones, air. One day, having started life on her egg salad, they would fly over rooftops, soar into the blue sky. Myra had found them beneath the plum tree after a night of high winds; the cat and kitty were homing in on them like pointer dogs.

"Oh, no! Don't get involved in a rescue mission again," Janet had said when Myra carried them into the house. "You know how they always die. Anything can go wrong—it always does. Then you'll be depressed for a week. Let nature work it out."

"Do you want to see Creamy bite off their heads?" Myra asked. "At least we can *try* to save them."

"But you mean *I* can try. It's always me that does it. You go away to school and *I* feed them, *I* watch them, *I* pray for them . . . and then *I* bury them."

"What can I do, Mom? I didn't blow them out of the tree."

"No," Janet agreed. "You didn't."

* * *

351

Now that the children were no longer babies, were all in school, Janet had finally begun to relax her vigilance just a little bit. Even Danny had commented on it. One night, coming to bed in a soft new nightgown, she had simply closed and locked the bedroom door behind her.

"Are you leaving the door closed?" he asked quietly, looking up from his magazine.

"Isn't that okay?"

"Well, yes, of course," he said. "But I thought you liked to be able to hear the children."

"They'll be okay," she said. "I'm not worried about them anymore. They're healthy. They breathe perfectly well all night. They've outgrown their croup attacks. If they want me, they can call me."

"Well . . ." Danny said, with a smile, putting aside the magazine and holding out his arms. "That's *certainly* a good idea."

The gray kitty had wandered into the driveway while Danny was washing the car one Sunday afternoon. It had a tiny face, the bluest eyes imaginable, and eight toes on each front paw. Janet had two contradictory reactions at once. "We can't keep it," she said, sounding a stern warning to Myra, who was in the driveway shining her bike while Danny washed the car. For Danny's benefit she added, "It's definitely not going to live here." The kitty began pitifully lapping at the bucket of soapsuds. "It would need shots, it would need to be sterilized, it would need worming. It probably has fleas." And even as she said it, as Myra picked up the kitten and began to stroke it, Janet felt a profound softening in her breast, a sweet weakness, an overwhelming tenderness toward the beautiful mewing creature.

In a glance, Myra knew what she could ask for and get. Secretly she met her mother at the side door and together they gave the kitten milk. "But I mean it," Janet whispered to her. "We really can't go on this way. It's adorable, I know. But Daddy doesn't like all these pets taking over the house. He'll accept Creamy because we've had him for so many years, but not *another* cat. Daddy doesn't understand animals. He never had any when he was little—his parents thought they were messy and dirty."

"So are kids," Myra said.

"But Daddy likes kids."

"Who knows?" Myra said. "Maybe not." She walked away and Janet felt something different in her breast, a hollow shock, some kind of fear. Maybe she had given her children the wrong father.

The baby birds went to sleep, one on top of the other, cuddled together under the light bulb. With no one home to pretend for, Janet sat and watched them a long time, remembering the looks on the faces of her sleeping babies, the way their hands had fallen out limply between the crib bars, their delicious soft cheeks, the curve of their eyelashes resting on the rosy skin. Refusing to care for the pets was a stance Danny had forced her to adopt—he thought she did enough work for the kids as it was, more than she ought to, now that they were growing up and ought to do more for themselves. He wanted to claim her back—she knew that. He was tired of having to share Janet as generously with the children as he had all these years, and now he wanted her to come back to him, to give him at last the lion's share of attention, which he was more than willing to lavish upon her.

She knew she was supposed to show exaggerated relief: Thank God, they're growing up. I have some peace now. She *was* glad to see them grow. Of course she was. But with it came Myra's turning her face away from her kisses.

Janet's anger at the birds, at the kitten, at the mess of bunnies and fish and frogs, had nothing to do with the creatures themselves but with Myra and her sisters, who no longer needed to be fed, teaspoon by loving teaspoon. If pressed, Janet would have had to admit that she really loved the animals, loved their needing her, their unbiased affection, their goodness. When she fed and petted them, she felt a transcendent sense of contentment.

Now she went out into the yard to feed the bunny, and the gray kitty mewed at her from the yew tree. His tiny, triangular face peered out from the thickly twined leaves and branches and he cried pathetically.

"Are you in there *again*, you little mischief head?" Janet said. "Come on, now—reach out to me and I'll put you down."

The kitty offered a paw, but when she moved to grasp it he pulled back, disappearing into the depths of the tree. She heard a scrambling and a rustling, and in a moment he appeared three feet higher, crying more loudly and desperately.

"Well," she said, "shall I wait till you figure it out or shall I get the ladder?"

She went inside and came out carrying the stepladder, and found that now the kitty was at the very top of the tree. She climbed up the ladder and reached perilously to get him; it was risky, she knew. No one was home and she could break her neck doing this. With both arms up in the air for him, she had no way to balance herself or to catch hold of anything. She hoped for the best and then pulled his front legs toward her. Tiny as he was, he resisted leaving his safe perch. They struggled; she caught him but lost her balance. Together they flew through the air, separated, and came down, each of them, on all fours. After a minute she managed to stand up and brush off her hands. A close call. Her heart was pounding. She scooped the kitty up in her arms and carried him into the house, where she sat down on the couch, holding him close against her. She could feel the pulsing of his heart. Soon, though, he began to purr, a rough, sweet rumbling deep under his fur. His coat was smooth, electric, magnificent to stroke. She petted him till they both calmed down and dozed off. Later, when she woke up, she left him on the couch, still sleeping, till just before the children came home from school.

What's this?" Danny asked, holding something between his thumb and forefinger as they sat having their breakfast at the dining-room table. "And look! There's another one that just landed in my coffee!"

"Fleas!" Myra gasped.

Bonnie and Jill automatically lifted their feet off the floor. "Yuck!"

"Don't blame me, Daddy," Myra said. "I haven't let the kitty in once."

"Then who did?" Danny demanded, looking around the table.

"Not *I,*" said Myra.

"Not *I,*" said Bonnie.

"Not *I*," said Jill.

"What is this? 'The Little Red Hen'?" said Janet.

"Fleas don't have their own key to the house," Danny said, "do they?"

Just then something stung Janet's ankle. She looked down and saw four black dots digging into her tender flesh. When she leaned down to grab one of them, they all leaped as if on tiny springs to her other leg.

"My God," Danny said, "they're all over the place!"

"We *can't* have fleas," Jill said. "Creamy has a flea collar."

"The kitty doesn't have a flea collar," Bonnie said.

"The kitty doesn't come in the house!" Myra pleaded.

"Never mind how it happened—that's it!" Danny said. "No more cats in the house from now on. That means Creamy too."

"You can't do that," Myra said. "He'll be insulted. He *lives* here."

"Well, now he will live in the backyard," Danny said. "In fact, *only* Creamy will live in the backyard. As for that kitten, you will just have to find someone to take it, or give it to the pound. You absolutely cannot keep it."

"You're cruel!" Myra cried. "Anyone who doesn't love animals is sick."

"With bubonic plague, which fleas carry, I'll be even sicker," Danny said, pushing away his contaminated coffee cup.

"Danny," Janet said quietly, "would you like me to pour you another cup of coffee?"

When they all had gone for the day, Janet went through the house and stood in the center of each room. Within seconds, fleas clung to her legs like iron filings to a magnet. It was her fault. She had let the kitty in every day, let it follow her around, let it sleep on the beds. Now she was in bad trouble.

She fed the baby birds their breakfast—mashed egg that was laced with cooked oatmeal—and then drove to the pet store in the mall and had a long talk with the proprietor.

"Aah, fleas," he said. "They're like wild armadillos on pogo sticks. You can't catch 'em, can't find 'em, can't kill 'em. *Unless* you're willing to go to war."

"I'm willing," Janet said. "Under these circumstances I can't conscientiously object."

He outlined a plan for her. She would have to vacuum every inch of the house, strip the beds, wash the blankets and bedspreads, seal the food boxes in plastic, remove the eating utensils and plants from the house, and buy insecticide bombs at the hardware store. The bombs would cover the fleas and everything else in the house with a poisonous mist. Luckily, human beings were bigger than fleas, so the chemicals that would kill the fleas would probably just give human beings cancer in thirty years or so—which was better than being eaten alive now. "Life is a trade-off," the pet-store owner said philosophically. Then he added that the cats would have to have a flea treatment on the same day as the bombing.

"Anything else?" Janet asked.

"Wear a gas mask," the man said.

At the hardware store Janet was told the bombs didn't work too well because they couldn't get the flea eggs. In a week the eggs would hatch and there'd be twice as many fleas in the house as there were to begin with. So instead of bombs, she was persuaded to buy "Murder 'Em Kennel Dust," which, if raked into the rugs, would get the eggs too. Coming home, she hid the lethal materials in the trunk of her car, determined to get rid of the fleas so that she wouldn't have to get rid of the kitten. She wasn't sure just how to work on Danny; he had spoken his final word on the subject. But she certainly couldn't approach him about keeping the kitten while scratching her shins!

The next morning, Janet fed the baby birds and then drove them—with all her houseplants and cereal boxes—a block away from the house, where she parked the car. Returning to the house, she put on plastic eye goggles, a surgeon's mask, rubber gloves, and an orange poncho (nonporous) and began skulking through the house, bent over, shaking "Murder 'Em Kennel Dust" over her pure-nylon rugs. When every room in the house was covered with a layer of powder, she got the red garden rake and began earnestly raking the stuff deep down into the rugs. She was worried. Ecologists had warned that by wiping out the snail darter, humanity might have changed the whole ecological balance. God only knew what would happen if fleas became extinct. She began to cough, sure that the poison was penetrating her surgeon's mask. She saw clusters of fleas holding on to the laces of her tennis shoes as if to a life raft. She was sweating under the poncho. Once she looked up into the mirror on the living-room wall and screamed in surprise.

"It's all right," she said to herself. "It's only me."

The doorbell rang and she opened the front door.

"Can I help you?" she said to the fleeing backs of two women and a child. They had left religious literature on her doorstep. Maybe they didn't feel that mutants needed to be given a conversion speech.

She walked from room to room through the powdery fog till she was convinced she had raked the seeds of destruction deeply enough. Then, gasping for breath, she ran out into the yard, where Creamy and the gray kitty lay in the sun, playing with each other's tails.

"Come over here, you guys—you're next. I bought you peppermint-scented 'Murder 'Em Pet Spray'—I'm doing this all the way!"

She didn't want Danny to know that the fleas had invaded the entire house, or that she could possibly be the cause of a cancer he might get in thirty years, so she vacuumed the powder sooner than she was supposed to. That night, collapsed, exhausted, in front of the TV, she ordered Myra up off the poisonous floor. "It's drafty," Janet said. "I don't want you to sit down there."

"We always sit on the floor," Myra complained.

"The TV gives off radioactive rays," Janet said. "Sit on a chair."

"Tell her the truth," Danny said. "Just tell her you don't want her to get bitten by fleas."

"I forgot to tell you," Janet said. "The fleas are all gone. Miraculously. There isn't a single one around. Maybe they weren't fleas. Maybe they were just ashes blowing out of the fireplace."

"*Biting* ashes?" Danny said. "By the way, where are the cats now?"

357

"Outside," Myra said. "Banned from their own home. Creamy is having a mental breakdown."

"Let him call the family-counseling talk show on KABC," Danny said.

"Phooey," Myra said, getting up off the floor and throwing her arms around her father's shoulders. "Who wants to watch TV anyway?"

"Mommy and I do." Danny said. *"Alone,* if you don't mind."

"You don't love me," Myra accused him. "It's obvious."

" 'Torn between two lovers,' " Danny sang, imitating one of Myra's favorite songs. " 'Breaking every rule. . . .' We have to try to keep it a secret from Mommy, sweetheart."

"Oh, shut up," Myra said, and stormed off to her room.

Janet was reassured. It was clear that they were friends. She wondered if she ought to tell Danny what a good father she knew he was, after all. But enervated from her day's labors, she lay there like a dead person, too weak to move, to speak, even to return the pressure of her husband's hand. Danny had been right. If the children were no longer exhausting her, now it was the pets who drained all her energy. Like the poisoned fleas in the carpet, her very libido was lying limp and impotent in her hidden crevices. If she weren't preoccupied with the fleas, it would be the birds, and if it weren't the birds, it would be the cats. Poor Danny—there never seemed to be a time and place for him. She would have to give up the kitten. It was her destiny. She lay there, beaten, sorrowful, while Danny switched channels with the remote-control device.

A program zipped by showing a woman giving another woman a sensual massage. Danny clicked back to it.

"This program will explore," the voice-over said, "the hidden meanings and power of human touch and the exquisite responsiveness of the touch-receptive cells in the human skin."

Danny ran his finger across Janet's upper arm. She wondered if he could tell it was made of numb rubber, the arm of a mannequin. A cluster of monkeys came on the screen, hugging and embracing one another. A mother and her baby were shown entwined, and then the little monkey was separated by a glass barrier from its mother and almost at once it displayed symptoms of extreme grief—first a desperate pawing at the glass and then, later, a slumped-over posture, head bowed, little hand to its forehead—classic sorrow. "Monkeys who are deprived of touch," the voice-over said, "eventually display signs of severe disturbance and aggression."

Now there were happier scenes—of an infant at his mother's breast, of parents cuddling a crying child, of an old woman playing with her cat, of a young man roughhousing with his dog, of a little girl rubbing noses with a kitten. "Pets," the voice-over said, "enhance the lives of those who live with them. The give-and-take of affection, particularly the cuddling, holding, and stroking of pets, has been shown to improve the quality of life for their owners. Touch is the matrix of our social and emotional relationships with others. People who own pets are calmer, more secure—and may even live longer."

Danny, still resting his arm on Janet's shoulder, reached up and gently stroked her cheek with his forefinger.

"Ummm," she sighed. Feeling seemed to be returning to her flesh. She shifted on the couch and embraced him, sliding her hand up his sleeve. As the TV screen flashed again to the restful expression on the face of the woman being given a massage, Janet massaged Danny's biceps muscle. As the picture returned to the monkeys, then panned to the old woman playing with her cat, to the young man with his dog and to the child with the kitten, Janet stroked Danny's skin with sweet sensuality. Then very quietly she stood up and excused herself for a second. She opened the patio door and returned with the gray kitten in her arms.

"Look," she whispered to her husband, placing his large hand on the luxurious fur of the kitten's back. "Feel that," she said. "When I stroke him, I feel calm, happy, full of well-being. All my senses come alive."

"They do?" Danny asked.

"Feel," she said softly drawing his fingers through the fur. "It's almost electric." She placed her own hand over his and together they stroked the kitten, who had begun to purr loudly in contentment.

"He keeps me company when no one is home," Janet said. "He's so sweet, and when I pet him, I can hardly wait for you to come home so I can pet you."

"Ummm," Danny murmured. He had put his head back against the edge of the couch and closed his eyes.

"I love his rough little tongue," she said. "It's scratchy, just like your cheek when you kiss me and your whiskers rub my face hard."

"Oh, yes," Danny nodded.

"And people who love pets live longer," Janet whispered. "They're better lovers. . . ."

Danny was totally relaxed, given up to the moment. Janet reached over and switched off the TV. In the dark silence she continued to nourish the touch-receptive cells of the three of them, breathing in, as she did so, the sweet, peppermint aroma of the kitten.

Alice Adams

THE ISLANDS

What does it mean to love an animal, a pet, in my case a cat, in the fierce, entire and unambivalent way that some of us do? I really want to know this. Does the cat (did the cat) represent some person, a parent or a child? some part of one's self? I don't think so—and none of the words or phrases that one uses for human connections sounds quite right: "crazy about," "really liked," "very fond of"—none of those describes how I felt and still feel about my cat. Many years ago, soon after we got the cat (her name was Pink), I went to Rome with my husband, Andrew, whom I really liked; I was crazy about Andrew, and very fond of him too. And I have a most vivid memory of lying awake in Rome, in the pretty bed in its deep alcove, in the nice small hotel near the Borghese Gardens—lying there, so fortunate to be in Rome, with Andrew, and missing Pink, a small striped cat with no tail— missing Pink unbearably. Even blaming Andrew for having brought me there, although he loved her too, almost as much as I did. And now Pink has died, and I cannot accept or believe in her death, any more than I could believe in Rome. (Andrew also died, three years ago, but this is not his story.)

A couple of days after Pink died (this has all been recent), I went to Hawaii with a new friend, Slater. It had not been planned that way; I had known for months that Pink was slowly failing (she was nineteen), but I did not expect her to die. She just suddenly did, and then I went off to "the islands," as my old friend Zoe Pinkerton used to call them, in her nasal, moneyed voice. I went to Hawaii as planned, which interfered with my proper mourning for Pink. I feel as though those islands interposed themselves between her death and me. When I needed to be alone, to absorb her death, I was over there with Slater.

Slater is a developer; malls and condominium complexes all over the world. Andrew would not have approved of Slater, and sometimes I don't think that I do either. Slater is tall and lean, red-haired, a little younger than I am, and very attractive, I suppose, although on first meeting Slater I was not at all drawn to him (which I have come to think is one of the reasons he found me so attractive, calling me the next day, insisting on dinner that night; he was probably used to women who found him terrific, right off). But I thought Slater talked too much about money, or just talked too much, period.

Later on, when I began to like him a little better (I was flattered by all that attention, is the truth), I thought that Slater's very differences from Andrew should be a good sign. You're supposed to look for opposites, not reproductions, I read somewhere.

Andrew and I had acquired Pink from Zoe, a very rich alcoholic, at that time a new neighbor of ours in Berkeley. Having met Andrew down in his bookstore, she invited us to what turned out to be a very long Sunday lunch party, in her splendidly decked and viewed new Berkeley hills house. "Getting to know some of the least offensive neighbors," is how

362

she probably thought of it. Her style was harsh, abrasive; anything-for-a-laugh was surely one of her mottoes, but she was pretty funny, fairly often. We saw her around when she first moved to Berkeley (from Ireland: a brief experiment that had not worked out too well). And then she met Andrew in his store, and found that we were neighbors, and she invited us to her party, and Andrew fell in love with a beautiful cat. "The most beautiful cat I ever saw," he told Zoe, and she was, soft and silver, with great blue eyes. The mother of Pink.

"Well, you're in luck," Zoe told us. "That's Molly Bloom, and she just had five kittens. They're all in a box downstairs, in my bedroom, and you get to choose any one you want. It's your doorprize for being such a handsome couple."

Andrew went off to look at the kittens, and then came back up to me. "There's one that's really great," he said. "A tailless wonder. Must be part Manx."

As in several Berkeley hills houses, Zoe's great sprawl of a bedroom was downstairs, with its own narrow deck, its view of the bay and the bridge, and of San Francisco. The room was the most appalling mess I had ever seen. Clothes, papers, books, dirty glasses, spilled powder, more clothes dumped everywhere. I was surprised that my tidy, somewhat censorious husband even entered, and that he was able to find the big wicker basket (filled with what looked to be discarded silk underthings, presumably clean) in which five very tiny kittens mewed and tried to rise and stalk about, on thin, uncertain legs.

The one that Andrew had picked was gray striped, a tabby, with a stub of a tail, very large eyes and tall ears. I agreed that she was darling, how great it would be to have a cat again; our last cat, Lily, who was sweet and pretty but undistinguished, had died some years ago. And so Andrew and I went back upstairs and told Zoe, who was almost very drunk, that we wanted the one with no tail.

"Oh, Stubs," she rasped. "You don't have to take that one. What are you guys, some kind of Berkeley bleeding hearts? You can have a whole cat." And she laughed, delighted as always with her own wit.

No, we told her. We wanted that particular cat. We liked her best.

Aside from seeing the cats—our first sight of Pink!—the best part of Zoe's lunch was her daughter, Lucy, a shy, pretty and very gentle young woman—as opposed to the other guests, a rowdy, oil-rich group, old friends of Zoe's from Texas.

"What a curious litter," I remarked to Andrew, walking home, up Marin to our considerably smaller house. "All different. Five different patterns of cat."

"Five fathers." Andrew had read a book about this, I could tell. Andrew read everything. "It's called multiple insemination, and occurs fairly often in cats. It's theoretically possible in humans, but they haven't come across any instances." He laughed, really pleased with this lore.

"It's sure something to think about."

"Just don't."

Andrew. An extremely smart, passionate, selfish and generous man, a medium-successful bookstore owner. A former academic: he left teaching in order to have more time to read, he said. Also (I thought) he much preferred being alone in his store to the company of students or, worse, of other professors—a loner, Andrew. Small and almost handsome, competitive, a gifted tennis player, mediocre pianist. Gray hair and gray-green eyes. As I have said, I was crazy about Andrew (usually). I found him funny and interestingly observant, sexy and smart. His death was more grievous to me than I can (or will) say.

"You guys don't have to take Stubs, you can have a whole cat all your own." Zoe Pinkerton on the phone, a few days later. Like many alcoholics, she tended to repeat herself, although in Zoe's case some vast Texan store of self-confidence may have fueled her repetitions.

And we in our turn repeated: we wanted the little one with no tail.

Zoe told us that she would bring "Stubs" over in a week or so; then the kittens would be old enough to leave Molly Bloom.

Andrew: "Molly Bloom indeed."

I: "No wonder she got multiply inseminated."

Andrew: "Exactly."

* * *

We both, though somewhat warily, liked Zoe. Or, we were both somewhat charmed by her. For one thing, she made it clear that she thought we were great. For another, she was smart, she had read even more than Andrew had.

A very small woman, she walked with a swagger; her laugh was loud, and liberal. I sometimes felt that Pink was a little like Zoe—a tiny cat with a high, proud walk; a cat with a lot to say.

In a couple of weeks, then, Zoe called, and she came over with this tiny tailless kitten under her arm. A Saturday afternoon. Andrew was at home, puttering in the garden like the good Berkeley husband that he did not intend to be.

Zoe arrived in her purple suede pants and a vivid orange sweater (this picture is a little poignant; fairly soon after that the booze began to get the better of her legs, and she stopped taking walks at all). She held out a tiny kitten, all huge gray eyes and pointed ears. A kitten who took one look at us and began to purr; she purred for several days, it seemed, as she walked all over our house and made it her own. This is absolutely the best place I've ever been, she seemed to say, and you are the greatest people—you are my people.

From the beginning, then, our connection with Pink seemed like a privilege; automatically we accorded her rights that poor Lily would never have aspired to.

She decided to sleep with us. In the middle of the night there came a light soft plop on our bed, which was low and wide, and then a small sound, *mmrrr,* a little announcement of her presence. "Littlest announcer," said Andrew, and we called her that, among her other names. Neither of us ever mentioned locking her out.

Several times in the night she would leave us and then return, each time with the same small sound, the littlest announcement.

In those days, the early days of Pink, I was doing a lot of freelance editing, for local small presses, which is to say that I spent many waking hours at my desk. Pink assessed my habits early on, and decided to make them her own; or perhaps she decided that she too was an editor. In any case she would come up to my lap, where she would sit, often looking up with something to say. She was in fact the only cat I have ever known with whom a sort of conversation was possible; we made sounds back and forth at each other, very politely, and though mine were mostly nonsense syllables, Pink seemed pleased.

Pink was her main name, about which Zoe Pinkerton was very happy. "Lordy, no one's ever named a cat for me before." But Andrew and I used many other names for her. I had an idea that Pink liked a new name occasionally: maybe we all would? In any case we called her a lot of other, mostly P-starting names: Peppercorn, Pipsy Doodler, Poipu Beach. This last was a favorite place of Zoe's, when she went out to "the islands." Pink seemed to like all these names; she regarded us both with her great gray eyes—especially me; she was always mostly my cat.

I find that this is very hard, describing a long relationship with a cat. For one thing, there is not much change of feeling, on either side. The cat gets a little bigger, and you get older. Things happen to both of you, but mostly there is just continuation.

Worried about raccoons and Berkeley free-roaming dogs, we decided early on that Pink was to be a house cat, for good. She was not expendable. But Andrew and I liked to take weekend trips, and after she came to live with us we often took Pink along. She liked car travel right away; settled on the seat between us, she would join right in whenever we broke what had been a silence—not interrupting, just adding her own small voice, a sort of soft clear mew.

This must have been in the early 70s; we talked a lot about Nixon and Watergate. "Mew if you think he's guilty," Andrew would say to Pink, who always resonded satisfactorily.

Sometimes, especially on summer trips, we would take Pink out for a semi-walk; our following Pink is what it usually amounted to, as she bounded into some meadow grass, with miniature leaps. Once, before I could stop her, she suddenly raced ahead—to a chipmunk. I was horrified. But then she raced back to me with the chipmunk in her mouth, and after a tiny shake she let him go, and the chipmunk ran off, unscathed. (Pink had what hunters call a soft mouth. Of course she did.)

* * *

We went to Rome and I missed her, very much; and we went off to the Piazza Argentina and gave a lot of lire to the very old woman there who was feeding all those mangy, half-blind cats. In honor of Pink.

I hope that I am not describing some idealized "perfect" adorable cat, because Pink was never that. She was entirely herself, sometimes cross and always independent. On the few occasions when I swatted her (very gently), she would hit me right back, a return swat on the hand—though always with sheathed claws.

I like to think that her long life with us, and then just with me, was a very happy one. Her vision, though, would undoubtedly state that she was perfectly happy until Black and Brown moved in.

Another Berkeley lunch. A weekday, and all the women present work, and have very little time, and so this getting together seems a rare treat. Our hostess, a diminutive and brilliant art historian, announces that her cat, Parsley, is extremely pregnant. "Honestly, any minute," she laughs, and this is clearly true; the poor burdened cat, a brown Burmese, comes into the room, heavy and uncomfortable and restless. Searching.

A little later, in the midst of serving our many-salad lunch, the hostess says that the cat is actually having her kittens now, in the kitchen closet. We all troop out into the kitchen to watch.

The first tiny sac-enclosed kitten to barrel out is a black one, instantly vigorous, eager to stand up and get on with her life. Then three more come at intervals; it is hard to make out their colors.

"More multiple insemination," I told Andrew that night.

"It must be rife in Berkeley, like everyone says."

"It was fascinating, watching them being born."

"I guess, if you like obstetrics."

A month or so later the art historian friend called with a very sad story: she had just been diagnosed as being very clearly allergic to cats. "I thought I wasn't feeling too well, but I never thought it could be the cats. I know you already have that marvelous Pink, but do you think—until I find someone to take them? Just the two that are left?"

Surprisingly, Andrew, when consulted, said, "Well, why not? Be entertainment for old Pink, she must be getting pretty bored with just us."

We did not consult Pink, who hated those cats on sight. But Andrew was right away crazy about them, especially the black one (maybe he had wanted a cat of his own?). We called them, of course, Black and Brown. They were two Burmese females, or semi-Burmese, soon established in our house and seeming to believe that they lived there.

Black was (she is) the more interesting and aggressive of the two. And from the first she truly took to Pink, exhibiting the sort of clear affection that admits of no rebuff.

We had had Pink spayed as soon as she was old enough, after one quite miserable heat. And now Black and Brown seemed to come into heat consecutively, and to look to Pink for relief. She raged and scratched at them, as they, alternatively, squirmed and rubbed toward her. Especially Brown, who gave all the signs of a major passion for Pink. Furious, Pink seemed to be saying, Even if I were the tom cat that you long for, I would never look at you.

Black and Brown were spayed, and relations among the cats settled down to a much less luridly sexual pattern. Black and Brown both liked Pink and wished to be close to her, which she would almost never permit. She refused to eat with them, haughtily waiting at mealtimes until they were through.

It is easy for me to imagine Black and Brown as people, as women. Black would be a sculptor, I think, very strong, moving freely and widely through the world. Unmarried, no children. Whereas Brown would be a very sweet and pretty, rather silly woman, adored by her husband and sons.

But I do not imagine Pink as a person at all. I only see her as herself. A cat.

Zoe was going to move to Hawaii, she suddenly said. "Somewhere on Kauai, natch, and probably Poipu, if those grubby developers have kept their hands off anything there." Her hatchet laugh. "But I like the idea of living on the islands, away from it all. And so does Gordon. You guys will have to come visit us there. Bring Pink, but not those other two strays."

"Gordon" was a new beau, just turned up from somewhere in Zoe's complex Dallas childhood. With misgivings, but I think mostly good will, we went over to meet him, to hear about all these new plans.

Gordon was dark and pale and puffy, great black blotches under his narrow, dishonest eyes, a practiced laugh. Meeting him, I right off thought, They're not going to Hawaii, they're not going anywhere together.

Gordon did not drink at all, that day, although I later heard that he was a famous drunk. But occasionally he chided Zoe, who as usual was belting down vodka on ice. "Now, Baby," he kept saying. (Strident, striding Zoe—Baby?) "Let's go easy on the sauce. Remember what we promised." (We?)

At which Zoe laughed long and loud, as though her drinking were a good joke that we all shared.

A week or so after that Zoe called and said she was just out of the hospital. "I'm not in the greatest shape in the world," she said—and after that there was no more mention of Gordon, nor of a move to Hawaii.

And not very long after that Zoe moved down to Santa Barbara. She had friends there, she said.

Pink by now was in some cat equivalent to middle age. Still quite small, still playful, at times, she was almost always talkative. She disliked Black and Brown, but sometimes I would find her nestled against one of them, usually Black, in sleep. I had a clear sense that I was not supposed to know about this occasional rapport, or whatever. Pink still came up to my lap as I worked, and she slept on our bed at night, which we had always forbidden Black and Brown to do.

We bought a new, somewhat larger house, further up in the hills. It had stairs, and the cats ran happily up and down, and they seemed to thrive, like elderly people who benefit from a new program of exercise.

* * *

369

Andrew got sick, a terrible swift-moving cancer that killed him within a year, and for a long time I did very little but grieve. I sometimes saw friends, and I tried to work. There was a lot to do about Andrew's bookstore, which I sold, but mostly I stayed at home with my cats, all of whom were now allowed to sleep with me, on that suddenly too-wide bed.

Pink at that time chose to get under the covers with me. In a peremptory way she would tap at my cheek or my forehead, demanding to be taken in. This would happen several times in the course of the night, which was not a great help to my already fragile pattern of sleep, but it never occurred to me to deny her. And I was always too embarrassed to mention this to my doctor, when I complained of lack of sleep.

And then after several years I met Slater, at a well-meaning friend's house. Although as I have said I did not much like him at first, I was struck by his nice dark red hair, and by his extreme directness; Andrew had a tendency to be vague, it was sometimes hard to get at just what he meant. Not so with Slater, who was very clear—immediately clear about the fact that he liked me a lot, and wanted us to spend time together. And so we became somewhat involved, Slater and I, despite certain temperamental obstacles, including the fact that he does not much like cats.

And eventually we began to plan a trip to Hawaii, where Slater had business to see to.

Pink as an old cat slept more and more, and her high-assed strut showed sometimes a slight arthritic creak. Her voice got appreciably louder; no longer a littlest announcer, her statements were loud and clear (I have to admit, it was not the most attractive sound). It seems possible that she was getting a little deaf. When I took her to the vet, a sympathetic, tall and handsome young Japanese woman, she always said, "She sure doesn't look her age—" at which both Pink and I preened.

The vet, Dr. Ino, greatly admired the stripes below Pink's neck, on her breast, which looked like intricate necklaces. I admired them too (and so had Andrew).

Needless to say, the cats were perfectly trained to the sandbox, and very dainty in their habits. But at a certain point I began to notice small accidents around the house, from time to time. Especially when I had been away for a day or two. It seemed a punishment, cat turds in some dark corner. But it was hard to fix responsibility, and I decided to blame all three—and to take various measures like the installation of an upstairs sandbox, which helped. I did think that Pink was getting a little old for all those stairs.

Since she was an old cat I sometimes, though rarely, thought of the fact that Pink would die. Of course she would, eventually—although at times (bad times: the weeks and months around Andrew's illness and death) I melodramatically announced (more or less to myself) that Pink's death would be the one thing I could not bear. "Pink has promised to outlive me," I told several friends, and almost believed.

At times I even felt that we were the same person-cat, that we somehow inhabited each other. In a way I still do feel that—if I did not her loss would be truly unbearable.

I worried about her when I went away on trips. I would always come home, come into my house with some little apprehension that she might not be there. She was usually the last of the three cats to appear in the kitchen, where I stood confused among baggage, mail and phone messages. I would greet Black and Brown, and then begin to call her, "Pink, Pink?"—until, very diffident and proud, she would stroll unhurriedly toward me, and I would sweep her up into my arms with foolish cries of relief, and of love. *Ah, my darling old Pink.*

As I have said, Slater did not particularly like cats; he had nothing against them, really, just a general indifference. He eventually developed a fondness for Brown, believing that she liked him too, but actually Brown is a whore among cats; she will purr and rub up against anyone who might feed her. Whereas Pink was always discriminating, in every way, and fussy. Slater complained that one of the cats deposited small turds on the bathmat in the room where he sometimes showered, and I am afraid that this was indeed old Pink, both angry and becoming incontinent.

One night at dinner at my house, when Slater and I, alone, were admiring my view of the bay and of romantic San Francisco, all those lights, we were also talking about our trip to Hawaii. Making plans. He had been there before and was enthusiastic.

Then the phone rang, and it was Lucy, daughter of Zoe, who told me that her mother had died the day before, in Santa Barbara. "Her doctor said it was amazing she'd lived so long. All those years of booze."

"I guess. But, Lucy, it's so sad, I'm so sorry."

"I know." A pause. "I'd love to see you sometime. How's old Pink?"

"Oh, Pink's fine," I lied.

Coming back to the table, I explained as best I could about Zoe Pinkerton, how we got Pink. I played it all down, knowing his feelings about cats. But I thought he would like the multiple insemination part, and he did—as had Andrew. (It is startling when two such dissimilar men, Andrew, the somewhat dreamy book person, and Slater, the practical man, get so turned on by the same dumb joke.)

"So strange that we're going to Poipu," I told Slater. "Zoe always talked about Poipu." As I said this I knew it was not the sort of coincidence that Slater would find remarkable.

"I'm afraid it's changed a lot," he said, quite missing the point. "The early developers have probably knocked hell out of it. The greedy competition."

So much for mysterious ways.

Two days before we were to go to Hawaii, in the morning Pink seemed disoriented, unsure when she was in her sandbox, her feeding place. Also, she clearly had some bad intestinal disorder. She was very sick, but still in a way it seemed cruel to take her to the vet, whom I somehow knew could do nothing for her. However, at last I saw no alternative.

She (Dr. Ino, the admirable vet) found a large hard mass in Pink's stomach, almost certainly cancer. Inoperable. "I just can't reverse what's wrong with her," the doctor told me, with great sadness. And succinctness: I saw what she meant. I was so terribly torn, though: should I bring Pink home for a few more days, whatever was left to her—although she was so miserable, so embarrassed at her own condition?

I chose not to do that (although I still wonder, I still am torn). And I still cannot think of the last moments of Pink. Whose death I chose.

I wept on and off for a couple of days. I called some close friends who would have wanted to know about Pink, I thought; they were all most supportively kind (most of my best friends love cats).

And then it was time to leave for Hawaii.

Sometimes, during those days of packing and then flying to Hawaii, I thought it odd that Pink was not more constantly on my mind, even odd that I did not weep more than I did. Now, though, looking back on that trip and its various aftermaths, I see that in fact I was thinking about Pink all that time, that she was totally in charge, as she always had been.

We stayed in a pretty condominium complex, two-story white buildings with porches and decks, and everywhere sweeping green lawns, and flowers. A low wall of rocks, a small coarsely sanded beach, and the vast and billowing sea.

Ours was a second-floor unit, with a nice wide balcony for sunset drinks, or daytime sunning. And, looking down from that balcony one night, our first, I saw the people in the building next door, out on the grass beside what must have been their kitchen, *feeding their cats.* They must have brought along these cats, two supple gray Siamese, and were giving them their supper. I chose not to mention this to Slater, I thought I could imagine his reaction, but in the days after that, everytime we walked past that building I slowed my pace and looked carefully for the cats, and a couple of times I saw them. Such pretty cats, and very friendly, for Siamese. Imagine: traveling to Hawaii with your cats—though I was not at all sure that I would have wanted Black and Brown along, nice as they are, and pretty.

Another cat event (there were four in all) came as we drove from Lihue back to Poipu, going very slowly over those very sedate tree- and flower-lined streets, with their decorous, spare houses. Suddenly I felt—we felt—

a sort of thump, and Slater, looking startled, slowed down even further and looked back.

"Lord God, that was a cat," he said.

"A cat?"

"He ran right out into the car. And then ran back."

"Are you sure? she's all right?"

"Absolutely. Got a good scare though." Slater chuckled.

But you might have killed that cat, I did not say. And for a moment I wondered if he actually had, and lied, saying the cat was okay. However Slater would never lie to spare my feelings, I am quite sure of that.

The third cat happening took place as we drove down a winding, very steep mountain road (we had been up to see the mammoth gorges cut into the island, near it western edge). On either side of the road there was thick green jungular growth—and suddenly, there among the vines and shrubs I saw a small yellow cat staring out, her ears lowered. Frightened. Eyes begging.

Slater saw her too and even he observed, "Good Lord, people dumping off animals to starve. It's awful."

"You're sure she doesn't live out there? a wilderness cat?"

"I don't think so." Honest Slater.

We did not talk then or later about going back to rescue that cat—not until the next day when he asked me what I would like to do and I said, "I'd like to go back for that cat." He assumed I was joking, and I guess I mostly was. There were too many obvious reasons not to save that particular cat, including the difficulty of finding her again. But I remembered her face, I can see it still, that expression of much-resented dependence. It was a way that even Pink looked, very occasionally.

Wherever we drove, through small neat impoverished "native" settlements (blocks of houses that Slater and his cohorts planned to buy, and demolish, to replace with fancy condos), with their lavish flowers all restrained into tidy beds, I kept looking at the yards, and under the houses. I wanted to see a cat, or some cats (I wanted to see Pink again). Realizing what I was doing, I continued to do it, to strain for the sight of a cat.

* * *

The fourth and final cat event took place as we walked home from dinner one night, in the flower-scented, corny-romantic Hawaiian darkness. To our left was the surging black sea; and to our right large tamed white shrubbery, and a hotel swimming pool, glistening blackly under feeble yellow floodlights. And then quite suddenly, from nowhere, a small cat appeared in our path, shyly and uncertainly arching her back against a bush. A black cat with some yellow tortoise markings, a long thin curve of a tail.

"He looks just like your Pink, doesn't he." Slater actually said this, and I suppose he believed it to be true.

"What—Pink? But her tail—Jesus, didn't you even see my cat?"

I'm afraid I went on in this vein, sporadically, for several days. But it did seem so incredible, not remembering Pink, my elegantly striped, my tailless wonder. (It is also true that I was purposely using this lapse, as one will, in a poor connection.)

I dreaded going home with no Pink to call out to, as I came in the door. And the actuality was nearly as bad as my imaginings of it: Black and Brown, lazy and affectionate, glad to see me. And no Pink, with her scolding *hauteur,* her long delayed yielding to my blandishments.

I had no good pictures of Pink, and to explain this odd fact I have to admit that I am very bad about snapshots; I have never devised a really good way of storing and keeping them, and tend rather to enclose any interesting ones in letters to people who might like them, to whom they would have some meaning. And to shove the others into drawers, among old letters and other unclassifiable mementos.

I began then to scour my house for Pink pictures, looking everywhere. In an album (Andrew and I put together a couple of albums, early on) I found a great many pictures of Pink as a tiny, tall-eared brand-new kitten, stalking across a padded window seat, hiding behind an oversized Boston fern—among all the other pictures from those days: Zoe Pinkerton, happy and smoking a long cigarette and almost drunk, wearing outrageous colors, on the deck of her house. And Andrew and I, young and very happy, silly, snapped by someone at a party. Andrew in his bookstore, horn-rimmed and quirky. Andrew uncharacteristically working in our garden. Andrew all over the place.

But no middle-year or recent pictures of Pink. I had in fact (I then remembered) sent the most recent shots of Pink to Zoe; it must have been just before she (Zoe) died, with a silly note about old survivors, something like that. It occurred to me to get in touch with Lucy, Zoe's daughter, to see if those pictures had turned up among Zoe's "effects," but knowing the chaos in which Zoe had always lived (and doubtless died) I decided that this would be tactless, unnecessary trouble. And I gave up looking for pictures.

Slater called yesterday to say that he is going back to Hawaii, a sudden trip. Business. I imagine that he is about to finish the ruination of all that was left of Zoe's islands. He certainly did not suggest that I come along, nor did he speak specifically of our getting together again, and I rather think that he, like me, has begun to wonder what we were doing together in the first place. It does seem to me that I was drawn to him for a very suspicious reason, his lack of resemblance to Andrew: why ever should I seek out the opposite of a person I truly loved?

I do look forward to some time alone now. I will think about Pink—I always feel her presence in my house, everywhere. Pink, stalking and severe, ears high. Pink, in my lap, raising her head with some small soft thing to say.

And maybe, since Black and Brown are getting fairly old now too, I will think about getting another new young cat. Maybe, with luck, a small gray partially Manx, with no tail at all, and beautiful necklaces.

Gina Berriault

FELIS CATUS

W hen they awoke their first Sunday morning in their very own house and slippered across their sea-grass rugs to eat their breakfast on orange pottery, with the soft blue bay and the dark green trees and the houses farther down the hill all blurring together beyond the bamboo screen like an impressionist painting; when now, after four years of apartments, they were settled at last, they talked together about finding a cat to live with them.

Mayda, chatting with the girls under her supervision at the telephone company, let it be known that she and her husband were in the market for a cat. After all, it was one of those homey, prosaic subjects that she was always looking for to maintain common ground with the girls, ground fast slipping away; for they were resentful, she knew, that her interest in the arts had procured for her, tall and homely as she was, a tall and cultured husband, and they suspected that he had sat down and planned with her, like a military strategy, a cultural life together that ruled out her fraternizing with the girls. But when one of the switchboard operators showed up in the morning with a gray-striped kitten in a shoebox, Mayda regretted having touched upon the subject. Unable to refuse it, she grew quite attached to it in the first week, for it did have a great deal of whirligig energy that one would never have anticipated from the *paleness* of it. Afraid, however, that their friends would think them indiscriminate, they drove up one weekend to a Siamese cattery near Guerneville and returned home with two seal points, adolescent brothers. Charles, watching the lean, beige brothers slide under the furniture and step high and bouncy upon the piles of cushions, said, with satisfaction, that they were losing no time in making themselves at home. But Mayda was a bit intimidated by the formality of their purebred bodies and went into the kitchen to get down on her knees and try to coax the gray one out from behind the stove.

In his browsing in the secondhand bookstore a few blocks from the London Men's Shop where he clerked, Charles came upon many a reference to cats in books that, topically, were in no way concerned with them, and he began to buy books that he would not otherwise have cared for—a Victorian era travel book on Italy because of some wonderful passages about the cats of the Forum Romanum, and a biography of a famous English surgeon because of the photograph it contained of that bearded gentleman with a huge tabby cat upon his lap. For the first time he was made aware of the predilection for cat companionship on the part of many renowned persons who had made their contribution to society in every field from entomology to religion, and the resemblance he bore to those persons in that respect increased his dissatisfaction with his job and reinforced the tantalizing idea, always in the back of his mind, of trying his hand as a novelist or an art critic. In Chinatown one afternoon he spied, in a window crowded with kimonos and carven teak boxes, a hanging glass shelf holding an assortment of tiny, painted ivory cats that overcame his antipathy for bric-a-brac, and he bought one—a yellow-striped tomcat on its haunches, a dazed, lopsided, pugilist's look in its face no bigger than an orange seed; and at the Museum of Modern Art one evening they bought two Fujita prints of feathery young cats, and Charles matted them on black silk.

When they had been living in their new home for six weeks, Mayda found time to reply to her sister Martha in Sacramento. She told how happy they were to be breathing what Charles called "green air," tending their garden and their cats, and told what a relief it was to drive out of San Francisco every evening, what a pleasure to drive back across the bridge to their charming hill town of Sausalito and contemplate across the bay the city where they worked all day; and she commented wryly that Charles's mother, in leaving him a sum of money large enough to make a down payment on a home, had finally contributed something to his comfort. Martha replied promptly, as usual, glad to hear they'd found a house "all cut out for them," and in uncomplaining comparison told them about the disrepair into which her own house had fallen. She'd taken a lot of time off from her work, she said, because she hadn't been feeling well for the past few months, and the money she had set aside for repainting and reroofing was used up. *Oh, well,* she wrote, *it doesn't look any worse than its neighbors, and that goes for me, too.* One of the items in her letter was about a college girl who had taken a room for a while in Martha's house. The girl had followed a state assemblyman to the capital, Martha wrote, but just before the assembly recessed the fellow must have broken everything off, because the girl cried all night long, so loudly that the children kept waking up and whimpering. *She was a strange girl,* Martha wrote. *The next morning she said she was going to Mexico and that we could have her cat. Then she packed her clothes and drove off in her foreign car. Peter tells me it's a Jaguar. You can have the cat if you want it. It's a handsome sir. She told me once what kind it was, something rare, but I can't remember. The kids always forget to feed the poor thing. Usually, I wouldn't mind seeing to it myself, but my chores seem to be piling up on me lately. Did I tell you I was down to 109 pounds?*

The following Sunday they drove up to Sacramento, leaving early in the morning and knocking at Martha's door at ten o'clock with tender surprise smiles on their faces. Martha, in a faded housecoat, was eating breakfast alone, the children having run out to play. She pushed aside the dishes and served the visitors coffee, repeating what a nice surprise this was—How long was it now since they'd visited last? A year come August? They said they had come because they were alarmed by her letter, and Mayda, pulling up a chair to the table, thought her sister's appearance gave them ample reason for a visit. And when Martha, her eyes rickracked by teary eyelashes, reached spontaneously across the table to pinch Mayda's cheek, to plump it out as one fondly does a baby's cheek, crying, "Maydine, you rascal!" utterly forgetting that her younger sister's every letter in the past four years had been signed by the new name Charles had chosen, even the displeasure Mayda felt over the discarded name was quashed by the pleasure the ailing woman took in saying it.

"Charlie," Martha said, when they had hardly lifted their heads from the first sip of coffee, "why don't you poke your head out the back door and call the kids? Just call loud, they're somewhere around."

He got up reluctantly. "Don't they come home for lunch?"

"But they've just had their breakfast," Martha said.

"Well, why can't we wait?" he asked querulously. "We're not leaving so soon." And he sat down again, frowning.

"Never mind!" Martha cried hastily. "If you'd rather just sit and talk that suits me fine. Once they come, we won't get a chance." Then with sincere concern she asked him, "And how is your asthma these days?"

He shrugged, surprised that he should be questioned about something that had not bothered him for almost four years, not since the early months of his marriage. But Mayda, perceiving that her sister was tracing his petulance to some lurking illness, cried with obliging cheer, "Oh, he's much better now. But we keep our fingers crossed."

The sisters took up again, as if their letters had been actual conversation between them, the news about themselves, and, stimulated by this sitting face to face with each other, they recalled their parents, recalled their friends, and soon Martha was recalling again that rainy day, six years ago, when her husband, a taxi driver, had lost his life in the streets not far from the capitol building. They had heard it all before, but, to Mayda, it was more tragic now than it had been even the first telling, because of Martha's thinly striving voice. And so she was dismayed when she felt

Charles's hand upon her knee, and, glancing at him, saw that he was sorry about his disagreeableness. His hand was reminding her that he was always upset to the point of surliness by the suffering of others, by their physical deterioration. It was because he wanted so badly to express his sympathy and yet sympathy seemed so inadequate. *Darling, you know how it is with me?* his hand said. She did not respond. All this under the table apologetics was an affront to Martha, who could see that he was not listening. But when, a few moments later, a cat brushed against Mayda's ankle and was gone, her own eyes lost their listening, she moved her feet searchingly.

The cat leaped onto Martha's lap and from there onto the table, where it stepped knowingly among the dishes in the manner of a prince slumming along narrow, winding streets. Martha feigned a sideways brush-off, rising from her chair and crying, "Did you ever?" But Mayda reached for it, lifting it from the table and setting it down on the floor, not attempting to take it into her lap, for it had the inviolable weight of someone else's property. It belonged to the girl in the Jaguar.

"What kind is it, Charles?" she asked eagerly.

"Peter knows," Martha said. "He remembers brand names and things like that."

The cat elongated itself toward a cracked white saucer under the high-legged stove, found the food there not to its liking, and sat down with its back to everyone, musing in the heat that still remained in the region of the stove. Never had they seen a cat with fur of rich brown, and the combination of topaz eyes and glossy brown coat and long, thin legs was the height of elegance.

"How old is Peter now?" Charles asked, lifting the percolator from the hot pad and shaking it.

"Here, here, I'll make some more!" Martha cried, reaching for it.

"No, no! I can do it!" Charles rose, glancing up at her cupboards. "Just tell me where you keep the coffee."

"Peter's nine now," Martha said, while Charles was filling the percolator, jostling the aluminum parts around and making himself at home. "And Norine's seven. Could I borrow a cigarette, I wonder?" she asked, leaning back and smiling a pale flirtation. "I'm not supposed to smoke, and so I've got none in the house. Peter caught me smoking once and he really had a tantrum. He's terribly worried about me, that boy. They're both as nice as pie, it almost makes me cry. They're so tidy! But you know the way kids tidy things up? Everything looks kind of odd, like there were little shrines all over the house." She leaned forward to accept a light from Mayda, holding the cigarette clumsily to her lips. "They're angels, but I'm not going to brag about it."

"Suppose we call them?" Charles suggested, setting the percolator on the flame.

"Wait'll I finish this cigarette," Martha begged, and Charles put his hands into his pockets and strolled about the kitchen, gazing at trinkets and potted cactus plants on the windowsill, and he leaned against the door frame, gazing out through the screen and remarking about the huge fig tree in the yard. Then he was purposefully gone, and they heard him calling. A few minutes later he held open the screen door, and under his arm, as under a bridge, the children entered, and he came in after them, smiling.

"God, they've grown!" he exclaimed. "They didn't even remember me, they couldn't imagine who'd be calling them. You should have seen their faces when they came through the hedge."

"It's Uncle Charles," Martha assured them. "Don't you remember Uncle Charles and Aunt Maydine? How can you forget so fast?" she cried. "He got afraid of a man's voice," Martha explained. "He thought something was wrong, he thought it was the doctor calling."

"I'm sorry, old man," Charles said, and Mayda shot an unbelieving glance at him, never having heard him use that term before. The triteness of it must surely, she thought, go against his grain. "I didn't mean to frighten you, but your mother was telling me all about you. About how tall you are and what an enormous memory you've got. She said you know what kind of cat the girl left."

"That cat? It's a Burmese," the boy said, not yet able to look Charles in the face. Beckoned by the sound of the children, the cat, having wandered up the hallway, now wandered in again and poked its muzzle at the food in the saucer, this time eating it reluctantly, its tongue smacking a delicate distaste. Ambivalently, its slender body seemed to be backing away from the saucer, for its front legs were in a low crouch while its hind legs were up straight and shifting weight, as if the cat were unwilling to admit to spectators that it was finally accepting this gray, crumbly food.

"Its name is Rangoon," the boy said, warming up. "She called it Baby all the time, and I asked her if that was his real name, and she said it was Rangoon. I thought that was a funny name. I'd never call a pet of mine a goon like that. I didn't say that, I just asked her why she wanted to call it Rangoon, and she said Rangoon was the name of a river in Burma and Burma was where the cat's ancestors came from. She said a guy who loved cats, he was in Burma when a war broke out, and he escaped with the cats with bullets flying all around him and brought them to the United States." He had slid from his mother's knee and was standing in a pose of jaunty authority, his ankles crossed and his hand on his hip.

"I should think she'd want to keep it," Charles asked, "with all the history it's got."

"She was spoiled," Martha said.

"She cried all night," Norine told the visitors.

"That's because she was spoiled," Martha explained to the child, who was leaning against her. "Norine feels sorry for her, but I say it did her good to lose that man. You couldn't contradict that girl one little bit."

All at once Peter and the cat were wrestling amicably in the hall doorway, and no one knew whether Peter had intercepted the cat's flight or whether the cat had seen Peter moving toward it. After a moment the cat hung down from Peter's hands, the long body tentatively resigned, the tail swishing.

"If you want that cat you take him," Martha said to Charles.

A grimace wrinkled up Peter's face. It wasn't a prelude to a weeping kind of frown but had a senility to it. He looked, Mayda thought, like an old man attempting to read fine print.

"But you never take care of it," his mother reminded him.

"Never mind," Charles said. "We've got our hands full of cats."

"But this is a rare one," Martha insisted above the sudden rattling of the percolator as it shot up jets of steam.

Charles fumbled the pot to a cold grill, all the comfortable agility gone from his movements. "Rare, smare," he said. "At night all cats are gray."

"Take it! I don't want it!" Peter had dropped the cat and turned his back on them, and was standing rigid, shouting up the hallway as if to someone at the other end.

Not at all dismayed by her brother's shouting, the girl said recitingly, "Once we had a cat that ate clam chowder. But this one can't keep nothing on its stomach. Peter told me he'd rather have a tabby cat because they can eat anything. He said he didn't think this one could even eat a mouse. He said he wasn't sure it was a real cat."

"Well then, it's good riddance, isn't it, Peter?" his mother asked, and chidingly, "People like you more when you're generous."

The jagged atmosphere was soon dispelled by Charles's blandishments and by the children's desire to be swayed by him. After a while the girl took his hand and led him into the backyard to see her vegetable garden. Peter followed them out, and towed Charles back through the kitchen to examine the boy's collection of rocks and gems, and, emerging from the children's bedroom, Charles informed Mayda that Peter had given him the name of a firm that sold Arizona rubies for 25 cents a packet. At lunch they sat crowded around the kitchen table, and Charles made jokes, the halting way he had of relating an anecdote or posing a riddle interfering to no degree with the children's appreciation of him, expressed in whoops and sputtering attempts to tell as funny a joke. In the midst of it, Mayda wondered with an unpleasant shock if he appeared naturally comic to the children. Sometimes children saw things and people disproportionately, and perhaps they misconstrued his tall, thin body and the sharp contrast of his black crew cut with his large, pale eyes. Even the pink shirt, so popular in the city with young career men, might appear to the youngsters to be comically inappropriate for a grown man, and part of a clown's costume. After a time, the children got overexcited, and Martha's weary voice darted in among their cries. She clasped Peter's wrist, and to force him to pay attention to her, shook his hand until it was limp and tractable.

At three o'clock they left, after an hour or so of parlor sitting with Martha. Under his arm Charles carried Rangoon, and as soon as they were alone in the car and the cat was leaping in leisurely curiosity from Mayda's lap to the back of the seat and down again, they were immediately silenced by their feeling of uneasy gain. The fact that they were taking Rangoon home with them made their whole visit suspect, even in the stronghold of their mated minds, and there was nothing they wanted to say to each other.

Within a few days, Mayda wrote to her sister, addressing the letter placatingly to Peter, too, and to Norine, and reported that Rangoon was getting along famously, that a friend of theirs who was a reporter for a daily paper and who had covered a cat show once had been over for supper, and he thought Rangoon was championship quality. But they weren't going to enter the cat in any competition, since they had no record of its ancestry. Can you imagine?—there was a studbook for cats wherein cats of known ancestry through four generations were listed, and another listing called the Foundation Record for cats of less than four generations of traceable ancestry. Wasn't that a kick? The reply came from Peter. It was written with pencil on lined tablet paper, and folded crookedly into the envelope, and he said that he was writing because his mother thought he ought to because Rangoon had been his cat; he told them about his and Norine's trip to a swimming pool and how they came home with their hair wet, and closed the letter on the same page he had begun it, hoping it found them in good health and signing it, *Your dear nephew, Peter.*

"Martha dictated it," Charles commented, and later, when the bomb had exploded, he remembered that casual observation of his and was able to say with sickly triumph, "What did I tell you?" Two weeks later, a letter from Martha came, the longest she had ever written to them, and following the news that her doctor had called in a bone specialist for consultation and that they had persuaded her to enter a sanitarium, *They think I'm such a rare duck, they don't want to lose hold of me;* following the information that the few silver serving spoons left to her by her mother, and the family photographs, were being sent to Maydine railway express, for she didn't want to be leaving precious things to the mercy of the tenants who'd be renting the house; following the details of upheaval, and the prediction, *You wait, Maydine, I'll bet my new boudoir slippers I'll be waltzing out of there in no time,* she at last asked them, Charles and Maydine, to take her two children into their home until she was well and could fetch them.

As customary on their return from work, they had taken the mail from the box that stood at street level, and, climbing the long flight of brick steps, had opened first that which promised to be most interesting. On that evening their choice was a letter from a couple vacationing in Spain and from whom they had expected no letter at all, being, as they were, on the outer edge of that couple's circle, and they had paused halfway up the steps to read it, this recognition of them arousing on the instant a sharp delight in their home up ahead of them and the feeling of the bay at their backs. It was not until they were already in lounging clothes and sipping their wine that she opened her sister's letter. They ate their supper with no appetite, and Charles asked, picking at the casserole and green salad on his plate, "Do we have to decide tonight?"

"Don't be silly," she said, feeling an impending annoyance with him. "She's not leaving for three weeks yet. We've all that time."

She recalled to herself with a kind of pain, with a feeling of lameness, how plain the children were. If they were beautiful, they'd be a little easier to have around; the admiration of visitors would compensate for the trouble of caring for them, and their beauty would reflect, in a way, upon herself, for they were her sister's children. But they were as plain as the rest of the family, as she herself had been, and now that she had taken the edge off a bit with the way she bound up her dark hair, with the wearing of Mexican silver necklaces that sometimes seemed as heavy and eliciting of favor as a religious ornament between her breasts, did she want to be constantly reminded by the children of her own essential plainness? Idling her fork around her plate, she was overcome by an irrational anger against Charles, and drew her feet in farther under her chair. What was the matter with being plain? What was the matter with being big-boned, lanky, and plain, as long as your heart was in the right place? Why must he be so particular about how she appeared to other people?

"This place isn't big enough," he was saying.

"There's an extra bedroom," she said, not to be persuasive but simply to state a fact.

"That's not an extra bedroom," he bristled. "It's got a north light, and it's going to be my studio. There's no *bed* in it, is there?"

She made no reply, scourging herself for her rural mentality that called a room a bedroom just because it was empty. But at once she felt allied with Martha, with her own dear sister, her own dear, honest, and uncomprehending sister who continued to call her by her real name, and she stood up, choking on her misery.

He followed her into the front room and stroked her bowed head and made her get up a minute from the chair so he could sit down and take her onto his lap, and he comforted her and said he was sorry and if she wanted the children to come and live with them, it was all right with him. They were nice kids and old enough to take care of themselves after school. It was all right with him. But she didn't *know,* she wailed. She had a closeness with him, she told him, that she had never had with anyone, with her mother or father or even with Martha, and she didn't want it destroyed by any relatives of hers imposing on them, by the children who would probably shatter this affinity by denying it nourishment like time and seclusion and the indulgence of happy, little idiosyncrasies. She didn't know, she wailed. She didn't know.

Only once did they bring themselves to mention the problem, when one evening Charles, bending over to set down upon the floor the large blue platter spread with canned mackerel, asked Mayda, "Where'll they go if they don't come here?" and gently with his foot pushed aside the cats who were rising up on their hind legs or running against one another just beneath the descending plate.

"Go? They'll go to some neighbor, I guess," she said. "If there are any that generous."

"Will they wonder if we don't take the kids?"

"Who?"

"The neighbors, the neighbors," he said.

"They're not *your* neighbors," she replied acridly.

That night he came down with an asthma attack the likes of which he had not experienced since his childhood. He sat bolt upright in bed, his chest hollowed out by his long, hoarse breaths that drew her up beside him in terror. She switched on the lamp above their bed and saw that the four cats, bedded down over the expanse of comforter, had already been watching him in the darkness, their heads high and alerted. So frightened were the animals by the sounds he was making that when she slipped from under the covers and ran in her bare feet to fetch his nebulizer, they fled the room. She sat beside him on the bed, fervently kissing his shoulder, and when at last he had some relief and lay back, she asked him, "What could have done it, darling?"

"My life's slipping by," he replied in hoarse sarcasm. "It worries me."

"It might be the cats," she speculated.

"The cats?" he cried, tossing her cooling hand off his brow. "Why not pollen, or eggs, or anything? That little lost cat we smuggled up to our apartment that time—it slept on my neck all night, it liked to sleep there, and did I get an attack?"

Already shaken by his spell, she could only stare down at him timidly, her long hair falling around her arms like a shawl protecting her from his cruelty. He softened, stroking her arm and explaining to her that he was sick of his job, literally sick of it, that he didn't have it in him to be a salesman, no matter how well he was doing at it. He tried hard to be capable, he said, just because he hated it so. She agreed that it was time for him to quit the London Shop. If he wanted, she said, to take a few months off and look around for something more congenial, or even do a critical article, why they'd get along for a time with just her salary. They'd meet the house payments and the car payments all right, they just wouldn't be able to bank anything or buy clothes or things like recordings.

The next evening he told her that he could not bring himself that day to give his notice of resignation. Maybe he wouldn't have another attack for a long time, he told her. Maybe the one last night had been a fluky thing. But a few hours later, when he had barely laid his head on the pillow, he came down with an attack the nebulizer was not equal to, and she called in the local doctor, who gave Charles a shot and left some pills and told him to drop by for a checkup when he got the chance. In the morning he was too weak to rise, and he agreed to her proposal that she would phone his shop as soon as she got to work and inform the manager that Charles was suffering from asthma and suggest that, since she didn't know how long he'd be away from work, they'd better interview some other man for the job.

When she came home that evening she sprawled in the canvas butterfly chair. No words spoken, he brought her a whiskey and water as if she had ordered it, and sat down on some pillows on the floor, sat awkwardly, his long bones at odds with one another. Whenever, before, he had revealed a momentary fear of her, her vantage had put her into a panic, but now she took a cloudy pleasure in seeing him uncomfortable. He was leading her by the nose into a conspiracy against the children, and he *ought* to be uncomfortable about it. He *ought* to be feeling guilty. She slid farther down into her chair, stretching her legs out like a slattern into a position he had chided her about in the past and cured her of.

Not long after supper he retired to the bedroom as if he had been banished there. Until it grew dark she busied herself in the garden, troweling here and there, and three of the cats kept her company. Enlivened by the cool of the evening, they were scuffling together, or calling throatily, or darting at insects she could not see in the dimness. She had no view of the bay from this rear garden, but the absence only increased her appreciation of the place, for she knew the bay was there, waiting, while she occupied herself within this garden that was filled with absolving fragrances and enclosed by plum and madrona trees. Charles had closed the bedroom windows against the garden with as much finality as if a decree had been read to him, denying him the pleasures of the evening; the bamboo screens and tan silk curtains were both in use, and through this double film she saw only the glow of the lamp above the bed and that was all. She thought of him propped up by a mountain of colored pillows from the living room and suffering pangs of guilt, and her resentment of his maneuvering against Peter and Norine was dispersed by her gratitude to him for the composite gift he had given her—for marriage and this home and this garden. She troweled under the bedroom windows, thinking of her childhood and what she had learned of his. They hadn't been happy, either. No happier than Peter or Norine. Charles in military school, seeing his mother once a year and his father never, and herself going to work at fourteen, passing for eighteen because she was so tall and overgrown, and crying at night for all the things so bountifully possessed by the small-size girls. Now, for the first time, they were on compatible terms with life. They had each other and they had this house that, although it was built to the specifications of the previous owner, seemed built for themselves, and in its interior decoration expressed Charles's talents that had been so frustrated by his years spent in stuffy, small apartments. After an evening at a concert, they could return here and find a certain leisure in which to remember and assimilate. They had no more time than they had before, but they had room and graciousness in this little house that gave the impression of being time. And did they not deserve this?

She stood in the doorway of the bedroom, clasping the lapels of her sweater across each other as if she had caught a chill in the garden, and said to him, "I'll write Martha tonight. I'll say we're sorry, but we can't possibly take the children because we're having some trouble . . . you've got your asthma again, and this time it's so bad you've had to quit your job. I'll explain it as a kind of nervous breakdown, and say that we'll just be able to make ends meet for a while."

He said, "Oh, God, Mayda, I feel like a dog," and laid his book on the comforter and could not look at her, and then, in a moment, broke, bowing his head and rubbing his hand over his face, saying to her, "Come here, come here."

She went down on her knees by the bed, and they embraced, and he stroked her hair back to kiss her brow, while she assured him that it was not his fault he was laid low by his desire to do more than just sell clothes for the rest of his life. It was not his fault at all that they couldn't take the children. They wept together in relief, for now they were again in accord, and they wept for Martha and the kids and the whole tragic situation in that little family.

In the days that followed he set himself a regimen of reading and researching for the article on Paul Klee he had in mind, and this activity, and Mayda's enthusiasm about his project, had a calming effect upon his nights and he slept well. But on the fifth night he was again victimized by his asthma; not so severe a spell, but distressing enough, and he coughed, off and on, until morning. In the last gray hour before she arose, she suggested to him that he really ought to go down and see the doctor for some allergy tests, and, feeling that their accord was certain enough now that he would not think she was belatedly accusing him, she again brought up the possibility that the cats might be causing his spells. Lying upon his back, his hand spread appeasingly upon his chest, he considered this at length, and they agreed to experiment. They would prohibit the cats from entering the bedroom, and twice a week she would brush the cats thoroughly and throw away the brushings in a paper bag, precautions that would rid the air of the irritant, to an extent. And to further convince her of his amenability all along, he began to muse upon who, among their friends, would be most glad to receive the cats, if the experiment did not work and they might be forced to give the cats away. The Siamese brothers could go to that young couple who had bought the house on upper Broadway in the city and who said they were going to get around some day to buying a Siamese; they were just acquaintances, but at least he knew them well enough to see that they would be appreciative. The gray cat Grisette could go to the child next door, and Rangoon? Well, Rangoon could go to Lizbeth, that elderly photographer who kept the most exquisite cats. It was six months now since the evening they'd been introduced to her at her exhibit in the Museum and had gone up to her studio afterward. She hadn't been by to visit them, and they'd phone her once more and say they had a surprise for her.

So when, a few days later, Charles strolled down the hill to the doctor's office and the doctor told him to get rid of the cats that had been underfoot that night of his house call, Charles was able to say that Mayda and he were already experimenting. And when he told Mayda about it that evening, repeating what the doctor had said—that the asthma was only a symptom and that what he really had was an extravagant fondness for cats, a disease, said the doctor, called *Felis catus*—Charles laughed pleasurably in the manner of one recalling a compliment.

They needn't have fretted where to place Rangoon, for one Sunday afternoon, a few weeks after the experimenting was begun, while Charles was cutting away the grass from between the brick steps, a white Jaguar drew up in the street below and through the trees he saw a girl bend from under the low, sleek top and stretch her leg to the road. Turning to his cutting again, he heard a girl's heels on the bricks below him, and gazing around to her and prepared to tell her where this neighbor or that lived, he saw her paused below, her face lifted. "I'm looking for Charles Corbett," she told him, "or his wife."

At once he recalled the Jaguar of the girl who had roomed in Martha's house, and he smiled a sweet quirk of a smile, replying, "You flatter us. It's Rangoon you're looking for."

They laughed together, and he put his clippers aside and led the way up to the house, not in any hurry, moving with an erect ease in his long body to convey to her that they had her kind of visitor every day. Under the fuchsia bushes by the front door, one of the Siamese brothers was sitting drowsily. The girl bent to stroke it, but it sprang away from her and bellied out of sight, setting the little red flowers aquiver. "One has to introduce oneself, of course," the girl said.

Charles chuckled ruminatively, opened the door, and called Mayda. Fortunately, she had just freshened herself after a day in the garden and was in a crisp yellow frock and Japanese sandals.

"Mayda, this is Rangoon's mistress," he said, and they all laughed because the cat was given more importance than the girl.

Charles went in search of Rangoon, returned in a minute, when Mayda was asking the girl what drink she preferred, with the cat riding backwards in his arms, paws upon his shoulder, muzzle delicately examining his ear. He placed the cat in the girl's lap, and Rangoon stood for a moment startled, balancing on spindly legs. The girl cupped the cat's narrow face, cooed its name, and asked if it had missed her.

"They thought I'd forsaken it, can you believe it?" she cried to Mayda. "When I left I was so upset, I was mad at everybody, even Rangoon, and I said I didn't know when I'd be back." She had, Charles thought, the languidly clutching manner of the University Beauty, and he wondered if she'd left the cat with a certain design, a studied carelessness. "Believe me," she said, "I couldn't have gone back any sooner because I couldn't bear it. The town, I mean. Emotionally, you know. But yesterday I drove up, and there were absolute strangers in the house. The woman said there was no cat around like I described. She told me her landlady was in a hospital, and the kids were staying with friends down the street. She pointed the house out to me, and I went over and knocked on the door, and there were about six kids swarming to answer it, and I thought, Oh, my God, they've skinned it! And I recognized the boy and shook him and screamed at him, What have you done with my cat? Well, he told me you'd taken it, but he didn't know your address, so I had to put in a call to the hospital and get his mother on the line, and she told me where you live."

"And how is she?" Mayda asked, alarmed, and happening at that moment to be seating herself with drink in hand, she hoped that the activity of her body—the flouncing skirt, the crossing of legs—obscured her voice so that the girl would neither hear nor answer.

"She didn't say, she just said to give you her love and that she hoped Charles was better. She said she was awfully sorry to hear about Charles's breakdown . . ." The girl looked him over, and Mayda hastened to explain that it wasn't a breakdown, really. "It's only that the cats bring on his asthma," Mayda said. "He went through several awful spells of it and had to take a vacation from his work. We're so attached to the creatures that we really can't bring ourselves to part with them. You can't do it at the drop of a hat, you know," she said. "So we're in the midst of experimenting now, we're forbidding them to come into the bedroom, and I brush their fur ritually. If that doesn't work we'll simply have to give them away."

"Oh, for God's sake, Mayda," Charles protested, as if she were praising him, for the girl was gazing at him with glittering sympathy.

"But how selfless of you!" the girl cried at him. "Rangoon couldn't have asked for nicer folks to live with. He won't want to come home with me now. But things were so upset," she explained, and, bowing her head and stroking the cat alongside her hip, she was pouring out the story of the assemblyman and herself: that she had followed him to the capital and met him in an East Indian restaurant she'd discovered for them and that he had his opposition to her all jotted down on a card, like notes for a speech, and that she had prevailed against him. She was discreet enough to withhold his name and the part of the state she was from, but that was her only discretion in the rambling story.

With misgivings, Rangoon went along with the girl, cradled in her arms. Going down the brick steps, she felt her way with the pointy toes of her high-heeled pumps, for she had to bend her head to soothe him so he wouldn't bolt, and Mayda and Charles, following after her, were poised to catch him if he ran back up the steps. In the car Rangoon inhaled the odor of the red leather upholstery, and, standing on his hind legs, rediscovered the familiarity of the top of the seat. Leaping up there and stretching out, the cat gazed with mollified yellow eyes at Mayda and Charles, who had bent their heads under the top to gaze at him.

"Thanks again, awfully," the girl said, and her white cotton dress slipped back from her young knee as she put her foot to the clutch. They waited in the middle of the road until the car reached the turn that went downhill, where the girl slowed and waved to them. They stood waving back with an appealing awkwardness, like two wise persons attempting to be less serious, until the car was hidden by the trees.

E. Nesbit

THE CAT-HOOD OF MAURICE

To have your hair cut is not painful, nor does it hurt to have your whiskers trimmed. But round wooden shoes, shaped like bowls, are not comfortable wear, however much it may amuse the onlooker to see you try to walk in them. If you have a nice fur coat like a company promoter's, it is most annoying to be made to swim in it. And if you had a tail, surely it would be solely your own affair; that any one should tie a tin can to it would strike you as an unwarrantable impertinence—to say the least.

Yet it is difficult for an outsider to see these things from the point of view of both the persons concerned. To Maurice, scissors in hand, alive and earnest to snip, it seemed the most natural thing in the world to shorten the stiff whiskers of Lord Hugh Cecil by a generous inch. He did not understand how useful those whiskers were to Lord Hugh, both in sport and in the more serious business of getting a living. Also it amused Maurice to throw Lord Hugh into ponds, though Lord Hugh only once permitted this liberty. To put walnuts on Lord Hugh's feet and then to watch him walk on ice was, in Maurice's opinion, as good as a play. Lord Hugh was a very favourite cat, but Maurice was discreet, and Lord Hugh, except under violent suffering, was at that time anyhow, dumb.

But the empty sardine-tin attached to Lord Hugh's tail and hind legs—this had a voice, and, rattling against stairs, banisters, and the legs of stricken furniture, it cried aloud for vengeance. Lord Hugh, suffering violently, added his voice, and this time the family heard. There was a chase, a chorus of 'Poor pussy!' and 'Pussy, then!' and the tail and the tin and Lord Hugh were caught under Jane's bed. The tail and the tin acquiesced in their rescue. Lord Hugh did not. He fought, scratched, and bit. Jane carried the scars of that rescue for many a long week.

When all was calm Maurice was sought and, after some little natural delay, found—in the boot-cupboard.

'Oh, Maurice!' his mother almost sobbed, 'how *can* you? What will your father say?'

Maurice thought he knew what his father would do.

'Don't you know,' the mother went on, 'how wrong it is to be cruel?'

'I didn't mean to be cruel,' Maurice said. And, what is more, he spoke the truth. All the unwelcome attentions he had showered on Lord Hugh had not been exactly intended to hurt that stout veteran—only it was interesting to see what a cat would do if you threw it in the water, or cut its whiskers, or tied thing to its tail.

'Oh, but you must have meant to be cruel,' said mother, 'and you will have to be punished.'

'I wish I hadn't,' said Maurice, from the heart.

'So do I,' said his mother, with a sigh; 'but it isn't the first time; you know you tied Lord Hugh up in a bag with the hedgehog only last Tuesday week. You'd better go to your room and think it over. I shall have to tell your father directly he comes home.'

Maurice went to his room and thought it over. And the more he thought the more he hated Lord Hugh. Why couldn't the beastly cat have held his tongue and sat still? That, at the time would have been a disappointment, but now Maurice wished it had happened. He sat on the edge of his bed and savagely kicked the edge of the green Kidderminster carpet, and hated the cat.

He hadn't meant to be cruel; he was sure he hadn't; he wouldn't have pinched the cat's feet or squeezed its tail in the door, or pulled its whiskers, or poured hot water on it. He felt himself ill-used, and knew that he would feel still more so after the inevitable interview with his father.

But that interview did not take the immediately painful form expected by Maurice. His father did *not* say, 'Now I will show you what it feels like to be hurt.' Maurice had braced himself for that, and was looking beyond it to the calm of forgiveness which should follow the storm in which he should so unwillingly take part. No; his father was already calm and reasonable—with a dreadful calm, a terrifying reason.

'Look here, my boy,' he said. 'This cruelty to dumb animals must be checked—severely checked.'

'I didn't mean to be cruel,' said Maurice.

'Evil,' said Mr. Basingstoke, for such was Maurice's surname, 'is wrought by want of thought as well as want of heart. What about your putting the hen in the oven?'

'You know,' said Maurice, pale but determined, 'you *know* I only wanted to help her to get her eggs hatched quickly. It says in "Fowls for Food and Fancy" that heat hatches eggs.'

'But she hadn't any eggs,' said Mr. Basingstoke.

'But she soon would have,' urged Maurice. 'I thought a stitch in time—'

'That,' said his father, 'is the sort of thing that you must learn not to think.'

'I'll try,' said Maurice, miserably hoping for the best.

'I intend that you shall,' said Mr. Basingstoke. 'This afternoon you go to Dr. Strongitharm's for the remaining week of term. If I find any more cruelty taking place during the holidays you will go there permanently. You can go and get ready.'

'Oh, father, *please* not,' was all Maurice found to say.

'I'm sorry, my boy,' said his father, much more kindly; 'it's all for your own good, and it's as painful to me as it is to you—remember that. The cab will be here at four. Go and put your things together, and Jane shall pack for you.'

So the box was packed. Mabel, Maurice's kiddy sister, cried over everything as it was put in. It was a very wet day.

'If it had been any school but old Strong's,' she sobbed.

She and her brother knew that school well: its windows, dulled with wire blinds, its big alarm bell, the high walls of its grounds, bristling with spikes, the iron gates, always locked, through which gloomy boys, imprisoned, scowled on a free world. Dr. Strongitharm's was a school 'for backward and difficult boys.' Need I say more?

Well, there was no help for it. The box was packed, the cab was at the door. The farewells had been said. Maurice determined that he wouldn't cry and he didn't, which gave him the one touch of pride and joy that such a scene could yield. Then at the last moment, just as father had one leg in the cab, the Taxes called. Father went back into the house to write a cheque. Mother and Mabel had retired in tears. Maurice used the reprieve to go back after his postage-stamp album. Already he was planning how to impress the other boys at old Strong's, and his was really a very fair collection. He ran up into the schoolroom, expecting to find it empty. But some one was there: Lord Hugh, in the very middle of the ink stained table-cloth.

'You brute,' said Maurice; 'you know jolly well I'm going away, or you wouldn't be here.' And, indeed, the room had never, somehow, been a favourite of Lord Hugh's

'Meaow,' said Lord Hugh.

'Mew!' said Maurice, with scorn. 'That's what you always say. All that fuss about a jolly little sardine-tin. Any one would have thought you'd be only too glad to have it to play with. I wonder how you'd like being a boy? Lickings, and lessons, and impots, and sent back from breakfast to wash your ears. You wash yours anywhere—I wonder what they'd say to me if I washed my ears on the drawing-room hearthrug?'

'Meaow,' said Lord Hugh, and washed an ear, as though he were showing off.

'Mew,' said Maurice again; 'that's all you can say.'

'Oh, no, it isn't,' said Lord Hugh, and stopped his ear-washing

'I say!' said Maurice in awestruck tones.

'If you think cats have such a jolly time,' said Lord Hugh, 'why not *be* a cat?'

'I would if I could,' said Maurice, 'and fight you—'

'Thank you,' said Lord Hugh.

'But I can't,' said Maurice.

'Oh, yes, you can,' said Lord Hugh. 'You've only got to say the word.'

'What word?'

Lord Hugh told him the word; but I will not tell you, for fear you should say it by accident and then be sorry.

'And if I say that, I shall turn into a cat?'

'Of course,' said the cat.

'Oh, yes, I see,' said Maurice. 'But I'm not taking any, thanks. I don't want to be a cat for always.'

'You needn't,' said Lord Hugh. 'You've only got to get some one to say to you, Please leave off being a cat and be Maurice again,' and there you are.'

Maurice thought of Dr. Strongitharm's. He also thought of the horror of his father when he should find Maurice gone, vanished, not to be traced. 'He'll be sorry, then,' Maurice told himself, and to the cat he said, suddenly:—

'Right—I'll do it. What's the word, again?'

'—,' said the cat.

'—,' said Maurice; and suddenly the table shot up to the height of a house, the walls to the height of tenement buildings, the pattern on the carpet became enormous, and Maurice found himself on all fours. He tried to stand up on his feet, but his shoulders were oddly heavy. He could only rear himself upright for a moment, and then fell heavily on his hands. He looked down at them; they seemed to have grown shorter and fatter, and were encased in black fur gloves. He felt a desire to walk on all fours—tried it—did it. It was very odd—the movement of the arms straight from the shoulder, more like the movement of the piston of an engine than anything Maurice could think of at that moment.

'I am asleep,' said Maurice—'I am dreaming this. I am dreaming I am a cat. I hope I dreamed that about the sardine-tin and Lord Hugh's tail, and Dr. Strong's.'

'You didn't,' said a voice he knew and yet didn't know, 'and you aren't dreaming this.'

'Yes, I am,' said Maurice; 'and now I'm going to dream that I fight that beastly black cat, and give him the best licking he ever had in his life. Come on, Lord Hugh.'

A loud laugh answered him.

'Excuse my smiling,' said the voice he knew and didn't know, 'but don't you see—you *are* Lord Hugh!'

A great hand picked Maurice up from the floor and held him in the air. He felt the position to be not only undignified unsafe, and gave himself a shake of mingled relief and resentment when the hand set him down on the inky table-cloth.

'You are Lord Hugh now, my dear Maurice,' said the voice, and a huge face came quite close to his. It was his own face, as it would have seemed through a magifying glass. And the voice—oh, horror!—the voice was his own voice—Maurice Basingstoke's voice. Maurice shrank from the voice, and he would have liked to claw the face, but he had had no practice.

'You are Lord Hugh,' the voice repeated, 'and I am Maurice. I like being Maurice. I am so large and strong. I could drown you in the water-butt, my poor cat—oh, so easily. No, don't spit and swear. It's bad manners—even in a cat.'

'Maurice!' shouted Mr. Basingstoke from between the door and the cab.

Maurice, from habit, leaped towards the door.

'It's no use *your* going,' said the thing that looked like a giant reflection of Maurice; 'it's *me* he wants.'

'But I didn't agree to your being me.'

'That's poetry, even if it isn't grammar,' said the thing that looked like Maurice. 'Why, my good cat, don't you see that if you are I, I must be you? Otherwise we should interfere with time and space, upset the balance of power, and as likely as not destroy the solar system. Oh, yes—I'm you, right enough, and shall be, till some one tells you to change from Lord Hugh into Maurice. And now you've got to find some one to do it.'

('Maurice!' thundered the voice of Mr. Basingstoke.)

'That'll be easy enough,' said Maurice.

'Think so?' said the other.

'But I sh'n't try yet. I want to have some fun first. I shall catch heaps of mice!'

'Think so? You forget that your whiskers are cut off—Maurice cut them. Without whiskers, how can you judge of the width of the places you go through? Take care you don't get stuck in a hole that you can't get out of or go in through, my good cat.'

'Don't call me a cat,' said Maurice, and felt that his tail was growing thick and angry.

'You *are* a cat, you know—and that little bit of temper that I see in your tail reminds me—'

Maurice felt himself gripped round the middle, abruptly lifted, and carried swiftly throught the air. The quickness of the movement made him giddy. The light went so quickly past him that it might as well have been darkness. He saw nothing, felt nothing, except a sort of long sea-sickness, and then suddenly he was not being moved. He could see now. He could feel. He was being held tight in a sort of vice—a vice covered with chequered cloth. It looked like the pattern, very much exaggerated, of his school knickerbockers. It *was.* He was being held between the hard, relentless knees of that creature that had once been Lord Hugh, and to whose tail he had tied a sardine-tin. Now *he* was Lord Hugh, and something was being tied to *his* tail. Something mysterious, terrible. Very well, he would show that he was not afraid of anything that could be attached to tails. The string rubbed his fur the wrong way—it was that that annoyed him, not the string itself; and as for what was at the end of the string, what *could* that matter to any sensible cat? Maurice was quite decided that he was—and would keep on being—a sensible cat.

The string, however, and the uncomfortable, tight position between those chequered knees—something or other was getting on his nerves.

'Maurice!' shouted his father below, and the be-catted Maurice bounded between the knees of the creature that wore his clothes and his looks.

'Coming, father,' this thing called, and sped away, leaving Maurice on the servant's bed—under which Lord Hugh had taken refuge, with his tin-can, so short and yet so long time ago. The stairs re-echoed to the loud boots which Maurice had never before thought loud; he had often, indeed, wondered that any one could object to them. He wondered now no longer.

He heard the front door slam. That thing had gone to Dr. Strongitharm's. That was one comfort. Lord Hugh was a boy now; he would know what it was to be a boy. He, Maurice, was a cat, and he meant to taste fully all catty pleasures, from milk to mice. Meanwhile he was without mice or milk, and, unaccustomed as he was to a tail, he could not but feel that all was not right with his own. There was a feeling of weight, a feeling of discomfort, of positive terror. If he should move, what would that thing that was tied to his tail do? Rattle, of course. Oh, but he could not bear it if that thing rattled. Nonsense; it was only a sardine-tin. Yes, Maurice knew that. But all the same—if it did rattle! He moved his tail. But he couldn't be sure unless he moved. But if he moved the thing would rattle, and if it rattled Maurice felt sure that he would expire or go mad. A mad cat. What a dreadful thing to be! Yet he couldn't sit on that bed for ever, waiting, waiting, waiting, for the dreadful thing to happen.

'Oh, dear,' sighed Maurice the cat. 'I never knew what people meant by "afraid" before.'

His cat-heart was beating heavily against his furry side. His limbs were getting cramped—he must move. He did. And instantly the awful thing happened. The sardine-tin touched the iron of the bed-foot. It rattled.

'Oh, I can't bear it, I can't,' cried poor Maurice, in a heartrending meaow that echoed through the house. He leaped from the bed and tore through the door and down the stairs, and behind him came the most terrible thing in the world. People might call it a sardine-tin, but he knew better. It was the soul of all the fear that ever had been or ever could be. *It rattled.*

Maurice who was a cat flew down the stairs; down, down—the rattling horror followed. Oh, horrible! Down, down! At the foot of the stairs the horror, caught by something—a banister a stair-rod—stopped. The string on Maurice's tail tightened, his tail was jerked, he was stopped. But the noise had stopped too. Maurice lay only just alive at the foot of the stairs.

It was Mabel who untied the string and soothed his terrors with strokings and tender love-words. Maurice was surprised to find what a nice little girl his sister really was.

'I'll never tease you again,' he tried to say, softly—but that was not what he said. What he said was 'Purrr.'

'Dear pussy, nice poor pussy, then,' said Mabel, and she hid away the sardine-tin and did not tell any one. This seemed unjust to Maurice until he remembered that, of course, Mabel thought that he was really Lord Hugh, and that the person who had tied the tin to his tail was her brother Maurice. Then he was half grateful. She carried him down, in soft, safe arms, to the kitchen, and asked cook to give him some milk.

'Tell me to change back into Maurice,' said Maurice who was quite worn out by his cattish experiences. But no one heard him. What they heard was, 'Meaow—Meaow—Meeeaow!'

Then Maurice saw how he had been tricked. He could be changed back into a boy as soon as any one said to him, 'Leave off being a cat and be Maurice again,' but his tongue had no longer the power to ask any one to say it.

He did not sleep well that night. For one thing he was not accustomed to sleeping on the kitchen hearthrug, and the blackbeetles were too many and too cordial. He was glad when cook came down and turned him out into the garden, where the October frost still lay white on the yellowed stalks of sunflowers and nasturtiums. He took a walk, climbed a tree, failed to catch a bird, and felt better. He began also to feel hungry. A delicious scent came stealing out of the back kitchen door. Oh, joy, there were to be herrings for breakfast! Maurice hastened in and took his place on his usual chair.

His mother said, 'Down, puss,' and gently tilted the chair so that Maurice fell off it. Then the family had herrings. Maurice said, 'You might give me some,' and he said it so often that his father, who, of course, heard only mewings, said:—

'For goodness' sake put that cat out of the room.'

Maurice breakfasted later, in the dust-bin, on herring heads.

But he kept himself up with a new and splendid idea. They would give him milk presently, and then they should see.

He spent the afternoon sitting on the sofa in the dining-room, listening to the conversation of his father and mother. It is said that listeners never hear any good of themselves. Maurice heard so much that he was surprised and humbled. He heard his father say that he was a fine, plucky little chap, but he needed a severe lesson, and Dr. Strongitharm was the man to give it to him. He heard his mother say things that made his heart throb in his throat and the tears prick behind those green cat-eyes of his. He had always thought his parents a little bit unjust. Now they did him so much more than justice that he felt quite small and mean inside his cat-skin.

'He's a dear, good, affectionate boy,' said mother. 'It's only his high spirits. Don't you think, darling, perhaps you were a little hard on him?'

'It was for his own good,' said father.

'Of course,' said mother; 'but I can't bear to think of him at that dreadful school.'

'Well—,' father was beginning, when Jane came in with the tea-things on a clattering tray, whose sound made Maurice tremble in every leg. Father and mother began to talk about the weather.

Maurice felt very affectionately to both his parents. The natural way of showing this was to jump on to the sideboard and thence on to his father's shoulders. He landed there on his four padded feet, light as a feather, but father was not pleased.

'Bother the cat!' he cried. 'Jane, put it out of the room.'

Maurice was put out. His great idea, which was to be carried out with milk, would certainly not be carried out in the dining-room. He sought the kitchen, and, seeing a milk-can on the window-ledge, jumped up beside the can and patted it as he had seen Lord Hugh do.

'My!' said a friend of Jane's who happened to be there, 'ain't that cat clever—a perfect moral, I call her.'

'He's nothing to boast of this time,' said cook. 'I will say for Lord Hugh he's not often taken in with a empty can.'

This was naturally mortifying for Maurice, but he pretended not to hear, and jumped from the window to the tea-table and patted the milk-jug.

'Come,' said the cook, 'that's more like it,' and she poured him out a full saucer and set it on the floor.

Now was the chance Maurice had longed for. Now he could carry out that idea of his. He was very thirsty, for he had had nothing since that delicious breakfast in the dust-bin. But not for worlds would he have drunk the milk. No. He carefully dipped his right paw in it, for his idea was to make letters with it. on the kitchen oil-cloth. He meant to write: 'Please tell me to leave off being a cat and be Maurice again,' but he found his paw a very clumsy pen, and he had to rub out the first 'P' because it only looked like an accident. Then he tried again and actually did make a 'P' that any fair-minded person could have read quite easily.

'I wish they'd notice,' he said, and before he got the 'l' written they did notice.

'Drat the cat,' said cook; 'look how he's messing the floor up.'

And she took away the milk.

Maurice put pride aside and mewed to have the milk put down again. But he did not get it.

Very weary, very thirsty, and very tired of being Lord Hugh, he presently found his way to the schoolroom, where Mabel with patient toil was doing her home-lessons. She took him on her lap and stroked him while she learned her French verb. He felt that he was growing very fond of her. People were quite right to be kind to dumb animals. Presently she had to stop stroking him and do a map. And after that she kissed him and put him down and went away. All the time she had been doing the map, Maurice had had but one thought: *Ink!*

The moment the door had closed behind her—how sensible people were who closed doors gently—he stood up in her chair with one paw on the map and the other on the ink. Unfortunately, the inkstand top was made to dip pens in, and not to dip paws. But Maurice was desperate. He deliberately upset the ink—most of it rolled over the table-cloth and fell pattering on the carpet, but with what was left he wrote quite plainly, across the map:—

> 'Please tell Lord Hugh
> to stop being
> a cat and be Mau
> rice again'

'There!' he said; 'they can't make any mistake about that.' They didn't. But they made a mistake about who had done it, and Mabel was deprived of jam with her supper bread.

Her assurance that some naughty boy must have come through the window and done it while she was not there convinced nobody, and, indeed, the window was shut and bolted.

Maurice, wild with indignation, did not mend matters by seizing the opportunity of a few minutes' solitude to write:—

> 'It was not Mabel
> it was Maur
> ice I mean Lord Hugh,'

because when that was seen Mabel was instantly sent to bed.

'It's not fair!' cried Maurice.

'My dear,' said Maurice's father, 'if that cat goes on mewing to this extent you'll have to get rid of it.'

Maurice said not another word. It was bad enough to be a cat, but to be a cat that was 'got rid off'! He knew how people got rid of cats. In a stricken silence he left the room and slunk up the stairs—he dared not mew again, even at the door of Mabel's room. But when Jane went in to put Mabel's light out Maurice crept in too, and in the dark tried with stifled mews and purrs to explain to Mabel how sorry he was. Mabel stroked him and he went to sleep, his last waking thought amazement at the blindness that had once made him call her a silly little kid.

If you have ever been a cat you will understand something of what Maurice endured during the dreadful days that followed. If you have not, I can never make you understand fully. There was the affair of the fishmonger's tray balanced on the wall by the back door—the delicious curled-up whiting; Maurice knew as well as you do that one mustn't steal fish out of other people's trays, but the cat that he was didn't know. There was an inward struggle—and Maurice was beaten by the cat-nature. Later he was beaten by the cook.

Then there was that very painful incident with the butcher's dog, the flight across gardens, the safety of the plum tree gained only just in time.

And, worst of all, despair took hold of him, for he saw that nothing he could do would make any one say those simple words that would release him. He had hoped that Mabel might at last be made to understand, but the ink had failed him; she did not understand his subdued mewings, and when he got the cardboard letters and made the same sentence with them Mabel only thought it was that naughty boy who came through locked windows. Somehow he could not spell before any one—his nerves were not what they had been. His brain now gave him no new ideas. He felt that he was really growing like a cat in his mind. His interest in his meals grew beyond even what it had been when they were schoolboy's meals. He hunted mice with growing enthusiasm, though the loss of his whiskers to measure narrow places with made hunting difficult.

He grew expert in bird-stalking, and often got quite near to a bird before it flew away, laughing at him. But all the time, in his heart, he was very, very miserable. And so the week went by.

Maurice in his cat shape dreaded more and more the time when Lord Hugh in the boy shape should come back from Dr. Strongitharm's. He knew—who better?—exactly the kind of things boys do to cats, and he trembled to the end of his handsome half-Persian tail.

And then the boy came home from Dr. Strongitharm's, and at the first sound of his boots in the hall Maurice in the cat's body fled with silent haste to hide in the boot-cupboard.

Here, ten minutes later, the boy that had come back from Dr. Strongitharm's found him.

Maurice fluffed up his tail and unsheathed his claw. Whatever this boy was going to do to him Maurice meant to resist, and his resistance should hurt the boy as much as possible. I am sorry to say Maurice swore softly among the boots, but cat-swearing is not really wrong.

'Come out, you old duffer,' said Lord Hugh in the boy shape of Maurice. 'I'm not going to hurt you.'

'I'll see to that,' said Maurice, backing into the corner, all teeth and claws.

'Oh, I've had such a time!' said Lord Hugh. 'It's no use, you know, old chap; I can see where you are by your green eyes. My word, they do shine. I've been caned and shut up in a dark room and given thousands of lines to write out.'

'I've been beaten, too, if you come to that,' mewed Maurice. 'Besides the butcher's dog.'

It was an intense relief to speak to some one who could understand his mews.

'Well, I suppose it's Pax for the future,' said Lord Hugh; 'if you won't come out, you won't. Please leave off being a cat and be Maurice again.'

And instantly Maurice, amid a heap of goloshes and old tennis bats, felt with a swelling heart that he was no longer a cat. No more of those undignified four legs, those tiresome pointed ears, so difficult to wash, that furry coat, that contemptible tail, and that terrible inability to express all one's feelings in two words—'mew' and 'purr.'

He scrambled out of the cupboard, and the boots and goloshes fell off him like spray off a bather.

He stood upright in those very chequered knickerbockers that were so terrible when their knees held one vice-like, while things were tied to one's tail. He was face to face with another boy, exactly like himself.

'*You* haven't changed, then—but there can't be two Maurices.

'There sha'n't be; not if I know it,' said the other boy; 'a boy's life a dog's life. Quick, before any one comes.'

'Quick what?' asked Maurice.

'Why tell me to leave off being a boy, and to be Lord Hugh Cecil again.'

Maurice told him at once. And at once the boy was gone, and there was Lord Hugh in his own shape, purring politely, yet with a watchful eye on Maurice's movements.

'Oh, you needn't be afraid, old chap. It's Pax right enough,' Maurice murmured in the ear of Lord Hugh. And Lord Hugh, arching is back under Maurice's stroking hand, replied with a purrr-meaow that spoke volumes.

'Oh, Maurice, here you are. It *is* nice of you to be nice to Lord Hugh, when it was because of him you—'

'He's a good old chap,' said Maurice, carelessly. 'And you're not half a bad girl. See?'

Mabel almost wept for joy at this magnificent compliment, and Lord Hugh himself took on a more happy and confident air.

Please dismiss any fears which you may entertain that after this Maurice became a model boy. He didn't. But he was much nicer than before. The conversation which he overheard when he was a cat makes him more patient with his father and mother. And he is almost always nice to Mabel, for he cannot forget all that she was to him when he wore the shape of Lord Hugh. His father attributes all the improvement in his son's character to that week at Dr. Strongitharm's—which, as you know, Maurice never had. Lord Hugh's character is unchanged. Cats learn slowly and with difficulty.

Only Maurice and Lord Hugh know the truth—Maurice has never told it to any one except me, and Lord Hugh is a very reserved cat. He never at any time had that free flow of mew which distinguished and endangered the cathood of Maurice.

E. Nesbit

THE WHITE CAT

The White Cat lived at the back of a shelf at the darkest end of the inside attic which was nearly dark all over. It had lived there for years, because one of its white china ears was chipped, so that it was no longer a possible ornament for the spare bed-room.

Tavy found it at the climax of a wicked and glorious afternoon. He had been left alone. The servants were the only other people in the house. He had promised to be good. He had meant to be good. And he had not been. He had done everything you can think of. He had walked into the duck pond, and not a stitch of his clothes but had had to be changed. He had climbed on a hay rick and fallen off it, and had not broken his neck, which, as cook told him, he richly deserved to do. He had found a mouse in the trap and put it in the kitchen tea-pot, so that when cook went to make tea it jumped out at her, and affected her to screams followed by tears. Tavy was sorry for this, of course, and said so like a man. He had only, he explained, meant to give her a little start. In the confusion that followed the mouse, he had eaten all the black-currant jam that was put out for kitchen tea, and for this too, he apologised handsomely as soon as it was pointed out to him. He had broken a pane of the greenhouse with a stone and . . . But why pursue the painful theme? The last thing he had done was to explore the attic, where he was never allowed to go, and to knock down the White Cat from its shelf.

The sound of its fall brought the servants. The cat was not broken—only its other ear was chipped. Tavy was put to bed. But he got out as soon as the servants had gone downstairs, crept up to the attic, secured the Cat, and washed it in the bath. So that when mother came back from London, Tavy, dancing impatiently at the head of the stairs, in a very wet night-gown, flung himself upon her and cried, 'I've been awfully naughty, and I'm frightfully sorry, and please may I have the White Cat for my very own?'

He was much sorrier than he had expected to be when he saw that mother was too tired even to want to know, as she generally did, exactly how naughty he had been. She only kissed him, and said:

'I am sorry you've been naughty, my darling. Go back to bed now. Good-night.'

Tavy was ashamed to say anything more about the China Cat, so he went back to bed. But he took the Cat with him and talked to it and kissed it, and went to sleep with its smooth shiny shoulder against his cheek.

In the days that followed, he was extravagantly good. Being good seemed as easy as being bad usually was. This may have been because mother seemed so tired and ill; and gentlemen in black coats and high hats came to see mother, and after they had gone she used to cry. (These things going on in a house sometimes make people good; sometimes they act just the other way.) Or it may have been because he had the China Cat to talk to. Anyhow, whichever way it was, at the end of the week mother said:

'Tavy, you've been a dear good boy, and a great comfort to me. You must have tried very hard to be good.'

It was difficult to say, 'No, I haven't, at least not since the first day,' but Tavy got it said, and was hugged for his pains.

'You wanted,' said mother, 'the China Cat. Well, you may have it.'

'For my very own?'

'For your very own. But you must be very careful not to break it. And you mustn't give it away. It goes with the house. Your Aunt Jane made me promise to keep it in the family. It's very, very old. Don't take it out of doors for fear of accidents.'

'I love the White Cat, mother,' said Tavy. 'I love it better'n all my toys.'

Then mother told Tavy several things, and that night when he went to bed Tavy repeated them all faithfully to the China Cat, who was about six inches high and looked very intelligent.

'So you see,' he ended, 'the wicked lawyer's taken nearly all mother's money, and we've got to leave our own lovely big White House, and go and live in a horrid little house with another house glued on to its side. And mother does hate it so.'

'I don't wonder,' said the China Cat very distinctly.

'*What!*' said Tavy, half-way into his nightshirt.

'I said, I don't wonder, Octavius,' said the China Cat, and rose from her sitting position, stretched her china legs and waved her white china tail.

'You can speak?' said Tavy.

'Can't you see I can?—hear I mean?' said the Cat. 'I belong to you now, so I can speak to you. I couldn't before. It wouldn't have been manners.'

Tavy, his night-shirt round his neck, sat down on the edge of the bed with his mouth open.

'Come, don't look so silly,' said the Cat, taking a walk along the high wooden mantel-piece, 'any one would think you didn't *like* me to talk to you.'

'I *love* you to,' said Tavy recovering himself a little.

'Well then,' said the Cat.

'May I touch you?' Tavy asked timidly.

'Of course! I belong to you. Look out!' The China Cat gathered herself together and jumped. Tavy caught her.

It was quite a shock to find when one stroked her that the China Cat, though alive, was still china, hard, cold, and smooth to the touch, and yet perfectly brisk and absolutely bendable as any flesh and blood cat.

'Dear, dear white pussy,' said Tavy, 'I do love you.'

'And I love you,' purred the Cat, 'otherwise I should never have lowered myself to begin a conversation.'

'I wish you were a real cat,' said Tavy.

'I am,' said the Cat. 'Now how shall we amuse ourselves? I suppose you don't care for sport—mousing, I mean?'

'I never tried,' said Tavy, 'and I think I rather wouldn't.'

'Very well then, Octavius,' said the Cat. 'I'll take you to the White Cat's Castle. Get into bed. Bed makes a good travelling carriage, especially when you haven't any other. Shut your eyes.'

Tavy did as he was told. Shut his eyes, but could not keep them shut. He opened them a tiny, tiny chink, and sprang up. He was not in bed. He was on a couch of soft beast-skin, and the couch stood in a splendid hall, whose walls were of gold and ivory. By him stood the White Cat, no longer china, but real live cat—and fur—as cats should be.

'Here we are,' she said. 'The journey didn't take long, did it? Now we'll have that splendid supper, out of the fairy tale, with the invisible hands waiting on us.'

She clapped her paws—paws now as soft as white velvet—and a table-cloth floated into the room; then knives and forks and spoons and glasses, the table was laid, the dishes drifted in, and they began to eat. There happened to be every single thing Tavy liked best to eat. After supper there was music and singing, and Tavy, having kissed a white, soft, furry forehead, went to bed in a gold four-poster with a counterpane of butterflies' wings. He awoke at home. On the mantelpiece sat the White Cat, looking as though butter would not melt in her mouth. And all her furriness had gone with her voice. She was silent—and china.

413

Tavy spoke to her. But she would not answer. Nor did she speak all day. Only at night when he was getting into bed she suddenly mewed, stretched, and said:

'Make haste, there's a play acted to-night at my castle.'

Tavy made haste, and was rewarded by another glorious evening in the castle of the White Cat.

And so the weeks went on. Days full of an ordinary little boy's joys and sorrows, goodnesses and badnesses. Nights spent by a little Prince in the Magic Castle of the White Cat.

Then came the day when Tavy's mother spoke to him, and he, very scared and serious, told the China Cat what she had said.

'I knew this would happen,' said the cat. 'It always does. So you're to leave your house next week. Well, there's only one way out of the difficulty. Draw your sword, Tavy, and cut off my head and tail.'

'And then will you turn into a Princess, and shall I have to marry you?' Tavy asked with horror.

'No, dear—no,' said the Cat reassuringly. 'I sha'n't turn into anything. But you and mother will turn into happy people. I shall just not *be* any more—for you.'

'Then I won't do it,' said Tavy.

'But you must. Come, draw your sword, like a brave fairy Prince, and cut off my head.'

The sword hung above his bed, with the helmet and breast-plate. Uncle James had given him last Christmas.

'I'm not a fairy Prince,' said the child. 'I'm Tavy—and I love you.'

'You love your mother better,' said the Cat., 'Come cut my head off. The story always ends like that. You love mother best. It's for her sake.'

'Yes.' Tavy was trying to think it out. 'Yes, I love mother best. But I love *you*. And I won't cut off your head,—no, not even for mother.'

'Then,' said the Cat, 'I must do what I can!'

She stood up, waving her white china tail, and before Tavy could stop her she had leapt, not, as before, into his arms, but on to the wide hearthstone.

It was all over—The China Cat lay broken inside the high brass fender. The sound of the smash brought mother running.

'What is it?' she cried. 'Oh, Tavy—the China Cat!'

'She would do it,' sobbed Tavy. 'She wanted me to cut off her head'n I wouldn't.'

'Don't talk nonsense, dear,' said mother sadly. 'That only makes it worse. Pick up the pieces.'

'There's only two pieces,' said Tavy. 'Couldn't you stick her together again?'

'Why,' said mother, holding the pieces close to the candle. 'She's been broken before. And mended.'

'I knew that,' said Tavy, still sobbing. 'Oh, my dear White Cat, oh, oh, oh!' The last 'oh' was a howl of anguish.

'Come, crying won't mend her,' said mother. 'Look, there's another piece of her, close to the shovel.'

Tavy stooped.

'That's not a piece of cat,' he said, and picked it up.

It was a pale parchment label, tied to a key. Mother held it to the candle and read: 'Key of the lock behind the knot in the mantelpiece panel in the white parlour.'

'Tavy! I wonder! But . . . where did it come from?'

'Out of my White Cat, I s'pose,' said Tavy, his tears stopping. 'Are you going to see what's in the mantelpiece panel, mother? Are you? Oh, do let me come and see too!'

'You don't deserve,' mother began, and ended,—'Well, put your dressing-gown on then.'

They went down the gallery past the pictures and the stuffed birds and tables with china on them and downstairs on to the white parlour. But they could not see any knot in the mantel-piece panel, because it was all painted white. But mother's fingers felt softly all over it, and found a round raised spot. It was a knot, sure enough. Then she scraped round it with her scissors, till she loosened the knot, and poked it out with the scissors point.

'I don't suppose there's any keyhole there really,' she said. But there was. And what is more, the key fitted. The panel swung open, and inside was a little cupboard with two shelves. What was on the shelves? There were old laces and old embroideries, old jewelry and old silver; there was money, and there were dusty old papers that Tavy thought most uninteresting. But mother did not think them uninteresting. She laughed, and cried, or nearly cried, and said:

'Oh, Tavy, this was why the China Cat was to be taken such care of!' Then she told him how, a hundred and fifty years before, the Head of the House had gone out to fight for the Pretender, and had told his daughter to take the greatest care of the China Cat. 'I will send you word of the reason by a sure hand,' he said, for they parted on the open square, where any spy might have overheard anything. And he had been killed by an ambush not ten miles from home,—and his daughter had never known. But she had kept the Cat.

'And now it has saved us,' said mother. 'We can stay in the dear old house, and there are two other houses that will belong to us too, I think. And, oh, Tavy, would you like some pound-cake and ginger-wine, dear?'

Tavy did like. And had it.

The China Cat was mended, but it was put in the glass-fronted corner cupboard in the drawing-room, because it had saved the House.

Now I dare say you'll think this is all nonsense, and a made-up story. Not at all. If it were, how would you account for Tavy's finding, the very next night, fast asleep on his pillow, his own white Cat—the furry friend that the China Cat used to turn into every evening—the dear hostess who had amused him so well in the White Cat's fairy Palace?

It was she, beyond a doubt, and that was why Tavy didn't mind a bit about the China Cat being taken from him and kept under glass. You may think that it was just any old stray white cat that had come in by accident. Tavy knows better. It has the very same tender tone in its purr that the magic White Cat had. It will not talk to Tavy, it is true; but Tavy can and does talk to it. But the thing that makes it perfectly certain that it is the White Cat is that the tips of its two ears are missing—just as the China Cat's ears were. If you say that it might have lost its ear-tips in battle you are the kind of person who always *makes* difficulties, and you may be quite sure that the kind of splendid magics that happened to Tavy will never happen to *you*.

P. G. Wodehouse

SIR RODERICK COMES TO LUNCH

The blow fell at precisely one forty-five (summer-time). Benson, my Aunt Agatha's butler, was offering me the fried potatoes at the moment, and such was my emotion that I lofted six of them on the sideboard with the spoon. Shaken to the core, if you know what I mean.

I've told you how I got engaged to Honoria Glossop in my efforts to do young Bingo Little a good turn. Well, on this particular morning she had lugged me round to Aunt Agatha's for lunch, and I was just saying "Death, where is thy sting?" when I realized that the worst was yet to come.

"Bertie," she said, suddenly, as if she had just remembered it, "what is the name of that man of yours—your valet?"

"Eh? Oh, Jeeves."

"I think he's a bad influence for you," said Honoria. "When we are married you must get rid of Jeeves."

It was at this point that I jerked the spoon and sent six of the best and crispest sailing on to the sideboard, with Benson gamboling after them like a dignified old retriever.

"Get rid of Jeeves!" I gasped.

"Yes. I don't like him."

"I don't like him," said Aunt Agatha.

"But I can't. I mean—why, I couldn't carry on for a day without Jeeves."

"You will have to," said Honoria. "I don't like him at all."

"I don't like him at all," said Aunt Agatha. "I never did."

Ghastly, what? I'd always had an idea that marriage was a bit of a wash-out, but I'd never dreamed that it demanded such frightful sacrifices from a fellow. I passed the rest of the meal in a sort of stupor.

The scheme had been, if I remember, that after lunch I should go off and caddy for Honoria on a shopping tour down Regent Street; but when she got up and started collecting me and the rest of her things, Aunt Agatha stopped her.

"You run along, dear," she said. "I want to say a few words to Bertie."

So Honoria legged it, and Aunt Agatha drew up her chair and started in.

"Bertie," she said, "dear Honoria does not know it, but a little difficulty has arisen about your marriage."

"By Jove! not really?" I said, hope starting to dawn.

"Oh, it's nothing at all, of course. It is only a little exasperating. The fact is, Sir Roderick is being rather troublesome."

"Thinks I'm not a good bet? Wants to scratch the fixture? Well, perhaps he's right."

"Pray do not be so absurd, Bertie. It is nothing so serious as that. But the nature of Sir Roderick's profession unfortunately makes him— over-cautious."

I didn't get it. "Over-cautious?"

"Yes. I suppose it is inevitable. A nerve specialist with his extensive practice can hardly help taking a rather warped view of humanity."

I got what she was driving at now. Sir Roderick Glossop, Honoria's father, is always called a nerve specialist, because it sounds better, but everybody knows that he's really a sort of janitor to the loony bin. I mean to say, when your uncle the Duke begins to feel the strain a bit and you find him in the blue drawing-room sticking straws in his hair, old Glossop is the first person you send for. He toddles round, gives the patient the once-over, talks about over-excited nervous systems, and recommends complete rest and seclusion and all that sort of thing. Practically every posh family in the country has called him in at one time or another, and I suppose that being in that position—I mean, constantly having to sit on people's heads while their nearest and dearest 'phone to the asylum to send round the wagon—does tend to make a chappie take what you might call a warped view of humanity.

"You mean he thinks I may be a loony, and he doesn't want a loony son-in-law?" I said.

Aunt Agatha seemed rather peeved than otherwise at my ready intelligence.

"Of course, he does not think anything so ridiculous. I told you he was simply exceedingly cautious. He wants to satisfy himself that you are perfectly normal." Here she paused, for Benson had come in with the coffee. When he had gone, she went on: "He appears to have got hold of some extraordinary story about your having pushed his son Oswald into the lake at Ditteredge Hall. Incredible of course. Even you would hardly do a thing like that."

"Well, I did sort of lean against him, you know, and he shot off the bridge."

"Oswald definitely accuses you of having pushed him into the water. That has disturbed Sir Roderick, and unfortunately it has caused him to make inquiries, and he has heard about your poor Uncle Henry."

She eyed me with a good deal of solemnity, and I took a grave sip of coffee. We were peeping into the family cupboard and having a look at the good old skeleton. My late Uncle Henry, you see, was by way of being the blot on the Wooster escutcheon. An extremely decent chappie personally, and one who had always endeared himself to me by tipping me with considerable lavishness when I was at school; but there's no doubt he did at times do rather rummy things, notably keeping eleven pet rabbits in his bedroom, and I suppose a purist might have considered him more or less off his onion. In fact, to be perfectly frank, he wound up his career, happy to the last and completely surrounded by rabbits, in some sort of a home.

"It is very absurd, of course," continued Aunt Agatha. "If any of the family had inherited poor Henry's eccentricity—and it was nothing more—it would have been Claude and Eustace, and there could not be two brighter boys."

Claude and Eustace were twins, and had been kids at school with me in my last summer term. Casting my mind back, it seemed to me that "bright" just about described them. The whole of that term, as I remembered it, had been spent in getting them out of a series of frightful rows.

"Look how well they are doing at Oxford. Your Aunt Emily had a letter from Claude only the other day, saying that they hoped to be elected shortly to a very important college club, called The Seekers."

"Seekers?" I couldn't recall any club of the name in my time at Oxford. "What do they seek?"

"Claude did not say. Truth or Knowledge, I should imagine. It is evidently a very desirable club to belong to, for Claude added that Lord Rainsby, the Earl of Datchet's son, was one of his fellow candidates. However, we are wandering from the point, which is that Sir Roderick wants to have a quiet talk with you quite alone. Now I rely on you, Bertie, to be—I won't say intelligent, but at least sensible. Don't giggle nervously; try to keep that horrible glassy expression out of your eyes; don't yawn or fidget; and remember that Sir Roderick is the president of the West London branch of the anti-gambling league, so please do not talk about horse-racing. He will lunch with you at your flat tomorrow at one-thirty. Please remember that he drinks no wine, strongly disapproves of smoking, and can only eat the simplest food, owing to an impaired digestion. Do not offer him coffee, for he considers it the root of half the nerve-trouble in the world."

"I should think a dog-biscuit and a glass of water would about meet the case, what?"

"Bertie!"

"Oh, all right. Merely persiflage."

"Now it is precisely that sort of idiotic remark that would be calculated to arouse Sir Roderick's worst suspicions. Do please try to refrain from any misguided flippancy when you are with him. He is a very serious-minded man. . . . Are you going? Well, please remember all I have said. I rely on you, and if anything goes wrong, I shall never forgive you."

"Right-ho!" I said.

And so home, with a jolly day to look forward to.

I breakfasted pretty late next morning and I went for a stroll afterwards. It seemed to me that anything I could do to clear the old lemon ought to be done, and a bit of fresh air generally relieves that rather foggy feeling that comes over a fellow early in the day. I had taken a stroll in the Park, and got back as far as Hyde Park Corner, when some blighter sloshed me between the shoulder-blades. It was young Eustace, my cousin. He was arm-in-arm with two other fellows, the one on the outside being my cousin Claude and the one in the middle a pink-faced chappie with light hair and an apologetic sort of look.

"Bertie, old egg!" said young Eustace, affably.

"Hallo!" I said, not frightfully chirpily.

"Fancy running into you, the one man in London who can support us in the style we are accustomed to! By the way, you've never met old Dog-Face, have you? Dog-Face, this is my cousin Bertie. Lord Rainsby— Mr. Wooster. We've just been round to your flat, Bertie. Bitterly disappointed that you were out, but were hospitably entertained by old Jeeves. That man's a corker, Bertie. Stick to him."

"What are you doing in London?" I asked.

"Oh, buzzing round. We're just up for the day. Flying visit, strictly unofficial. We oil back on the three-ten. And now touching that lunch you very decently volunteered to stand us, which shall it be? Ritz? Savoy?

Carlton? Or, if you're a member of Ciro's or the Embassy, that would do just as well."

"I can't give you lunch. I've got an engagement myself. And by Jove," I said, taking a look at my watch, "I'm late." I hailed a taxi. "Sorry."

"As man to man, then," said Eustace, "lend us a fiver."

I hadn't time to stop and argue. I unbelted the fiver and hopped into the cab. It was twenty to two when I got to the flat. I bounded into the sitting room, but it was empty.

Jeeves shimmied in.

"Sir Roderick has not yet arrived, sir."

"Good egg!" I said. "I thought I should find him smashing up the furniture." My experience is that the less you want a fellow, the more punctual he's bound to be, and I had had a vision of the old lad pacing the rug in my sitting-room, saying "He cometh not!" and generally hotting up, "Is everything in order?"

"I fancy you will find the arrangements quite satisfactory, sir."

"What are you giving us?"

"Cold consommé, a cutlet, and a savory, sir. With lemon-squash, iced."

"Well, I don't see how that can hurt him. Don't go getting carried away by the excitement of the thing and start bringing in coffee."

"No, sir."

"And don't let your eyes get glassy, because if you do, you're apt to find yourself in a padded cell before you know where you are."

"Very good, sir."

There was a ring at the bell.

"Stand by, Jeeves," I said. "We're off!"

I had met Sir Roderick Glossop before, of course, but only when I was with Honoria; and there is something about Honoria which makes almost anybody you meet in the same room seem sort of undersized and trivial by comparison. I had never realized till this moment what an extraordinarily formidable old bird he was. He had a pair of shaggy eyebrows which gave his eyes a piercing look which was not at all the sort of thing a fellow wanted to encounter on an empty stomach. He was fairly tall and fairly broad, and he had the most enormous head, with practically no hair on it, which made it seem bigger and much more like the dome of St. Paul's. I suppose he must have taken about a nine or something in hats. Shows what a rotten thing it is to let your brain develop too much.

"What-ho! What-ho! What-ho!" I said, trying to strike the genial note, and then had a sudden feeling that that was just the sort of thing I had been warned not to say. Dashed difficult it is to start things going properly on an occasion like this. A fellow living in a London flat is so handicapped. I mean to say if I had been the young squire greeting the visitor in the country, I could have said "Welcome to Meadowsweet Hall!" or something zippy like that. It sounds silly to say "Welcome to Number 6a, Crichton Mansions, Berkeley Street, W.I."

"I am afraid I am a little late," he said as we sat down. "I was detained at my club by Lord Alastair Hungerford, the Duke of Ramfur-line's son. His Grace, he informed me, had exhibited a renewal of the symptoms which have been causing the family so much concern. I could not leave him immediately. Hence my unpunctuality, which I trust has not discommoded you."

"Oh, not at all. So the Duke is off his rocker, what?"

"The expression which you use is not precisely the one I should have employed myself with reference to the head of perhaps the noblest family in England, but there is no doubt that cerebral excitement does, as you suggest, exist in no small degree." He sighed as well as he could with his mouth full of cutlet. "A profession like mine is a great strain, a great strain."

"Must be."

"Sometimes I am appalled at what I see around me." He stopped suddenly and sort of stiffened. "Do you keep a cat, Mr. Wooster?"

"Eh? What? Cat? No, no cat."

"I was conscious of a distinct impression that I had heard a cat mewing either in the room or very near to where we are sitting."

"Probably a taxi or something in the street."

"I fear I do not follow you."

"I mean to say, taxis squawk, you know. Rather like cats in a sort of way."

"I had not observed the resemblance," he said, rather coldly.

"Have some lemon-squash," I said. The conversation seemed to be getting rather difficult.

"Thank you. Half a glassful, if I may." The hell-brew appeared to buck him up, for he resumed in a slightly more pally manner: "I have a particular dislike for cats. But I was saying—Oh, yes. Sometimes I am positively appalled at what I see around me. It is not only the cases which come under my professional notice, painful as many of those are. It is what I see as I go about London. Sometimes it seems to me that the whole world is mentally unbalanced. This very morning, for example, a most singular and distressing occurrence took place as I was driving from my house to the club. The day being clement, I had instructed my chauffeur to open my landaulette, and I was leaning back, deriving no little pleasure from the sunshine, when our progress was arrested in the middle of the thoroughfare by one of those blocks in the traffic which are inevitable in so congested a system as that of London."

I suppose I had been letting my mind wander a bit, for when he stopped and took a sip of lemon-squash, I had a feeling that I was listening to a lecture and was expected to say something.

"Hear, hear!" I said.

"I beg your pardon?"

"Nothing, nothing. You were saying . . ."

"The vehicles proceeding in the opposite direction had also been temporarily arrested, but after a moment they were permitted to proceed. I had fallen into a meditation when suddenly the most extraordinary thing took place. My hat was snatched abruptly from my head! And as I looked back I perceived it being waved in a kind of feverish triumph from the interior of a taxi-cab, which, even as I looked, disappeared through a gap in the traffic and was lost to sight."

I didn't laugh, but I distinctly heard a couple of my floating ribs part from their moorings under the strain.

"Must have been meant for a practical joke," I said. "What?"

This suggestion didn't seem to please the old boy.

"I trust," he said, "I am not deficient in an appreciation of the humorous, but I confess that I am at a loss to detect anything akin to pleasantry in the outrage. The action was beyond all question that of a mentally unbalanced subject. These mental lesions may express themselves in almost any form. The Duke of Ramfurline, to whom I had occasion to allude just now, is under the impression—this is in the strictest confidence—that he is a canary; and his seizure today, which so perturbed Lord Alastair, was due to the fact that a careless footman had neglected to bring him his morning lump of sugar. Cases are common, again, of . . . Mr. Wooster, there *is* a cat close at hand! It is *not* in the street! The mewing appears to come from the adjoining room."

This time I had to admit there was no doubt about it. There was a distinct sound of mewing coming from the next room. I punched the bell for Jeeves, who drifted in and stood waiting with an air of respectful devotion.

"Sir?"

"Oh, Jeeves," I said. "Cats! What about it? Are there any cats in the flat?"

"Only the three in your bedroom, sir."

"What!"

"Cats in his bedroom!" I heard Sir Roderick whisper in a kind of stricken way, and his eyes hit me amidships like a couple of bullets.

"What do you mean," I said, "only the three in my bedroom?"

"The black one, the tabby, and the small lemon-colored animal, sir."

"What on earth—?"

I charged round the table in the direction of the door. Unfortunately, Sir Roderick had just decided to edge in that direction himself, with the result that we collided in the doorway with a good deal of force and staggered out into the hall together. He came smartly out of the clinch and grabbed an umbrella from the rack.

"Stand back!" he shouted, waving it over his head. "Stand back, sir! I am armed!"

It seemed to me that the moment had come to be soothing.

"Awfully sorry I barged into you," I said. "Wouldn't have had it happen for worlds. I was just dashing out to have a look into things."

He appeared a trifle reassured and lowered the umbrella. But just then the most frightful shindy started in the bedroom. It sounded as though all the cats in London, assisted by delegates from outlying suburbs, had got together to settle their differences once for all. A sort of augmented orchestra of cats.

"This noise is unendurable," yelled Sir Roderick. "I cannot hear myself speak."

"I fancy, sir," said Jeeves, respectfully, "that the animals may have become somewhat exhilarated as the result of having discovered the fish under Mr. Wooster's bed."

The old boy tottered.

"Fish! Did I hear you rightly?"

"Sir?"

"Did you say that there was a fish under Mr. Wooster's bed?"

"Yes, sir."

Sir Roderick gave a low moan and reached for his hat and stick.

"You aren't going?" I said.

"Mr. Wooster, I *am* going! I prefer to spend my leisure time in less eccentric society."

"But I say. Here, I must come with you. I'm sure the whole business can be explained. Jeeves, my hat."

Jeeves rallied round. I took the hat from him and shoved it on my head.

"Good heavens!"

Beastly shock it was! The bally thing had absolutely engulfed me, if you know what I mean. Even as I was putting it on I got a sort of impression that it was a trifle roomy, and no sooner had I let go of it than it settled down over my ears like a kind of extinguisher.

"I say! This isn't my hat!"

"It is *my* hat!" said Sir Roderick in about the coldest, nastiest voice I'd ever heard. "The hat which was stolen from me this morning as I drove in my car."

"But—"

I suppose Napoleon or somebody like that would have been equal to the situation, but I'm bound to say it was too much for me. I just stood there goggling in a sort of coma while the old boy lifted the hat off me and turned to Jeeves.

"I should be glad, my man," he said, "if you would accompany me a few yards down the street. I wish to ask you some questions."

"Very good, sir."

"Here, but, I say—!" I began, but he left me standing. He stalked out, followed by Jeeves. And at that moment the row in the bedroom started again, louder than ever.

I was about fed up with the whole thing. I mean, cats in your bedroom—a bit thick, what? I didn't know how the dickens they had got in, but I was jolly well resolved that they weren't going to stay picnicking there any longer. I flung open the door. I got a momentary flash of about a hundred and fifteen cats of all sizes and colors scrapping in the middle of the room, and then they all shot past me with a rush and out of the front door; and all that was left of the mob scene was the head of a whacking big fish, lying on the carpet and staring up at me in a rather austere sort of way, as if it wanted a written explanation and apology.

There was something about the thing's expression that absolutely chilled me, and I withdrew on tiptoe and shut the door. And, as I did so, I bumped into someone.

"Oh, sorry!" he said.

I spun round. It was the pink-faced chappie, Lord Something-or-other, the fellow I had met with Claude and Eustace.

"I say," he said, apologetically, "awfully sorry to bother you, but those weren't my cats I met just now legging it downstairs, were they? They looked like my cats."

"They came out of my bedroom."

"Then they *were* my cats!" he said, sadly. "Oh, dash it!"

"Did you put cats in my bedroom?"

"Your man, what's his name, did. He rather decently said I could keep them there till my train went. I'd just come to fetch them. And now they've gone! Oh, well, it can't be helped, I suppose. I'll take the hat and the fish, anyway."

427

I was beginning to dislike this bird.

"Did you put that bally fish there, too?"

"No, that was Eustace's. The hat was Claude's."

I sank limply into a chair.

"I say, you couldn't explain this, could you?" I said.

The chappie gazed at me in mild surprise.

"Why, don't you know all about it? I say!" He blushed profusely. "Why, if you don't know about it, I shouldn't wonder if the whole thing didn't seem rather rummy to you."

"Rummy is the word."

"It was for The Seekers, you know."

"The Seekers?"

"Rather a blood club, you know, up at Oxford, which your cousins and I are rather keen on getting into. You have to pinch something, you know, to get elected. Some sort of a souvenir, you know. A policeman's helmet, you know, or a door-knocker or something, you know. The room's decorated with the things at the annual dinner, and everybody makes speeches and all that sort of thing. Rather jolly. Well, we wanted rather to make a sort of special effort and do the thing in style, if you understand, so we came up to London to see if we couldn't pick up something here that would be a bit out of the ordinary. And we had the most amazing luck right from the start. Your cousin Claude managed to collect a quite decent top-hat out of a passing car, and your cousin Eustace got away with a really goodish salmon or something from Harrods, and I snaffled three excellent cats all in the first hour. We were fearfully braced, I can tell you. And then the difficulty was to know where to park the things till our train went. You look so beastly conspicuous, you know, tooling about London with a fish and a lot of cats. And then Eustace remembered you, and we all came on here in a cab. You were out, but your man said it would be all right. When we met you, you were in such a hurry that we hadn't time to explain. Well, I think I'll be taking the hat if you don't mind."

"It's gone."

"Gone?"

"The fellow you pinched it from happened to be the man who was lunching here. He took it away with him."

"Oh, I say! Poor old Claude will be upset. Well, how about the goodish salmon or something?"

"Would you care to view the remains?"

He seemed all broken up when he saw the wreckage.

"I doubt if the committee would accept that," he said, sadly. "There isn't a frightful lot of it left, what?"

"The cats ate the rest."

He sighed deeply.

"No cats, no fish, no hat. We've had all our trouble for nothing. I do call that hard! And on top of that—I say, I hate to ask you, but you couldn't lend me a tenner, could you?"

"A tenner? What for?"

"Well, the fact is, I've got to pop round and bail Claude and Eustace out. They've been arrested."

"Arrested!"

"Yes. You see, what with the excitement of collaring the hat and the salmon or something, added to the fact that we had rather a festive lunch, they got a bit above themselves, poor chaps, and tried to pinch a motor-lorry. Silly, of course, because I don't see how they could have got the thing to Oxford and shown it to the committee. Still, there wasn't any reasoning with them, and, when the driver started making a fuss, there was a bit of a mix-up, and Claude and Eustace are more or less languishing in Vine Street police station till I pop round and bail them out. So if you could manage a tenner—Oh, thanks, that's fearfully good of you. It would have been too bad to leave them there, what? I mean, they're both such frightfully good chaps, you know. Everybody likes them up at the 'Varsity. They're fearfully popular."

"I bet they are!" I said.

When Jeeves came back, I was waiting for him on the mat. I wanted speech with the blighter.

"Well?" I said.

"Sir Roderick asked me a number of questions, sir, respecting your habits and mode of life, to which I replied guardedly."

"I don't care about that. What I want to know is why you didn't explain the whole thing to him right at the start? A word from you would have put everything clear."

"Yes, sir."

"Now he's gone off thinking me a loony."

"I should not be surprised, from his conversation with me, sir, if some such idea had not entered his head."

I was just starting in to speak when the telephone-bell rang. Jeeves answered it.

"No, madam, Mr. Wooster is not in. No, madam, I do not know when he will return. No, madam, he left no message. Yes, madam, I will inform him." He put back the receiver.

"Mrs. Gregson, sir."

Aunt Agatha! I had been expecting it. Ever since the luncheon party had blown out a fuse, her shadow had been hanging over me, so to speak.

"Does she know? Already?"

"I gather that Sir Roderick has been speaking to her on the telephone, sir, and . . ."

"No wedding bells for me, what?"

Jeeves coughed.

"Mrs. Gregson did not actually confide in me, sir, but I fancy that some such thing may have occurred. She seemed decidedly agitated, sir."

It's a rummy thing, but I'd been so snootered by the old boy and the cats and the fish and the hat and the pink-faced chappie and all the rest of it that the bright side simply hadn't occurred to me till now. By Jove, it was like a bally weight rolling off my chest! I gave a yelp of pure relief.

"Jeeves," I said. "I believe you worked the whole thing!"

"Sir?"

"I believe you had the jolly old situation in hand right from the start."

"Well, sir, Benson, Mrs. Gregson's butler, who inadvertently chanced to overhear something of your conversation when you were lunching at the house, did mention certain of the details to me; and I confess that, though it may be a liberty to say so, I entertained hopes that something might occur to prevent the match. I doubt if the young lady was entirely suitable to you, sir."

"And she would have shot you out on your ear five minutes after the ceremony."

"Yes, sir. Benson informed me that she had expressed some such intention. Mrs. Gregson wishes you to call upon her immediately, sir."

"She does, eh? What do you advise, Jeeves?"

"I think a trip to the south of France might prove enjoyable, sir."

"Jeeves," I said, "you are right, as always. Pack the old suitcase, and meet me at Victoria in time for the boat-train. I think that's the manly, independent course, what?"

"Absolutely, sir!" said Jeeves.

Honoré de Balzac

THE AFFLICTIONS OF AN ENGLISH CAT

When the report of your first meeting arrived in London, O! French Animals, it caused the hearts of the friends of Animal Reform to beat faster. In my own humble experience, I have so many proofs of the superiority of Beasts over Man that in my character of an English Cat I see the occasion, long awaited, of publishing the story of my life, in order to show how my poor soul has been tortured by the hypocritical laws of England. On two occasions, already, some Mice, whom I have made a vow to respect since the bill passed by your august parliament, have taken me to Colburn's, where, observing old ladies, spinsters of uncertain years, and even young married women, correcting proofs, I have asked myself why, having claws, I should not make use of them in a similar manner. One never knows what women think, especially the women who write, while a Cat, victim of English perfidy, is interested to say more than she thinks, and her profuseness may serve to compensate for what these ladies do not say. I am ambitious to be the Mrs. Inchbald of Cats and I beg you to have consideration for my noble efforts, O! French Cats, among whom has risen the noblest house of our race, that of Puss in Boots, eternal type of Advertiser, whom so many men have imitated but to whom no one has yet erected a monument.

I was born at the home of a parson in Catshire, near the little town of Miaulbury. My mother's fecundity condemned nearly all her infants to a cruel fate, because, as you know, the cause of the maternal intemperance of English Cats, who threaten to populate the whole world, has not yet been decided. Toms and females each insist it is due to their own amiability and respective virtues. But impertinent observers have remarked that Cats in England are required to be so boringly proper that this is their only distraction. Others pretend that herein may lie concealed great questions of commerce and politics, having to do with the English rule of India, but these matters are not for my paws to write of and I leave them to the *Edinburgh-Review.* I was not drowned with the others on account of the whiteness of my robe. Also I was named Beauty. Alas! the parson, who had a wife and eleven daughters, was too poor to keep me. An elderly female noticed that I had an affection for the parson's Bible; I slept on it all the time, not because I was religious, but because it was the only clean spot I could find in the house. She believed, perhaps, that I belonged to the sect of sacred animals which had already furnished the she-ass of Balaam, and took me away with her. I was only two months old at this time. This old woman, who gave evenings for which she sent out cards inscribed *Tea and Bible,* tried to communicate to me the fatal science of the daughters of Eve. Her method, which consisted in delivering long lectures on personal dignity and on the obligations due the world, was a very successful one. In order to avoid these lectures one submitted to martyrdom.

One morning I, a poor little daughter of Nature, attracted by a bowl of cream, covered by a muffin, knocked the muffin off with my paw, and lapped the cream. Then in joy, and perhaps also on account of the weakness of my young organs, I delivered myself on the waxed floor to the imperious need which young Cats feel. Perceiving the proofs of what she called my intemperance and my faults of education, the old woman seized me and whipped me vigorously with a birchrod, protesting that she would make me a lady or she would abandon me.

"Permit me to give you a lesson in gentility," she said. "Understand, Miss Beauty, that English Cats veil natural acts, which are opposed to the laws of English respectability, in the most profound mystery, and banish all that is improper, applying to the creature, as you have heard the Reverend Doctor Simpson say, the laws made by God for the creation. Have you ever seen the Earth behave itself indecently? Learn to suffer a thousand deaths rather than reveal your desires; in this suppression consists the virtue of the saints. The greatest privilege of Cats is to depart with the grace that characterizes your actions, and let no one know where you are going to make your little toilets. Thus you expose yourself only when you are beautiful. Deceived by appearances, everybody will take you for an angel. In the future when such a desire seizes you, look out of the window, give the impression that you desire to go for a walk, then run to a copse or to the gutter."

As a simple Cat of good sense, I found much hypocrisy in this doctrine, but I was so young!

"And when I am in the gutter?" thought I, looking at the old woman.

"Once alone, and sure of not being seen by anybody, well, Beauty, you can sacrifice respectability with much more charm because you have been discreet in public. It is in the observance of this very precept that the perfection of the moral English shines the brightest: they occupy themselves exclusively with appearances, this world being, alas, only illusion and deception."

I admit that these disguises were revolting to all my animal good sense, but on account of the whipping, it seemed preferable to understand that exterior propriety was all that was demanded of an English Cat. From this moment I accustomed myself to conceal the titbits that I loved under the bed. Nobody ever saw me eat, or drink, or make my toilet. I was regarded as the pearl of Cats.

Now I had occasion to observe those stupid men who are called savants. Among the doctors and others who were friends of my mistress, there was this Simpson, a fool, a son of a rich landowner, who was waiting for a bequest, and who, to deserve it, explained all animal actions by religious theories. He saw me one evening lapping milk from a saucer and complimented the old woman on the manner in which I had been bred, seeing me lick first the edges of the saucer and gradually diminish the circle of fluid.

"See," he said, "how in saintly company all becomes perfection: Beauty understands eternity, because she describes the circle which is its emblem in lapping her milk."

Conscience obliges me to state that the aversion of Cats to wetting their fur was the only reason for my fashion of drinking, but we will always be badly understood by the savants who are much more preoccupied in showing their own wit, than in discovering ours.

When the ladies or the gentlemen lifted me to pass their hands over my snowy back to make the sparks fly from my hair, the old woman remarked with pride, "You can hold her without having any fear for your dress; she is admirably well-bred!" Everybody said I was an angel; I was loaded with delicacies, but I assure you that I was profoundly bored. I was well aware of the fact that a young female Cat of the neighbourhood had run away with a Tom. This word, Tom, caused my soul a suffering which nothing could alleviate, not even the compliments I received, or rather that my mistress lavished on herself.

"Beauty is entirely moral; she is a little angel," she said. "Although she is very beautiful she has the air of not knowing it. She never looks at anybody, which is the height of a fine aristocratic education. When she does look at anybody it is with that perfect indifference which we demand of our young girls, but which we obtain only with great difficulty. She never intrudes herself unless you call her; she never jumps on you with familiarity; nobody ever sees her eat; and certainly that monster of a Lord Byron would have adored her. Like a tried and true Englishwoman she loves tea, sits, gravely calm, while the Bible is being explained, and thinks badly of nobody, a fact which permits one to speak freely before her. She is simple, without affectation, and has no desire for jewels. Give her a ring and she will not keep it. Finally, she does not imitate the vulgarity of the hunter. She loves her home and remains there so perfectly tranquil that at times you would believe that she was a mechanical Cat made at Birmingham or Manchester, which is the *ne plus ultra* of the finest education."

What these men and old women call education is the custom of dissimulating natural manners, and when they have completely depraved us they say that we are well-bred. One evening my mistress begged one of the young ladies to sing. When this girl went to the piano and began to sing I recognized at once an Irish melody that I had heard in my youth, and I remembered that I also was a musician. So I merged my voice with hers, but I received some raps on the head while she received compliments. I was revolted by this sovereign injustice and ran away to the garret. Sacred love of country! What a delicious night! I at last knew what the roof was. I heard Toms sing hymns to their mates, and these adorable elegies made me feel ashamed of the hypocrisies my mistress had forced upon me. Soon some of the Cats observed me and appeared to take offence at my presence, when a Tom with shaggy hair, a magnificent beard, and a fine figure, came to look at me and said to the company, "It's only a child!" At these condescending words, I bounded about on the tiles, moving with that agility which distinguishes us; I fell on my paws in that flexible fashion which no other animal knows how to imitate in order to show that I was no child. But these calineries were a pure waste of time. "When will some one serenade me?" I asked myself. The aspect of these haughty Toms, their melodies, that the human voice could never hope to rival, had moved me profoundly, and were the cause of my inventing little lyrics that I sang on the stairs. But an event of tremendous importance was about to occur which tore me violently from this innocent life. I went to London with a niece of my mistress, a rich heiress who adored me, who kissed me, caressed me with a kind of madness, and who pleased me so much that I became attached to her, against all the habits of our race. We were never separated and I was able to observe the great world of London during the season. It was there that I studied the perversity of English manners, which have power even over the beasts, that I became acquainted with that cant which Byron cursed and of which I am the victim as well as he, but without having enjoyed my hours of leisure.

Arabella, my mistress, was a young person like many others in England; she was not sure whom she wanted for a husband. The absolute liberty that is permitted girls in choosing a husband drives them nearly crazy, especially when they recall that English custom does not sanction intimate conversation after marriage. I was far from dreaming that the London Cats had adopted this severity, that the English laws would be cruelly applied to me, and that I would be a victim of the court at the terrible Doctors' Commons. Arabella was charming to all the men she met, and every one of them believed that he was going to marry this beautiful girl, but when an affair threatened to terminate in wedlock, she would find some pretext for a break, conduct which did not seem very respectable to me. "Marry a bow-legged man! Never!" she said of one. "As to that little fellow he is snub-nosed." Men were all so much alike to me that I could not understand this uncertainty founded on purely physical differences.

Finally one day an old English Peer, seeing me, said to her: "You have a beautiful Cat. She resembles you. She is white, she is young, she should have a husband. Let me bring her a magnificent Angora that I have at home."

Three days later the Peer brought in the handsomest Tom of the Peerage. Puff, with a black coat, had the most magnificent eyes, green and yellow, but cold and proud. The long silky hair of his tail, remarkable for its yellow rings, swept the carpet. Perhaps he came from the imperial house of Austria, because, as you see, he wore the colours. His manners were those of a Cat who had seen the court and the great world. His severity, in the matter of carrying himself, was so great that he would not scratch his head were anybody present. Puff had travelled on the continent. To sum up, he was so remarkably handsome that he had been, it was said, caressed by the Queen of England. Simple and naïve as I was I leaped at his neck to engage him in play, but he refused under the pretext that we were being watched. I then perceived that this English Cat Peer owed this forced and fictitious gravity that in England is called respectability to age and to intemperance at table. His weight, that men admired, interfered with his movements. Such was the true reason for his not responding to my pleasant advances. Calm and cold he sat on his unnamable, agitating his beard, looking at me and at times closing his eyes. In the society world of English Cats, Puff was the richest kind of catch for a Cat born at a parson's. He had two valets in his service; he ate from Chinese porcelain, and he drank only black tea. He drove in a carriage in Hyde Park and had been to parliament.

My mistress kept him. Unknown to me, all the feline population of London learned that Miss Beauty from Catshire had married Puff, marked with the colours of Austria. During the night I heard a concert in the street. Accompanied by my lord, who, according to his taste, walked slowly, I descended. We found the Cats of the Peerage, who had come to congratulate me and to ask me to join their Ratophile Society. They explained that nothing was more common than running after Rats and Mice. The words, shocking, vulgar, were constantly on their lips. To conclude, they had formed, for the glory of the country, a Temperance Society. A few nights later my lord and I went on the roof of Almack's to hear a grey Cat speak on the subject. In his exhortation, which was constantly supported by cries of "Hear! Hear!" he proved that Saint Paul in writing about charity had the Cats of England in mind. It was then the special duty of the English, who could go from one end of the world to the other on their ships without fear of the sea, to spread the principles of the *morale ratophile*. As a matter of fact English Cats were already preaching the doctrines of the Society, based on the hygienic discoveries of science. When Rats and Mice were dissected little distinction could be found between them and Cats; the oppression of one race by the other then was opposed to the Laws of Beasts, which are stronger even than the Laws of Men. "They are our brothers," he continued. And he painted such a vivid picture of the suffering of a Rat in the jaws of a Cat that I burst into tears.

Observing that I was deceived by this speech, Lord Puff confided to me that England expected to do an immense trade in Rats and Mice; that if the Cats would eat no more, Rats would be England's best product; that there was always a practical reason concealed behind English morality; and that the alliance between morality and trade was the only alliance on which England really counted.

Puff appeared to me to be too good a politician ever to make a satisfactory husband.

A country Cat made the observation that on the continent, especially at Paris, near the fortifications, Tom Cats were sacrificed daily by the Catholics. Somebody interrupted with the cry of "Question!" Added to these cruel executions was the frightful slander of passing the brave animals off for Rabbits, a lie and a barbarity which he attributed to an ignorance of the true Anglican religion which did not permit lying and cheating except in the government, foreign affairs, and the cabinet.

He was treated as a radical and a dreamer. "We are here in the interests of the Cats of England, not in those of continental Cats!" cried a fiery Tory Tom. Puff went to sleep. Just as the assembly was breaking up a young Cat from the French embassy, whose accent proclaimed his nationality, addressed me these delicious words:

"Dear Beauty, it will be an eternity before Nature forms another Cat as perfect as you. The cashmere of Persia and the Indies is like camel's hair when it is compared to your fine and brilliant silk. You exhale a perfume which is the concentrated essence of the felicity of the angels, an odour I have detected in the salon of the Prince de Talleyrand, which I left to come to this stupid meeting. The fire of your eyes illuminates the night! Your ears would be entirely perfect if they would listen to my supplications. There is not a rose in England as rose as the rose flesh which borders your little rose mouth. A fisherman would search in vain in the depths of Ormus for pearls of the quality of your teeth. Your dear face, fine and gracious, is the loveliest that England has produced. Near to your celestial robe the snow of the Alps would seem to be red. Ah! those coats which are only to be seen in your fogs! Softly and gracefully your paws bear your body which is the culmination of the miracles of creation, but your tail, the subtle interpreter of the beating of your heart, surpasses it. Yes! Never was there such an exquisite curve, more correct roundness. No Cat ever moved more delicately. Come away from this old fool of a Puff, who sleeps like an English Peer in parliament, who besides is a scoundrel who has sold himself to the Whigs, and who, owing to a too long sojourn at Bengal, has lost everything that can please a Cat."

Then, without having the air of looking at him, I took in the appearance of this charming French Tom. He was a careless little rogue and not in any respect like an English Cat. His cavalier manner as well as his way of shaking his ear stamped him as a gay bachelor without a care. I avow that I was weary of the solemnity of English Cats, and of their purely practical propriety. Their respectability, especially, seemed ridiculous to me. The excessive naturalness of this badly groomed Cat surprised me in its violent contrast to all that I had seen in London. Besides my life was so strictly regulated, I knew so well what I had to count on for the rest of my days, that I welcomed the promise of the unexpected in the physiognomy of this French Cat. My whole life appeared insipid to me. I comprehended that I could live on the roofs with an amazing creature who came from that country where the inhabitants consoled themselves for the victories of the greatest English general by these words:

Malbrouk s'en va-t-en guerre,
Mironton, TON, TON, *MIRONTAINE!*

Nevertheless I awakened my lord, told him how late it was, and suggested that we ought to go in. I gave no sign of having listened to this declaration, and my apparent insensibility petrified Brisquet. He remained behind, more surprised than ever because he considered himself handsome. I learned later that it was an easy matter for him to seduce most Cats. I examined him through a corner of my eye: he ran away with little bounds, returned, leaping the width of the street, then jumped back again, like a French Cat in despair. A true Englishman would have been decent enough not to let me see how he felt.

Some days later my lord and I were stopping in the magnificent house of the old Peer; then I went in the carriage for a drive in Hyde Park. We ate only chicken bones, fishbones, cream, milk, and chocolate. However heating this diet might prove to others my so-called husband remained sober. He was respectable even in his treatment of me. Generally he slept from seven in the evening at the whist table on the knees of his Grace. On this account my soul received no satisfaction and I pined away. This condition was aggravated by a little affection of the intestines occasioned by pure herring oil (the Port Wine of English Cats), which Puff used, and which made me very ill. My mistress sent for a physician who had graduated at Edinburgh after having studied a long time in Paris.

Having diagnosed my malady he promised my mistress that he would cure me the next day. He returned, as a matter of fact, and took an instrument of French manufacture out of his pocket. I felt a kind of fright on perceiving a barrel of white metal terminating in a slender tube. At the sight of this mechanism, which the doctor exhibited with satisfaction, Their Graces blushed, became irritable, and muttered several fine sentiments about the dignity of the English: for instance that the Catholics of old England were more distinguished for their opinions of this infamous instrument than for their opinions of the Bible. The Duke added that at Paris the French unblushingly made an exhibition of it in their national theatre in a comedy by Molière, but that in London a watchman would not dare pronounce its name.

"Give her some calomel."

"But Your Grace would kill her!" cried the doctor.

"The French can do as they like," replied His Grace. "I do not know, no more do you, what would happen if this degrading instrument were employed, but what I do know is that a true English physician should cure his patients only with the old English remedies."

This physician, who was beginning to make a big reputation, lost all his practice in the great world. Another doctor was called in, who asked me some improper questions about Puff, and who informed me that the real device of the English was: *Dieu et mon droit congugal!*

One night I heard the voice of the French Cat in the street. Nobody could see us; I climbed up the chimney and, appearing on the housetop, cried, "In the raintrough!" This response gave him wings; he was at my side in the twinkling of an eye. Would you believe that this French Cat had the audacity to take advantage of my exclamation. He cried, "Come to my arms," daring to become familiar with me, a Cat of distinction, without knowing me better. I regarded him frigidly and, to give him a lesson, I told him that I belonged to the Temperance Society.

"I see, sir," I said to him, "by your accent and by the looseness of your conversation, that you, like all Catholic Cats, are inclined to laugh and make sport, believing that confession will purge you, but in England we have another standard of morality. We are always respectable, even in our pleasures."

This young Cat, struck by the majesty of English cant, listened to me with a kind of attention which made me hope I could convert him to Protestantism. He then told me in purple words that he would do anything I wished provided I would permit him to adore me. I looked at him without being able to reply because his very beautiful and splendid eyes sparkled like stars; they lighted the night. Made bold by my silence, he cried "Dear Minette!"

"What new indecency is this?" I demanded, being well aware that French Cats are very free in their references.

Brisquet assured me that on the continent everybody, even the King himself, said to his daughter, *Ma petite Minette,* to show his affection, that many of the prettiest and most aristocratic young wives called their husbands, *Mon petit chat,* even when they did not love them. If I wanted to please him I would call him, *Mon petit homme!* Then he raised his paws with infinite grace. Thoroughly frightened I ran away. Brisquet was so happy that he sang *Rule Britannia,* and the next day his dear voice hummed again in my ears.

"Ah! you also are in love, dear Beauty," my mistress said to me, observing me extended on the carpet, the paws flat, the body in soft abandon, bathing in the poetry of my memories.

I was astonished that a woman should show so much intelligence, and so, raising my dorsal spine, I began to rub up against her legs and to purr lovingly with the deepest chords of my contralto voice.

While my mistress was scratching my head and caressing me and while I was looking at her tenderly a scene occurred in Bond Street which had terrible results for me.

Puck, a nephew of Puff's, in line to succeed him and who, for the time being, lived in the barracks of the Life Guards, ran into my dear Brisquet. The sly Captain Puck complimented the *attaché* on his success with me, adding that I had resisted the most charming Toms in England. Brisquet, foolish, vain Frenchman that he was, responded that he would be happy to gain my attention, but that he had a horror of Cats who spoke to him of temperance, the Bible, etc.

"Oh!" said Puck, "she talks to you then?"

Dear French Brisquet thus became a victim of English diplomacy, but later he committed one of these impardonable faults which irritate all well-bred Cats in England. This little idiot was truly very inconsistent. Did he not bow to me in Hyde Park and try to talk with me familiarly as if we were well acquainted? I looked straight through him coldly and severely. The coachman seeing this Frenchman insult me slashed him with his whip. Brisquet was cut but not killed and he received the blow with such nonchalance, continuing to look at me, that I was absolutely fascinated. I loved him for the manner in which he took his punishment, seeing only me, feeling only the favour of my presence, conquering the natural inclination of Cats to flee at the slightest warning of hostility. He could not know that I came near dying, in spite of my apparent coldness. From that moment I made up my mind to elope. That evening, on the roof, I threw myself tremblingly into his arms.

"My dear," I asked him, "have you the capital necessary to pay damages to old Puff?"

"I have no other capital," replied the French Cat, laughing, "than the hairs of my moustache, my four paws, and this tail." Then he swept the gutter with a proud gesture.

"Not any capital," I cried, "but then you are only an adventurer, my dear!"

"I love adventures," he said to me tenderly. "In France it is the custom to fight a duel in the circumstances to which you allude. French Cats have recourse to their claws and not to their gold."

"Poor country," I said to him, "and why does it send beasts so denuded of capital to the foreign embassies?"

"That's simple enough," said Brisquet. "Our new government does not love money—at least it does not love its employees to have money. It only seeks intellectual capacity."

Dear Brisquet answered me so lightly that I began to fear he was conceited.

"Love without money is nonsense," I said. "While you were seeking food you would not occupy yourself with me, my dear."

By way of response this charming Frenchman assured me that he was a direct descendant of Puss in Boots. Besides he had ninety-nine ways of borrowing money and we would have, he said, only a single way of spending it. To conclude, he knew music and could give lessons. In fact, he sang to me, in poignant tones, a national romance of his country, *Au clair de la lune.* . . .

At this inopportune moment, when seduced by his reasoning, I had promised dear Brisquet to run away with him as soon as he could keep a wife comfortably, Puck appeared, followed by several other Cats.

"I am lost!" I cried.

The very next day, indeed, the bench of Doctors' Commons was occupied by a *procès-verbal* in criminal conversation. Puff was deaf; his nephews took advantage of his weakness. Questioned by them, Puff said that at night I had flattered him by calling him, *Mon petit homme!* This was one of the most terrible things against me, because I could not explain where I had learned these words of love. The judge, without knowing it, was prejudiced against me, and I noted that he was in his second child-hood. His lordship never suspected the low intrigues of which I was the victim. Many little Cats, who should have defended me against public opinion, swore that Puff was always asking for his angel, the joy of his eyes, his sweet Beauty! My own mother, come to London, refused to see me or to speak to me, saying that an English Cat should always be above suspicion, and that I had embittered her old age. Finally the servants testified against me. I then saw perfectly clearly how everybody lost his head in England. When it is a matter of a criminal conversation, all sentiment is dead; a mother is no longer a mother, a nurse wants to take back her milk, and all the Cats howl in the streets. But the most infamous thing of all was that my old attorney who, in his time, would believe in the innocence of the Queen of England, to whom I had confessed every-thing to the last detail, who had assured me that there was no reason to whip a Cat, and to whom, to prove my innocence, I avowed that I did not even know the meaning of the words, "criminal conversation" (he told me that the crime was so called precisely because one spoke so little while committing it), this attorney, bribed by Captain Puck, defended me so badly that my case appeared to be lost. Under these circumstances I went on the stand myself.

"My Lords," I said, "I am an English Cat and I am innocent. What would be said of the justice of old England if . . ."

Hardly had I pronounced these words than I was interrupted by a murmur of voices, so strongly had the public been influenced by the *Cat-Chronicle* and by Puck's friends.

"She questions the justice of old England which has created the jury!" cried some one.

"She wishes to explain to you, My Lords," cried my adversary's abominable lawyer, "that she went on the rooftop with a French Cat in order to convert him to the Anglican faith, when, as a matter of fact, she went there to learn how to say, *Mon petit homme,* in French, to her husband, to listen to the abominable principles of papism, and to learn to disregard the laws and customs of old England!"

Such piffle always drives an English audience wild. Therefore the words of Puck's attorney were received with tumultuous applause. I was condemned at the age of twenty-six months, when I could prove that I still was ignorant of the very meaning of the word, Tom. But from all this I gathered that it was on account of such practices that Albion was called Old England.

I fell into a deep miscathropy which was caused less by my divorce than by the death of my dear Brisquet, whom Puck had had killed by a mob, fearing his vengeance. Also nothing made me more furious than to hear the loyalty of English Cats spoken of.

You see, O! French Animals, that in familiarizing ourselves with men, we borrow from them all their vices and bad institutions. Let us return to the wild life where we obey only our instincts, and where we do not find customs in conflict with the sacred wishes of Nature. At this moment I am writing a treatise on the abuse of the working classes of animals, in order to get them to pledge themselves to refrain from turning spits, to refuse to allow themselves to be harnessed to carriages, in order, to sum up, to teach them the means of protecting themselves against the oppression of the grand aristocracy. Although we are celebrated for our scribbling I believe that Miss Martineau would not repudiate me. You know that on the continent literature has become the haven of all Cats who protest against the immoral monopoly of marriage, who resist the tyranny of institutions, and who desire to encourage natural laws. I have omitted to tell you that, although Brisquet's body was slashed with a wound in the back, the coroner, by an infamous hypocrisy, declared that he had poisoned himself with arsenic, as if so gay, so light-headed a Cat could have reflected long enough on the subject of life to conceive so serious an idea, and as if a Cat whom I loved could have the least desire to quit this existence! But with Marsh's apparatus spots have been found on a plate.

—Translated from the French by Carl Van Vechten.

James Herriot

OSCAR THE SOCIALITE CAT

One late spring evening, when Helen and I were still living in the little bed-sitter under the tiles of Skeldale House, Tristan shouted up the stairs from the passage far below.

"Jim! Jim!"

I went out and stuck my head over the bannisters. "What is it, Triss?"

"Sorry to bother you, Jim, but could you come down for a minute?" The upturned face had an anxious look.

I went down the long flights of steps two at a time and when I arrived slightly breathless on the ground floor Tristan beckoned me through to the consulting room at the back of the house. A teenage girl was standing by the table, her hand resting on a stained roll of blanket.

"It's a cat," Tristan said. He pulled back a fold of the blanket and I looked down at a large, deeply striped tabby. At least he would have been large if he had had any flesh on his bones, but ribs and pelvis stood out painfully through the fur and as I passed my hand over the motionless body I could feel only a thin covering of skin.

Tristan cleared his throat. "There's something else, Jim."

I looked at him curiously. For once he didn't seem to have a joke in him. I watched as he gently lifted one of the cat's hind legs. There was a large gash on his abdomen and innumerable other wounds. I was still shocked and staring when the girl spoke.

"I saw this cat sittin' in the dark, down Brown's yard. I thought 'e looked skinny, like, and a bit quiet and I bent down to give 'im a pat. Then I saw 'e was badly hurt and I went home for a blanket and brought 'im round to you."

"That was kind of you," I said. "Have you any idea who he belongs to?"

The girl shook her head. "No, he looks like a stray to me."

"He does indeed." I dragged my eyes away from the terrible wound. "You're Marjorie Simpson, aren't you?"

"Yes."

"I know your dad well. He's our postman."

"That's right." She gave a half smile, then her lips trembled. "Well, I reckon I'd better leave 'im with you. You'll be goin' to put him out of his misery. There's nothing anybody can do about . . . about that?"

I shrugged and shook my head. The girl's eyes filled with tears. She stretched out a hand and touched the emaciated animal, then turned and walked quickly to the door.

"Thanks again, Marjorie," I called after the retreating back. "And don't worry—we'll look after him."

In the silence that followed, Tristan and I looked down at the shattered animal. Under the surgery lamp it was all too easy to see. The injuries were very serious and the wounds were covered in dirt and mud.

"What d'you think did this?" Tristan said at length. "Has he been run over?"

"Maybe," I replied. "Could be anything. An attack by a big dog or somebody could have kicked him or struck him." All things were possible with cats because some people seemed to regard them as fair game for any cruelty.

Tristan nodded. "Anyway, whatever happened, he must have been on the verge of starvation. He's a skeleton. I bet he's wandered miles from home."

"Ah well," I sighed. "There's only one thing to do, I'm afraid. It's hopeless."

Tristan didn't say anything but he whistled under his breath and drew the tip of his forefinger again and again across the furry cheek. And, unbelievably, from somewhere in the scraggy chest a gentle purring arose.

The young man looked at me, round-eyed. "My God, do you hear that?"

"Yes . . . amazing in that condition. He's a good-natured cat."

Tristan, head bowed, continued his stroking. I knew how he felt because, although he preserved a cheerfully hard-boiled attitude to our patients, he couldn't kid me about one thing; he had a soft spot for cats. Even now, when we are both around the sixty mark, he often talks to me over a beer about the cat he has had for many years. It is a typical relationship—they tease each other unmercifully—but it is based on real affection.

"It's no good, Triss," I said gently. "It's got to be done." I reached for the syringe but something in me rebelled against plunging a needle into that pathetic body. Instead I pulled a fold of the blanket over the cat's head.

"Pour a little ether onto the cloth," I said. "He'll just sleep away."

Wordlessly Tristan unscrewed the cap of the ether bottle and poised it above the head. Then from under the shapeless heap of blanket we heard it again; the deep purring which increased in volume till it boomed in our ears like a distant motor cycle.

449

Tristan was like a man turned to stone, hand gripping the bottle rigidly, eyes staring down at the mound of cloth from which the purring rose in waves of warm, friendly sound.

At last he looked up at me and gulped. "I don't fancy this much, Jim. Can't we do something?"

"You mean, try to repair all this?"

"Yes. We could stitch the wounds, bit by little bit, couldn't we?"

I lifted the blanket and looked again. "Honestly, Triss, I wouldn't know where to start. And the whole thing is filthy."

He didn't say anything, but continued to look at me steadily. And I didn't need much persuading. I had no more desire to pour ether on to that comradely purring than he had.

"Come on, then," I said. "We'll have a go."

With the oxygen bubbling and the cat's head in the anaesthetic mask we washed the whole body with warm saline. We did it again and again but it was impossible to remove every fragment of caked dirt. Then we started the painfully slow business of stitching the many wounds, and here I was glad of Tristan's nimble fingers which seemed better able to manipulate the small round-bodied needles than mine.

Two hours and yards of catgut later, we were finished and everything looked tidy.

"He's alive, anyway, Triss," I said as we began to wash the instruments. "We'll put him on to sulphapyridine and keep our fingers crossed that peritonitis won't set in." There were still no antibiotics at that time but the new drug was a big advance.

The door opened and Helen came in. "You've been a long time, Jim." She walked over to the table and looked down at the sleeping cat. "What a poor skinny little thing. He's all bones."

"You should have seen him when he came in." Tristan switched off the steriliser and screwed shut the valve on the anaesthetic machine. "He looks a lot better now."

She stroked the little animal for a moment. "Is he badly injured?"

"I'm afraid so, Helen," I said. "We've done our best for him but I honestly don't think he has much chance."

"What a shame. And he's pretty, too. Four white feet and all those unusual colours." With her finger she traced the faint bands of auburn and copper-gold among the grey and black.

Tristan laughed. "Yes, I think that chap has a ginger tom somewhere in his ancestry."

Helen smiled, too, but absently, and I noticed a broody look about her. She hurried out to the stock room and returned with an empty box.

"Yes . . . yes . . ." she said thoughtfully. "I can make a bed in this box for him and he'll sleep in our room, Jim."

"He will?"

"Yes, he must be warm, mustn't he?"

"Of course, especially with such chilly nights."

Later, in the darkness of our bed-sitter, I looked from my pillow at a cosy scene: Sam the beagle in his basket on one side of the flickering fire and the cat cushioned and blanketed in his box on the other.

As I floated off into sleep it was good to know that my patient was so comfortable, but I wondered if he would be alive in the morning. . . .

I knew he was alive at 7:30 A.M. because my wife was already up and talking to him. I trailed across the room in my pyjamas and the cat and I looked at each other. I rubbed him under the chin and he opened his mouth in a rusty miaow. But he didn't try to move.

"Helen," I said. "This little thing is tied together inside with catgut. He'll have to live on fluids for a week and even then he probably won't make it. If he stays up here you'll be spooning milk into him umpteen times a day."

"Okay, okay." She had that broody look again.

It wasn't only milk she spooned into him over the next few days. Beef essence, strained broth and a succession of sophisticated baby foods found their way down his throat at regular intervals. One lunch time I found Helen kneeling by the box.

"We shall call him Oscar," she said.

"You mean we're keeping him?"

"Yes."

I am fond of cats but we already had a dog in our cramped quarters and I could see difficulties. Still I decided to let it go.

"Why Oscar?"

"I don't know." Helen tipped a few drops of chop gravy onto the little red tongue and watched intently as he swallowed.

One of the things I like about women is their mystery, the unfathomable part of them, and I didn't press the matter further. But I was pleased at the way things were going. I had been giving the sulphapyridine every six hours and taking the temperature night and morning, expecting all the time to encounter the roaring fever, the vomiting and the tense abdomen of peritonitis. But it never happened.

It was as though Oscar's animal instinct told him he had to move as little as possible because he lay absolutely still day after day and looked up at us—and purred.

His purr became part of our lives and when he eventually left his bed, sauntered through to our kitchen and began to sample Sam's dinner of meat and biscuit it was a moment of triumph. And I didn't spoil it by wondering if he was ready for solid food; I felt he knew.

From then on it was sheer joy to watch the furry scarecrow fill out and grow strong, and as he ate and ate and the flesh spread over his bones the true beauty of his coat showed in the glossy medley of auburn, black and gold. We had a handsome cat on our hands.

Once Oscar had recovered, Tristan was a regular visitor. He probably felt, and rightly, that he, more than I, had saved Oscar's life in the first place and he used to play with him for long periods. His favourite ploy was to push his leg round the corner of the table and withdraw it repeatedly just as the cat pawed at it.

Oscar was justifiably irritated by this teasing but showed his character by lying in wait for Tristan one night and biting him smartly in the ankle before he could start his tricks.

From my own point of view Oscar added many things to our menage. Sam was delighted with him and the two soon became firm friends; Helen adored him and each evening I thought afresh that a nice cat washing his face by the hearth gave extra comfort to a room.

Oscar had been established as one of the family for several weeks when I came in from a late call to find Helen waiting for me with a stricken face.

"What's happened?" I asked.

"It's Oscar—he's gone!"

"Gone? What do you mean?"

"Oh, Jim, I think he's run away."

I stared at her. "He wouldn't do that. He often goes down to the garden at night. Are you sure he isn't there?"

"Absolutely. I've searched right into the yard. I've even had a walk around the town. And remember," her chin quivered, "he . . . he ran away from somewhere before."

I looked at my watch. "Ten o'clock. Yes, that is strange. He shouldn't be out at this time."

As I spoke the front door bell jangled. I galloped down the stairs and as I rounded the corner in the passage I could see Mrs. Heslington, the vicar's wife, through the glass. I threw open the door. She was holding Oscar in her arms.

"I believe this is your cat, Mr. Herriot," she said.

"It is indeed, Mrs. Heslington. Where did you find him?"

She smiled. "Well, it was rather odd. We were having a meeting of the Mothers' Union at the church house and we noticed the cat sitting there in the room."

"Just sitting . . . ?"

"Yes, as though he were listening to what we were saying and enjoying it all. It was unusual. When the meeting ended I thought I'd better bring him along to you."

"I'm most grateful, Mrs. Heslington." I snatched Oscar and tucked him under my arm. "My wife is distraught—she thought he was lost."

It was a little mystery. Why should he suddenly take off like that? But since he showed no change in his manner over the ensuing week we put it out of our minds.

Then one evening a man brought in a dog for an inoculation and left the front door open. When I went up to our flat I found that Oscar had disappeared again. This time Helen and I scoured the market place and side alleys in vain and when we returned at half past nine we were both despondent. It was nearly eleven and we were thinking of bed when the door bell rang.

It was Oscar again, this time resting on the ample stomach of Jack Newbould. Jack was leaning against the doorpost and the fresh country air drifting in from the dark street was richly intermingled with beer fumes.

Jack was a gardener at one of the big houses. He hiccuped gently and gave me a huge benevolent smile. "Brought your cat, Mr. Herriot."

"Gosh, thanks, Jack!" I said, scooping up Oscar gratefully. "Where the devil did you find him?"

"Well, s'matter o' fact, 'e sort of found me."

"What do you mean?"

Jack closed his eyes for a few moments before articulating carefully. "Thish is a big night, tha knows, Mr. Herriot. Darts championship. Lots of t'lads round at t'Dog and Gun—lotsh and lotsh of 'em. Big gatherin'."

"And our cat was there?"

"Aye, he were there, all right. Sittin' among t'lads. Shpent t'whole evenin' with us."

"Just sat there, eh?"

"That 'e did." Jack giggled reminiscently. "By gaw, 'e enjoyed isself. Ah gave 'im a drop o' best bitter out of me own glass and once or twice ah thought 'e was goin' to have a go at chuckin' a dart. He's some cat." He laughed again.

As I bore Oscar upstairs I was deep in thought. What was going on here? These sudden desertions were upsetting Helen and I felt they could get on my nerves in time.

I didn't have long to wait till the next one. Three nights later he was missing again. This time Helen and I didn't bother to search—we just waited.

He was back earlier than usual. I heard the door bell at nine o'clock. It was the elderly Miss Simpson peering through the glass. And she wasn't holding Oscar—he was prowling on the mat waiting to come in.

Miss Simpson watched with interest as the cat stalked inside and made for the stairs. "Ah, good, I'm so glad he's come home safely. I knew he was your cat and I've been intrigued by his behaviour all evening."

"Where . . . may I ask?"

"Oh, at the Women's Institute. He came in shortly after we started and stayed till the end."

"Really? What exactly was your programme, Miss Simpson?"

"Well, there was a bit of committee stuff, then a short talk with lantern slides by Mr. Walters from the water company and we finished with a cake-making competition."

"Yes . . . yes . . . and what did Oscar do?"

She laughed. "Mixed with the company, apparently enjoyed the slides and showed great interest in the cakes."

"I see. And you didn't bring him home?"

"No, he made his own way here. As you know, I have to pass your house and I merely rang your bell to make sure you knew he had arrived."

"I'm obliged to you, Miss Simpson. We were a little worried."

I mounted the stairs in record time. Helen was sitting with the cat on her knee and she looked up as I burst in.

"I know about Oscar now," I said.

"Know what?"

"Why he goes on these nightly outings. He's not running away— he's visiting."

"Visiting?"

"Yes," I said. "Don't you see? He likes getting around, he loves people, especially in groups, and he's interested in what they do. He's a natural mixer."

Helen looked down at the attractive mound of fur curled on her lap. "Of course . . . that's it . . . he's a socialite!"

"Exactly, a high stepper!"

"A cat-about-town!"

It all afforded us some innocent laughter and Oscar sat up and looked at us with evident pleasure, adding his own throbbing purr to the merriment. But for Helen and me there was a lot of relief behind it; ever since our cat had started his excursions there had been the gnawing fear that we would lose him, and now we felt secure.

From that night our delight in him increased. There was endless joy in watching this facet of his character unfolding. He did the social round meticulously, taking in most of the activities of the town. He became a familiar figure at whist drives, jumble sales, school concerts and scout bazaars. Most of the time he was made welcome, but he was twice ejected from meetings of the Rural District Council—they did not seem to relish the idea of a cat sitting in on their deliberations.

At first I was apprehensive about his making his way through the streets but I watched him once or twice and saw that he looked both ways before tripping daintily across. Clearly, he had excellent traffic sense and this made me feel that his original injury had not been caused by a car.

Taking it all in all, Helen and I felt that it was a kind of stroke of fortune which had brought Oscar to us. He was a warm and cherished part of our home life. He added to our happiness.

When the blow fell it was totally unexpected.

I was finishing the morning surgery. I looked round the door and saw only a man and two little boys.

"Next, please," I said.

The man stood up. He had no animal with him. He was middle-aged, with the rough, weathered face of a farm worker. He twirled a cloth cap nervously in his hands.

"Mr. Herriot?" he said.

"Yes, what can I do for you?"

He swallowed and looked me straight in the eyes. "Ah think you've got ma cat."

"What?"

"Ah lost ma cat a bit since." He cleared his throat. "We used to live at Missdon but ah got a job as ploughman to Mr. Horne of Wederly. It was after we moved to Wederly that t'cat went missin'. Ah reckon he was tryin' to find 'is way back to his old home."

"Wederly? That's on the other side of Brawton—over thirty miles away."

"Aye, ah knaw, but cats is funny things."

"But what makes you think I've got him?"

He twisted the cap around a bit more. "There's a cousin o' mine lives in Darrowby and ah heard tell from 'im about this cat that goes around to meetin's. I 'ad to come. We've been huntin' everywhere."

"Tell me," I said, "this cat you lost. What did he look like?"

"Grey and black and sort o' gingery. Right bonny 'e was. And 'e was allus goin' out to gatherin's."

A cold hand clutched at my heart. "You'd better come upstairs. Bring the boys with you."

Helen was laying the table for lunch in our little bed-sitter.

"Helen," I said. "This is Mr.—er—I'm sorry, I don't know your name."

"Gibbons, Sep Gibbons. They called me Septimus because ah was the seventh in family and it looks like ah'm goin' t'same way 'cause we've got six already. These are our two youngest." The two boys, obvious twins of about eight, looked up at us solemnly.

I wished my heart would stop hammering. "Mr. Gibbons thinks Oscar is his. He lost his cat some time ago."

My wife laid down the plates. "Oh . . . oh . . . I see." She stood very still for a moment, then smiled faintly. "Do sit down. Oscar's in the kitchen, I'll bring him through."

She went out and reappeared with the cat in her arms. She hadn't got through the door before the little boys gave tongue.

"Tiger!" they cried. "Oh, Tiger, Tiger!"

The man's face seemed lit from within. He walked quickly across the floor and ran his big work-roughened hand along the fur.

"Hullo, awd lad," he said, and turned to me with a radiant smile. "It's 'im, Mr. Herriot, it's 'im awright, and don't 'e look well!"

"You call him Tiger, eh?" I said.

"Aye," he replied happily. "It's them gingery stripes. The kids called 'im that. They were brokenhearted when we lost 'im."

As the two little boys rolled on the floor our Oscar rolled with them, pawing playfully, purring with delight.

Sep Gibbons sat down again. "That's the way 'e allus went on wi' the family. They used to play with 'im for hours. By gaw we did miss 'im. He were a right favourite."

I looked at the broken nails on the edge of the cap, at the decent, honest, uncomplicated Yorkshire face so like the many I had grown to like and respect. Farm men like him got thirty shillings a week in those days and it was reflected in the thread-bare jacket, the cracked, shiny boots and the obvious hand-me-downs of the boys.

But all three were scrubbed and tidy, the man's face like a red beacon, the children's knees gleaming and their hair carefully slicked across their foreheads. They looked like nice people to me.

I turned towards the window and looked out over the tumble of roofs to my beloved green hills beyond. I didn't know what to say.

Helen said it for me. "Well, Mr. Gibbons." Her tone had an unnatural brightness. "You'd better take him."

The man hesitated. "Now then, are ye sure, Missus Herriot?"

"Yes . . . yes, I'm sure. He was your cat first."

"Aye, but some folks 'ud say finders keepers or summat like that. Ah didn't come 'ere to demand 'im back or owt of t'sort."

"I know you didn't, Mr. Gibbons, but you've had him all those years and you've searched for him so hard. We couldn't possibly keep him from you."

He nodded quickly. "Well, that's right good of ye." He paused for a moment, his face serious, then he stopped and picked Oscar up. "We'll have to be off if we're goin' to catch the eight o'clock bus."

Helen reached forward, cupped the cat's head in her hands and looked at him steadily for a few seconds. Then she patted the boys' heads. "You'll take good care of him, won't you?"

"Aye, missus, thank ye, we will that." The two small faces looked up at her and smiled.

"I'll see you down the stairs, Mr. Gibbons," I said.

On the descent I tickled the furry cheek resting on the man's shoulder and heard for the last time the rich purring. On the front door step we shook hands and they set off down the street. As they rounded the corner of Trengate they stopped and waved, and I waved back at the man, the two children and the cat's head looking back at me over the shoulder.

It was my habit at that time in my life to mount the stairs two or three at a time but on this occasion I trailed upwards like an old man, slightly breathless, throat tight, eyes prickling.

I cursed myself for a sentimental fool but as I reached our door I found a flash of consolation. Helen had taken it remarkably well. She had nursed that cat and grown deeply attached to him, and I'd have thought an unforeseen calamity like this would have upset her terribly. But no, she had behaved calmly and rationally. You never knew with women, but I was thankful.

It was up to me to do as well. I adjusted my features into the semblance of a cheerful smile and marched into the room.

Helen had pulled a chair close to the table and was slumped face down against the wood. One arm cradled her head while the other was stretched in front of her as her body shook with an utterly abandoned weeping.

I had never seen her like this and I was appalled. I tried to say something comforting but nothing stemmed the flow of racking sobs.

Feeling helpless and inadequate I could only sit close to her and stroke the back of her head. Maybe I could have said something if I hadn't felt just about as bad myself.

You get over these things in time. After all, we told ourselves, it wasn't as though Oscar had died or got lost again—he had gone to a good family who would look after him. In fact he had really gone home.

And of course, we still had our much-loved Sam, although he didn't help in the early stages by sniffing disconsolately where Oscar's bed used to lie, then collapsing on the rug with a long, lugubrious sigh.

There was one other thing, too. I had a little notion forming in my mind, an idea which I would spring on Helen when the time was right. It was about a month after that shattering night and we were coming out of the cinema at Brawton at the end of our half day. I looked at my watch.

"Only eight o'clock," I said. "How about going to see Oscar?"

Helen looked at me in surprise. "You mean—drive on to Wederly?"

"Yes, it's only about five miles."

A smile crept slowly across her face. "That would be lovely. But do you think they would mind?"

"The Gibbonses? No, I'm sure they wouldn't. Let's go."

Wederly was a big village and the ploughman's cottage was at the far end a few yards beyond the Methodist chapel. I pushed open the garden gate and we walked down the path.

A busy-looking little woman answered my knock. She was drying her hands on a striped towel.

"Mrs. Gibbons?" I said.

"Aye, that's me."

"I'm James Herriot—and this is my wife."

Her eyes widened uncomprehendingly. Clearly the name meant nothing to her.

"We had your cat for a while," I added.

Suddenly she grinned and waved her towel at us. "Oh, aye, ah remember now. Sep told me about you. Come in, come in!"

The big kitchen-living room was a tableau of life with six children and thirty shillings a week. Battered furniture, rows of much-mended washing on a pulley, black cooking range and a general air of chaos.

Sep got up from his place by the fire, put down his newspaper, took off a pair of steel-rimmed spectacles and shook hands.

He waved Helen to a sagging armchair. "Well, it's right nice to see you. Ah've often spoke of ye to t'missus."

His wife hung up her towel. "Yes, and I'm glad to meet ye both. I'll get some tea in a minnit."

She laughed and dragged a bucket of muddy water into a corner. "I've been washin' football jerseys. Them lads just handed them to me tonight—as if I haven't enough to do."

As she ran the water into the kettle I peeped surreptitiously around me and I noticed Helen doing the same. But we searched in vain. There was no sign of a cat. Surely he couldn't have run away again? With a growing feeling of dismay I realised that my little scheme could backfire devastatingly.

It wasn't until the tea had been made and poured that I dared to raise the subject.

"How—" I asked diffidently, "how is—er—Tiger?"

"Oh, he's grand," the little woman replied briskly. She glanced up at the clock on the mantelpiece. "He should be back any time now, then you'll be able to see 'im."

As she spoke, Sep raised a finger. "Ah think ah can hear 'im now."

He walked over and opened the door and our Oscar strode in with all his old grace and majesty. He took one look at Helen and leaped on to her lap. With a cry of delight she put down her cup and stroked the beautiful fur as the cat arched himself against her hand and the familiar purr echoed round the room.

"He knows me," she murmured. "He knows me."

Sep nodded and smiled. "He does that. You were good to 'im. He'll never forget ye, and we won't either, will we, Mother?"

"No, we won't, Mrs. Herriot," his wife said as she applied butter to a slice of gingerbread. "That was a kind thing ye did for us and I 'ope you'll come and see us all whenever you're near."

"Well, thank you," I said. "We'd love to—we're often in Brawton."

I went over and tickled Oscar's chin, then I turned again to Mrs. Gibbons. "By the way, it's after nine o'clock. Where has he been till now?"

She poised her butter knife and looked into space.

"Let's see, now," she said. "It's Thursday, isn't it? Ah yes, it's 'is night for the yoga class."

Carol Emshwiller

THE START OF THE
END OF IT ALL

First the distant sound of laughter. I thought it was laughter. Kind of chuckling . . . choking maybe . . . or spasms of some sort. Can't explain it. Scary laughter coming closer. Then they came in in a scary way, pale, with shiny raincoats and fogged glasses, sat down, and waited out the storm here. Asked only for warm water to sip. Crossed their legs with refined grace and watched late-night TV. They spoke of not wanting to end up in a museum . . . neither them, nor their talismans, nor their flags, their dripping flags. They looked so vulnerable and sad . . . chuckling, choking sad that I lost all fear of them. They left in the morning, most of them. All but three left. Klimp, their regional director, and two others stayed.

"It is important and salutary to speak of incomprehensible things," they said, and so we did till dawn. They also said that their love for this planet, "this splendid planet," knows no bounds and that they could take over with just a tiny smidgen of violence, especially as we had been softening up the people ourselves as though in preparation for them. I believed them. I saw their love for this place in their eyes.

"But am I"—and I asked them this directly—"am I, a woman, and a woman of, should I say, a certain age, am I really to be included in the master plan?" They implied, yes, chuckling (choking), but then everyone has always tried to give me that impression (former husband especially) and it never was true before. It's nice, though, that they said they couldn't do it without me and others like me.

What they also say is, "As sun to earth, so kitchen is to house, and so house is to the rest of the world. Politics," they say, "begins at home, and most especially in the kitchen, place of warmth, chemistry, and changes, means toward ends. Grandiose plans cooked up here. A house," they say, "hardly need be more than a kitchen and a few good chairs." Where they come from that's the way it is. And I agree that, if somebody wanted to take over the earth, it's true: they could do worse than to do it from the kitchen.

They also say that it will be necessary to let the world lie fallow and recoup for fifteen years. That's about step number three of their plan.

"But first," they say (step number one), "It will be necessary to get rid of the cats."

Klimp! His kind did not, absolutely not, descend from apelike creatures, but from higher beings. Sky folk. We can't understand that, he said. Their sex organs are, he told me, pure and unconnected to excretory organs in any way. Body hair in different patterns. None, and this is significant, under the arms, and, actually, what's on their head really isn't hair either. Just looks like it. They're a manifestation in living form of a kind of purity not to be achieved by any of us except by artificial means. They also say that, because of what they are, they will do a lot better with this world than we do. Klimp promises me that and I believe him. They're simply crazy about this world. "It's a treasure," Klimp keeps saying.

I ask, "How much time is there, actually, till doomsday, or whatever you call it?"

No special name, though Restoration Day or (even better) Resurrection Day might serve. No special time either. ("Might take a lifetime. Might not.") They live like that but without confusion.

But first, as they say, it is necessary to get rid of the cats, though I am trying to see both sides: (a) Klimp's and his friends' and (b) trying to come to terms with three hyperactive cats that I've had since the divorce. The white one is throwing up on the rug. Turns out to be a rubber band and a long piece of string.

Of the three, Klimp is clearly mine. He likes to pass his cool hands . . . his always-cold hands through my hair, but if I try to sit on his lap to confirm our relationship, he can't bear that. We've known each other almost two weeks now, shuffled along in the park (I name the trees), the shady side of streets, examined the different kinds of grasses. (I never noticed how many kinds there were.) He looks all right from every angle but one, and he always wears his raincoat so we don't have any trouble.

"I accept," I say, when he asks me a few days later, anthropomorphizing as usual, and tired of falling in love with TV stars and newsmen or the equivalent. I put on my old wedding ring and start, then, to keep a record of the takeover, kitchen by kitchen by kitchen . . .

Klimp says, "Let's get in bed and see what happens."

Something does, but I won't say what.

I haven't seen any of them, even Klimp, totally naked, though a couple of times I saw him wearing nothing but a teacup.

(They read our sex manuals before beginning their takeover.)

But willing servants (women are) of almost anything that looks or feels like male or has a raspy voice, regardless of the real sex whatever that may be, or if sex at all. And sometimes one has to make do (we older women do, anyway) with the peculiar, the alien or the partly alien, the egocentric, the disgruntled, the dissipated . . . But also, and especially, willing servants of things that can fly, or things, rather, that may have descended from things that could fly once or things that could almost fly

464

(though lots of things can *almost* fly). But I heard some woman say that someone told her that one had been seen actually vibrating himself into the sky, arched back, hands in pockets . . . had also, this person said, been seen throwing money off the Ambassador Bridge. The ultimate subversion.

Also I heard they may have already infiltrated the mayonnaise company. A great deal of harm can be done simply by loosening all the jar lids. Is this without violence! And when one of them comes up behind you on the street, grabs your arm with long, strong thumb and forefinger, quietly asking for money, and your watch, and promising not to hurt you . . . especially not to hurt you, then you give them. Afterward I hear they sometimes crumple the bills into their big, white pipes and smoke them on the spot. They flush the watches down toilets. This last I've seen myself.

But is all this without violence! Klimp takes the time to explain it to me. We're using the same word with two somewhat different meanings, as happens with people from different places. But then there's never any need to justify the already righteous. Sure of his own kindnesses, as look at him right now, Klimp, kiss to earlobe and one finger drawing tickly circles in the palm of my hand. He sees, he says, the Eastern Seabord as it could be were it the kind of perfection that it should be. He says it will be splendid and these are means toward that end.

Random pats, now, in the region of the belly button. (His pats. My belly button.) Asks me if I ever saw a cat fly. It's important. "Not exactly," I say, "but I saw one fall six stories once and not get hurt, if that counts."

As we sit here, the white cat eats a twenty-dollar bill.

I was divorced, as I mentioned. We were, all of us women who are in this thing with them, all divorced. DIVORCE. A tearing word. I was divorced in the abdomen and in the chest. In those days I sometimes telephoned just to hear "Hello." I was divorced at and against sunsets, hills, fall leaves, and, later on in the spring, I was divorced from spring. But now, suddenly, I have not failed everything. None of us has failed. And we want nothing for ourselves. Never have. We want to do what's best for the planet.

Sometimes lately, when the afternoon is perfect . . . a pale, humid day, the kind they like the most . . . cool . . . white sky . . . and Klimp or one of the others (it's hard to tell them apart sometimes, though Klimp usually wears the largest cap . . . yellow plastic cap) . . . when the one I think is Klimp is on the lawn chair figuring how to get rid of all the bees by too much spraying of fruit trees or how best to distribute guns to the quick-tempered or some such problem, then I think that life has turned perfect already, though they keep telling me that comes later . . . but perfect right now at least as far as I'm concerned. I like it with the takeover only half begun. Doing the job, it's been said, is half the fun. To me it's all the fun. And I especially like the importance of the kitchen for things other than mere food. Yesterday, for instance, I destroyed (at the self-cleaning setting) a bushel of important medical records plus several reference works and dictionaries, also textbooks, and a bin of brand-new maps. When I see Klimp, then, on the lawn, or all three sometimes, and all three gauzy, pale blue flags unfurled, and they're chuckling, and whispering, and choking together, I feel as though the kitchen itself, by its several motors, will take off into the air . . . hum itself into the sunset, riding smoothly on a warm updraft, all its engines turned to low. I want to tell them how I feel. "Perfect," I say. "Everything's perfect except for these three things: wet sand tracked into the vestibule, stepping on the tails of cats, and please don't look at me with such a steady, fishlike gaze, because when you do, I can't read the recipes you gave me for things that make people feel good, rot the brain, and cost a lot."

But I shouldn't have reminded them of the cats. They are saying again that I have to choose between the cats or them. They say their talismans are getting lost under the furniture, that some of their wafers have been found chewed on and spat out. They say I don't realize the politics of the situation and I suppose I don't. I never did pay much attention to politics. "You have to realize everything is political," they say, "even cats."

I'm thinking perhaps I'll take them to the state park outside of town. They'll do all right. Cats do. Get rid of them in some nice place I'd like to be in myself, by a river, near some hills . . . Leave them with full stomachs. Be up there and back by evening. Klimp will be pleased.

But look what's coming true now! Dead cats . . . drowned cats washed up on the beaches. I saw the pictures on the news. Great flocks of cats, as though they had been caught at sea in a storm, or as though they had flown too far from shore and fallen into the ocean from exhaustion. Perhaps I understand even less about politics than I thought.

I decide to please my cats with a big dish of fresh fish. (Klimp is out tonight turning up amplifiers in order to impair hearing, while the others are out pulling the hands off clocks.)

The house has a sort of air space above the attic. If the little vent were removed, a cat could live up there quite comfortably, climbing up and down by way of the roof of the garage and a tree near it. A cat could be fed secretly outside and might not be recognized as one who lived here. It isn't that I don't dedicate myself to Klimp and the others. I do, but, as for the cats, I also dedicate myself to them.

Klimp and the others come back at dawn, flags furled, tired but happy. "Job's well done," they say. I fill the bathtub, boil water for them to dip their wafers in. They chuckle, pat me. (They're so demonstrative. Not at all like my husband used to be.) They move their hands in cryptic signals, or perhaps it's nervousness. They blink at each other. They even blink at me. I'm thinking this is pure joy. Must never end. And now I have the cats and them also. I love. I love. Luff . . . loove . . . loofe . . . they can't pronounce it, but they use the word all the time. Sometimes I wonder exactly what they mean by it, it comes so easily to their lips.

At least I know what I mean by "love," and I know I've gone from having nothing and nobody (I had the cats, of course, but I have people now) to having all the best things in life: love, and a kind of family, and meaningful work to do . . . world-shaking work . . . All of us useless women, now part of a vast international kitchen network and I'm wondering if we can go even further. Get to be sort of a world-watching crew while the earth lies fallow. "Listen, what about us in all this?" I ask, my arm across Klimp's barrel chest. "We're no harm. We're all over childbearing age. What about if we watch over things for you during the time the earth rests up?"

He answers, "Is as does. Does as is." (If he really loves me, he'll do it.)

"Listen, we could see to it that no smart ape would start leveling out hills."

"What we need," he says, "are a lot of little, warm, wet places." He tells me he's glad the cats are no longer here. He says, "I know you love ('luff') me now," and wants me to eat a big pink wafer. I try to get out of it politely. Who knows what's in it? And the ones *they* always eat are white. But what has made me worthy of this honor, just that the cats are no longer in view?

"All right," I say, "but just one tiny bite." Tastes dry and chalky and sweet . . . too sweet. Klimp . . . but I see it's not Klimp this time . . . one of the others . . . urges another bite. "Where's Klimp?"

"I also love ('luff') you," he says and, "Time to find lots of little dark, wet places. We told you already."

I'm wondering what sort of misunderstanding is happening right now.

I have a vision of a skyful of minnows . . . silver schools of minnows . . . the buzz of air . . . the tinkling . . . the glitter . . . *my* minnows flashing by. Why not? And then more and more, until the sky is bursting with them and I can't tell any more which are mine. Somewhere a group of thirty-six . . . no, lots more than that . . . eighty-four . . . I'm not sure. One hundred and eight? Yes, my group among the others. They, my own, swim back to me, then swirl up and away. Forever. And forever mine. Why not?

I wake to the sound of sheep. I have a backyard full of them. Ewes, it turns out. They are contented. As I am. I watch the setting moon, eat the oranges and onions Klimp brings me, sip mint tea, feel slightly nauseous, get a call from a friend. Seems she's had sheep for a couple of weeks now. Took her cats up to the state park just as I'd thought of doing and had sheep the next day, though she wishes now she had put those cats in the attic as I've done, but she's wondering will I get away with it? She wants me to come over, secretly if I can. She says it's important. But there's a lot of work to be done here. Klimp is talking, even now, about important projects such as opening the wild animal cages at the zoo and the best way to drop water into mailboxes and how about digging potholes in the roads? How about handing out free cartons of cigarettes? He hangs up the phone for me and brings me another onion. I don't need any other friends.

She calls me again a few days later. She says she thinks she's pregnant, but we both know that can't be true. I say to see a doctor. It's probably a tumor. She says they don't want her to, that they drove her car away somewhere. She thinks they pushed it off the pier along with a lot of others. I say I thought they were doing just the opposite. Switching road signs and such to get people to drive around wasting gas. Anyway, she says, they won't let her out of the house. Well, I can't be bothered with the delusions of every old lady around. I have enough troubles of my own and I haven't been feeling so well lately either, tired all the time and a little sick. Irritable. Too irritable to talk to her.

The ewes in the backyard are all obviously pregnant. They swell up fast. The bitch dog next door seems pregnant, too, which is funny because I thought she was a spay. It makes you stop and think. I wonder, what if *I* wanted to go out? And is my old car still in the garage? They've been watching me all the time lately. I can't even go to the bathroom without one of them listening outside the door. I haven't been able to feed the cats. I used to hate it when they killed birds, but now I hope there are some winter birds around. I think I will put up a bird feeder. I think spring is coming. I've lost track, but I'm sure we're well into March now. Klimp says, "I luff, I luff," and wants to rub my back, but I won't let him . . . not any more . . . or not right now. Why won't they all three go out at the same time as they used to?

What's wrong with me lately? Can't sleep . . . itch all over . . . angry at nothing . . . They're not so bad, Klimp and the others. Actually better than most. Always squeeze the toothpaste from the bottom, leave the toilet seat down . . . they don't cut their toenails and leave them in little piles on the night table, use their own towels usually, listen to me when I talk. Why be so angry?

I must try harder. I will tell Klimp that he can rub my back later. I'll apologize for being angry and I'll try to do it in a nice way. Then I'll go into the bedroom, shut the door, brace it with a chair and be really alone for a while. Lie down and relax. I know I'll miss cooking up some important concoctions, but I've missed a lot of things lately.

Next thing I know I wake up and it's dark outside. I have a terrible stomach ache as if a lot of gas is rolling around inside. I feel strange. I have to get out of here.

I can hear one of them moving outside my door. I hear him brush against it . . . a chitinous scraping. "Let me in I loofe you." Then there's that kind of giggle. He can't help it, I know, but it's getting on my nerves. "Is as does," he says. "Now you see that." I put on my sneakers and grab my old sweatshirt.

"Just a minute, dear"—I try to say it sweetly—"I just woke up. I'll let you in in a minute. I need a cup of tea. I'd love it if you'd get one for me." (I really do need one, but I'm not going to wait around for it.) I open the window and step out on the garage roof, cross to the tree, and climb down. Not hard. I'm a chubby old woman, but I'm in pretty good shape. The cats follow me. All three.

As I trot by, I see all the ewes in the backyard lying down and panting. God! I have to get out of here. I run, holding my stomach. I know of an empty lot with an old Norway spruce tree that comes down to the ground all around. I think I can make that. I see cats all around me, more than just my own. Maybe six or eight. Maybe more. Hard to see because, and thank God, Klimp has broken all the streetlights. I cross vacant lots, tear through brambles, finally crawl under the spruce branches and lie down panting . . . panting. It feels right to pant. I saw my cat do that under similar circumstances.

I have them. I give birth to them, the little silvery ones squeaking . . . sparkling. I'll surprise Klimp with eighty-four . . . ninety-six . . . one hundred and eight? Look what we did together! But it wasn't Klimp and I. Suddenly I realize it. It was Klimp and that other. Through me. And all those ewes . . . fourteen ewes and one bitch dog times eighty-four or one hundred and eight. That's well over a thousand of them that I know about already.

My little ones cough and flutter, try to swim into the air, but only raise themselves an inch or so . . . hardly that. They smell of fish. They slither over one another as though looking for a stream. They are covered with a shiny, clear kind of slime. Do I love them or hate them?

So that's the way it is. As with us humans, it takes two, only I wasn't one of them. I might just as well have been a bitch or a ewe . . . better, in fact, to have been some dumb animal. "Lots of little warm, wet places!" It must have been a big night, that night. Some sacred sort of higher beings they turned out to be. That's not love . . . nor luff, nor loove. Whatever they mean by those words, this can't be it.

But look what all those hungry cats are doing. Eating up my minnows. I try to gather the little things up, but they're too slippery. I can't even get one. I try to push the cats away, but there are too many of them and they all seem very hungry. And then, suddenly, Klimp is there helping me, kicking out at the cats in a fury and gathering up minnows at the same time. For him it's easy. They stick to him wherever he touches them. He's up to his elbows in them. They cluster on his ankles like barnacles, but I'm afraid lots are eaten up already. And now he's kicking out at me. Hits me hard on the cheek and shoulder. Stamps on my hand.

"I'm confused," I say, getting up, thinking he can explain all this in a fatherly way, but now he stamps on my foot and knocks me down with his elbow. Then I see him give a kind of hop step, the standard dance way of getting from one foot to the other. He's going to lift. I don't know how I know, but I do. He has that look on his face, too, eyes half closed . . . ecstasy. I see it now—flying, or almost flying, is their ultimate orgasm . . . their true love (or loofe . . . if this is flying. Yes, he's up, but only inches, and struggling . . . pulling at my fingers. This is *not* flying.

"You call this flying!" I yell. "And you call this whole thing being a pure aerial being! I say, cloaca . . . cloaca, I say, is your only orifice." I have, by now, one leg hooked around his neck and both hands grabbing his elbow, and he's not really more than one foot off the ground at the very highest, if that, and struggling for every inch. "Cloaca! You and your

'luff'!" The slime and minnows are all over him. He seems dressed in them
. . . sparkling like sequins. He's too slippery with them. I can't hang on.
I slip off and drop lightly into the brambles. Klimp slides away at a
diagonal, right shoulder leading, and glides, luminous with slime, just off
the ground. Disappears in a few seconds behind the trees. "Cloaca!" I
shout after him. It's the worst I've ever said to anyone. "Filthy fish thing!
Call that flying!"

Everything is going wrong. It always does, I should know that by now.
I'm thinking that my former husband slipped away in almost exactly the
same way. He was slippery too, sneaked out first with younger women and
then left me for one of them later on. I tried to grab at him the same way I
grabbed at Klimp. Tried to hold him back. I even tried to change my
ways to suit him. I know I've got faults. I talk too much. I worry about
things that never happen (though they did finally happen, almost all of
them, and *now* look).

   I hobble back (with cats), too angry to feel the pain of my bruises.
No sign of the ewes or the dog, but the backyard looks all silvery. No
minnows left there, though, just slime. I have to admit it's lovely. Makes
me feel romantic feelings for Klimp in spite of myself. I wonder if he saw
it. They're so sensitive to beautiful things and they love glitter. I can see
why.

   The house is dark. I open the door cautiously. I let in all eight . . .
no, nine . . . maybe ten cats. I call. No answer. I lock all the windows
and the doors. I check under the beds and in the closts. Nobody. I go into
the bathroom and lock that door too. Fill tub. Take off my clothes. Find
two minnows stuck inside my sweatshirt. One is dead. The other very
weak. I put him in the tub and he seems to revive a little. He has big eyes,
four fins where legs and arms would be, a minnow's tail . . . actually big
blue eyes . . . pale blue, like Klimp's. He looks at me with such pleading. He comes to the surface to breathe and squeaks now and then. I keep
making reassuring sounds as if I were talking to the cats. Then I decide to
get in the tub with him myself. Carefully, though. With me in the tub,
the creature seems happier. Swims around making a kind of humming

sound and blowing bubbles. Follows my hand. Lets me pick it up. I'm thinking it's a clear case of bonding, perhaps for both of us.

Now that I'm relaxing in the water, I'm feeling a lot better. And nothing like a helpless little blue-eyed creature of some sort to care for to bring brightness into life. The thing needs me. And so do all those cats.

I lie quietly, cats miaowing outside the door, but I just lie here and Charles (Charles was my father's name) . . . Charles? Howard? Henry? He falls asleep in the shallows between my breasts. I don't dare move. The phone rings and there's the thunk of something knocked over by the cats. I don't move. I don't care.

So what about ecology? What about our favorite planet, Klimp's and mine? How best save it? And who for? Make it safe for this thing on my chest? (Charles Bird? Henry Fishman?) Quietly breathing. Blue eyes shut. And what about all those thousands of others? Department of fisheries? Department of lakes and streams? Gelatin factory? Or the damp basements of those housing developments built in former swamps?

I blame myself. I really do. Perhaps if I'd been more understanding of their problems . . . accepted them as they are. Not criticize all that sand tracked in. And so what if they did step on the tails of cats? I've been so irritable these last few days. No wonder Klimp kicked out at me. If only I had controlled myself and thought about what they were going through. It was a crucial time for them too. But all I thought about was myself and my blowing-up stomach. Me, me, me! No wonder my former husband walked out. And now the same old pattern. Another breakup, another identity crisis. It shows I haven't learned a thing.

I almost fell asleep lying here, but when the water begins to get cold we both wake up, Charles and I. I rig up a system, then, with the electric frying pan on the lowest setting and two inches of water on top of a piece of flannel. Put Charles . . . Henry? . . . inside, sprinkle in crumbs of wafer. Lid on. Vent open. Lock the whole business in my bedroom on top of the knick-knack shelves. Then I check out their room, Klimp's and the others'. It's a mess, wafers scattered around . . . several pink ones, bed not made. If they were, all three, men, I'd understand it, but that can't be. I wonder if they used servants where they come from . . . or slaves? Well, Charles will be brought up differently. Learn to pick up his underwear and help out around the house, cook something besides telephone books and such. I find a talisman under the bed. I shut my eyes, squeeze hard, wondering can I lift with it? Maybe, on the other hand, it's some sort of anchor to stop with or to be let down by. Something thrown out to keep from flying. I'll save it for Charles.

I sit down to rest with a cup of tea, two cats on my lap and one across my shoulders. All the cats seem fat and happy; and I really feel pretty happy too . . . considering.

The telephone rings again and this time I answer it. It's a love call. I think I recognize Klimp's voice, but he won't say if it's him and they do all sound a lot alike, sort of muffled and slurred. Anyway, he says he wants to do all those things with me, things, actually, he already did. I suppose this call is part of a new campaign. I don't think much of it and I tell him so. "How about breaking school windows and stealing library books?" I say. But whose side am I on now? "Listen," I say, "I know of a nice wet place devoid of cats. It's called the Love Canal and you'll love it. Lots of empty houses. And there's another place in New Jersey that I know of. Call me back and I'll have the exact address for you." I think he believes me. (Evidently they haven't read *all* the books about women.)

Political appointees. I'll bet that's what they are. Makes a lot of sense. I could do as well myself. And did, actually. Who was it sent them out with spray-paint cans? Who told them how to cause static on TV? Who had thousands of stickers made up reading: NO DANGER, NONTOXIC, and GENERALLY REGARDED AS SAFE?

We can do all this by ourselves. Let's see: number 1, day-care-aquarium centers; number 2, separate cat-breeding facilities; number 3, the takeover proper; number 4, the lying fallow period. And we have time . . . plenty of time. Our numbers keep increasing, too, though slowly . . . the rejected, the divorced, the growing older, the left out . . .

Maybe they've already started it. I can't be the only one thinking this way. Maybe they're out there just waiting for my call, kitchens all warmed up. I'll dial my old friend. "Include me in," I'll say.

Everything will be perfect, and I even have Charles. We don't need them. Bunch of bureaucrats. *That* wasn't flying.

Roger Caras

TEDDY'S TALE

Teddy could become an American icon. His is a real-life saga. He is a legend-type cat, a living folk song, although no one has yet sat down to write the banjo and guitar music appropriate to his tale. Teddy is the stuff of folklore. Teddy is a soap opera. If there is a great cat in the sky he probably looks at least a little like Teddy, or he would like to. He came to us a Damien. It didn't suit. Since he has certain teddy-bear qualities he got his new, much more suitable, name.

As far as we know Teddy originated in the vicinity of San Francisco; at least it was in the Queen of American Cities that we found him (which shows good taste on his part). We were visiting the wonderful San Francisco Society for the Prevention of Cruelty to Animals (SFSPCA), and Jill spotted this oversized, somewhat too dark, certainly overage and well-used neutered Seal-Point Siamese tom. There is not a great deal of logic to adopting a shelter cat in California when you live in Maryland, but as a character on the Jack Benny radio show back in the 1940s used to say, *"If you look, you'll see; if you like, you'll buy."* Jill looked, she saw, she liked, and Teddy went into the hold of our 747 for the trip back to Baltimore. Who needs logic? And besides, the SFSPCA executive director, Rich Avanzino, egged Jill on behind my back.

All we knew of his history was that someone unknown was in the process of bringing him to the SFSPCA to turn him in when, just outside the shelter door, he wriggled out of his carrier and escaped into the maze of industrial buildings in the area. For six months the SFSPCA tried to trap him, and at last they were successful. Teddy was checked over by a veterinarian and declared to be "OK, if somewhat used," and he was certainly that. He was a well-scarred, fat-faced old tom of heroic, even Falstaffian, proportions and was obviously considerably older than the "5 years plus" notation on his documents suggested. But he was and is a great purrer, one of the greatest of our time, and he has a certain comfortable bulk to him. He does, though, have no center of gravity, and picking him up is like trying to hoist a well-greased, half-filled water mattress onto a towel rack.

What his records didn't show was that those early years in the port of San Francisco had allowed him to move only halfway across the bridge toward the human lifestyle dictate. He is an all-out card-carrying people lover, but he immediately made it clear that that was as far as he would go—one species. All four-legged types were out. At the sight of another cat or dog, however benign the other animal's intent, Teddy went ballistic. The first time a Greyhound came yowling down the hall wearing Teddy, all of him, like a snood, spitting and snarling, we knew we would have to address the matter sooner rather than later.

Fortunately, the main house at Thistle Hill Farm has three ample living rooms, and it was possible to lock one off just for big, old, tough Teddy alone. It has a great antique English oak door with a frosted glass pane that carries the quaint legend H. Babb Builder and Undertaker. It also had a heavy brass hook and eye so Teddy could be kept from chance encounters. He had become the prisoner in the tower. At least, we could console ourselves, his isolation was self-imposed. It was not the way we would prefer it.

There are a number of places in the house where we can hook up VCRs and enjoy the art and history of film, but we inevitably chose what became known as *Teddy's room,* to give him as much company as we could. Many a fine film have we watched with that badly stuffed pillow of a cat smothering one lap or another and purring up a storm. An important architectural detail: because the carpeting is thick at the portal to Teddy's room, there is no sill installed under the door, but there is space, an inch or so. That is important to remember.

Now we must leave Teddy alone in his tower in order to introduce the next character to play a key role in his tale. Up in coastal Connecticut a rather pretty tortoiseshell cat my grandson, Joshua, would eventually name Emmy, was working over a neighborhood trying to decide on her next home, even as Teddy was defining the terms of his world in Maryland. What her life before had been we can't even speculate. We would come to know that neither dogs nor other cats bothered her in the slightest. She hears celestial music, I am sure. She has proven to be a very self-assured young queen, very pulled together, definitely a NOW cat. If cats think about such things, Emmy is a feminist and quite properly so.

On several occasions during her selection trials the little queen stopped off at the home of our physician son, Clay, his wife, and their two children. Despite the fact that daughter-in-law Sheila is seriously allergic to cats, Emmy-to-be was allowed in, fed, and invited to bed down for the night. Joshua and his younger sister, Abaigeal, were delighted with the little, cuddly stranger who always arrived at dusk. The Emmy business only became serious when her drop-in frequency rate increased enough to make it clear that she had made her choice. She would be yet another Caras cat, Connecticut Chapter. But Sheila was still coughing and wheezing. The obvious solution—Emmy would come to Maryland and always be here at Thistle Hill Farm for Joshua and Abaigeal when they came to visit.

All of that was pretty routine, and sauntering, self-possessed, easygoing Emmy had her surgery, then her shots, and settled in as a Regular. She began exploring at once, of course, and quickly discovered the door to Teddy's dungeon. It seemed to fascinate her. She just had to find out who the beguiling stranger was behind the great oak door. What were we hiding, what was in the family closet? We often found her in the hall outside the H. Babb door gazing at it unblinkingly. She hunkered down and stared as if she thought she could eventually burn a hole through it.

One day I was going into our bedroom and had to pass close to the door to Teddy's lockup. Emmy was lying on her back on our side of the door with one paw stretched out as far as it could go. She was reaching under the H. Babb door! I got down and peered along Emmy's arm. She and Teddy were holding paws. With Jill standing by in case we had to separate one cat from the other surgically, I opened the door. With such supreme confidence that it suggested a prior agreement, Emmy strode into Teddy's chamber. He just watched her as we watched them. She ignored him and investigated the room she had never visited before. He watched and then slowly, almost hesitantly, walked over to her. She rolled over on her side and then her back, and he began to bathe her. It was as simple as that. When in doubt, try a little of that good old social-grooming stuff. Teddy was not a cat without a soul after all. He was more than just a thunderous purr. He was, in truth, all heart.

So Teddy the Solitary gained a companion. Each day we would find Emmy outside his door, sometimes holding paws with Teddy under the door, sometimes just rubbing against the door, purring. Sometimes Emmy would spend the night with Teddy, but every day, one way or another, they spent hours together. Emmy had developed other imperatives of her own both inside the house and out on the farm, but she always found time for a visit with the dark stranger in the tower. And when Emmy arrived, there was rubbing and bathing. They often slept rolled up together on either the couch or an old oak doll's bed they both seemed to favor. Several of the dozens of teddy bears that live all over this house are always perched at one end of the bed watching over them, Teddy and his visiting mistress, Emmy. (The teddy bears are in almost every room of the

479

house, but they do come together once a year. On Boxing Day—the day after Christmas—all the teddy bears assemble, and our grandchildren, each by written invitation, join in the Teddy Bears' Tea Party. The children are expected to dress for the event. The bears come as they are.)

Is that it, then? An unknown beginning, the attempted turn-in at the SFSPCA, the escape, evasion of capture for six months, the flight across America, the initial shock of the Thistle Hill population, solitary confinement, the burgeoning love affair with Emmy that began through an inch and a half of solid oak? Is that how the story closes? By no means. That is how it begins. Teddy has apparently no end of secret dimensions.

The next stage of the saga was shaping up in nearby rural Pennsylvania. Faithful Karen Dorn, farm manager here at Thistle Hill, brought us, in rapid succession, our three youngest cats: Martha Custis Washington, without a tail, and Mary Todd Lincoln and Marmalade, both with tails.

MARMALADE was abandoned with two littermates beside a country road in southern Pennsylvania. They were much too young to survive. I have never figured out what people say to themselves when they do that. Marmalade, an orange tabby, was generally in good shape and obviously socialized, so one can conjecture that she was handled a good deal if not loved before being abandoned to die. She hasn't really gotten over the shock of whatever it was that happened. She may be suspicious the rest of her life. You never know. Cats are not always ready or perhaps able to set aside the baggage they arrive with. If they have to live with it, so do the people who take them on. Cats are not neurotic by choice any more than people are. They are forgiving and we must be, too. Fair is fair.

MARY TODD LINCOLN is gray and pinky white. She is a very sweet little cat with a huge purr. When she really gets going she sounds like James Earl Jones doing a voice-over. She is just one more case of inexplicable abandonment in nearby Pennsylvania, in an area we know as Pennsyltucky. She is very people-oriented.

MARTHA CUSTIS WASHINGTON is pretty and pleasantly meddlesome, a gray job that someone didn't want. Our records are not perfect so we don't know why she was dumped. Perhaps because she was threatening—she threatened to grow up. She has no tail. The vet says she is a true, naturally born bobtail. Until you get used to her, it seems as if half a cat has just come into the room or out from under the couch.

I had threatened Karen's life if she didn't stop bringing us eating machines, and she pouted. So did Jill. Granddaughter Sarah swung into her awesome seven-year-old's let's-manipulate-granddad mode, and the terrible trio came on board. They are permanent, and surgery has been done. The good life lies ahead. They will never know hunger, neither will they know truculent weather unless they opt for it. They have it made! (When I die, if all that Hindu circular stuff is right, I want to come back as an animal in my house.)

One evening the awful three were playing in the hall near Teddy's H. Babb door when either Jill or I got the bright idea of seeing what Teddy's reaction would be to tiny kittens. He still had shown no signs of ever accepting anything with four legs except Emmy. And we had tested him—under tightly controlled conditions—from time to time. It would be nice to let H. Babb stand ajar. Teddy's room is one of the prettiest in the house, and it is a shame to have to slip in and out of it. Besides, it means an extra cat litter box, extra food and water dishes, just more things to remember not to forget.

On that fateful evening Jill and I carried the kittens into Teddy and Emmy's trysting place, ready to beat a quick retreat and save the kittens should our Jekyll-and-Hyde cat opt to play Mr. Hyde in response to our latest imposition.

But that is not how it went at all. Teddy came toward us with only the slightest hesitancy. In fact, he seemed to get giddier with every step he took. In minutes he was on his back with the mauling mites all over him. He pinned them one at a time and bathed them. Emmy did the strangest thing! Obviously miffed, she stalked out and hasn't been back to see Teddy since. Easy come, I guess, easy go. The kittens stayed.

Teddy mothered the kittens to an incredible degree. He is extraordinarily nurturing for a male, particularly a misanthrope-cat. The kittens insisted upon nursing, and Teddy accommodated by assuming the appropriate position. Amazingly, over the days, his nipples began to grow.

What all of this actually means, I don't know. An awful lot of genetic data have gotten twisted around one another and skewed out of shape. There have been misplaced responses to confusing signals, and the genders involved have become absolutely meaningless. Nothing, in fact, has dictated the scenario except Teddy's incredible tolerance on the one hand and total lack thereof on the other.

Bottom line, so to speak? Teddy found his true love in Emmy and then lost her within a few months. He now has three other companions who spend much of their time pouncing on his tail, which he obligingly swishes back and forth for them. They also nibble his whiskers and chew on his already well-scarred ears. He loves every minute of it. We have never seen him even a little cross with them, he of the ballistic trajectory at the sight of cat or dog.

What will happen when Mary, Martha, and Marmalade are old, too, I do not know. In all fairness they cannot be assigned for life to mollycoddle Teddy's neuroses unless they elect to play that role. The strange foursome led by "mother" Teddy have emerged from solitary without becoming wacko over the other animals. They are now indoor-outdoor cats who hang out near Jill's orchid greenhouse. Teddy does not seek the company of other animals except the three "kids." And Emmy is very standoffish when she and Teddy encounter each other. Is there life after Emmy and M, M, and M? Stay tuned.

Saki

THE PENANCE

Octavian Ruttle was one of those lively cheerful individuals on whom amiability had set its unmistakable stamp, and, like most of his kind, his soul's peace depended in large measure on the unstinted approval of his fellows. In hunting to death a small tabby cat he had done a thing of which he scarcely approved himself, and he was glad when the gardener had hidden the body in its hastily dug grave under a lone oak tree in the meadow, the same tree that the hunted quarry had climbed as a last effort towards safety. It had been a distasteful and seemingly ruthless deed, but circumstances had demanded the doing of it. Octavian kept chickens; at least he kept some of them; others vanished from his keeping, leaving only a few bloodstained feathers to mark the manner of their going. The tabby cat from the large grey house that stood with its back to the meadow had been detected in many furtive visits to the hen-coops, and after due negotiation with those in authority at the grey house a sentence of death had been agreed on: "The children will mind, but they need not know," had been the last word on the matter.

The children in question were a standing puzzle to Octavian; in the course of a few months he considered that he should have known their names, ages, the dates of their birthdays, and have been introduced to their favourite toys. They remained, however, as non-committal as the long blank wall that shut them off from the meadow, a wall over which their three heads sometimes appeared at odd moments. They had parents in India—that much Octavian had learned in the neighbourhood; the children, beyond grouping themselves garmentwise into sexes, a girl and two boys, carried their life-story no further on his behoof. And now it seemed he was engaged in something which touched them closely, but must be hidden from their knowledge.

The poor helpless chickens had gone one by one to their doom, so it was meet that their destroyer should come to a violent end, yet Octavian felt some qualms when his share of the violence was ended. The little cat, headed off from its wonted tracks of safety, had raced unfriended from shelter to shelter, and its end had been rather piteous. Octavian walked through the long grass of the meadow with a step less jaunty than usual. And as he passed beneath the shadow of the high blank wall he glanced up and became aware that his hunting had had undesired witnesses. Three white set faces were looking down at him, and if ever an artist wanted a threefold study of cold human hate, impotent yet unyielding, raging yet masked in stillness, he would have found it in the triple gaze that met Octavian's eye.

"I'm sorry, but it had to be done," said Octavian, with genuine apology in his voice.

"Beast!"

The answer came from three throats with startling intensity.

Octavian felt that the blank wall would not be more impervious to his explanations than the bunch of human hostility that peered over its coping; he wisely decided to withhold his peace overtures till a more hopeful occasion.

Two days later he ransacked the best sweet-shop in the neighbouring market town for a box of chocolates that by its size and contents should fitly atone for the dismal deed done under the oak tree in the meadow. The two first specimens that were shown him he hastily rejected; one had a group of chickens pictured on its lid, the other bore the portrait of a tabby kitten. A third sample was more simply bedecked with a spray of painted poppies, and Octavian hailed the flowers of forgetfulness as a happy omen. He felt distinctly more at ease with his surroundings when the imposing package had been sent across to the grey house, and a message returned to say that it had been duly given to the children. The next morning he sauntered with purposeful steps past the long blank wall on his way to the chicken-run and piggery that stood at the bottom of the meadow. The three children were perched at their accustomed look-out, and their range of sight did not seem to concern itself with Octavian's presence. As he became depressingly aware of the aloofness of their gaze he also noted a strange variegation in the herbage at his feet; the greensward for a considerable space around was strewn and speckled with a chocolate-coloured hail, enlivened here and there with gay tinsel-like wrappings or the glistening mauve of crystallized violets. It was as though the fairy paradise of a greedy-minded child had taken shape and substance in the vegetation of the meadow. Octavian's blood-money had been flung back at him in scorn.

To increase his discomfiture the march of events tended to shift the blame of ravaged chicken-coops from the supposed culprit who had already paid full forfeit; the young chicks were still carried off, and it seemed highly probable that the cat had only haunted the chicken-run to prey on the rats which harboured there. Through the flowing channels of servant talk the children learned of this belated revision of verdict, and Octavian one day picked up a sheet of copy-book paper on which was painstakingly written: "Beast. Rats eated your chickens." More ardently than ever did he wish for an opportunity for sloughing off the disgrace that enwrapped him, and earning some happier nickname from his three unsparing judges.

And one day a chance inspiration came to him. Olivia, his two-year-old daughter, was accustomed to spend the hour from high noon till one o'clock with her father while the nursemaid gobbled and digested her dinner and novelette. About the same time the blank wall was usually enlivened by the presence of its three small wardens. Octavian, with seeming carelessness of purpose, brought Olivia well within hail of the watchers and noted with hidden delight the growing interest that dawned in that hitherto sternly hostile quarter. His little Olivia, with her sleepy placid ways, was going to succeed where he, with his anxious well-meant overtures, had so signally failed. He brought her a large yellow dahlia, which she grasped tightly in one hand and regarded with a stare of benevolent boredom, such as one might bestow on amateur classical dancing performed in aid of a deserving charity. Then he turned shyly to the group perched on the wall and asked with affected carelessness, "Do you like flowers?" Three solemn nods rewarded his venture.

"Which sorts do you like best?" he asked, this time with a distinct betrayal of eagerness in his voice.

"Those with all the colours, over there." Three chubby arms pointed to a distant tangle of sweet-pea. Child-like, they had asked for what lay farthest from hand, but Octavian trotted off gleefully to obey their welcome behest. He pulled and plucked with unsparing hand, and brought every variety of tint that he could see into his bunch that was rapidly becoming a bundle. Then he turned to retrace his steps, and found the blank wall blanker and more deserted than ever, while the foreground was void of all trace of Olivia. Far down the meadow three children were pushing a go-cart at the utmost speed they could muster in the direction of the piggeries; it was Olivia's go-cart and Olivia sat in it, somewhat bumped and shaken by the pace at which she was being driven, but apparently retaining her wonted composure of mind. Octavian stared for a moment at the rapidly moving group, and then started in hot pursuit, shedding as he ran sprays of blossom from the mass of sweet-pea that he still clutched in his hands. Fast as he ran the children had reached the piggery before he could overtake them, and he arrived just in time to see Olivia, wondering but unprotesting, hauled and pushed up to the roof of the nearest sty. They were old buildings in some need of repair, and the

486

rickety roof would certainly not have borne Octavian's weight if he had attempted to follow his daughter and her captors on their new vantage ground.

"What are you going to do with her?" he panted. There was no mistaking the grim trend of mischief in those flushed but sternly composed young faces.

"Hang her in chains over a slow fire," said one of the boys. Evidently they had been reading English history.

"Frow her down and the pigs will d'vour her, every bit 'cept the palms of her hands," said the other boy. It was also evident that they had studied Biblical history.

The last proposal was the one which most alarmed Octavian, since it might be carried into effect at a moment's notice; there had been cases, he remembered, of pigs eating babies.

"You surely wouldn't treat my poor little Olivia in that way?" he pleaded.

"You killed our little cat," came in stern reminder from three throats.

"I'm very sorry I did," said Octavian, and if there is a standard of measurement in truths Octavian's statement was assuredly a large nine.

"We shall be very sorry when we've killed Olivia," said the girl, "but we can't be sorry till we've done it."

The inexorable child-logic rose like an unyielding rampart before Octavian's scared pleadings. Before he could think of any fresh line of appeal his energies were called out in another direction. Olivia had slid off the roof and fallen with a soft, unctuous splash into a morass of muck and decaying straw. Octavian scrambled hastily over the pigsty wall to her rescue, and at once found himself in a quagmire that engulfed his feet. Olivia, after the first shock of surprise at her sudden drop through the air, had been mildly pleased at finding herself in close and unstinted contact with the sticky element that oozed around her, but as she began to sink gently into the bed of slime a feeling dawned on her that she was not after all very happy, and she began to cry in the tentative fashion of the normally good child. Octavian, battling with the quagmire, which seemed to have learned the rare art of giving way at all points without yielding an inch, saw his daughter slowly disappearing in the engulfing slush, her smeared face further distorted with the contortions of whimpering wonder, while from their perch on the pigsty roof the three children looked down with the cold unpitying detachment of the Parcæ Sisters.

"I can't reach her in time," gasped Octavian, "she'll be choked in the muck. Won't you help her?"

"No one helped our cat," came the inevitable reminder.

"I'll do anything to show you how sorry I am about that," cried Octavian, with a further desperate flounder, which carried him scarcely two inches forward.

"Will you stand in a white sheet by the grave?"

"Yes," screamed Octavian.

"Holding a candle?"

"An' saying, 'I'm a miserable Beast'?"

Octavian agreed to both suggestions.

"For a long, long time?"

"For half an hour," said Octavian. There was an anxious ring in his voice as he named the time-limit; was there not the precedent of a German king who did open-air penance for several days and nights at Christmas-time clad only in his shirt? Fortunately the children did not appear to have read German history, and half an hour seemed long and goodly in their eyes.

"All right," came with threefold solemnity from the roof, and a moment later a short ladder had been laboriously pushed across to Octavian, who lost no time in propping it against the low pigsty wall. Scrambling gingerly along its rungs he was able to lean across the morass that separated him from his slowly foundering offspring and extract her like an unwilling cork from its slushy embrace. A few minutes later he was listening to the shrill and repeated assurances of the nursemaid that her previous experience of filthy spectacles had been on a notably smaller scale.

That same evening when twilight was deepening into darkness Octavian took up his position as penitent under the lone oak tree, having first carefully undressed the part. Clad in a zephyr shirt, which on this occasion thoroughly merited its name, he held in one hand a lighted candle and in the other a watch, into which the soul of a dead plumber seemed to have passed. A box of matches lay at his feet and was resorted to on the fairly frequent occasions when the candle succumbed to the night breezes. The house loomed inscrutable in the middle distance, but as Octavian conscientiously repeated the formula of his penance he felt certain that three pairs of solemn eyes were watching his moth-shared vigil.

And the next morning his eyes were gladdened by a sheet of copy-book paper lying beside the blank wall, on which was written the message "Un-Beast."

Lilian Jackson Braun

PHUT PHAT
CONCENTRATES

Phut Phat knew, at an early age, that humans were an inferior breed. They were unable to see in the dark. They ate and drank unthinkable concoctions. And they had only five senses; the pair who lived with Phut Phat could not even transmit their thoughts without resorting to words.

For more than a year, ever since arriving at the townhouse, Phut Phat had been trying to introduce his system of communication, but his two pupils had made scant progress. At dinnertime he would sit in a

"Phut Phat Concentrates" was first published in *Ellery Queen's Mystery Magazine,* December 1963.

corner, concentrating, and suddenly they would say: "Time to feed the cat," as if it were their own idea.

Their ability to grasp Phut Phat's messages extended only to the bare necessities of daily living, however.

Beyond that, nothing ever got through to them, and it seemed unlikely they would ever increase their powers.

Nevertheless, life in the townhouse was comfortable enough. It followed a fairly dependable routine, and to Phut Phat routine was the greatest of all goals. He deplored such deviations as tardy meals, loud noises, unexplained persons on the premises, or liver during the week. He always had liver on Sunday.

It was a fashionable part of the city in which Phut Phat lived. The three-story brick townhouse was furnished with thick rugs and down-cushioned chairs and tall pieces of furniture from which he could look down on questionable visitors. He could rise to the top of a highboy in a single leap, and when he scampered from first-floor kitchen to second-floor living room to third-floor bedroom, his ascent up the carpeted staircase was very close to flight, for Phut Phat was a Siamese. His fawn-colored coat was finer than ermine. His eight seal brown points (there had been nine before that trip to the hospital) were as sleek as panne velvet, and his slanted eyes brimmed with a mysterious blue.

Those who lived with Phut Phat in the townhouse were identified in his consciousness as ONE and TWO. It was ONE who supplied the creature comforts, fed his vanity with lavish compliments, and sometimes adorned his throat with jeweled collars taken from her own wrists.

TWO, on the other hand, was valued chiefly for games and entertainment. He said very little, but he jingled keys at the end of a shiny chain and swung them back and forth for Phut Phat's amusement. And every morning in the dressing room he swished a necktie in tantalizing arcs while Phut Phat leaped and grabbed with pearly claws.

These daily romps, naps on downy cushions, outings in the coop on the fire escape, and two meals a day constituted the pattern of Phut Phat's life.

Then one Sunday he sensed a disturbing lapse in the household routine. The Sunday papers, usually scattered on the library floor for him to shred with his claws, were stacked neatly on the desk. Furniture was rearranged. The house was filled with flowers, which he was not allowed to chew. ONE was nervous, and TWO was too busy to play. A stranger in a white coat arrived and clattered glassware, and when Phut Phat investigated an aroma of shrimp and smoked oysters in the kitchen, the maid shooed him away.

Phut Phat seemed to be in everyone's way. Finally he was deposited in his wire coop on the fire escape, where he watched sparrows in the garden below until his stomach felt empty. Then he howled to come indoors.

He found ONE at her dressing table, fussing with her hair and unmindful of his hunger. Hopping lightly to the table, he sat erect among the sparkling bottles, stiffened his tail, and fastened his blue eyes on ONE's forehead. In that attitude he proceeded to concentrate—and concentrate—and concentrate. It was never easy to communicate with ONE. Her mind hopped about like a sparrow, never relaxed, and Phut Phat had to strain every nerve to convey his meaning.

Suddenly ONE darted a look in his direction. A thought had occurred to her.

"Oh, John," she called to TWO, who was brushing his teeth, "would you ask Millie to feed Phuffy. I forgot his dinner until this very minute. It's after five o'clock and I haven't fixed my hair yet. You'd better put your coat on; people will start coming soon. And please tell Howard to light the candles. You might stack some records on the stereo, too. . . . No, wait a minute. If Millie is still working on the hors d'oeuvres, would you feed Phuffy yourself? Just open a can of anything."

At this, Phut Phat stared at ONE with an intensity that made his thought waves almost visible.

"Oh, John, I forgot," she corrected. "It's Sunday, and he'll expect liver. But before you do that, would you zip the back of my dress and put my emerald bracelet on Phuffy? Or maybe I'll wear the emerald myself, and he can have the amethyst . . . John! Do you realize it's five-fifteen! I wish you'd put your coat on."

"And I wish you'd simmer down," said TWO. "No one ever comes at the stated hour. Why do you insist on giving big parties, Helen, if it makes you so nervous?"

"Nervous? I'm not nervous. Besides, it was *your* idea to invite your clients and my friends at the same time. You said we should kill a whole blasted flock of birds with one blasted stone. . . . Now, *please*. John, are you going to feed Phuffy? He's staring at me and making my head ache."

Phut Phat scarcely had time to swallow his creamed liver, wash his face, and arrange himself on the living room mantel before people started to arrive. His irritation at the disrupted routine was lessened somewhat by the prospect of being admired by the guests. His name meant "beautiful" in Siamese, and he was well aware of his pulchritude. Lounging between a pair of Georgian silver candlesticks, with one foreleg extended and the other exquisitely bent under at the ankle, with his head erect and gaze withdrawn, with his tail drooping nonchalantly over the edge of the marble mantel, he awaited compliments.

It was a large party, and Phut Phat observed that very few of the guests knew how to pay their respects to a cat. Some talked nonsense in a false voice. Others made startling movements in his direction, or worse still, tried to pick him up.

There was one knowledgeable man, however, who approached with the proper attitude of deference and reserve. Phut Phat squeezed his eyes in appreciation. The admirer was a distinguished-looking man who leaned heavily on a shiny stick. Standing at a respectful distance, he slowly held out his hand with one finger extended, and Phut Phat twitched his whiskers politely.

"You are a living sculpture," said the man.

"That's Phut Phat," said ONE, who had pushed through the crowded room toward the fireplace. "He's the head of our household."

"He is obviously of excellent stock," said the man with the shiny cane, addressing his hostess in the same courtly manner that had charmed Phut Phat.

"Yes, he could probably win ribbons if we wanted to enter him in shows, but he's strictly a pet. He never goes out except in his coop on the fire escape."

"A splendid idea!" said the guest. "I should like such an arrangement for my own cat. She's a tortoiseshell longhair. May I inspect this coop before I leave?"

"Certainly. It's just outside the library window."

"You have a most attractive house."

"Thank you. We've been accused of decorating it to complement Phut Phat's coloring, which is somewhat true. You'll notice we have no breakable bric-a-brac. When he flies through the air, he recognizes no obstacles."

"Indeed, I have noticed you collect Georgian silver," the man said. "You have some fine examples."

"Apparently you know silver. Your cane is a rare piece."

He frowned in self-pity. "An attempt to extract a little pleasure from a sorry necessity." He hobbled a step or two.

"Would you like to see my silver collection downstairs in the dining room?" asked ONE. "All early examples, around the time of Wren."

Phut Phat, aware that the conversation no longer centered on his superlative qualities, jumped down from the mantel and stalked out of the room with several irritable flicks of the tail. He found an olive and pushed it down the heat register. Several feet stepped on him. In desperation he went upstairs to the guest room, where he discovered a mound of sable and mink and went to sleep.

After this upset in the household routine Phut Phat needed several days to catch up on his rest, so the coming week was a sleepy blur. But soon it was Sunday again, with creamed liver for breakfast, Sunday papers scattered over the floor, and everyone lounging around being pleasantly routie.

"Phuffy! Don't roll on those newspapers," said ONE. "John, the ink rubs off on his fur. Give him the *Wall Street Journal;* it's cleaner."

"Maybe he'd like to go out into his coop and get some sun."

"That reminds me, dear. Who was that charming man with the silver cane at our party? I didn't catch his name."

"I don't know," said TWO. "I thought he was someone you invited."

494

"Well, he must have come with one of the other guests. At any rate, he was interested in getting a coop like ours. He has a long-haired torty. And did I tell you the Hendersons have two Burmese kittens? They want us to go over and see them next Sunday and have a drink."

Another week passed, during which Phut Phat discovered a new perch. He found he could jump to the top of an antique armoire—a towering piece of furniture in the hall outside the library. Otherwise it was a routine week, followed by a routine weekend, and Phut Phat was content.

ONE and TWO were going out on Sunday evening to see the Burmese kittens, so Phut Phat was served an early dinner, after which he fell asleep on the library sofa.

When the telephone rang and waked him, it was dark and he was alone. He raised his head and chattered at the instrument until it stopped its noise. Then he went back to sleep, chin on paw.

The second time the telephone started ringing, Phut Phat stood up and scolded it, arching his body in a vertical stretch and making a question mark with his tail. To express his annoyance he hopped on the desk and sharpened his claws on *Webster's Unabridged.* Then he spent quite some time chewing on a leather bookmark. After that he felt thirsty. He sauntered toward the powder room for a drink.

No lights were on, and no moonlight came through the windows, yet he moved through the dark rooms with assurance, sidestepping table legs and stopping to examine infinitesimal particles on the hall carpet. Nothing escaped his attention.

Phut Phat was lapping water, the tip of his tail was waving rapturously, when something caused him to raise his head and listen. His tail froze. Sparrows in the backyard? Rain on the fire escape? There was silence again. He lowered his head and resumed his drinking.

A second time he was alerted. Something was happening that was not routine. His tail bushed like a squirrel's, and with his whiskers full of alarm he stepped noiselessly into the hall, peering toward the library.

Someone was on the fire escape. Something was gnawing at the library window.

Petrified, he watched—until the window opened and a dark figure slipped into the room. With one lightning glide Phut Phat sprang to the top of the tall armoire.

There on his high perch, able to look down on the scene, he felt safe. But was it enough to feel safe? His ancestors had been watch-cats in Oriental temples centuries before. They had hidden in the shadows and crouched on high walls, ready to spring on any intruder and tear his face to ribbons—just as Phut Phat shredded the Sunday paper. A primitive instinct rose in his breast, but quickly it was quelled by civilized inhibitions.

The figure in the window advanced stealthily toward the hall, and Phut Phat experienced a sense of the familiar. It was the man with the shiny stick. This time, though, his presence smelled sinister. A small blue light now glowed from the head of the cane, and instead of leaning on it, the man pointed it ahead to guide his way out of the library and toward the staircase. As the intruder passed the armoire, Phut Phat's fur rose to form a sharp ridge down his spine. Instinct said: "Spring at him!" But vague fears held him back.

With feline stealth the man moved downstairs, unaware of two glowing diamonds that watched him in the blackness, and Phut Phat soon heard noises in the dining room. He sensed evil. Safe on top of the armoire, he trembled.

When the man reappeared he was carrying a bulky load, which he took to the library window. Then he crept to the third floor, and there were muffled sounds in the bedroom. Phut Phat licked his nose in apprehension.

Now the man reappeared, following a pool of blue light. As he approached the armoire, Phut Phat shifted his feet, bracing himself against something invisible. He felt a powerful compulsion to attack, and yet a fearful dismay.

"Get him!" commanded a savage impulse within him.

"Stay!" warned the fright throbbing in his head.

"Get him! . . . Now . . . now . . . *NOW!*"

Phut Phat sprang at the man's head, ripping with razor claws wherever they sank into flesh.

The hideous scream that came from the intruder was like an electric shock; it sent Phut Phat sailing through space—up the stairs—into the bedroom—under the bed.

For a long time he quaked uncontrollably, his mouth parched and his ears inside-out with horror at what had happened. There was something strange and wrong about it, although its meaning eluded him. Waiting for time to heal his confusion, he huddled there in darkness and privacy. Blood soiled his claws. He sniffed with distaste and finally was compelled to lick them clean.

He did it slowly and with repugnance. Then he tucked his paws under his warm body and waited.

When ONE and TWO came home, he sensed their arrival even before the taxicab door slammed. He should have bounded to meet them, but the experience had left him in a daze, quivering internally, weak and unsure. He heard the rattle of the front door lock, feet climbing the stairs, and the click of the light switch in the room where he waited in bewilderment under the bed.

ONE gasped, then shrieked. "John! Someone's been in this room. We've been robbed!"

TWO's voice was incredulous. "How do you know?"

"My jewel case! Look! It's open—and empty!"

TWO threw open a closet door. "Your furs are still here, Helen. What about money? Did you have any money in the house?"

"I never leave money around. But the silver! What about the silver? John, go down and see. I'm afraid to look . . . No! Wait a minute!" ONE's voice rose in panic. "Where's Phut Phat? What happened to Phut Phat?"

"I don't know," said TWO with alarm. "I haven't seen him since we came in."

They searched the house, calling his name—unaware, with their limited senses, that Phut Phat was right there under the bed, brooding over the upheaval in his small world, and now and then licking his claws.

When at last, crawling on their hands and knees, they spied two eyes glowing red under the bed, they drew him out gently. ONE hugged him with a rocking embrace and rubbed her face, wet and salty, on his fur, while TWO stood by, stroking him with a heavy hand. Comforted and reassured, Phut Phat stopped trembling. He tried to purr, but the shock had contracted his larynx.

ONE continued to hold Phut Phat in her arms—and he had no will to jump down—even after two strange men were admitted to the house. They asked questions and examined all the rooms.

"Everything is insured," ONE told them, "but the silver is irreplaceable. It's old and very rare. Is there any chance of getting it back, Lieutenant?" She fingered Phut Phat's ears nervously.

"At this point it's hard to say," the detective said, "but you may be able to help us. Have you noticed any strange incidents lately? Any unusual telephone calls?"

"Yes," said ONE. "Several times recently the phone has rung, and when we answered it, no one was there."

"That's the usual method. They wait until they know you're not at home."

ONE gazed into Phut Phat's eyes. "Did the phone ring tonight while we were out, Phuffy?" she asked, shaking him lovingly. "If only Phut Phat could tell us what happened! He must have had a terrifying experience. Thank heaven he wasn't harmed."

Phut Phat raised his paw to lick between his toes, still defiled with human blood.

"If only Phuffy could tell us who was here!"

Phut Phat paused with toes spread and pink tongue extended. He stared at ONE's forehead.

"Have you folks noticed any strangers in the neighborhood?" the lieutenant was asking. "Anyone who would arouse suspicion?"

Phut Phat's body tensed, and his blue eyes, brimming with knowledge, bored into that spot above ONE's eyebrows.

"I can't think of anyone. Can you, John?"

TWO shook his head.

"Poor Phuffy," said ONE. "See how he stares at me; he must be hungry. Does Phuffy want a little snack?"

The cat squirmed.

"About those bloodstains on the windowsill," said the detective. "Would the cat attack anyone viciously enough to draw blood?"

"Heavens, no!" said ONE. "He's just a pampered little house pet. We found him hiding under the bed, scared stiff."

"And you're sure you can't remember any unusual incident lately? Has anyone come to the house who might have seen the silver or jewelry? Repairman? Window washer?"

"I wish I could be more helpful," said ONE, "but honestly, I can't think of a single suspect."

Phut Phat gave up!

Wriggling free, he jumped down from ONE's lap and walked toward the door with head depressed and hind legs stiff with disgust. He knew who it was. He knew! The man with the shiny stick. But it was useless to try to communicate. The human mind was so tightly closed that nothing important would ever penetrate. And ONE was so busy with her own chatter that her mind . . .

The jingle of keys caught Phut Phat's attention. He turned and saw TWO swinging his key chain back and forth, back and forth, and saying nothing. TWO always did more thinking than talking. Perhaps Phut Phat had been trying to communicate with the wrong mind. Perhaps TWO was really Number One in the household and ONE was Number Two.

Phut Phat froze in his position of concentration, sitting tall and compact with tail stiff. The key chain swung back and forth, and Phut Phat fastened his blue eyes on three wrinkles just underneath TWO's hairline. He concentrated. The key chain swung back and forth, back and forth. Phut Phat kept concentrating.

"Wait a minute," said TWO, coming out of his puzzled silence. "I just thought of something. Helen, remember that party we gave a couple of weeks ago? There was one guest we couldn't account for—a man with a silver cane."

"Why, yes! He was curious about the coop on the fire escape. Why didn't I think of him? Lieutenant, he was terribly interested in our silver collection."

TWO said: "Does that suggest anything to you, Lieutenant?"

"Yes, it does." The detective exchanged nods with his partner.

"This man," ONE volunteered, "had a very cultivated voice and a charming manner. He walked with a limp."

"We know him," the detective said grimly. "The limp is phony. We know his method and what you tell us fits perfectly. But we didn't know he was operating in this neighborhood again."

ONE said: "What mystifies me is the blood on the windowsill."

Phut Phat arched his body in a long, luxurious stretch and walked from the room, looking for a soft, dark, quiet place. Now he would sleep. He felt relaxed and satisfied. He had made vital contact with a human mind, and perhaps—after all—there was hope. Some day they might learn the system, learn to open their minds and receive. They had a long way to go before they realized their potential. But there was hope.